The Burning Hour

Jessica Barksdale Inclan

UFP Fiction Series
Detroit, Michigan, USA
Windsor, Ontario, Canada

Published in the United States of America and Canada by

Urban Farmhouse Press
www.urbanfarmhousepress.com

First Edition. First Print Run.
April 2016

ISBN: 978-1-988214-04-7

Book cover design: D.A. Lockhart
Book cover image: fire rises by Amella Wells
Book layout: D.A. Lockhart

The UFP Fiction Series is a line of books that showcases established and emerging poetic voices from across North America. The books in this series represent what the editors at UFP believe to be some of the strongest voices in both American and Canadian fiction writing. Burning Hour is the second book in this series.

Printed in Garamond font

For Julien Inclan

Contents

Ten Standard Firefighting Orders

1. Keep informed on fire weather conditions and forecasts.
2. Know what your fire is doing at all times.
3. Base all actions on current and expected behavior of the fire.
4. Identify escape routes and safety zones and make them known.
5. Post lookouts when there is possible danger.
6. Be alert. Keep calm. Think clearly. Act decisively.
7. Maintain prompt communications with your forces, your super visor, and adjoining forces.
8. Give clear instructions and ensure they are understood.
9. Maintain control of your forces at all times.
10. Fight fire aggressively, having provided for safety first.

Eighteen Watch Out Situations

1. Fire not scouted and sized up.
2. In country not seen in daylight.
3. Safety zones and escape routes not identified.
4. Unfamiliar with weather and local factors influencing fire behavior.
5. Uninformed on strategy, tactics, and hazards.
6. Instructions and assignments not clear.
7. No communication link with crewmembers/supervisors.
8. Constructing line without safe anchor point.
9. Building fireline downhill with fire below.
10. Attempting frontal assault on fire.
11. Unburned fuel between you and the fire.
12. Cannot see main fire, not in contact with anyone who can.
13. On a hillside where rolling material can ignite fuel below.
14. Weather is getting hotter and drier.
15. Wind increases and/or changes direction.
16. Getting frequent spot fires across line.
17. Terrain and fuels make escape to safety zones difficult.
18. Taking a nap near the fire line.

Chapter One

Northern Nevada
Mapp Ranch
Summer 1985

Stanley Mapp yanked his pickup to a stop in the middle of the dirt road, flung himself out of the cab, and jumped up on the flatbed. He stripped off his shirt, the sun scathing. He filled with one single emotion, as fierce as the sun, the heat outside matching the boil of anger inside him. Swallowing, breathing as if suffocating, he ignored his trembling knees and found balance. So he closed his eyes, pictured his family's ranch, wide open fields full of horses and cows, animals all the way to the mountains. Eight-hundred acres of grass and hill and sagebrush.

The image held. Opening his eyes, he pulled in a deep breath and stood legs spread, hands on hips, and waited for the convoy of horse-packed Bureau of Land Management livestock trucks that were just now leaving the Mapp Ranch, plumes of dust rising from the valley. He only had minutes. All day, the BLM and their helicopters and cowboys had rustled up Mapp Ranch horses, the air full of horse scream, thick with metal and heat and anger.

His older sisters Wanda and Birdie had stood their ground for as long as they could in front of the ranch house, Birdie speaking the truth.

"You have no right to disrupt our livelihood," she said as she stood in front of the convoy, her arms stretched out wide. Dust swirled around her, but she stood brilliant in her red shirt, her long black braids smooth down her back.

Wanda stood to the side, her eyes never wavering from the men and their guns, from the horses stomping and screaming in the trailers. She stared so hard, the men turned away. But neither sister could change the men's minds because what could the Mapps do without reinforcements? The agents yelled out, "Government land," and, "No grazing rights," and "Too many horses," and then got back in their trucks and pulled the horses away from where they'd run, bred, and lived all their lives.

That's when Stanley slipped away into the barn, knowing that today was a good day to change the world. He coasted away in his truck, hoping that his sisters would stay behind at the ranch house. Just like the agents, he couldn't bear the force of his sisters' gaze.

Now, sweat ran fine streams from his neck to his belt loops. His hair slid like hot snakes across his back. Arms raised, he cried out, hoping for a return message. What would his ancestors have done? What would his father have done? When Dempsey Mapp was alive, the BLM had kept their distance, circling the ranch but not spiriting away one foal or calf. But the minute Dempsey died, those vultures flew back, wanting this and that and everything. They cawed their reasons. Claimed the treaty that ceded the Mapps this land was bunk. Brought proof. Papers that showed long ago, rights had been sold for cash.

Squinting, Stanley could imagine his father, hands on hips, gaze forward. Boots planted, jeans stiff with dirt and manure that ringed with sweat and wear, ponytail dark and flat against his strong back.

"Land," Dempsey might say.

Newe Segobia.

Nevada.

The land wasn't really theirs or his, but Stanley had been borrowing it with the land's permission his whole life. It had given him what he'd needed, and he had cared for it. No government he didn't believe in was going to change that, no matter what the papers said. And no bunch of damn hatted assholes was going to take the horses.

He heard the motors, breathed in the diesel fuel, watched the dust whisk around the seven trucks headed his way. Stanley grabbed the can of gasoline and unscrewed the cap, the fumes wavering, visible, the odor harsh and vital.

The trucks rumbled forward, slowed, and then stopped, one door slowly opening. Cal Templeton stepped out, all insect-eyed and tall-hatted, one hand on his gun belt. A hot rush of air billowed as the trucks slowed and idled.

"Stanley!" he yelled from behind his open truck door. "Get off the damn road."

"Not going anywhere!" Stanley shouted back.

Other BLM agents jumped from cabs, all watching, waiting, palms flat on holsters. Radios crackled from inside cruisers. As Stanley stood on the flatbed, breathing light, his skin pulsed. With each second, each inhale, rage burned around his every edge.

"I told your sisters," Cal said. "I told you, too. You don't own these horses. This is public land. Bought fair and square from you people."

"Mother Earth is not for sale!" Stanley lifted up the gas can so Cal and all his BLM goons could see it. "You're not taking what isn't yours."

"Get off the truck," Cal said, stepping around the door and walking closer, motioning to other agents who seemed to be suddenly busy looking for things in their trucks. Behind the parked convoy, Wanda's truck bumped down the road at high speed. Time to get to it.

"You're not taking them anywhere." Stanley splashed the gas on his arms, the liquid cool and hot at the same time, his skin chilled and heated, each arm a river of burning gooseflesh. But he rose above it, held and guided by something bigger than himself, a power from within and without.

"Listen to me." Cal moved closer and closer. Two other agents slid along with him, holding fire extinguishers. "Let's be reasonable."

Stanley shook his head. He raised his hands upward again, the can dangling in one hand. Be reasonable? No reasoning with these people.

Eyes closed, he shook the last few drops on his head, his eyes burning, the fumes sucking away oxygen. This was what he was doing. But what would it feel like, all that flame? How much would it burn, this terrible heat?

"Steady now." Cal approached slowly, hands held up, palms white stars in the blinding noon sun. Other agents began to circle the truck, one step, two step, extinguishers shiny red and aimed. Behind them, the sheriff's men crept along like spiders.

"I'm going to do it!" Stanley yelled, the world folding down into a bright triangle of action. He squeezed the can's handle, heard the slosh. "Don't get near me!"

From his jeans pocket, he pulled out a lighter and lifted it high. The agents and the officers stopped moving, watching his hand liked trained dogs.

"You let those horses go, or I'll do it. Right here! Right now! And I won't stop till I take some of you sons-of-bitches with me."

"Not going to change things." Cal's boots crunching on rock and hard packed earth. "Even if you got your horses back, you aren't going to keep this land."

You'll see, Stanley thought, flicking the lighter once, twice, staring at the wheel under his thumb. One spark would change everything. He stamped on the flatbed, waved his hand, whooped. But then Birdie and Wanda got out of the truck. Stanley tried to ignore his sisters' sweet voices crying and calling out in the background. Even Birdie looked small from up here.

Don't, he thought. *Oh, stop. Let me do this.*

"Stanley," Cal called, his voice smooth.

"You'll see!" Stanley cried. But then something whacked him from behind. He crumbled, fell to his knees on the flatbed. He lashed out, trying to hit at something, someone. He struggled to hold onto the lighter, flinging the can and hearing a loud ting as it connected. He kicked, he struck out, he tried to move away from the bodies on top of him.

"Get him down! Get him down!" Cal yelled. "Break his fucking arm!"

Stanley flailed and struggled to his feet but was brought down again, face smashed hard on steel. His eyes burned, his lungs ached from want of air. But he could still make it happen. Birdie wasn't the only warrior in the family.

"Leave him be!" Birdie yelled. "Stop! You're hurting us both!"

"Quit your damn struggling," some agent yelled.

One last time, Stanley flicked the lighter wheel. A scream. Wanda? Then he heard nothing but his own rage roaring. But in the pause of metal flick and possibility, there was a hiss and whoosh, and he was blown back, covered in stinging foam. He slipped across the truck bed, hands scrabbling, the lighter slipping away. Fists pounded his back before angry hands grabbed and pulled at him. Men yanked him up and off the truck, onto the hot road, slamming him once more to his knees.

Someone kicked him hard and then again, harder. Stanley toppled, gravel and grit biting his palms, foam oozing between his fingers. Yanked back to kneeling, he tried to twist away from all the hands, but no matter which way he moved, they forced him still, pressing, shutting him down.

"God...damn...fucking...stubborn...Injun," one of them huffed with each boot strike.

"Let him go!" Birdie cried out. At the sound of her voice, Stanley wrenched free to see two agents grip her by the shoulders, wrangling Birdie just as they had the horses. He had to get to her. But the officers wrested him up, whacked on cuffs, and shoved him in the back of a baking hot sheriff's vehicle. No one bothered to protect his head, his temple hitting the top of the door, the strike ringing in his ears as the door slammed and the engine started. Dripping with fire retardant, the sharp chemical tang stuck on his face like a hot plastic bag, he collapsed against the seat. His left cheek bloomed with bruise. One eye filled with blood from the gash on his forehead. He breathed in gas, sweat, and failure.

Chapter Two

Wildland Firefighter Camp
Salida, Colorado
March 2012

One afternoon late in the first week of camp, Nick Delgado's training captain Chris led the class of twenty would-be firefighters out onto the compound grounds to a spot a few hundred feet beyond the buildings. The morning had been cold, in the 30's, but now the temperature was peaking at almost sixty.

"Downright balmy," Chris said as he handed out drip torches. "Fire just might make a run for it."

Nick held his breath as Chris poured his drip torch's burning oil onto a pile of duff, thick and heavy with dry pine needles, dead grass, and brown leaves.

"Okay, people. Eyes on the green. Head on a swivel. Keep focused. Let's burn."

For a few seconds, only smolder and smoke. But then it caught and grew. Nick breathed in the fire's hot tang, felt it reach a slim hand down his throat.

During his first few days at camp, Nick hadn't gotten close to a real fire. None of them had. He'd stared at whiteboard and then the PowerPoint presentations, trying to focus as the dude behind him crunched on Corn Nuts. Nick studied diagrams about the head and the heel of the fire and how humidity and wind effected both. He was quizzed on proper use of firefighting gear, the chain-of-command, the types of fire crews, and the correct implementation of tools and fire shelters. Nick learned about the black—what the fire had raged through and burned—and the green—what it hadn't. Yet.

But now, finally, ash swirled and heat rushed around him. As Nick watched the breeze comb through the duff and tease the fire hot and crackling, he clenched his teeth. None of the reading had bothered to describe this feeling. No "Ten Ways to Shit Yourself" when looking at something you had to actually put out. He was as ready as he could be. Helmet, gloves, and proper boots, the ones he'd bought for camp, thick-soled, hard-toed. Even so, he was sweating under his helmet, a trickle running down his spine.

The flames waved, hot and yellow, taking to the warming air, spreading out, digging hard into the pine needles, the air pulsing as the ground lit up in flame.

Chris backed up, trip torch at his side, "Cut line."

Nick grabbed his shovel and dug into the soil, turning up the earth that would stop the fire should the wind change course, should the fire blow high. He worked alongside his classmates, none of them saying anything. After a few minutes, Chris called him over. "Delgado, man the portable pump. If things get out-of-hand, don't let it jump this section."

Nick stepped back from the line, dropped the shovel, and wheeled the pump toward the fire. As the flames spit and hissed, flaring and moving, the yellow licks reaching higher, deepening to orange, smoke blowing into his face, he noticed it creeping toward a light pole and the wires that connected it to the main compound building a hundred or so yards away.

"Delgado," Chris yelled. "Put it out."

Nick swallowed, his heart lurching as he grabbed the hose and, just as he had been taught, directed the stream at the bottom of the flames that leaped toward the wires. At first, the fire jumped, skittering, flared. He moved forward, feeling the heat, the water on his face, his breath hard and tight in his chest. But then, the fire stilled, clumped and waiting. Then it burst forward with hot fingers. The fire bent, grew, arced. Limber, agile. He saw how it could twirl up a structure. Up his body. How it could run. Gallop.

He heard his girlfriend Megan's voice. "Be careful." Her eyes, her face, the expression she'd worn for the last year that said he couldn't. Didn't know how. Didn't know what he was doing.

"It's so dangerous," she had said when he left the apartment with his gear, the cab waiting.

As if he didn't know that.

He gripped the hose harder and aimed at the base of the fire, worked high, until the area around the pole, and then more and more, was just smoldering and black. He wanted all the fire out, nothing left but cold wet dirt.

"Hey! Hold it, Chief," Chris said. "Don't put it all out. We need some to practice on. But hell, you're a natural."

Chris laughed, and Nick felt a blush start as he wheeled the pump back toward the compound. Now that all was safe, the sweat trickled down his spine, his armpits soaked. There was truth in what Chris said. Just now, what he'd done? It was natural. Good. Something he could do in the real world, if only he could get a district to hire him. If only he could do this work.

Chapter Three

Northern Nevada
Mapp Ranch
March 2012

Just before five-thirty, the air sliced wide open with steel and wind. Wanda Mapp snapped straight in her kitchen table chair. The pre-dawn filled with a harsh *whap whap whap*. Behind her, Wanda's younger sister Birdie dropped something on the kitchen counter, a cereal bowl, a saucer; crack, smash, a clatter of cutlery.

"The horses!" Birdie dashed toward the front door. "Round up."

"Sisters!" Stanley called out, muffled and anxious in the folds of his sofa bed. "What is it?"

Standing painfully, Wanda lurched and creaked to the coat rack, grabbed up a sweater, and shoved her stiff arms in the sleeves, her breath fast and shallow.

"I'll go see," she called to Stanley. "Don't you worry. Don't you move. Just stay put."

She shuffled onto the front porch and stood next to Birdie, stunned by the brutal whack of noise. Their mother used to call this soft grayness the "breath of day," but nothing seemed to be breathing now, the air shocked, live-wired, and terrifying with sound. Wanda clung to Birdie's elbow and blinked into the darkness, their ranch lands coming into focus. What she saw on the horizon reminded her of a war movie, helicopters in whirring silhouette against the pinkish dawn.

"We have to stop them," Birdie said, a fist to her throat.

They'd been warned. Every year. All the Crescent Valley ranchers had been given notice. Imminent round up. Too many horses, way too many on Mapp Ranch, at least according to the BLM. Not Mapp land anyway, officials said. Had always said. Gave the government the right to round up all the wild horses without one lick of notice.

Besides, the officials with thumbs in belt loops had told them at meetings and in unscheduled visits to the ranch. *Come on! These horses aren't really wild. Just abandoned. Left to breed. Only wild 'cause no one bothers to care for them. Crusher of native grasses, ruiner of soil. Malingering Nevada nuisance. Needs taking care of, once and for all.*

Taken care of as in exterminated. *Taken care of* as in sold for dog food or sinister lasagna, though no one admitted the ugly truth that kill farms across the borders were still in the horse meat business.

"Get dressed quick," Birdie said. "I'll get the truck."

Ten minutes later, Wanda and Birdie sped from the house, bumped over sage and field, tracked the helicopters the mile or so toward the bluff above the valley that curved up and toward the highway. Soon they saw trucks and the riders on horseback, all of them pushing the wild horses into flight.

The truck's seatbelts only a memory and never used anyway, Wanda held onto the Jesus handle and the seat. She turned to watch her sister. Birdie's fingers—knotted but thin and strong—clutched the steering wheel, but every so often, she would lift a hand and push her fingers through her long unbraided hair. Birdie's only nervous habit. When her hair was tight in braids, she'd pull free one lock and worry it with her fingers. Never good news, Birdie's loose hair. Through the open windows, the sharp, wet-metal smell of terrified horse blew in. Wanda shuddered at the whoops of the Bureau folk, all of them so damn happy with themselves as they flushed the horses from gully and gulch, scaring the animals into the funnel between bluff and mountain. Their Jeeps tore deep welts in the soil, their horses pounded over grass and brush. One wrangler galloped by, a foal slung across his saddle.

Birdie jerked to a stop at the bluff's edge. They banged out of the truck cab, stabs in Wanda's feet as she hit the cold earth, the early morning unkind to her eighty-four-year-old bones. The sky lightened, the sun golden on the grass as horses tore by, ripping black lines across the fields.

Wanda took Birdie's arm again. She couldn't shield her eyes. These horses were family, most not full wild, some used to human hands and noises, familiar with machine and engine, truck and tractor. Part quarter horse, part Morgan, part Indian, part wild, some had been broken, others sired by those broken before, a chain of horse from before the before. Greys, roans, palominos, pintos, browns spotted like spring starlings, stallions black as oil, mares with white blazes on their noses or stars on their foreheads, foals new as yesterday—these were kin to horses no one had rustled before. Kin to horses Wanda remembered from her childhood, horses her father fed from his palm. Horses her mother saddled up and road into town. Horses ranch hands had ridden for over three generations on Mapp Ranch.

Three helicopters flew low, buzzing the herd fast and hard from the sides, from the rear, zinging them forward, the horses in a froth of spit and scream. Caught in the cup of the Cortez Mountain Range, the animals fanned out in wild panic, manes and tails flying. Confused, they stumbled and lurched into tangled remnants of rusted barbed wire fences, lunged up rocky hills, and skidded down the other sides, unaware that BLM personnel were over the bluff, waiting in the boxed canyon with cowboys and ropes and horse trailers, a perfect trap. There were guns, too, for the horses that fought back or the ones damaged and broken—pelvises, legs—from the run and terror.

"*Ataa,*" Birdie said, using their father's language. She shook her head, one hand at her throat, fingers gripping skin. "We didn't save them!"

Wanda swallowed down the sob stuck under her breastbone, the pain like a tired heart attack. Two weeks ago and under the cover of night and cloud, Wanda and Birdie and members of the ranching and tribal communities had moved 400 horses and 250 head of cattle to tribal lands. They managed it all without any helicopters. Community leaders had called around for volunteers and equipment. People came, bringing their gear and relatives. Pickups with pulls and trailers, cowboys on loan from other ranches, ropes and hay and feed. Those animals were now safe, tucked away where the BLM couldn't find them. But Birdie was right. They hadn't been able to get them all.

Wanda forced herself to watch, miles and miles of chase in the growing morning heat. Birdie's daughter Tanya, grandson Dwayne, tribal members, and neighboring ranchers soon joined them. The horses ran until they were corralled in pens like prisoners or unwanted refugees, exhausted and so sweaty they changed colors. They were loaded up, pulled and wrenched into trailers, mares separated from foals, herd separated into groups. The neighing of loss was unbearable, a calling to kin—to her, Wanda thought—unrelenting.

She wanted to stumble down the bluff and save them all. She turned to Birdie, expecting an answer, but Birdie stared ahead, worrying her hair.

Wanda turned back to the sea of horses. The right answer had to be struggling to get out. But once Wanda had the solution, could she fight like Birdie usually did? Could she stand up like Stanley and threaten to burn himself to get them to stop?

Would anything stop this? Nothing had stopped before.
She wanted to scream out, "Nothing ever changes."

But Wanda knew what happened when anyone said that to Birdie. Right now, she couldn't bear Birdie's reply. "Sister, just you wait."

She didn't want Birdie to say, "I'll make them all change."

Even now, next to her sister, high on the bluff as they watched trailer after trailer of horses yanked away, she saw Birdie's back as she left once again to try to do what Wanda had no words for.

Chapter Four

San Francisco Bay Area
California
Early May 2012

Nick sat folded tight on his career counselor's couch, his legs awkward and huge, long, bony, and mountainous in the dainty room. He fidgeted, slipping slightly on the plush velvet fabric, and then he leaned back and crossed his arms, his hands resting in the damp rounds of sweat just under his armpits. "My uncle Dean called again last night."

Joanne nodded, her yellow pencil poised in her hand. "How did that conversation go?"

"As usual."

"Meaning what?" Joanne's writing hand hovered, and Nick considered the three months' worth of Nick notes in the wooden cabinet behind her cluttered desk. The room itself was a large purple square, shades from grape bubblegum to lavender jellybean on the walls and the ceiling. The carpet was tan, but the welcome mat and the small rugs under the desk and low table between his chair and Joanne's were purple: striped, flowered, polka-dotted.

Nick rubbed his eyebrows with thumb and forefinger, one of the many habits his girlfriend Megan teased him about.

"Oh, the worries of the world," she'd say when she caught him. "The thinker at thought."

Joanne waited, her face quiet and calm and without reaction. Even after all these sessions, Nick was surprised she'd never broken character once, so much her steady self he had to conclude this was who she really was.

"Dean made some calls at work. He's in IT. 'Pulled in all my chits,' he said. I don't really know what a chit is. Only Dean would use a word like that. But anyway, one of his colleagues gave him first dibs on this entry level job. The only thing needed is a college degree. Sitting behind a desk. Customer service from five in the morning to one in the afternoon. I'd get there early for the East Coast calls. 'It's a great opportunity,' Dean said. 'Room for advancement.'"

Nick waited for Joanne to tell him that he should snatch up this miraculous job offer with its annual salary of sixty thousand plus benefits and paid vacation.

"These don't come around very often," Dean had said just before he'd hung up. "Who knows? You could eventually work your way up. End up being my boss."

Boss of Dean. A role Nick truly did not want.

As he waited for Joanne to speak, he felt her objects pressing in on him, her little Indian-from-India statues, goddesses with several arms, gods with elephant heads. Then there were seashells on the bookshelves, photos of her family in carved wooden frames on her desk, brass bells along the window sill. It was like doing therapy in a shop on Telegraph Avenue, incense in the air, chimes on the door.

Joanne continued to look at him, her straight dark hair framing her placid, neutral expression, her body still and calm in her leather chair.

"Opportunities like this don't fall from trees," his father had said when Nick told him about Dean's offer. "Jesus, Nick. Why haven't you already signed on the dotted line?"

"Do it for a year," his mother had said. "Then you can do this fire-fighting thing. Really, Nick. Think about it. You'd have health insurance."

Megan had just shrugged, but he felt her relief. After a couple of months, the desk job was transferable to a Seattle office. That way, that maybe he wouldn't be gone for six months out of the year. When she went to the University of Washington for her PhD program, she wouldn't be dragging around a seasonal firefighter. What to do with a boyfriend like that at department parties? What would he have to say to all those professors? And even if he got a wildland gig, he wouldn't be considered a real firefighter, the hero kind that raced up structures in blinding smoke, pried motorists from their burning cars, and saved babies suffocating in their cribs. He would be the kind of firefighter no one paid much attention to unless he or she died.

As Joanne gazed at him steady and clear, Nick held his breath. If she told him he was a douche bag (words she would never use) for even questioning the job offer, he would take it. After all, he was twenty-four, two years out of college, his history degree hanging like an old, moldy coat in a dark closet. History. Who gave a shit about what happened in the past? No one even read the paper any more, much less questioned what was in it. And what about television or films? Every single war movie had anachronisms, the wrong guns in the wrong wars in the wrong countries.

"How do you feel about the job Dean offered?" Joanne asked.

Nick sat back, exhaled. "It's in an office. Eight hours a day."

"That's not what you want," she said, no question in her words.

Nick shook his head, imagining himself pulling into the parking lot, adjusting the tie he didn't know how to tie, the black one he did own in a permanent knot in a drawer, brought out for graduations, funerals, weddings, and interviews. But for this job, he'd be stuck with it. He'd tuck in his shirt, sling on his tie, strap on a leather belt and shoes, sigh, and sit on his ass for eight hours, minus breaks, all of which he'd spend eating some kind of shit food he'd buy from a vending machine. He'd grow soft and flabby and pale, his high school acne coming back, his hair greasing up, his back slumping, rounding into a permanent, fatty hump.

But, as his mother indicated, he'd have health insurance, and he'd probably need it for the heart attack he'd have next year or the next. Nick knew himself. If he got stuck, sometimes he stayed put rather than save his own life. It was that way with his high school girlfriend Claire. Months and months of their relationship turned into years before he could break up with her, college finally doing the job, but they weren't really done until the summer after his freshman year. And what about that job at The Evergreen State College alumni office? Every night, he called people who had no money to give and even sometimes people who had died. His best conversations were with the wrong numbers, the people who had never even attended the college much less lived in Olympia, Washington. The guy with the three Harleys and a Standard poodle puppy. The woman with the triplet granddaughters and a bum hip. The old man who lived in a log cabin in Sand Beach. Nick didn't want to hang up on those calls because he knew when he did, he'd have to make another. How long had he stayed in that job? A year before he was fired for "lack of enthusiasm"?

"No, I don't want it," he said to Joanne, shaking his head. "Not at all."

"Then there's not really anything to discuss," she said.

"What do I tell my uncle?" Nick thought about how Dean had

pulled a few easy strings and came up with 55,000 more dollars a year than Nick was currently making driving folks from the assisted living facility to Trader Joe's and the park on Wednesdays and Fridays.

"Tell him 'Thank you very much,'" Joanne said. "He did you a favor."

Nick shrugged. Tight-assed Dean wasn't exactly a cream puff do-gooder, but he had gone out of his way, no doubt because Nick's mom asked him. A few times, more than likely.

"Then there's my dad." Nick imagined his father's dark eyes. Jess Delgado—Jesus to no one but his mother—retold the family legends, the first being the tale of his father loading up Jess and his siblings in the old Ford and barreling up from Mexico City into Los Angeles, possible back then, green cards easier to get. But then followed the backbreaking work at the auto body shop, the laundry Nick's grandmother did with her bare hands over a tin tub, the miles everyone walked to school. And now? Who was Nick to turn down money and benefits like this? Who in the hell did he think he was?

"Think about this, Nick," Joanne said, her gaze steady. "You worked hard on identifying your interests. You picked the career you wanted based on your skills and desires. You researched the job. Frankly, more than most of my clients do. Then you trained at fire camp. When you got back, you sent out applications. You had a couple of interviews and a job offer that met your requirements. There you go. You're living your life, not someone else's." Joanne wrote on her pad, the pencil tip scratch-scratching. Nick breathed in and tried to stretch his legs, flexing one foot and then the other. When she finished, he said, "Thank you."

"You did it," Joanne said, smiling for the first time, the serious portion of this session over. "You'll do great. Give yourself time on the job. Everything takes practice."

Before Nick left the Bay Area, he hiked one last time with his father on a trail they'd hiked hundreds of times together. The April day had warmed to at least seventy, seventy-two degrees, the grass tall and green and dotted with mustard and lupine. Red-tail hawks circled overhead, lesser goldfinches and juncos called out from bay, oak, and manzanita.

As Jess powered up the hill, Nick stared at his father's calves, rock hard, Jess strong and fit, not a bit of fat on him, even at fifty-three. They weren't built anything alike. Nick was cobbled from his mother's side of the gene tree, all long bones and lean, smooth muscle. His father was shorter, built like a welterweight boxer, sturdy powerful arms, solid of thigh.

From the time before the time he could remember much, Nick was always outside with his father, digging holes for redwood saplings, raking mountainous piles of oak leaves, carrying fresh cut logs to the wood pile by the side of the house. He and his father camped—his mother joining them those first few times in Big Sur and Monterey and then opting out when Nick got older. Later, Nick and Jess backpacked in Yosemite, Tahoe-Donner, the Siskiyous, setting up tents on snow-covered mountainsides, hanging their food in trees, boiling water and adding tablets to ward away giardia and general stomach cramps. And they hiked on weekends and during school vacations. All his life there had been these strong brown calves, Nick second in line, following, keeping up the pace.

"Well," Jess said, reaching the top of the hill and stopping, his hands on his hips as he looked out over the Bay and caught his breath. The water was flat and blue, the sky an opalescent swirl of white and aqua and filled with clouds. They breathed hard together for a while. Nick closed his eyes as he took in air. "You'll always have work. There's never a shortage of fire."

"At least in the summers. Till I can get on year-round."

Jess shot Nick a glance. "How long will that take? Any way to push that process along? Will your college education help?"

"Maybe," Nick said, not wanting to tell his father that the track to full-time was longer that he'd let on: temporary seasonal, permanent seasonal, permanent year-round. But those spots were coveted, fought-over, complete with health benefits and retirement packages.

Nick opened his eyes, not seeing the vista but thinking of the rules his father lived by: pick up your room, drink a lot of water, and get outside. All his life, during school failures, bad behavior, upset and sadness, Nick got one of these commands as comfort. The dictums were simple and clear, practical, and within reach and served Nick at surprising times: when sick, confused, or anxious. And yet, always his father wanted brilliance and genius and surprise—straight A's, a first place science project, stunning conversational twists—even as he taught Nick only the basics.

"Get on a lot of fires," Jess said. "If they happen."

"They will. Lightning," Nick said. "Matches. Spark."

"Be careful," Jess said, still looking out to the water. "Don't do anything stupid."

Nick nodded, thought to add that command to the list of rules to live by, one that worked for auto mechanics and neurosurgeons alike.

"I won't," he said, and that's when his father reached over and put his arm around Nick's shoulder, pulled him close, hugging but not. Nick willed himself not to cry because that just wasn't how the Delgadaos did things. They hugged and didn't look at each other. They said goodbye while looking at anything other than each other.

Chapter Five

Northern Nevada
Mapp Ranch
March 2012

As she washed last night's dinner dishes, Wanda's hands were deep in the warm soapy water, the bubbles tinged a slight red from Tanya's chili. Two days after the horse roundup, twelve folks met around the table and planned over full bowls how to fight back against the BLM. Nothing was settled, but the chili was good. That and Kestrel Jackson's corn bread.

Wanda looked out the window as her fingers played the instruments of dirty plate and fork, the movement relaxing kinks from old fingertips to wrist bones. She liked doing the dishes. Back when he could still see well, Stanley had busted down the old kitchen counter and built one that fit Wanda just so. The smooth edge came to her waist, the sink reachable without having to stand on a step-stool. Even after their daddy died and Wanda took over the barn and herds, she still did at least one sink full of dishes every day, letting her hands and mind linger.

Her odd dream from the night before flickered and spun in her mind, the one with the boy out on the ranch in the dark. He'd been from BLM fire, that was for sure, yellow-jacketed, thick- booted. And what had he said to her? His face obscured, the voice familiar.

"What do you want from us?" he blurted.

Wanda hadn't known what to tell him. So many things to choose from. The cattle. Grazing rights. Her grand-nephew Dwayne and his secrets. Birdie's trip to DC. Wanda's old, groaning body. Finally, the light pushing up from the east, she'd said, "Breakfast."

The boy had laughed. "Well, okay. How about a ham sandwich?"

"Holy moly," Wanda said. "That'll do."

Then she'd woken up, Birdie snoring next to her in the old iron bed. Wanda sighed. If only a ham sandwich could fix everything.

But now, awake and on alert, Birdie stood behind Wanda, talking on the phone to a New York journalist. She paced back and forth, the long, kinked cord trailing behind her like a yellow pigtail. Every morning, Birdie griped about being out here with wavery cell reception and no internet connection, nothing but the spotty land line. In DC in her rented apartment, Birdie had all the machines she needed. Even so, Wanda didn't know why Birdie complained: nothing had ever been able to shut her down.

"BLM used a nonexistent ruling to get on our land and take those horses," Birdie was saying now. "They can talk all they want about too many horses for the acreage. They can say we should pay grazing fees, but this is our land by treaty rights. We make the rules here. Not the US government." The floorboards chattered under Birdie's feet. "No, no. We aren't ignoring the environment. We are the environment!"

Wanda turned to look at her sister, younger by six years but twice as smart and still pretty, even though her face was a map of a long, fighting life. *Just call us Mapp maps*, Wanda thought when looking at her sister or her own beat up reflection in the bathroom mirror. There were directions to just about everywhere on Mapp faces. Pick a wrinkle and go.

Stanley might have looked just as pruned, but he'd been inside and away from the sun for most of the last decade, sitting on the couch listening to stupid TV show soundtracks picked up with the crooked antenna perched on the roof. Smooth-cheeked, bald-headed, he sat silent and irritated, crunching on Cheetos and sipping lemonade. But before? Stanley had been something. Nowadays, it was hard to imagine Stanley as he'd been, angry, braided, standing on the flatbed bare skinned and shaking the gas can.

But neither Stanley nor Wanda had ever been much to look at. Birdie, though, was another story. When she was a girl, oh, watch out. Her hair had been long, black, and thick, flowing all the way down to the backs of her thighs, her dark eyes wide, her skin smooth as summer hills. Five inches taller than Wanda, three over Stanley, it was as if their parents had saved up all their good genes for Birdie. Wanda and Stanley were made up of broken parts and faulty wiring, Stanley not only blind as a bat but partially deaf to boot, and Wanda stiff with the arthritis everywhere.

Wanda turned back to her dishes, adding in a little more hot water. Birdie was leaving again as she always did: Kellogg City, Carson City, South Dakota, DC, New York City, Geneva. Some years, she'd been more gone than home.

"Listen," Birdie said, the command strong. "The BLM round-ups are the least of our worries. We've got the mining in the Cortez Mountains. You can talk about damage to the soil with horses. But a herd of wild animals is nothing compared to a mine. You know they use cyanide to leach the gold."

Wanda rinsed off two plates, ears on alert. As she put the dishes in the drainer, she thought of her mare Six, who pretended to ignore Wanda, but then there were her ears, flicking from back and front, just waiting for the sound of a carrot. That horse could hear a carrot in the kitchen all the way from the barn. Six probably heard the carrot growing in Wanda's garden patch behind the house. Probably heard the seed talking in Wanda's palm.

She moved her fingers one more time in the water, her hands almost warmed up enough to grab hammer and nails and get going on the fence. Maybe later after Dwayne finished his ranch work, she could get him to head into Kellogg City to pick up feed and a few movies to entertain Stanley. When Birdie left, Stanley was antsy, the agitator in him opening one angry eye.

Wanda pulled the plug, the water draining, rosy soap scum clinging to the sides of the battered and cracked porcelain sink. She picked up a runaway fork and rinsed it and then swished the sink.

"Thought you'd escape, heh?" Wanda laughed as she slipped the fork in the drainer. "There's no hiding from me."

Birdie cupped a hand over the receiver, whispering, "What?"

Wanda shook her head and went to the kitchen table, lowering herself down onto a rickety chair, part of the set their mother brought with her from Pine Ridge Reservation in South Dakota. Dempsey Mapp was Nevada born and bred; Margaret Keen, Oglala Sioux from South Dakota. But one hot evening in August 1928 at a courting dance in Billings, Montana was all it took. This was in the good times, after The Great War and before the crash and Depression, love something two visiting kids from different tribes could hope for.

That night, the dance and songs worked their magic. A month later and just before the wedding, Margaret lugged her belongings to Nevada in a rickety wagon. What had her daddy said?

"Wheels turned to splinters," her daddy said. "Shoulda watched the way she gripped them reins. It was me next. Said my vows, and she hauled out the paint cans. Made me build her a respectable floor. No dirt for her. Brought her sister Edie down here, too."

At this point of the story, he sat back, hands resting on his belt. "Next thing I know we have indoor plumbing and Wanda."

And what do you know? All these years later, a set of Margaret's curtains still hung by the kitchen window. More likely, Aunt Edie hung some up later, searching out the same color her sister had favored, a morning sky blue. But now they were the color and texture of used-up gauze.

Wanda gazed at her boots by the front door and then at Birdie, who was listening to whatever the journalist had to say, hand on one strong hip. If Wanda could still put her old, cracked leather boots on by herself, she would, but her toes resided in another country, a faraway trip with too many painful check points. It took help to yank them on, and there wasn't time for any of that nonsense. Stanley wasn't even awake yet, snoring up a sonata on the couch.

Slippers today, Wanda knew, Birdie not even close to done. The conversation started with the horses and had curled back around to the Ruby Treaty.

"A treaty with this government is like a treaty with a foreign nation."

All their lives, Birdie had said the true things while Wanda and Stanley waited to see what would happen nest. Birdie told their father to stop drinking, this after Margaret died of the cancer that ate her from the inside out until only a shell was left. Birdie was about six, Wanda almost twelve. Birdie's small, wiry stood next to this same kitchen table, saying, "No, Daddy. No more."

He bleared at her, red eyes weepy. Then slumped, sagging into the truth.

When Dempsey put away his bottle and his grief, he stopped yelling and throwing things against the wall. He stopped coming home with bloody noses and busted cheekbones. Her Daddy's sad anger had followed them around the house for a year or two, but by the time Dempsey Mapp died, Wanda wondered if that bad time had been a dream, the way her mother felt like a dream, a hazy memory of a terse, loving voice, arms and hands on Wanda's shoulders, laughter flat and fast like a slap. Her mother was as present as her curtains, fluttery and almost invisible. But now anyway, pretty much everything felt like a dream, except the current moment.

Wanda stood and shuffled over to the door.

"Where are you going?" Birdie mouthed.

Wanda shook her head, lifted a hand, and put on her slippers over her socks. She didn't dare tell Birdie she was going to take out the ATV, lest Birdie hang up the phone and start prying.

"Barn," Wanda said, a lie that wouldn't cause a ruckus.

Birdie gave her a hard one-two stare and then nodded, turning her attention back to the voice on the other end of the line. "If all American people want to live in freedom, you've got to protect the freedom of all America's people. Not just the lucky ones. Not only for yourselves but us, too."

Wanda waved again and then lifted her coat off the coat rack. Then leaving her sister and her arguments inside, Wanda pushed out into the morning, the dark sky just pulling up its skirts from the ranch, the rest of Nevada still hidden. It was early yet, Dwayne and his buddies not at work, the ranch quiet.

Wanda breathed in, squinting into the eastern sky, and then gazed at the gray, grainy landscape, hill and sagebrush and heat.

At the sound of the front door closing, Ruby crawled out from under the planks. Outside the oval of porch light, the old dog scratched herself, stretched, and then yawned. Now nearing ten, she was the sixth mutt named Ruby. The first Ruby was her father's, Ruby Treaty, named for the ignored treaty of 1863, the one that promised this land to the Mapp family forever.

"Ruby Treaty!" Dempsey would call, Dempsey the grandson of treaty signers. And sure enough, the dog would come, wagging her scruffy tail. All the Rubys since then had been the same no-breed mix of happy. But this Ruby was something special, a devilish catcher of rats, a fine chaser of hares, scared only by irritated mules and the sound of a hairdryer, not that such a device got much play in this house. Ruby looked part shepherd, part Aussie, part terrier, her nose fine and keen. She snuffled as she stretched.

Wanda pulled down her sleeves, looking back into the house, the phone cord coiled around Birdie's chair. The government had been trying to undo what it did since doing it in the first place, wanting back what it had unhappily given. So Birdie was headed to DC to fight them once again. If Birdie had her way, she'd come back with the original treaty, frame it, and hang it on the wall. Not that Birdie was telling Wanda any of this.

They were all too careful. Too worried. No matter the clinic doc told them Wanda's old heart was fine. Weight middling. Blood pressure passable. Arthritis okay with the medication. But Birdie treated her like a fragile flower that wilted in the midday heat. Wanda wasn't going to keel over if Birdie took another trip. Besides, if Birdie and her group lost the ruling, Wanda would be standing here forty miles southwest of Kellogg City on a ranch no longer Mapp. Then moved to reservation soil and buried in it, soon enough.

Ruby trotted over for a pet, sidling next to Wanda's leg, snout up. Wanda scratched the dog behind her ears, looking up when she heard the morning *quick-quick-quick* of a burrowing owl. Pretty soon, Birdie's phone call would end. Wanda needed to hightail.

"Come on, old lady," she said to Ruby. "Got some fences to mend. Can't let no cows bust out. BLM's on the case."

The air smelled like fire or the wet, put-out aftermath of one, a burn somewhere close. During the long hot summer months—spring and fall, too—the horizon was a constant smudge of black to brown, the Cortez Mountains a tinder box, what with lightning strikes and idiot campers and boys riding motor bikes and ATVs all over the dry hills.

Day and night, the BLM fire engines roared by in a flash of nuclear insect green, whirring their giant tires and billowing exhaust and dust. They made a big fuss about protecting the sage grouse, fighting fires in rugged, dangerous terrain no one lived on or near, just to save the darn bird, rare and fancy as it was, big feathers and all. Special in some kind of endangered way.

Anyway, the firefighters weren't really the bad ones—mostly young kids needing the summer work—but they had walkie-talkies or radios or whatnot dialed into dispatch. If they saw Wanda on her ATV, it would only be a scant hour before Sherriff Bryant would come tooling by, nonchalant, asking questions. He always pretended to know everything, acting nice in order to angle for stories about horse and cattle count, wanting a tiny excuse to call in the troops for a roundup.

"Let's go, girl." Wanda moved a bit faster and easier now, leaving the protection of the house and the cottonwood trees and heading toward the barn. Above her on the flagpole, the slap slap of the tribal flag Dwayne had brought home from a tribal meeting. On days with a slight, now-and-again breeze, the red, white, and green flag flickered and swung. Ahead, she could hear the horses in their stalls, their big warm bodies shifting, their snorts, their nostrils pulling in her scent. Most mornings after her kinks unkinked, Wanda took out Six, fine and muscular, barely fifteen hands, easy for her to get a good seat.

Wanda and Ruby passed the corral and then the barn and headed behind it to the ATV parked next to the tractor. Dwayne had tried to do some work on the contraption a few days back, clacking and rattling his tools like a big shot, fixing something that was "Big trouble, Aunt Wanda." The clutch tended to slip, the thing lurching around like an unbroken stallion.

"Aunt Wanda, I don't think you should be riding this." He'd looked at her with his odd green eyes, the ones his daddy gave him, that boy Tanya had taken up with for a year or so during high school. Paul Tall Weather.

"I've been riding it forever."

"Point 'zactly," Dwayne said as he hovered over the ATV's open hood, jiggling this, jiggling that. But then he packed up his tools, turned and left to get a beer, setting himself down with Stanley for an hour of soap operas.

Wanda had bent down to gaze at the 110 cc engine, four-stroke, the replacement for the overworked two-stroke she'd ridden for years. Last time the thing broke down, it was the timing piston. She'd fixed that herself. Now? Wanda thought it was the rocker arm. When it all finally fell to pieces, she thought she might just buy one of those retired post office Jeeps. Easy to break, easy to fix.

Now, Wanda adjusted Ruby's box on the back of the ATV. "Go on. Get in."

Ruby whined but then did her little gingerly jump-and-step into the cardboard box that Wanda fastened tight onto the back with bungee cords and a piece of rope. So far, the dog hadn't fallen out, and after five minutes, she always seemed to enjoy herself.

Wanda got on the ATV, adjusted herself on the battered seat, and zipped up her coat. "Okay, Ruby, time to fly."

She started the old engine. Putting her hand on the clutch, she turned it a little to feel for glitch and lurch. But Dwayne, good with his hands and tools, had done some magic.

Wanda put her feet up on the rests and turned the other handle gently, just enough for the ATV to creep forward, not enough to flood the whole thing and give Birdie time to run outside and holler Wanda back into the house.

The ATV bumped and jerked forward, Wanda holding tight, Ruby whining, her dog claws scratching the bottom and sides of the box. Birdie had horse ears, too, so Wanda went slow, bumping along the dirt driveway. In a few seconds, she was past the gravel by the barn (silently promising to give Six a good ride later) then onto the smoother dirt of Dempsey Mapp Road, headed southwest toward her work.

After a few minutes, she felt Ruby's warm breath on her neck, her snout on her shoulder. And there was the day opening up its palms. The road was wide, clear, smooth sailing. And what a thing it was to feel the fresh, clean air when in a couple of hours, it would be as hot as Hades. So what if there was a lick of fire in her nose. Right now, it was morning, a bloom of cool air overhead, and all hers.

Chapter Six

On the Road,
Oakland to Devlin
May 2012

At some point on I-80 just after he passed Sacramento, Nick clenched the steering wheel, gripped by the truth of the first thing his father said to him when Nick accepted the BLM job: "No Delgado ever fought fire."

That wasn't true, of course. Nick had fought fire. At firecamp. But he'd been protected, insured, supervised, and ordered. He'd been wearing his gear; he was prepared with mask, fire shelter, water, and tools (some of which he'd never seen before, like the Pulaski, a combination ax and grub hoe, and a combi, a shovel and hoe) and, most importantly, fellow firefighters at the ready. Nearby were Chris and the rest of the trainers, the people who could stop the fires before they turned deadly. But when that second controlled fire roared up and into the hill above the compound, there was that second he'd stepped back instead of moving forward and toward the fireline.

"They don't train you enough," he'd heard Megan say. "They send you in there to die."

Nick had tugged down his jacket and moved forward with his combi, pushing Megan out of his head.

"Keep one foot in the black," Chris had said as they worked, the black an escape, a place to run. In the black, the fire triangle of heat, oxygen, and fuel was already broken, nothing left to flicker into flame.

Now as Nick drove through the brown Sacramento flood plain and stared up at the looming white-blonde Sierra foothills, he zipped by nothing but fire triangle. California was ready for a burn. By the end of the summer, there would be more black than green.

Another firefighting concept wasn't as safe, as far as Nick could tell. No one foot anywhere.

"Bring your black with you," Chris had said, and at first Nick didn't understand, imagining picking up the burned ground as though it were a carpet, yanking hard, pulling it along behind him.

But bringing the black was risky, ironically dangerous though it was a common safety practice. You had to create the black, not rely on black already there. But together with his fellow fire campers, Nick burned the fallen leaves and grasses with a drip torch and pushed forward, digging with a combi and cutting at shrubs and trees with a chainsaw, pulling the burnt earth with them as they put out the blaze.

"Fuel. And heat. But never forget the other parts of the fire triangle," Chris said. "Oxygen. Especially wind. That's your unknown. Wind's the tricky part. Pay attention. One shift as you're burning the edge, and there might not be any black to run to. Nowhere to escape."

As Nick had mopped up the controlled burns, sweated inside his jacket, his helmet heavy and hot on his head, he thought about the black, how it was like the past, the life that had already been lived. The black—an area where there is no longer any flammable material—was like the last second, the last minute, the day before, a year before, childhood.

As he drove on past Roseville toward Auburn and Tahoe, he knew Megan was clicking on her seatbelt, waiting for her flight to Seattle to depart. She lived in his head like a photo, dark and silent, hunched over her books and laptop. He thought of his high school girlfriend Claire, off in her life somewhere. She wasn't a Facebook friend. Too much baggage. But he carried her in his head as well. Claire, short, blonde—a non-stop talker. That year between high school and college, she'd been like a barnacle, almost impossible to pry off, needing a knife to loosen her grip. But now he reached out, touching the memory.

But even she'd fluttered away. Nothing was easy to grab tight. The past was like smoke. Thick but impossible to hold. Nothing to do with it but wait for it to clear. At least with fire, you could put it out. Watch it die.

Once off 80 and in Devlin, Nick headed up a street, passed first what looked like another fire station and a small green-lawn park with a playground and swings, and then pulled up next to the flat, squat BLM station, his Subaru kicking up dust in the large gravel turnaround space. Parked in front of a large four-door garage was a huge lime green engine, two guys wearing long-sleeved t-shirts, work pants and boots washing it. Inside the open garage were two additional engines and a smaller truck, a chase rig used to hunt down fires.

Nick took in a big breath and got out of his car, his boots crunching on the gravel. He put his hands to his lower back and stretched. He glanced around at the burst of lawn by the station and then out toward the dry brown hills surrounding it. This dandelion-spotted patch seemed to be the last gasp of green.

"Hey," one of the guys called out, giving a wave. The other guy looked over and nodded, his eyebrows V'd in a slash. But then he went back to cleaning the engine's windows.

The friendlier one walked over, loped really, like some kind of horse or a big dog, a Great Dane or a wolfhound. Nick imagined he could hear him panting.

"Hi. You new?"

Nick shook the guy's warm hand. "Nick Delgado."

"Jim Mackenzie. Mac. First day here. Got here this morning. Most everyone else came yesterday. Or the day before. That's Thompson," he said, jerking his head toward the guy washing windows. "Engine captain. Third year. Takes a lot of pride in that rig."

Mac winked, and Nick felt the tension he hadn't even known he was carrying diminish. He was just about to ask after Andrew Jarchow, the fire operation supervisor who had hired him, when the door to the main building flew open. The man in the door frame was a tree trunk. Short and solid, he looked like he could bench press somewhere north of 300 pounds and run a fast 100 meter dash. He stood legs spread, arms akimbo, and at attention to the army of the environment. The man's right forearm flexed, the movement creating a wave in the tattooed plume of orange and red fire. Nick was just close enough to read the script above the tat: *Fight Always.*

His skin was the color of the polished wood in Nick's parents' house, the color of a roasted—maybe poisonous—nut.

"Glad you could make it, Delgado," he said. "Jarchow."

Nick nodded, his voice caught at the back of his throat. He took a couple of steps and thrust out his hand. Jarchow's grip wasn't viselike but held the promise it could be. "Hey," Nick managed.

Jarchow twitched his lips, irritated maybe or at least impatient with

Nick's obvious inability to converse. "Your room's 9. Unload and pull your car around back. See you in the mess in an hour."

Jarchow nodded and walked over to Thompson and the gleaming engine, both men examining the passenger door. Thompson worked the handle and swore a little, Jarchow akimbo again, nodding. Thompson might not want anything to do with newbies Nick or Mac, but he looked directly at Jarchow, face open. And in that instant, likeable.

"I'd like to tell you the FOS is a real softie inside, all cuddly and nice," Mac said as they headed back to Nick's car, Nick working to keep up with the guy's long strides. "But at this point, I'd be lying."

"Together, they could run a prison," Nick said, surprising himself. Mac laughed, hit him lightly on the shoulder.

"Then we're the inmates."

Nick smiled and pulled his gear out of his car. The station looked recently constructed, house-like, with a big main room, kitchen, and a long hallway with what seemed like twelve or so bedroom doors, some open, most closed. Mac helped lug his bags and backpacks to room 9, which was small and spare but clean with a bed long enough for Nick's 6'3" body.

"Two shared bathrooms," Mac said. "Deb gets her own. And from the common room, we can steal the internet from the county volunteer fire station next door. There's one corner that works best."

"Good," said Nick. When he had planned for the coming months, he'd assumed he'd have to drive into downtown Devlin or all the way to Kellogg City to get online. "But how come they have it and we don't?"

"You know. They're structural dudes. *Real* firefighters, according to everyone else. They're voluntary and get perks from the locals."

Real, thought Nick. Just like Megan said the day he'd gotten the job.

"Real firefighters train for years," she'd said at the end of their long fight that day, her voice ragged, hoarse. "Real districts don't just send you out to die."

"It is a 'real' district," he'd said. "What do you know about it?"

She'd started, eyes big and then hurt. She'd turned back to her laptop, ignoring him for the rest of the night. Angry because he'd what? Told her the truth? But to Megan deep into her Master's degree, only her books and ideas were real and true. Old stories about imaginary people that were safe tucked away in their stories.

But to be fair, no one had been wide-eyed with joy and excitement when Nick had told them about his job. As it had been his entire life, his parents had reacted differently to his decision to fight fire. His father was calm and cool with his list of practical advice. His mother was emotional, sad, proud, saying everything on her mind.

"You can study fire, but it doesn't keep you from getting hurt by it," she told him as they ate greasy hash breakfasts at the Rockridge Cafe.

"Great advice, Mom," Nick said. "I know what you've been reading. Giving the books to Megan when you're done, too. You've got to stop."

"The stories. My god. You know about that terrible—"

"They have better technology now. GPS. Weather radar. Cell phones. All the districts have Facebook and Twitter pages. People know what's going on and can stay connected."

"A fire doesn't have a cell phone, Nick. And Facebook? Please."

"It will help you keep track of what I'm doing." He reached over and took her hand.

"Oh, Nick. Why fire? Nine hundred firefighters have died since the forest service started."

"I know."

"People burn from the inside out. Their lungs melt first."

"Mom, stop." He was irritated now, wishing he could tell her to knock it off. But that's not how he spoke to her, especially since his Grandma Rosa scared the hell out of him when he was eight. She caught him giving his mother some lip, and later she said, "You know, *mi'jo,* what you do in life leaves a mark."

Nick had hoped this was just one of her Mexican superstitions, but ever since, he'd not been rude to his mother, imagining a scar for every one of his ugly remarks or fibs.

So he looked at his mother, saw her fear.

"Mom," he said.

"And those flimsy metallic fire shelters they give you? They don't work. They're hardly better than foil. They call them 'shake and bakes.' The fire races over you and you're all cooked up."

Nick had read the books. He'd seen the photos of the smiling firefighters, snapped the day—the hour—before they'd gone off to their deaths. His mom was right. Death was just part of the deal, but he couldn't worry the various tragedies like beads on Grandma Rosa's rosary. He'd never leave. He'd never go anywhere.

"Mom, come on." He let go of her hand and looked up at the server who held up a carafe of tea-colored coffee. He shook his head, and she smiled, moving to the next table. "I'll be okay. I promise."

He'd made her other promises, such as to keep her posted on fires and text her when he was called out. He'd made promises to Megan, too.

Megan's face had been a mix of yes and no, pride and horror when he told her he'd gotten the job. "Really?" She'd looked down at her hands folded in her lap, fingers lightly shaking, her breath a too-quick one, two. "It's for sure?"

"Yes." Nick tried to keep the up in his voice, the up that had carried him to their Lakeshore apartment. Up the stairs. Up to the open door. Up into the apartment to wait for Megan, who had just come home, put her books on the kitchen table, and was now sitting next to him.

"When do you go?"

"May 18th," he said.

"But you're not ready."

What did Megan know about anything? Had she even noticed what he'd been reading for months? What he'd been talking about as he searched for job openings? Had she paid attention to anything beyond what her next paper was about? Did it even really matter to her if he was here at all? Nick more furniture than boyfriend, more prop than useful appliance.

Megan waited. He looked at her knee, wishing he felt as he had just ten minutes before. He might reach out and touch her. Instead, he rubbed his forehead, closed his eyes. "I've got six weeks to workout hard. And there's boot camp when I get there."

"I mean real training. You've had what? Two weeks in a Colorado fire camp? Real firefighters train for years," Megan said. "Real districts don't just send you out to die."

"What's not real about this?" Nick asked.

Megan shook her head, closed her eyes. Their dining room table was full of all of Megan's work that had eventually taken over the entire apartment. Work that dominated their lives. Their schedule was dictated by her due dates for papers and tests; they could go out if she had crafted the perfect introduction or when she turned the last page of a novel. They could travel, eat, talk depending on if she'd emailed her professor her finished, perfect, worried-over, endlessly talked-about final draft.

Everything of hers was so important. *So real.* Obviously, these two years as he'd worked the odd, irritating jobs, his efforts had been fake. To her, wildland firefighting was fake? Maybe nothing was real to her but made up stories written by people dead for two hundred years. And it was true that all her studies would probably lead to a job. But so had his. Taking Joanna's advice, Nick had filled out one of those online surveys and put two and two together. The wild. Nature. And a clear task. Something he could do and learn to do better. When he came up with the job description, it all made sense to him. On paper, he'd thought it had made sense to Megan, too.

But now that it was one hundred percent real, it was fake.

"You're going to get hurt. They're going to send you into a place you're not prepared for, and you're going to die."

"I'm not going to die!" He stood up, the setting sun hitting him in the eyes, so he yanked on the blinds to close them.

"Fifteen wildland firefighters die a year."

"It's not going to be me."

"How can you possibly predict that?" Now Megan stood, wrenching off her sweater and throwing it on the couch. She walked to the kitchen and wiped her eyes with the back of a hand. Her hair was a tangle in the back, the way it had been in the morning. She'd been so busy, she'd not even bothered to shower before she went to campus. Her life was a pinprick of focus, a glimmer of light at the end that shone only on herself and her studies.

"I'll be careful," he said quietly. "Nothing bad is going to happen."

"How can you even know that?"

"I just do," he said.

She slumped into a chair at the table and put her head into her hands. "I didn't think it would work out. I thought you'd end up taking that job. The office work. You could transfer. We could have stayed together."

"I couldn't."

Megan was crying hard now, her words jagged and full of sadness. "But I hoped it would change."

"I'd change."

"You'd change."

"That's great, Megan. What if I said that about all your stuff?" He opened his arms, turned to take in her piles of words.

But she didn't follow him down the fight. He wished she would. He wanted her to say things he wouldn't be able to forgive her for. But all she said was, "My work doesn't kill anyone."

"The office job would kill me," he said.

Megan shook her head.

"Why doesn't anyone trust me to do this?" he asked, anger flaring in his throat. "I'm not some fucking idiot."

The fight floating around them spun, shimmered, and then fell to the old carpet.

"Firefighting," Megan said finally, looking up, walking toward him, her brown eyes wide and full of everything.

"I'm going to be on an engine. We always have water. That's what an engine does. We go in, spray, dig line, mop up. It's the hotshot crews and smokejumpers and helitack guys that are in all of those books my mom's been giving you. They're the ones who die. They get dropped into the action and are caught in the blowups. They're the ones right there, smack in the middle of fires burning in 60 foot trees. Not me. Not guys who dig line. Not the guys with the chainsaws and the hoes. We start on the edge and work our way in. We've always got one foot in the black."

Nick felt the heat in his face, his words hot in his mouth. He almost believed his own words.

Megan blinked, listening.

"I've got to do this," he said, pulling her close, her head against his chest. She smelled like their rumpled bed and laundry soap and lavender, the things that reminded him of their life together.

"I hate it," she said.

Nick wasn't sure what she hated: the job or what this job meant to them. About them. What were the chances they'd be together after all this? His job, her studies. In college, he'd always thought they'd grow up and then old together. Corny, trite, but he used the word soulmates during their first years.

But after graduation, they were no longer sharing much of anything. They didn't study together or laugh about things that happened at school. They no longer had shared friends. They didn't go to the same cafeteria or café and read while they ate the same food. Until the job offer, Nick had fallen off track. But he was back on now. No matter what everyone said, he was leaving for Nevada.

Nick had breathed in again, held her tight.

After pulling the Subaru around back and parking next to a Mustang (Thompson?) and a Matrix (Mac?) and admiring a brand new Ford 2500 (Jarchow, for sure), Nick went to the common room that was attached to the mess hall, where a long wooden table with benches on either side dominated the space next to a kitchen stocked with gigantic stainless steel appliances. On the stove, something bubbled, the steam fragrant with meat, tomatoes, and rosemary. Nick's stomach growled, loud enough that Mac laughed.

"Thompson says Jarchow cooks a mean stew," he said. "There's a cooking schedule. I'm up tomorrow."

Nick looked up at the whiteboard, reading the names for the week. Mac walked over and scrawled Delgado on Wednesday's open slot.
"Hope you got more than grilled cheese with tomatoes. That's my specialty."
Thank god for his four memorized recipes. If Mac threw him a smoked ham hock and a bag of lentils, he could make soup right now. As Mac showed him around the kitchen (two refrigerators, two sinks), Nick was suddenly grateful for all the long, dull down time in Oakland, if only for the recipes he'd learned to prepare.

Thompson, six other men, and one woman banged into the room, the screen door flying open, all of them talking. They seemed confident and easy with each other, that extra day or two having created some mysterious alchemy of personality. They sat down in the yard-sale-reject chairs and sofa. "How the hell did you end up in this shithole?" one guy asked Nick, his voice loud and full of laughter. He was huge, hard-muscled, freckled. Probably need about 100 SPF sunscreen. "No offense, or anything."

"You're here, too, Hamm bone," the woman said. "You explain it to all of us."

By the obvious process of elimination, Nick knew this was Deb.

"Devlin has a special place in my heart," the guy Hamm said. "It's a dream come true to drink at The Big Tap Bar with all the miners."

"Seriously," Deb said. "Why Devlin?"

Nick shifted on his feet and tried not to think of Megan agreeing with this conversation, saying "Yes, why Devlin? Why not a 'real' station?"

"Not much to explain. This was the district that hired me."

They all laughed. "Same for me," Deb said. "Same for all of us."

"Yep," another guy said. They introduced themselves, asked where Nick was from, where he'd trained, how long it took to drive from the Bay Area. Then they turned their attention to the big flat-screen television, tuned to ESPN, two giant men in kilts throwing enormous logs long distances.

Nick, having answered their questions, felt himself sitting in the corner of himself as he tried to figure out who *they* all were. This was like freshman year at the dorm, or even earlier when his parents moved them from Oakland to suburban Orinda. The terror of fourth grade, the way he was taller than all the other kids, unsure, wanting to hold onto his mother at the school door but also wanting to join in. For a second as the class stood in line waiting for the teacher to collect them, he'd felt a kinship with another boy, also named Nick. Later, he found out this Nick was Nic. No K. In the classroom as they sat at their desks, he chanced to see Nic's name card and the hope he'd felt turned to panic. It was true. He was really stuck in this town, at this school, with all these strangers. All he wanted was to run out and find his mother and beg to go home—not to their new house, but to the one they'd left in Oakland. Forget the good schools or the safe neighborhood. He wanted his shabby grammar school with the dinosaur computers and all the kids he'd known since kindergarten. He wanted to stay where he understood what was going to happen next, not this strange school where people misspelled ordinary names.

But he hadn't tried to run to find his mother. He and all the others sat at their clean, new desks with the shiny textbooks stacked on top. Nick faced his teacher and the blackboard and swallowed down the strangeness.

Now Nick longed to do the relaxed thing, be like these people, already comfortable with each other. When would he finally learn to be a piece of the bigger thing, whatever that bigger thing was? All his life he'd hovered and then moved in when the situation was vetted, good and safe, when he knew his way in and knew the escape routes. He hadn't asked Claire to go to the movies until she'd basically thrown her body in front of him in the P hall between classes. He didn't take his driving test until he was sure he could parallel park.

"Jesus, Nick," his mother had finally said as he slipped in between a motorcycle and minivan on College Avenue. "It's time. I can't even do this as well as you."

He didn't apply for the fire jobs until he'd passed both trainings and had taken a refresher course.

But maybe his caution was why he was a natural at wildfire fighting, as Chris at firecamp had said.

The kilted guys yelling on the screen, Nick stepped in closer, listening, collecting information, getting everyone straight in his mind. Their names: Johnson, Mac, Wicks, Hamm, Lehman, Schraeder, Thompson, Cowley. Schraeder, Wicks, and Thompson captained the engines, taking orders from Jarchow. Johnson, Lehman, and Hamm were the engine operators, the guys who drove where the captains told them to go. That left Cowley, Mac, and Nick as the crew members, one in each engine.

He wasn't surprised to have a woman at the station, but he was surprised by how slight Deb Cowley was, dark, lean, short hair, sharp pretty features. A tiny mole on her left cheek. A wide smile. Wicks was big and funny; Hamm bigger, louder, and bulky, with thoughtful, green eyes. Lehman looked half Asian or something, the other half white. Schraeder? Irish or Scottish or maybe even Swedish, pale and blond. Johnson was quiet, dark-haired, and muscular, fully ready for all the exercise ahead of them. When turned to Thompson, Nick almost flinched at his politically incorrect thought. But there it was despite himself. The guy was as black as the clarinet Nick was forced to play in seventh grade and seemed as intricate and difficult to understand.

Nick sat down on a high metal stool and listened to the chatter, adding in comments here and there, still wary, still but making the turn inside himself.

"Hope you're ready for boot camp," Wicks said, shaking his close-to-shaved head. He must be former Army or Marines, blue-eyed, square-jawed, muscled as hell. His work shirt sleeves rolled up, Wicks' forearms bulged from the fabric like the wrong appendage. Like legs-- like calves. And if that were true, Nick wasn't sure what his calves looked like.

"Boot camp!" Deb almost snorted. "Hardly. We're going to be in Kellogg City almost all day tomorrow for lame-ass refresher classes."

"More like Ruby Fire District cover-your-asses classes," Hamm said.

"Lawsuits," Thompson said. "District can't even afford to pay us. If we don't sue them, maybe we'll get some overtime."

"Yeah, but don't worry," Lehman said to Nick and Mac who came to sit down with them. "The FOS will get in a workout before we go. Probably a three-mile run with our packs just for good measure."

"Great." Thompson leaned back in his chair and stretching his legs. "Another run. I could barely walk this morning. And today wasn't even for reals. You newbies are in for a treat."

Nick had been running and lifting all winter and spring, hiking on the weekends with his father, doing sit-ups and pushups every night before bed. On Sunday mornings, he ran around Lake Merritt with a backpack weighted with forty pounds of rocks. His boots were broken in, his skin browned from the sun. His lungs and heart and quads were ready for heat and distance. He was the strongest he'd ever been in his life, and though he was sure boot camp or whatever they were calling it would really hurt, he could handle it.

"Chow's on," Jarchow said. Deb and Hamm jumped up, grabbing utensils and plates and setting the table as if it were a game board, forks sliding, cups rolling. Nick walked toward the table and almost stopped, surprised by something but what? He watched the action around the table, the bustle of passing plates and settling down, and then he knew what surprised him. He was smiling. More than that. He felt a satisfaction he'd never really believed in, something that started at his feet, something that was working its way up to his chest, his heart, his face.

The long months in Oakland slipped away. What had started out as Nick and Megan's great Bay Area adventure, had turned into two years of one day and then the next and the next. Nick learning to make hot and spicy pork stir fry and fried chicken. Megan slumping in after class, spreading her work across the table or falling asleep sprawled on the bed. Megan and he eating together, not talking, her face in a book, Nick on his laptop scrolling through fire district sites.

"Sit down," Thompson said. "Eat now or just don't eat. There aren't ever any leftovers."

Nick sat and pulled his steaming bowl close.

Chapter Seven

Kellogg City, Nevada
May 2012

KelloggCityFreePress.Com—The Daily Donnelly
A Year in Nevada by Em Donnelly

Okay all you from everywhere else. Next time you're sitting around bored, try to conjure a few details about any of our fine fifty states. It's a good way to pass the time while on line at the post office or sitting in a dentist's chair, your mouth numbed up. Also, not a bad way to fall asleep when you have insomnia. You don't have to pull up something profound. It goes like this:

Massachusetts: Pilgrims. Paul Revere. Oysters.

Mississippi: Mark Twain, riverboats, floods. Easier to spell than Missouri.

California: Marijuana, Berkeley, the Pacific.

Next?

Okay, well, try Nevada.

When I played this game in the nervous morning hours before I set out by rickety car to drive 2500 miles from Boston to Kellogg City more than a year ago, here's what I came up with: Nuclear testing, gambling, prostitution, heat. Heat. Oh, yes—wait for it—heat.

But you get my point. As a Boston girl raised near the Atlantic Ocean, an East Coast native brought up in the land of historical American myth, fable, and folklore, I didn't think to expect more than the above from Nevada, certain as I pressed down on the gas pedal that my list wouldn't improve. As I slipped into the state for my first job after running away from grad school, I wasn't exactly bowled over by the flat expanse of I-80 around East Wendover, the nondescript blue sky, the murk of white haze on the horizon, the bare, rocky Goshute mountain range.

But I didn't know everything. Yes, the list I conjured in my child-hood bedroom is true. After over a year on the Kellogg City blog beat, I can tell you I'm already familiar with the acronyms EPA, BLM, DOE, and the DOD. There are a lot of folks out there worrying the environment, the land, and what's under the land and how to get it out and use it to make things go boom!

There's the BIA and the IHS, a whole native population and their affairs and health to understand.

But more than anything, I've been surprised by the natural beauty. Yes, call me crazy (my Boston friends do). For instance, the Ruby Mountains on a cold spring day, a dusting of snow on top, the sun a flare of pink. Early morning sparrow song in Lamoille Canyon. Wild-flowers. Oh, my god. A ton of wildflowers, even alongside that damn I-80. Yellow bells, creeping jenny, poppies, and lupine flaring against the particular blue of a clear Nevada sky. Not just a watery I-80 pale. But something cliché, extreme even, maybe cerulean. Maybe navy. Then a fleet of clouds heading south, underneath them shadows as big as cities. And wait, surprise, a whirl of red-winged blackbirds in an evening sky.

And that sky. Out in the open, under the sun, I can see, well, a lot of stuff, so much and so damn far in all directions.

I know nature isn't my beat per se, but Kellogg City and northern Nevada are, both filled with many more details than I could have ever imagined (Cowboy Poetry Gathering? Every winter!) But there are troubles afoot, and I'm here to report on land management, mining and grazing rights, zoning laws. Mine workers living in tents in the Walmart parking lot, undocumented workers at the local casinos, shake-ups at Tribal meetings. Just you wait. More is coming for you newcomers wanting the lay of the land and those of you who want the perspective of someone seeing things for the first time. But let me just declare I've officially changed my list. Who knows what else I'll find?

Chapter Eight

Northern Nevada
Mapp Ranch
May 2012

"Hey there, Ms. Mapp," Sheriff Jeff Bryant said from his open cruiser window. His tanned elbow and the glare from his thick stainless steel watch were the only things Wanda could see as she crouched at a fence post, bending a curling, truculent loop of barbed wire with her gloved hands. His car blew dusty air toward her, and she closed her eyes against the unavoidable waft of exhaust. The big V8 engine glugged like a bear on beer. She could smell the thick rubber tread of his brand-new tires.

Nine in the morning, and for sure the day was going to be a scorcher. The spring had burst open with heat and dryness, the winter too short, the ground already parched and cracked, parting in dusty brown veins along the fence line. That noxious cheat grass had invaded the ranch and was near white from heat even as it spread its beasty tentacles. Milkweed sprouted up like green mistakes here and there, but everything else was blond to tan, dead to deader. Wanda could almost see black ticks in the brush, scorpions buried under debris and twigs and such, tarantulas hiding in their burrows. Sweat dripped down the sides of her face, her neck, and along her sides, finding slip and safety in the flesh around her middle. Ruby had curled up in a tight dog roll and was sleeping in the tiny piece of shade cast by the ATV. Wanda could imagine a Coke crackling in a tall glass with ice.

But first this wire wrapped tight in her hands. And then the sheriff. She wrestled the wire into place and then took hammer and nail and battened it down, hoping that the post could take one more good pound. But pretty soon, she'd have to replace it instead of the wire.

"Looks like the wind'll blow that fence right on over. Don't know how it'll keep all those head on your land."

Wanda smirked. Oh, how he was trying to suss out the Mapp herd.

She searched her mind for the truly evil word that would sit on the Sheriff's head like a bad hat. Problem was, he wasn't an evil man, and he was already wearing a bad hat, that sheriff's thing a pretend-to-be- cowboy hat but not quite. Bryant was nothing but ignorant with a frosting of stupid. His momma Irene ran a second-hand store in Kellogg City on Utah Street, a good woman who did charity work, proud of her son, despite his toady behavior and all that BLM shoulder rubbing.

But it didn't pay to irritate Bryant. The more Wanda resisted, the closer he came, driving down from Kellogg City every odd chance he got. He'd ask questions about Birdie's visitors. A journalist who had flown into Reno and stayed nights in Kellogg City. He'd ask what Stanley was doing at the tribal meetings. He'd poke around a bit with Wanda, asking about the herd count. If those topics didn't dislodge a fact he could chew on, he'd mention Linda Quinn, the state BLM supervisor who came armed with new plans to enforce stricter laws. He'd talk about grazing rights. He'd say something irksome like, "Why can't Indians get with the program? Why can't you all forget this tribal nonsense?" On and on he'd go, his voice slow and calm and sweet.

What did he think she'd say? Maybe, "Sheriff, I've got a thousand head of cattle just over that hill yonder. Yes, sir. Go get the BLM cowboys and you can sell them off."

Or maybe, "Birdie and I are fixing to sell every acre. Maybe a mining company will snap it up."

It was just too damn hot to bicker, parry, or wrangle, so Wanda closed her eyes, and then pushed up to standing, holding onto the fence post that wobbled slightly at her pressure. The heat radiated from the hot earth into her boots.

"Morning," she said.

The sheriff took off his glasses, his bright blue eyes locked on her. "Morning. Where's that flea-tick bag of yours you call a dog?"

"Fell asleep the minute you drove up. Already knew the tiresome conversation."

Bryant nodded, a slight smirk on his full red lips, almost like a woman's, but then he had those two big white teeth. Birdie had invented and often used her own special word for the Sheriff's teeth—*bucksome*—and that's what came to mind as Wanda glared into the full and forward gleam of his smile.

"Need a hand?"

There he goes, Wanda thought. He knew she never needed or accepted a hand. "All done," she said. "Only four thousand more to go. The whole ranch a tangle of barbed wire."

Bryant's eyes took in a little morning light, his expression softening. She remembered when he was a little boy at Irene's store, sitting on the counter as he watched TV and ate a Snickers, his face and fingers gooey brown smears.

"Jeez, get Dwayne out here. Good work'll keep him out of trouble."

Here it was. All she had to do was stare and be silent.

"I saw him talking with Len Dunning day or two ago," the sheriff said. "That dude is bad news."

"Stole a car once. Wrote a bad check, maybe. That's all."

"That's not all," Bryant said.

Wanda forced herself to stay still, even as a rivulet of sweat zoomed down her spine and joined her sisters in the pool on her waistband.

"Talking isn't a crime. At least, not yet. Anyway, last I heard, Len's living in Yomba," Wanda said.

Len Dunning. Twelve in her memory. Sharp, skinny, more anger than brains. A chip on his shoulder than weighed more than he did.

"Used to be," the sheriff said. "Not anymore. Moved with some Indian girl up to Kellogg City. Living in a place behind the movie theater. Working at the rez convenience shop."

Indian girl. Wanda wiped her forehead, looking down at the dead grass, the scurry of a big black ant over an obstacle course of pebble and stick.

"Dwayne and Len came up together," Wanda said. "Same age in school. Not a crime, far's I know."

Bryant slipped his sunglasses back on. "Dunning was in jail. Got in with a bad bunch."

Now Wanda was losing her patience, the sun cupping her neck with an insistent hand, her whole body a shimmering slick.

"They were protesting, Sheriff. You know that. Got arrested for blocking the Devlin mine. Banners and words and maybe a rock or two banging against the metal entrance sign. Not murder."

"Not yet," Bryant said, winking.

Wanda thought of her horse Six, the way the mare stamped down her front hooves, one, two, blowing air out her nostrils, rearing back until Wanda pulled down on the reins. Right now, she wished she sat atop Six, able to tower over the cruiser, horse against car. Today, right now, on this land? Horse would win.

"If Dwayne sees his old high school friend, that's a good thing."

"Okay, okay," the sheriff said, and at his tone, Wanda realized she'd spoken loudly, her words heavy in the air. She didn't want to yell. She didn't want to fight. She wanted to finish the fence and go home and sit at the kitchen table and read the paper with her glass of Coke. She wanted to slide next to Stanley on the couch and watch one of those soap operas, maybe the one in the hospital where no one seemed sick, just mad crazy in love. Birdie had left the day before, and Tanya would stop by in the afternoon with a pot of stew or a pan of macaroni all crispy on the edges. Maybe a teeny pint of ice cream, if her niece was feeling lenient. If Dwayne came along, Wanda might figure out this Len Dunning business, though business was the wrong word. Piffle. Rigmarole. Bunch of hooey.

But breath was hard for a second. She didn't think of her nephew in the barn banging down loose boards or riding with the herd. Or even sitting at the table laughing over a bowl of chili. No, there was Dwayne holding Stanley's arm as they came home from Kellogg City, both of them dark and shining with something secret.

Wanda turned toward the ATV, Ruby's scratching jiggling the machine, a *whick, whick, whick* of claws against tough old dog skin.

Bryant put his car in gear and turned his steering wheel, the midday sun topaz in his glasses. He looked fake, a robot, something made of metal and heat.

"Just tell Dwayne to stay away from Dunning," Bryant said. "Trust me on this one, Ms. Mapp, even though I know you don't want to."

A nod, a smooth roll of the wheel, a triangle of dust wide and thick, and Bryant was headed back down Dempsey Mapp Road, Wanda watching him go.

Wanda found Stanley sitting on the couch in the cool cave of the house, remote in hand, the caterwaul of characters filling the room, the television on the highest volume. He couldn't see everything in front of him, but he could make out the periphery, sometimes turning his head to look from the corners of his eyes, especially during exciting scenes. But he knew his TV shows' main characters by voice, picking up others' names and settings through the non-stop, quick-as-a-wink dialogue. At the clack of the closing door, he glanced up as Wanda walked in and hung her hat on the rack.

"Hey, Sister," Stanley said. "Just in time for some good stuff. Marissa is about to tell Jared she can't marry him. He's big trouble for sure. She found his email to Cindy."

"Sounds good, Brother," Wanda said, Marissa a character Wanda knew too much about. "Want a Coke?"

"What?"

"Want a Coke?"

"What?"

"A Coke? Want a Coke?"

"Oh, nah," he said. "Dwayne and me had one before."

Wanda stared at Stanley, struck again by how he looked both old and young at the same time, bald, wispy haired, round of face. He looked exactly like a seventy-four-year-old man, but also like a child, his face as unlined as his conscience. What bad could he have done? For years now, he'd sat on the couch or, at the most, shuffled out to the deck to sit with Wanda and Birdie and whoever else on warm evenings. Sometimes, he and Dwayne played "Name That Indian," Stanley asking questions like, "Who's the only Indian to win an Oscar?"

Wanda hadn't known the answer to that one, surprised when Stanley finally said, "Buffy Sainte-Marie."

"Damn! What kinda hell Indian name is that?" Dwayne asked, but Stanley just shouted out another question.

Lately, Tanya and Dwayne had been taking Stanley to council meetings, Stanley coming back fired up about water pollution and property rights. One day when she was doing the wash, she found Stanley's dungaree pockets packed with gum wrappers, folded pamphlets, and phone numbers of people she didn't know. And Wanda had been alive long enough to know most everyone.

After a jaunt with Dwayne, Stanley would come through the door, dropping the arm that helped him in. He'd stamp his feet a bit and bluster about something or another. But as soon as he sat down, he turned back into couch Stanley. It was hard to imagine how angry he'd been years before, protesting and even traveling around the country with Birdie well into his fifties. The worst had been when he stood on that truck, slick with gasoline. It took her breath still. The way his shoulders glistened as he held up the gas can. The sound of his wet body thumping on the ground as the agents jammed on the handcuffs. His head bloodied, his voice loud. She'd wanted to run to him, beat the men off, pull him to safety. There that spark was still, flaming up and over them all before she had the chance.

But they'd grabbed her and Birdie, too. They'd only been able to watch as Stanley, the agents, and the horses headed down Mapp Ranch Road. Nothing left but fumes and smashed grass.

Some days, Wanda thought she smelled that angry, desperate gasoline on Stanley's neck, in his hair, the fumes floating around him still.

Wanda took out a Coke from the old fridge and popped the top, deciding to forego ice and glass. The freezer didn't do more than halfway ice anyway, skinny half melted moons. Sitting slowly, she let herself be drawn closer to her brother by the couch itself, the cushions worn into slopes by their rear ends. By the time she finished sliding, their shoulders touched. The soap opera squawked the sounds of those betrayed, loud and with gusto, enough so that Stanley might almost see it. Wanda sipped her drink, feeling the heat of the day on her skin and Bryant's words in her heart, that old sow of muscle that beat out a hard one two, one, one two.

When the show went to a commercial for some green cleaner that bubbled like a science experiment, she turned down the volume. "So Dwayne was here?"

"For sure." Stanley nodded, listening for the sound of the show to return. The fingers of his left hand absently stroked the cat arm of the couch.

Wanda waited. Stanley shifted, sighed, and then said, "Meeting on Saturday."

"About what?"

Stanley stroked the cat a bit faster, his fingernails scratching the worn fabric. As Wanda waited for his answer, he pressed his lips together, the way he had as a boy seventy years ago when their father told him to go to bed or clean up his damn mess. Wanda stared at her brother's wet lip. How it was possible they were both so old? That boy and this man couldn't be of the same bone and blood and mind. And she? Wanda looked down at her Coke bottle in her chapped, rough, wrinkled hands. Her skin was old, but she was the same person inside, the same as she'd always been. Think all she did about Stanley ass down on this very couch, but she'd never stood up to men with guns while trying to protect her kith and kin. Nothing had changed her, and she was pretty sure something needed to. What did Birdie always say, "A journey of a thousand miles begins with a single step." Of course, Wanda rolled her eyes every time she heard it. But, as usual, her sister was right. No step? No travel. No marriage. No children.

Or with Birdie? Too many steps. And look what she left behind while taking them. Family, the ranch, her own baby girl.

"There's some talk about trouble," Wanda said, watching his eyelids. Too much blinking and Stanley was lying.

Wanda turned up the volume, the TV flaring with dramatic music. Oh, the Coke had already worn off, the hot day's worth of work pulsing in her body. Wanda's old bones were still her old bones. No wonder they hurt. On the screen, Cindy and Marissa stalked each other like bobcats, fangs and claws out, ready to fight to the death for Jared. Wanda turned to look at her brother, but Stanley was watching the TV, blinking, blinking, blinking fast.

Wanda had one firm hand on Six's withers, the other on a brush as she worked out the last of the horse's winter coat, the smooth, constant sound what Wanda imagined the ocean was like. She'd never seen the sea. Once during a too-long stretch home, Birdie got the ants in her pants and begged Wanda to go with her on a trip to San Francisco.

"Let's go to Ocean Beach!" Birdie had said. "Carmel! The whole wide Pacific in front of us. We can dip in our toes."

Wanda had driven by car to Kellogg City, Reno, Carson City, once to Las Vegas for Tanya's college graduation, and a few times to Pine Ridge, Oglala, and Rapid City, South Dakota to visit their mother's family. But she'd never been on an airplane or a train. There'd been that one bus ride from Rapid City to Pine Ridge and back, Wanda gripping her bag the entire time, woozy as she never got on a horse. Horses had their own minds and clear opinions, but Wanda understood them. Right now, Six was under her very hands, warm and sure. She never got that from the ATV or the truck, so forget about an airplane.

The barn door opened with a triangle of sunlight, and Tanya came inside, brushing cobwebs out of her long black hair. She was taller than Birdie and sharper in the face. But softer in the eyes and quicker to smile. At her arrival, swallows spun and dove from their nests, arcs of whirling black dots outside. Up in the rafters, the busy whine of starlings. Somewhere up there, too, Wanda imagined an owl, maybe bats covering their blind eyes with thin wings. Ruby looked up from biting her back quarters, woofed, and then got back to work, snuffling as she searched out a flea.

"It's like a haunted house in here," Tanya said.

Wanda nodded. "Ride the spiders like horses."

"Giddy up!"

"Heh," Wanda laughed, standing up straight, a hand to her lower back.

Tanya put on her gloves and rolled down her shirt sleeves, Wanda watching her niece as she did. Tanya worked at the gym teaching health and exercise classes, trying to prevent the diabetes that the kids were getting, some of them so fat you couldn't see their eyes through the press of cheeks and foreheads. Other days, she worked at the tribal health clinic with the fattest young ones, trying to keep them from having to take insulin and whatnot.

"All the Coke," Tanya had told her. "Damn sodas. I've got to get you all off of it. I know you sneak it in for Stanley."

Tanya kicked at a hay bale and then maneuvered it to the barn floor.

"So Len Dunning goes to the tribal meetings?" Wanda laid a palm on Six's flank, feeling the quivering river of horse energy.

"Yep." Tanya pierced the bale with a pitchfork, a crackle of split hay filling the air. She worked, forking hay into the stalls. Tanya was the one precious child to come out of their pack. Thin but competent, her arms were strong, muscled, used to hard work. She'd had Dwayne too early, her fifteen-year-old pregnant body seeming so odd, wrong, but she'd pushed Dwayne out as if he were a baseball and not an eight pound screaming thing already grasping. When Dwayne was but a toddler, Birdie finally decided to wrangle things. While Wanda, Stanley, and sometimes Birdie took care of Dwayne, Tanya was packed off to the University of Nevada in Las Vegas on scholarship to major in sociology. Tanya graduated once and then again with her master's degree in public health and came home for good. Most days, though, she showed up at the ranch after long clinic hours to help Wanda in the barn with the horses and also in the middle of the night when mares foaled.

After they moved down the road to the small house Dempsey had built for his sister years ago, Tanya would drive up, Dwayne tucked tight in a sleeping roll in the car. Eventually, she had to force him to come with her, he sullen or spitting nails as he mucked out the stalls. But lately, Dwayne was here even when he wasn't on call. Working on the ATV. Laughing with Stanley at some dumb thing on the TV. Sometimes, she caught him on the porch staring up at the Cortez Mountains, just like Dempsey used to.

There was something Wanda needed to say, but her question was a turtle with its head pulled in.

"What is it, Auntie?" Tanya stopped moving, her eyes bright, a light sheen of sweat on her forehead.

If Birdie were around, all Wanda would have to do is mention what Bryant said, and Birdie would be at the bottom of it—or through the bottom, digging a hole around the problem and moving on to the next one. Even if Wanda knew what the boggle was, she was never sure what to do about it.

"They're really going to meetings?"

"Yep," Tanya said. "It's good. Get that boy on the right track."

"What track is that?"

"Anything but awful," Tanya said.

"So he's all about awful?"

Tanya put down the fork, leaning on it and wiping her forehead with the back of her forearm, whisking away sweat and probably irritation at her old crone aunt.

"Auntie, what did you hear?"

Wanda shrugged, something like shame beating a wing inside her. She saw Dwayne every single day. Why would she believe the sheriff?

"Sheriff Bryant—"

"Him? That big bucksome jerk. Don't pay any attention. Whatever he said, it doesn't mean anything."

"He said Dwayne is getting mixed up in something bad. With Len."

Tanya stilled. Wanda could see her niece's breath catch. For a little less than half Tanya's life, Dwayne had been a hardship. Not his fault for being born. He was a good boy at heart, but what was Tanya to do when he started all his mischief? Then she was away at school, her boy raised up partial by his grandmother and a crotchety old aunt whose bones creaked like an old bench. Some weekends, Tanya came home to a child who ran away when she walked through the door. When Dwayne was a teenager, he whirled up a great rage, missing the father who'd moved off rez long before he was born and left him stuck with the women. For a time, Stanley had been there, teaching Dwayne about the machines and horses. Taught him to hunt jackrabbit. But then his eyesight was going, so Wanda taught Dwayne to drive. Now they were all getting old now, not able to teach Dwayne much of anything.

He already knew plenty. Drinking, drugs maybe. Vandalized sign at the Devlin mine. That girl Sheree. Oh, her angry daddy and his baseball bat. A true wonder Dwayne didn't have one or two of his own children. A flat out miracle he hadn't been stabbed behind a bar or bruised up or worse in a car wreck on the interstate. Now, finally, grown and a true help on the ranch, Dwayne understood what Tanya had been through. But it hadn't made him stop the drinking or the driving around Kellogg City with people who shouldn't be behind the wheel of any car. Whatever might be going on, it wasn't like he'd take advice from his creaky aunt Wanda. But when she thought of Dwayne, she smelled that old gas can, heard the wheel of the lighter turn under an angry thumb.

"What's Len into?" Tanya asked.

"Don't know. Sheriff just said for Dwayne to steer clear."

"From Len?"

"From trouble."

"Oh." Tanya avoided Wanda's gaze and looked down at her boot, kicking at some hay.

From across the barn, Wanda could feel the sadness inside Tanya, exhausted tears from twenty-one years of a parenting worry Wanda would never be able to feel exactly, though now something like sorrow ached in her throat. But before either of them could shed a tear or say another word, Tanya stood straight and started baling hay.

"I'll find out," she said, hair falling in front of her face as she worked.

Wanda leaned against Six, the horse stomping, impatient to be in her stall eating, probably already feeling the crunch and crackle of oats between her teeth. But warm horse body or no, Wanda couldn't avoid the scariness of life.

As if she commiserated, there was Ruby, leaning against Wanda's right leg, panting a little.

"I'll kick his ass," Tanya said.

"It's okay, girl," Wanda said, part to Six, part to Ruby, part to Tanya and part to herself. "It'll be all right."

Tanya hefted hay, her forearms now lightly breaded with flecks of chaff and sawdust. Six nickered. As Wanda breathed in the sharp tang of horse urine mixed with hay, she felt her heart slow. Tanya's steady movements lulled them both.

Nodding, Wanda patted Ruby and then turned back to her work, the brush sliding smoothly over Six, who was minding patiently again, but by her flicks of muscle and flesh, readying to move on.

Neither Wanda nor Tanya spoke, both busy, and a wide hush filled the barn into which poured the sounds of swallows, their swooshes, dips, and arcs. Then there was sunlight, whirling dust motes, the sweet nickering of the other horses. Outside the barn, Nevada called like a good friend needing a visit, the earth lonely for horse hooves at a gallop and the laughter and whoops of riders.

But Wanda didn't take off on Six. Not that she could do that anymore without some preparation. No, she stayed in the barn, listening to the sounds of the pitchfork. The jab. The lift. The soft fall of hay in the stalls. The sound of Tanya's old sadness as it filled the air. Chaff and grief sparkled in chance rays of sun like jewels.

Chapter Nine

Devlin, Nevada
May 2012

Nick's first five days at the station were spent mostly driving to Kellogg City and sitting through classes, though the rumors about intense physical training were true enough. By six-thirty, they were all up, fed, and running in the hills above the station. They raced back on the final stretch, only to be told to do push-ups, pull-ups, squats, and lunges. Wednesday by six am, they were hiking in full gear and with loaded packs.

Thursday when they pulled up to the Fire Operation Center in Kellogg City, a half circle of protestors blocked the District's driveway.

"What's it this time?" Hamm slowed down and then braked sharp and hard as the groups surged around them. "The sage grouse?"

"Can't you read?" Thomason said, pointing. "Horses."

Nick bent down and looked out at the signs the protestors shook at them.

No Grazing Fees—Grazing rights and
Horses Not Horse Meat.

More to the point: *BLM Get Out*

"This has nothing to do with fire," Thompson said, dismissing the protestors with a one-hand beat on the dash.

"Feel free to go out and tell 'em that," Hamm said. "Tribe seems eager to listen."

Thompson shook his head. "Don't kill anyone. But get us the hell out of here, okay?"

"Yes, sir, Captain." Hamm pressed on the accelerator, moving the engine slowly through the group. The crowd parted to let the engine through, but they pressed close, looking up into the windows. On the other side of the glass, dark faces glared, some beneath fancy headdresses, one woman under a hat that looked like half a blue Easter egg. Two women in beaded dresses raised fists as the firefighters slid past. Indians. That was the word that popped into Nick's head, even though he knew he should think *Native Americans*. The first he'd seen since arriving in Nevada. Such festive clothes, but their gestures—the raised arms, the mouths forming angry shouts—were nothing close to celebratory. When they looked at him, did they think White Man, the way he'd just thought Indian?

"What's this horse thing?" he asked.

"BLM horse round ups," Thompson said. "Not us. Well, I've been to one. Anyway, BLM rounds up wild horses on their land. Tribal land. Or treatied land. Though apparently, it's not always their land. So it's them against the government."

"Good times," said Hamm, as he turned the wheel, forearm flexing, eyes flicking between his side view mirrors. "The wild west."

Just as they'd almost made it through, two guys about Nick's age caught his stare and stared back, both long-braided and dark-skinned, the taller sporting a scar under his jaw. The other dude held up his sign—*Ruby Treaty Breakers*—in front of his chest and strode toward the window. Nick swallowed, sat back in his seat, but the guy held his gaze, pointed at him, mouthed, "You."

Nick almost nodded, knowing yes, me. But no, not *me*. Not by half, literally. He wanted to jump out of the cab and talk to the guy, convince him he was no horse taker. He wasn't the bad guy. He wasn't white. But that wasn't completely true. His mom Susan was white. Raised middle-class. Her dad went to work, her mom stayed home until the kids were in school. Only then did Grandma Flo work part time at the library.

Susan met Jess at Cal, where he'd landed a scholarship. "Found me at a water fountain," she'd told Nick. "Saw me running every day and then waited for me to stop."

For the first week, she didn't know where Jess was from. "Dark eyes, dark hair, dark skin. Sexy as hell. Yes! I have to say it. But no clue," she said. "I thought maybe Hawaii."

Made sense. Jess had pulled himself out of the immigrant blue-collar world. From seventh-grade on after Grandpa Victor moved them to the LA suburbs, no accent. From that point too—often repeated—straight A's. Nick's mother called Jess "The All-American Mexican." Football, basketball, a cheerleader girlfriend.

Nick's racial identity was on his skin but covered by his fire-fighter gear. It was in his heart but once removed. And maybe, he thought, removed by choice. Or action. Or inaction.

So he turned away from the guy's dark, hard eyes and focused on the engine's slight jerking moves as Hamm inched them closer to the office.

"Jesus," Hamm said, as they cleared the group, the protestors turning toward another engine rumbling up into the drive. "Don't they know we're on their side? We're protecting their land."

"Maybe that's the point," Nick said. "The *their* part. Apparently, no one's using that possessive pronoun."

"Oh, don't go showing off," Thompson said. "You know I'm only three units shy of my BS in chemistry. Don't be going all smarty pants with that Evergreen degree of yours."

At least I have a degree, Nick wanted to say. But he was lucky to be in the engine and not stuck at another table now watching Megan start her Ph.D.

Hamm laughed and pulled around to the back of the building. Nick turned to look back. The protestors stabbed the air with their signs, yelled at the next engine and the one after that. Even as Hamm revved them out of sight and parked in the bay, Nick heard the yells, saw the guy's eyes, felt the *you* all the way to his heart.

Friday, they loaded up, Hamm behind the wheel headed to the center, his eyes intent on the road as he chewed on and then spit out sunflower seeds. As they roared by in the fluorescent green engines, people looked up. Nick noticed the faces. Other than the protestors from the day before and the influx of Mexican migrant workers, everyone seemed white. Really white. Pale, light-eyed, and light-haired, freckled, fat, and sunburned.

"Away from our little red-lined fire station, it feels like Utah or Idaho out here, doesn't it?" Thompson said, the edge of his words sharp. "Maybe Sweden."

Redlined? The real estate term? But then he got it. There they were, tucked away in Devlin, all the Americans with racial adjectives: Asian, Latino, African. Not to mention a woman. All lined up at one convenient station.

"Shit," Nick said.

"You've seen other stations, right?"

"Not really."

"But you've seen what kind of people live in Nevada?" Thompson asked. "Everyone with dark skin is working inside a casino. Or in a mine."

"What about on the ranches?" There had to be migrant workers somewhere. Back in the Bay Area, the world would literally collapse if the Latino workers disappeared.

Thompson shook his head. "I was at this barbeque last season, me and this other black dude and about a couple hundred white people. It was the volunteer firefighters' fundraiser, but all these drunk assholes crashed, racers from the Dusty Times 250 off-road event. The other guy is one of the only other black firefighters in Nevada, and he comes up to me, and we're talking about nothing really. Shooting the shit. Then this white guy walks up, a beer in his hand, and says, 'Wow! You're the only two black people around! It's like seeing two actual frigging unicorns or something. At the same time! We should set you two loose up in the hills and hunt you down.'"

"No way. For real?"

"Yeah," Thompson said, shaking his head. "I'm staying away from white men with grills this year. No offense, Hamm."

"None taken," Hamm said. "What're you talking about?"

"Fucking Nevada," Nick said. "This is where the tide of progress stopped."

"Trust me," Thompson said. "We can't even see the water from here."

"It's not your mother's Ford," Jarchow lectured to them in the final class of the long week. He strode alongside the gleaming Ruby District engine, bigger and newer than the three overhauled and overused engines at the Devlin station. Sweat trickled in clear, orderly paths down his temples. "BLM designed this four-door 667 for Western US off-road firefighting. Six-person crew, 865 gallon tank, 20 gallons foam concentrate, Navistar 4800. The pump here can deliver its full rating at elevations up to 5,000 feet and temperatures up to 100°F. The tank polypropylene. Body stainless steel.

Remember, as an engine crew, your first defense is water. Here's your delivery system."

After learning the specs about the engine, they took turns driving. When Nick was up, he sat with the enormous steering wheel in his hands. He was almost scared to turn it, much less press the large accelerator under his boot. The power from the engine radiated into his stomach, his breath slightly uneven. How was it that firefighter hadn't made it on his list of childhood dreams? In second-grade, he'd written them down in response to a homework prompt, and during his freshman year of college, his mother had emailed him the list. He'd been very specific: NASA pilot, Air Force radar controller, hockey goalie, SWAT team member, basketball player, superhero.

Firefighter wasn't even an alternate. So when he was researching careers at Joanna's request—Googling "outside careers" and "physical jobs"— he was surprised by this new list of possibilities: landscape architect, surveyor, archaeologist, mason, pest management, wildland firefighter. He clicked the last link and read on. Outside. Action. Doing something constructive. That research that led him to firecamp and eventually to this very steering wheel.

As Nick sat inside the gigantic beast, driving slowly through the District parking lot, he knew that his eight-year-old self should have put this on the top of the list. So what that he hit the parking bollards and over-steered, lurching as he rounded the space. This huge machine was in his hands, under his body, holding him up as they moved together. The roar and vibration as he accelerated was the answer to the question he'd asked all those years ago.

It took a week for Nick to get red carded and approved to fight fires, but that approval didn't lead to much action. Due to heighted fire weather conditions in southern Nevada, Schraeder, Johnson, and Deb left for the Ely District on a severity detail. Their voices and laughter gone, the Devlin station was more subdued, the PT sessions less intense. The relative humidity was low, hovering around 13%, but too high for easy combustion, so the only hope for a fire was a human start, some idiot with a spark. Nick found most of his days filled with waiting around, sharpening combis and hoes, sitting in the engine on the way to Kellogg City for classes. The big excitement came when they took the engine to Big 5 to shop for butane for the MSR stoves they used to boil water and heat soup when out on patrol. Jarchow had them doing pack drills, emergency checks on the equipment, and endless engine window washing, but it seemed to Nick that he'd come all this way to do absolutely nothing. In moments of stifling boredom as he sharpened tools, he was transported back to the Oakland apartment, scrolling through job postings as the ugly hum of the wall heater filled the room with stale hot air.

How weird was it, he wondered, that he was itching for something to burn?

"Jesus, it's hot," Nick said. A group of them sat on the porch, trying to pull the coolness from the concrete. He wondered how air so thin could feel so full.

"Hot as a motherfucker." Hamm squished an empty water bottle to fist size. "Wish this were a damn beer."

"Can you quantify the exact temperature of a motherfucker?" Nick asked.

Hamm snorted.

"You know what they say about the temperature," Mac said, as he rubbed Tiger Balm on his right triceps.

"No, asshole," Hamm said. "What do they say? Educate us."

Mac flushed. "If you want shade, carry your own."

Nick snickered, but Hamm shook his head.

"Damn, son. You need a parasol?" Hamm mimicked a little umbrella with his big hands. He batted his big green eyes.

"God, I wish we had a fire," Mac said quickly, looking away from Hamm. "Even a campfire, nothing smoking but a marshmallow."

"You'd need your helmet for that one, knucklehead," Lehman said. As a fourth year engine operator, Lehman knew how to wait. "A marshmallow is too much for you."

"I thought he was a marshmallow," Hamm said. "White and soft. And oh, so sweet!"

"He-y," Mac stutter-said.

"White sweetness." Thompson smacked his lips.

"Gooey and hot," Hamm said.

Mac stepped forward and then back, his eyes on Thompson. Sensing some ugly idea move to the guy's lips, Nick's scalp prickled. He stood up and put a hand on Mac's shoulder, his palm moving to the flex and quiver of Mac's tense muscles.

Mac flinched and tried to shake him off.

"Hey," Nick said, his words light, his fingers gripping hard enough to reach collarbone. "Hey, man."

Mac's body wanted to fight, so Nick hung on, not knowing what he would do when Mac swung wide. For a second, Nick thought Mac would let loose, the words floating free and changing everything. But they didn't. Mac breathed again and laughed a little, shrugging off Nick and moving away from Thompson.

Hamm snorted. "Can't take a fucking joke."

It wasn't a joke, really. But everything at the station became one. Wicks said "The immediacy of death" made everything funny.

"Dipshit reads too much," Hamm had said. "Everything's funny because it just is."

Whatever Wicks' theories, Mac was unused to teasing. Or just couldn't handle it. Even though he was an only child, Nick had a thick skin, his dad a jester, a teaser, a poker-in-the-ribber, a riding under so many of his words. Before Nick could barely remember, his father had him outside either hiking or running or playing at something he failed at miserably, at least at first. His father taught to throw a baseball and a football, even though Nick hated team sports. If they weren't outside sweating hard at something, Jess was tossing him around on the bed, the couch, the hardwood floors until his mother cried for "Peace for god's sake. *Jesus!*"

"Yes?" Jess—Jesus Delgado—would say, and they'd all laugh.

It was clear Mac wanted attention but didn't know how to take it when he got it. Probably in grammar school, he'd been shaking on the sidelines, anxious to be asked to play anything. Once included, he'd flip out, all wild arm pinwheels, kicking and screaming and calling names, unable to deal with the blows and curses. Finally, red in the face, he'd sobbed on the schoolyard pavement as he peed his pants.

Nick wanted to take Mac aside and give him a head's up (or a headlock, he wasn't sure which), but probably the guy's whole life, people had done that. And Mac was still who he was.

It was almost impossible to change. Besides, who was Nick to try to say anything? He had barely pulled himself out of Oakland. Fending off his mother's and Megan's worries and sadness until the last moment, it was a miracle he'd made it out of California at all.

Mac banged into the station. Hamm laughed and stood. Mincing, he shook his ass and pretended to hold a tiny parasol as he walked in the blazing heat. Lehman and Thompson laughed into their water bottles. Nick sat back down, ignoring them. How would it feel to just do something without thought or hesitation or years of preparation? Without anyone holding him back. In an instant. Just like that.

Chapter Ten

Kellogg City, Nevada
May 2012

"Call to order," Darlene Hightower barked, banging her gavel. The sound echoed in the small room at the tribal band office on Barrel Springs Road. Wanda hadn't been to this first Wednesday of the month, seven pm meeting in years. Though all the Mapps were enrolled tribal members, Birdie had been asked to stay away years ago after she threatened mutiny and caused a ruckus when the council leased a freeway spot for fast food billboards. Wanda stayed away in sisterly solidarity, maybe attending one or two meetings in the last decade. But tonight, she was on a covert mission to prove Sheriff Bryant wrong, though she'd probably fall asleep during the minutes. But while she was wide awake, she'd spy, mostly on Dwayne but also on Len Dunning, and anyone else who looked suspicious. Who knew what suspicious looked like or if she'd even notice? For now, she sat between Tanya and Stanley, her brother staring ahead, blinking and blinking some more. She stared at his hands cupping his knees, the cuticles around his thumbs bitten to the quick, red and raggedy.

"Miz Mapp?"

Len Dunning stood in the row, taller than when Wanda had last seen him. Twelve years old back then, all long bones and big teeth. But even then, the long hair worn in what Tanya called the "clichéd indigenous pony-tail."

"Len." Wanda thought to stand but her legs declined. "Good to see you."

She held out her hand and he shook it, his grip loose but his gaze sharp enough that she thought to turn away. For a second, shame beat a little drum in Wanda's throat. Wanda hadn't done anything wrong, had she? Wanda swallowed hard and met Len's gaze. Why did she feel this with Len? He was still a boy. Good looking. Strong. With some wild oats, but a boy nonetheless.

"Glad to see you." Len let go of her hand and moved on to greet Tanya.

After he'd moved down the row, Tanya leaned over, her mouth at Wanda's ear.

"Who knew he'd turn out like that?"

"Dwayne's just as handsome," Wanda said, casting a glance at her nephew, who sat tall in his seat next to Stanley. "And Dwayne don't have a scar on his chin."

Tanya paused. "Didn't mean that. I meant so . . . intense."

Wanda relaxed into her chair. Len was exactly that, a butter knife in a plugged in toaster. Her whole body still buzzed from meeting him, a zing in her arm. "What's with that scar?"

"Bar fight. Or maybe it was a car accident. Something with a girl, that's for sure."

"Call to order!" Darlene banged her gavel once more. The thirty or so people who'd been chatting and drinking coffee started to take their seats, the old metal chairs creaking and groaning. Somewhere behind them, Len took a chair. Wanda could feel him without even turning around.

"Call to order!" Darlene said one more time as the eight council members settled themselves up front behind a long table. Finally, everyone seated, the room filled with the silence of waiting. Since the last time Wanda had seen her, Darlene Hightower had grown as fat, round, and brown as a fallen summer apple. The council leader was clearly not participating in Tanya's health and exercise program, still sucking down the Cokes and probably whiskey, too. Wanda laughed inside, holding the sound tight on her tongue. As Darlene called roll, her face barely moved, her chins protecting her head from her neck.

"John Circle?"

"Present."

"Clarence Daily?"

"Present."

"Ruth Eagle?"

"Present."

For a heartbeat of a moment, John Circle's grandfather Wesley flung across Wanda's mind. There he was, racing across the Blackstock's ranch on his horse, faster than a lightning strike, Stephen Natchez behind him in his old 1932 Ford, the suspension whining.

"Gerben Falls Down?"

"Present."

"Kestrel Jackson?"

"Present."

"Marla Tenday?"

"Present."

And without even asking him to come forward, Jake Tenday sprung forth anyway, the only boy who'd shown Wanda an inkling, a wink, a thought. At fourteen, she'd found the courage to give Jake a smile, hardly sure how to contend with her all-over nerves. Her whole body had tingled so, as if she were about to shake out of her own skin. That one night near the open door of her family's barn, his eyes were pine needle green in the kerosene lamplight, his cheek near hers.

"Do you want to dance, Wanda Mapp?" Jake had asked.

But she hadn't been able to answer him, much less walk out of the barn to the dance floor where all the adults glided in smooth pairs. Why not? There'd been no joke in his offer. No laugh in his voice. No nagging tease, the one she'd heard from the other boys, she so short, so dark, so quiet. Maybe if her mother had been alive, Margaret could have taught Wanda how to translate his offer. How to say yes to something true. But back then? She'd let him leave the barn alone, her "no" in his ear. All these years later, she could still hear his feet scuff through dirt and scrub. By the time she'd changed her mind, the night and the party had swallowed him up whole.

She'd never learned to say yes on her own behalf. If he asked her now, she'd probably do the same stupid thing all over again.

He was still clear in her mind, paining her so. Wanda swallowed, took in a breath big enough for Tanya to notice, lean closer, ask, "Auntie, are you okay?"

Wanda blinked and reached out to pat her niece's knee, Jake stepping back into Wanda's long line of regrets.

"All council members accounted for," Darlene said. "Marla, could you read the minutes?"

Marla cast a glance at Darlene and rolled her eyes. "You didn't send me the notes in time. I told you that."

Darlene waved a hand. "Any unfinished business from last meeting?"

"For sure it's all unfinished business," Stanley blurted out, startling Wanda.

"Mr. Mapp?"

Wanda and Tanya both leaned toward Stanley who was blinking fast but not saying anything. Dwayne glanced at Stanley, cleared his throat, and then said, "The new mine."

"What new mine?" someone said from the row behind them.

"Big secret," Kestrel Jackson whispered loud in the row ahead. "Not in the newsletter, you know?"

John Circle, who sat to Darlene's right, shook his head. "This isn't on tonight's agenda. We voted last time on that permit. Done deal."

"Whose done deal?" Len said, his voice clear, loud, and calm. "Not mine. I never voted yes on anything."

"Order!" Darlene cried, banging the gavel again. "Order!"

"Kid's not a voting member," John Circle said. "What's he doing raising a fuss?"

Wanda's heart beat to the next gavel bang, but Darlene was done. The room swelled with noise, then filled with hush. Amongst the grumblings and warm air, Wanda smelled the unasked questions about payouts. She heard money jingling secretly in someone else's pockets.

"Reports," Darlene said, seemingly unflustered, except for the red dots on both cheeks.

Ruth Eagle raised her hand. "The Forest Service and the BIA sent us a prognostication for this coming fire season."

Tanya leaned over Stanley and whispered to Wanda, "She's never gotten over only finishing one year at Great Basin College. *Prog-nos-tication* my ass."

Wanda laughed. No matter how different they sometimes seemed, Tanya was one hundred percent Birdie's daughter.

"Do you have a report?" Darlene asked.

Ruth nodded. "It's going to be a very dangerous fire season. Snowfall has been below normal for three years and there's some kind of blight in the mountains. Trees are shriveling up. Lots of dead stuff."

"Fuel," Ruth Eagle's husband Dave called out from the front row of metal chairs.

"Lots of fuel. Also, the weather service is predicting a summer of very low—"   "Relative humidity," finished Dave. "RH they call it."

"Right." Ruth glared at him. "Look. This is what it all means. We're already in a high fire situation."

"Red," Dave said.

Ruth ignored him. "High fire alert. We're going to have a lot of firefighters here soon. The BLM and the Forest Service are calling in the troops. National Park and Fish and Wildlife are all over this. BIA is going to coordinate outreach. We need to get the ranchers involved as fire watchers."

"That's all we need," Dwayne said too loudly. He shifted in his chair, thighs flexing as if he were going to stand. "More BLM."

"Mrs. Hightower?" a woman called from the back of the room.

Wanda turned around, not able to place the tiny blonde woman, small and slight with bright blue eyes and a pointy, pixie nose.

"Who's that?" Wanda asked Tanya.

"I think she blogs for a local news site."

"Blogs?"

"She posts stuff on the internet. Covers the indigenous," Tanya said.

"She's indigenous?" Wanda asked. "Looks like she grew up in a snow globe."

"Whitest girl in the west," Tanya said, and they both laughed, just as Darlene banged her gavel.

"Yes, Miss Donnelly."

"Donnelly," Tanya whispered. "Irish. Totally indigenous."

"For sure, you went to the university and not a community college." They both laughed against their palms until Stanley shoved at them with his pointy elbows.

"I'd like to know more about the unfinished mining business." As Miss Donnelly talked, she kept her eyes locked on Darlene even as she typed with her fingers on one of those smart things. Phone. Tablet.

"We've moved onto reports—" Darlene began.

"From the reaction in the room, it seems that the case isn't closed," Miss Donnelly said. "Will there be a forum to express opinion?"

"We've voted al—" Darlene said.

"I'll tell you about the mining!" Len said, his chair skittering back.

Wanda turned to look at Len who stood tall, hands on hips. "These bastards granted mining leases to a new company. Now there are going to be two mines on sacred ground."

"This mine is on Mount Aurora?" Miss Donnelly asked.

"Sacred ground," Stanley whispered. Wanda turned to him, remembering the ceremonies she and her siblings had gone to with their father. The crackling fire in the ring, the flames leaping up against the sky soon to pale to grey. The Chief's voice as he welcomed the morning.

"When will it open?" Miss Donnelly asked.

"Sacred ground," Stanley said, louder this time, his whole body shaking in his chair.

"When it open's not the point!" At Len's shout, Dwayne and Stanley suddenly stood up. Wanda looked at her brother and nephew and then back at Len. But they weren't the only ones standing. Next to and behind Len, a half dozen others stood—mostly young men, though Wanda saw Ruth Eagle's niece Crystal standing, too.

Wanda spun in her seat, taking them all in. Should she stand? What would Birdie do? But of course, Wanda knew even as she thought the question. Taking hold of her seat chair, she started to push up. But Tanya put her hand on her arm.

"Auntie," she whispered, leaning close. Wanda relaxed.

Darlene sat stunned, as did the rest of the council. Len turned and faced Miss Donnelly. "Some of us have done everything not to take the government's bribes and payoffs. People here in this room sacrificed time and safety to keep our lands. Some 'advisory' committee met with the mining community without the rest of us knowing. Meanwhile, we worked hard to keep the mines out of the Cortez. The BLM and the US government lawyered up. Say our land isn't ours. Say they are granting us 'the right of occupancy,' which they can take away at any damn time. When they want something, they take it. So now there's gold under our sacred ground. Who cares people pray up in those mountains. People have ceremonies. So we fight the good fight and then what?"

Len turned to accuse the loop of eight council members, one hand outstretched, index finger pointing. "These people. Our own people. They just go ahead, 180 like, and give up mining rights, secret vote and all. Where do you think that money is going? If you want the answer, look in their pockets."

His face was flushed, eyes bright, the half dozen standing with him clapping hard and loud. Next to Wanda, Dwayne and Stanley clapped, too. A couple of people in other rows slapped hands together, chairs creaking with release as they pulled their old, tired butts from their seats.

Inflamed a little, hot under his t-shirt, Wanda supposed, Len turned in a full circle, arms wide. "So where's our mining rights money? Not on our reservations. Not in our schools and health clinics."

The group erupted, and even those not standing started to murmur, talk, and shout. For so long, the tribe had refused government payouts, knowing that once you took the money, there was no reclaiming what you sold. Land. Mining and timber rights. "Temporary" access, right of way, easement. Didn't matter what. That part of the mountain was gone, just like that, Sold, as Birdie always said, "For spending money, pennies from a big pocket."

Wanda turned back to look at the lady blogger, tapping away. Wanda never went on the internet, but she hoped the blogger was getting it right. Turning back, Wanda stared at Darlene, who looked like Ruby did when she was caught doing her business in the wide out open instead of behind the rabbitbrush, shamed at her big mess steaming right there in public.

"We've been betrayed!" Len cried out, inspired by the whistles and whoops.

"Big surprise," Wanda said, but no one heard her. "This is news?"

How many times had there been the big fight and then the seduction? Indians protesting and then taking the cash. What else was there to do sometimes? Uncle Sam had lots of money, but he was also nasty, vindictive, and treacherous, managing to turn tribal members against their own. Look what was happening with Indian gaming everywhere but Nevada. Birdie had talked about the thousands of Indians being kicked out of their tribes supposedly because they didn't have the proper bloodlines to collect their share.

"What it really means," Birdie had said to Wanda. "Is that the tribe doesn't want to pay them their cut of casino profits. In California, the casinos made 70 billion. Why not whittle down on the profit sharing? Get rid of some of those pesky, extra stipends. Who cares that the ones they dis-enroll lose their housing and the kids can't go to the rez schools anymore. More for the rest of them."

"Order!" Darlene screeched. "Order!"

But there was no order. No one cared about the meeting anymore. None of them were worried about the fires that would burn everywhere, threatening ranch homes, grazing lands, and small towns. All that mattered now was that some of them were making money and some weren't. Some had the power and others didn't. Some cared about traditions and the past and some wanted a new future. The same old story just with different characters, Wanda thought, leaning back against her metal chair waiting—as she always had—for the fighting to stop.

While everyone argued, Darlene tried to move past reports and onto new business and the official adjournment. Finally, she banged her gavel one more time and stormed out of the room, Ruth and Dave Eagle following behind her.

"Meeting's over," Len called out calmly, turning to face those who remained. He cocked his head toward the front door. "If you don't want them to take everything, let's go outside where we can see through all the smoke they've blown."

The group filed out, even Nan Hall nodded as she pushed her walker out the door. Outside in the soft Kellogg City spring night, Tanya and Wanda stood in the middle of the parking lot as Stanley and Dwayne made plans. Wanda could feel the day's heat still simmering in the asphalt under her feet, steady and comforting.

"Excuse me?" Miss Donnelly sidled next to Wanda's right. "You're Wanda Mapp, right? Birdie Mapp's sister?"

"That's right," Wanda said. Since Birdie had been born, that's what Wanda had been, Birdie's sister. "Miss Donnelly is it?"

"Em," Miss Donnelly said. "Emily. But everyone calls me Em."

"Em, you got one hell of a story in there," Tanya said, shrugging a little. Neither side of this fight wanted a disaster on the web. What was done was done. Good thing this Em seemed to not be half bad.

"Yeah, but it seems like just the beginning? Or the middle, maybe?" Em said. "I need to look into this mining lease. Sounds bad. Birdie probably knows something about it, right?"

"You'd think," Tanya said. "But she's off in DC."

"Could I come by one day and talk with her about it? And other tribal matters?"

Wanda listened, wondering if everything Em said was a question. Maybe everything was a question. Good to hedge your bets.

Wanda nodded. "Birdie likes a good interview."

"You can call me at work at the clinic," Tanya said, digging in her purse for her card. "Or email, but I don't have service at home."

Em Donnelly smiled, looking like an illustration from a white girl's story about white people's magic.

"Thanks," Em said, a statement at last. "I will."

She tucked the card in her pocket, then pulled out her tablet. She flicked it on, the thing glowing, and started typing. Still looking down, Em asked, "That fire report. Are you worried about it?"

Tanya laughed. "We have so much human fire around here, I don't know what we'll do when everything else goes up in flames."

Em laughed, and the two of them continued talking, Em tapping away and nodding as Tanya gave her facts and figures. Wanda turned to look back at Len's group, focusing on Stanley, seeing how he leaned against Dwayne, listening intently, but instead of looking up toward the sky as he usually did, he was watching Len, ignoring the dark hole in his vision. For a moment, it was as if Stanley was his old self, twenty years ago, readying for battle.

Wanda shook her head and listened to Tanya recount for Em the story of the Sadler Fire of 1999. The BLM and Fire Service made a hash out of that one. Firefighters here and there, scrambling out of harm's way. Three of them ended up in Kellogg City Hospital, and it was a miracle no one died. But the fire Wanda remembered most clearly wasn't really a fire but an almost-fire, the one that would have consumed her brother if he'd gone ahead and flicked the lighter. He would have flamed high and hot if he'd called the BLM's bluff. For about three seconds as the BLM officers stood stock still, mouths open, eyes wide, Wanda willed the world still. Stanley was doused, he had the lighter, and he was angry. That hot day on Dempsey Mapp Road, Stanley was ready to sacrifice everything. But it didn't matter. The BLM didn't leave the horses. Then or any of the other times. If Stanley had been able to flick the lighter and burned himself, he'd just be the dead crazy Mapp brother in their stories instead of the live crazy one.

They bumped down Highway 306, Wanda and Stanley in the back seat of Tanya's Bronco, Dwayne sitting up front, his arms crossed, his head toward the darkness outside the truck cab. But even from where she sat, Wanda felt Dwayne's energy. Took her breath sometimes, this man in front of her. How'd he get here? All fight and foam, wanting something Wanda hadn't noticed he'd missed? Maybe not as sure of himself as Len. Or his Grandma Birdie. But serious all the same.

Wanda wished she could put her hand on his head without worry he'd push it away. She knew he wasn't a boy, though he might not believe it. No, that little boy running around with Ruby was gone. Where did he go? The boy whose mother was at school, sitting at the table all lively and talking a string of forever? Sure, Wanda had been watching him grow up, but tonight he stood on his two man feet, full of his own opinions. He sat here now ready to crackle the cab to bright light with his indignation. Like the lighting that moves between clouds. Inter-cloud lightning, her father had said, explaining what that meant. "Cloud-to-cloud," he'd added. "Look how it beats and burns bright but doesn't strike."

Intra-cloud lightning pulses in one cloud alone, a beacon, a warning. Maybe Dwayne was a singular pulse right now, but earlier, on the sidewalk in front of the tribal offices? That was inter-cloud. Or maybe he was sheet lightning, a whole fabric of bright flash covering the entire sky. And then another. And another.

"What in the hell was that?" Tanya asked suddenly, waiting for miles to separate them from Kellogg City. "You could have warned us."

"The new mine isn't secret," Dwayne said.

"Yeah." Stanley's low voice jerked Wanda's mind out of the sky and away from light.

"For sure it isn't anymore," Tanya said. "All of Kellogg City and then Nevada going to know. Reporter saw it all. Your grandmother is going to be swooping back here—"

"It's too late," Wanda said.

Dwayne turned around to look at her. Tanya's eyes glinted white in the rearview mirror.

"What do you mean, Auntie?" Dwayne asked.

Wanda shrugged. "Money's passed hands. Probably been spent. Somewhere, there's important signatures at the bottom of legal papers. Some corporation's machines on their way or already here."

"We can stop it!" Dwayne said. "Len—"

Wanda almost laughed, but she couldn't make fun. This was serious, so she swallowed down the sound. "Len's young. He's strong. He's smart. But he doesn't have money or big business behind him. He'll never get the tribe to agree."

"He's got that people thing," Tanya said. "Gathers and riles them up. Like Birdie."

"There's nothing that we can do—" Wanda started to say.

"There is!" Stanley blurted. "When did you stop caring, sister! Daddy didn't teach us the giving up way."

"Uncle," Dwayne said.

"Look," Tanya said, slowing down the Bronco, the girl always calm even under pressure. "Who knows what we can do? Historically, not much. But let's not go crazy."

"Like being sane ever worked!" Dwayne hit the passenger's side door with his fist. "What does Grandma say? Nevada's all greed and need."

Wanda nodded at Birdie's oft repeated and true words. Their father used to say that the state motto should be: *Nevada: No One's Watching.* But Nevada or any other state, it didn't matter. America did what America wanted to. If there was money in the air, on the ground, or under the soil, America would gather, mine, cut, and harvest whatever it was. For her entire life, that's what had gone on. Probably, the blood of anyone born and raised in Nevada was half payoff, half uranium. Hang all Nevadans up at midnight, Birdie said, and they'd light the sky like radioactive stars.

Money. Everything was money. All Wanda wanted was to raise her cattle, ride her horses, tend the land. All she wanted was for her family to find their place in the bigger wide world. Not limited by who sold what or who they were. Not stuck in Nevada because of poor choices or worse, no choices at all.

"Let's call Birdie in the morning," Wanda said. "Let her decide."

Dwayne hit the door again, a dull *thwamp,* and Stanley blinked fast. Tanya accelerated, the road a whoosh under her near-to-dead tires. Wanda sat back, looking up at the sky, almost expecting to see lightning bounce from cloud to cloud to cloud, on and on. But for now, nothing but darkness outside the window as they sped past.

Chapter Eleven

Mapp Ranch
Northern Nevada
Late Summer 1939

When the local Indian Affairs agent Vern Tomah showed up on Dempsey Mapp's doorstep, the kids and some of their cousins and kin were down in the creek hollering and splashing, the creek running due to some strange, fluky weather, winter short and cold, spring long and lush, fall already licking at its heels. Dempsey had driven back to the house for lunch, Margaret's sister Edie still camped out on the sofa and making her soggy flatbread and tough-as-nails elk steak. Dempsey didn't know how to tell her to head back home to South Dakota nor did he really want her to. She'd been with them for over a year, sticking around through all his troubles. But now that the drinking was behind him, he couldn't just let her go home. The way she slowly drifted through the house, the songs she hummed, and the smell of her soap reminded him of Margaret when everything else about his wife was slowly fading away.

Gaseous from the oily bread and ticked raw by Vern's approach, Dempsey watched as the agent pulled up in his mostly new, mostly white Ford Deluxe. Vern got out, slipped on his suit jacket, and then turned toward the creek, listening to the kids whoop it up. And then, as if on cue, there were screams. Dempsey watched the kids throw a barrage of mud clods hoisted into the air and hitting their marks—shoulder, head, thigh—and then more screams, Ruby barking. Dempsey sighed, wishing his sister Bobbie hadn't dropped off her kids plus half the reservation. Vern always said tribal children were let run wild, a bunch of true heathen savages that needed the firm hands of God and the state to cure them of their Indianness.

Some cure if Vern was an example of government enforced Catholic boarding school. Truth was, when Dempsey was growing up, everyone was Catholic or pretended to be. He would have been sent away as his wife Margaret had been, shunted to some school in Pennsylvania or whatnot, but his mother had hidden both her children, moving them from house to house, leaving them uncounted, unnoted by Indian Affairs. He couldn't remember how many times she'd shaken him and Bobbie awake, all of them dressing by candlelight and then clattering off in the wagon for Auntie Selma's or Auntie Vida's houses. But his family acted Catholic when necessary, a rosary tucked into the back corner of some drawer, nestled in socks and mouse nests. Easier just to fake it, especially when going to boarding school was the law, one that Dempsey's mother fought against—and won—and that Dempsey fought, too. But Vern? He was the poster child of assimilation. He was tried and true in his almost-new Ford, ready to poach the world into perfection, converting one Indian child at a time, even if the boarding schools had finally closed down.

"Been thinking it was about time you showed up," Dempsey said. Every year since little Wanda turned four, Vern had appeared, wanting to fix things US government style. And as usual, Dempsey was unable to stop looking at the large raised mole on Vern's forehead. Try as he might, Dempsey couldn't avert his eyes. But Vern seemed used to people staring at the solid black growth that grew like a third eye just to the right of center.

"Looking fine and fit, Dempsey," Vern said.

"Wish I could say the same 'bout you, Vern. Don't you know it's summer? You look ready to burst into flame in that monkey suit."

"May be, but fall's coming," Vern said. "Setting up situations for the children."

"Happens every year, but darned if you don't seem to remember them schools are closed now. Five. No, six years," Dempsey replied, sitting back down on the bench, the old wood creaking beneath him. He put his boots up on the railing, never taking his eyes off Vern. The man was too easy to read, only part Indian on his daddy's side. But Vern wasn't from around here. Wisconsin, Dempsey thought. Or Michigan. Easier not to care about kids you don't know. Easier not to think about what them nuns or social workers do with their rulers and whips.

"Got to take the kids, Dempsey." Vern took off his suit jacket and leaned against a weathered column. "It's best for them."

"Don't need to send 'em." Dempsey kept his voice cool and calm, hiding the flare of gritty nerves under his words. No one was taking any of his family anywhere.

"It's the law," Vern said, his words slow, law heavy and Midwestern in his mouth.

"Was," Dempsey said. "They go to school. They eat their meals. No one's beating them with a leather strop."

"They need to fit in," Vern said. "Assimilate."

"Assimilate or die," Dempsey said with a snort. "US policy."

"Now, Dempsey. Look here—"

"You just want your bonus," Dempsey said. "What do you get per kid, anyway? For sure, you'll be trying to steal them next."

Vern raised his eyebrows and looked out at the creek. Little Stanley stood shirtless, crying, and covered in mud. All hell and back could hear the rest of them teasing and whistling and making a damn ruckus. Where was Edie?

"They need some structure. You send them to a better school and they'll learn English."

"They speak English." Hell if that wasn't what his children spoke best. How could Dempsey have known Margaret would die and her language along with her? By the time she was dead and buried, it just seemed too late to start with the kids. He tried not to think about what his momma used to say before he was married. After every baby was born. Before she died last year. "Don't ever learn your children that English before their Indian words. Indian comes first." Well, the Mapp children lost their mother and most of their Indian, too. But they weren't going to lose their connection to him. For sure, they wouldn't lose that.

And Stanley? He was just a babe. But English? These kids could wrap their grammar around the cottonwood trees and call it a bow. "Better than me."

"That's because you didn't teach them yours. Means you know they need to be part of civilization."

"You saying Indians aren't civilized? Damn, Vern. What kind of Indian are you?"

Vern pushed up from the column, his face beating red, his mole a dark spotlight taking in everything: the one room house, the swirling dust, the broken toys and dog shit on the porch. "As much as the rest of you, but you have to see getting involved is progress. Your kids will be able to make a living when they grow up. Work outside the reservation."

"That's just the thing," Dempsey said. "This isn't the reservation. We're on my land here. Mapp land. Treaty acknowledged. I'm not beholden to the US Government. They have no right telling me how to educate my kids. Kids're staying right here 'mongst their people. Pure and simple."

Vern let out a practiced sigh. "Listen, if it's not me taking them, it'll be someone else. Social worker. County nurse. They'll be put in a good home. Given regular meals. Clothes. Sent to decent schools. Do you really think you can raise them here? All by yourself?"

"Good home?" Dempsey repeated the phrase, stuck on the idea that his ranch, right here in the Crescent Valley, wasn't good. That his words, ideas, love, and land weren't enough. But wasn't that what he'd felt since Margaret died? Didn't he look around his own house think exactly what Vern was telling him now?

Dempsey looked down, but Vern had seen Dempsey's sorrow as well as an opportunity. "Think about it. Your wife's passed and with her, all the special things women do. The hugging and loving and singing. Braiding that long hair. Washing those dirty faces. And look at this house. One room. One toilet. No privacy. Out in the middle of nowhere. How can you work your ranch with all the distractions? You'd be doing everyone a favor."

"Really." Dempsey crossed his arms and glared at Vern, even as a terrible part of him wondered if Vern was right. Margaret and her kisses and songs and clean, bleached sheets were gone. Dinner was badly cooked and the kids' clothes hand-me-downs or worse. For a year, Dempsey had raged drunk and stupid, just now trying to live whole when half of him was gone.

In another home, his kids wouldn't have had to bear witness to that.

"You know it's like I said. Someone will take them." Vern took a white handkerchief out of a pant pocket and wiped his forehead. The air stilled to death, bloomed with radiant heat, smelled of cow dung and horse manure.

"Thanks for the warning," Dempsey said. "Now I know what to do."

"Huh?"

Dempsey stood and walked close to Vern, near enough to smell the blue of his aftershave as well as his fear. It didn't matter if Mapp Ranch life was raggedy around the edges. It was their life, an Indian life. That's what mattered.

"Get off my porch."

In the pause between them, there was a rustle, a branch under a small foot. They both turned. Near the creek, thirteen kids stood on the creek bank like expectant blackbirds, all of them facing the house, finally silent, finally still. They were muddy, wet, but now perfectly at attention, just like good little schoolchildren.

Dempsey'd be damned if these kids were going to go to any school but the one in town. For sure, if there was one thing Dempsey could do in this life, it would be to keep his children home. Margaret had wanted them to live here, looking out at grasslands from the front door, the Cortez Mountains from the back. Animals, air, sun, rain, and sometimes snow. This was their heritage. Not Reno or Las Vegas. Not Idaho. Not Pennsylvania. Not Catholic. Here, they'd be safe and always Indian. His family had been given this land through negotiation and treaty, and it was Mapp law here.

During Dempsey's grief, Chief Roundhouse had come up to him at a gathering. "Get that little boy singing. Make him a drum. Learn him how to sing."

Dempsey hadn't done it. Had done mostly nothing for poor Stanley. But he'd drawn the line with school.

"Dempsey," Vern started.

"Go home," Dempsey said. "And I mean to your tribe. Ruin someone else's life for a change."

Vern stared at him, shaking his head slightly. The man really thought he was doing a righteous deed. But that was thing about life. You had to learn to see when something was right and true and when it was a lie. Problem was, lies came disguised as good men in suits driving almost new Fords.

"Go home," Dempsey repeated. "Don't come back."

Chapter Twelve

Southern California
El Monte
Fall 1966

When his father's old Suburban rattled into the Los Angeles Basin, Jesus Guadalupe Delgado became another person, forced into another name by old Mrs. Krause, the Delgados' new next-door neighbor. She had knocked on their front door their second day in town, his mother surrounded by the boxes and bags that constituted their worldly possessions.

"You can't call them by those names," she'd told Jess's mother Rosa, Mrs. Krause's fat German hands resting on her thick, aproned hips. "You have to make them more American."

She bit her lip, shook her head, looking out at the half-dozen boys, dark brown, black-haired, wide-eyed.

"And they have to speak English."

The good news was that some of his brothers were able to still be who they were. For the eldest, Victor Junior, sixteen years Jess' senior, it was a given, Victor a name everyone knew and understood, even in Los Angeles, where life was in English. Later, Jess learned that victor meant winner, and who didn't want to win?

Luis was still Luis, but no longer Lou-eece. He was Lou-is. Lou-is. Lou to some of the kids from his school, the boys in jeans and white t-shirts, thick hair combed back, something smoky and dark on their breaths. Mario? He stayed Mario because that name could be Italian, too, not just Mexican. Mario could be a wop or a spic, but wops had been in their neighborhood longer.

Tomás was Tommy. Enrique was Ricky. Esteban was Stevie. All of them cut down to size, made smaller, sillier, younger than young.

And he? The brother dead set in the middle? Jesus? Hay-soos? Jesus Guadalupe Delgado, the boy named for all the holiness in the room when he was born blue and managed yet to survive? Jess. He became Jess.

"You can't keep to this meal schedule," Mrs. Krause said to Rosa three weeks later as the women sat at the small kitchen table in the three-bedroom house on the hill. "Breakfast is before school and work. Lunch is at noon. That's the time they eat at school. Snack is when they come home from school. Dinner's not at three in the afternoon. It's at night, when your husband comes home from his shop. It's not that Mexican food. It's American meals you should be eating, the kind everyone else prepares. Then all of you sit together and talk about your day. That's dinner. And for goodness sake, speak English."

And like that, instead of pans of enchiladas and rice and beans, there was Salisbury steak and mashed potatoes and the nine of them trying to cram around the table, Jess' father completely silent as they ate, ignoring their English conversation until he was done eating. Then he would move to the counter to read *El Opinión* with a cup of lukewarm tea.

Just as Mrs. Krause said, at school they ate at noon, sitting at long tables that pulled out from the cafeteria walls, the tops smelling of ammonia and the boiled hot dogs they ate every Wednesday. Spaghetti, macaroni and cheese, hot dogs, pizza, and fish sticks. Sometimes sides of corn or iceberg lettuce salad or carrot sticks. Tater tots with ketchup in little paper rounds. Wobbly pale yellow French fries. Tiny cartons of whole milk. Maybe chocolate, if they were lucky. Then recess, Jess burping up the grease of the food as he rushed around playing kickball.

At home, their mother gave them the snack foods they saw on commercials: brownies made from the box, Twinkies, sugary fruit pies, Fritos. Afterward, they ran wild outside in their play clothes, ignoring Mrs. Krause as she yelled at them to "Stop acting like monsters."

They knew English now, so they knew that they weren't acting like monsters. No *monstros* here. They were bandits and space invaders and superheroes.

Their house was second to the last on a long street up a big hill, most of the lots undeveloped, grass allowed to go green, yellow, and then stalk dry, year after year. There were some scrub oak and scraggly pine trees, and the burnt-out shell of a large house, an apricot tree in what was once the front yard. They raced around the ruins and over the hills. They built forts and slid down slick grass on cardboard rafts. Once Jess and his friend David from down the street two houses found a book of matches.

"Give it to me." Jess pulled out a match the way he'd seen his older brother Luis do as he lit a cigarette. Like his slick older brother, he pulled the match against the strike strip once, twice, and then the match bloomed, a petal of heat.

Jess threw the match on the grass and lit another.

"Stop it," David said. Then, "Give me one."

They lit the entire book, and as Jess threw down the last, it caught. He saw it happen, the way one dried grass stem burned, catching on another, and then another, until the line of fire pushed up the crackling hill.

At the first sign of smoke, Mrs. Krause called the fire department.

"Don't tell," David begged as the sirens wailed, his face pale, his eyes red. "My dad'll kill me."

Jess never told, not even when the fire chief finally asked, "Do you know anything about this used up book of matches?"

Jess shook his head, afraid that not only would David be beaten, but that he himself would be kicked out of the United States. All because of him and the stupid matches, he and his family would be shipped back to the place he could barely remember but that still smelled like a dream of dust and diesel fuel. If Jess admitted to anything, it would all end. No more school. No more fruit pies.

The fire chief looked down at him. He knew what Jess had done, even if Jess lied. The man saw through everything but finally sighed and mumbled something under his breath, a sound Jess never wanted to hear again, disapproval mixed with disgust.

"Let's go, boys," he called, walking toward the truck, his yellow jacket swinging behind him like a cape. "All done. Nothing here."

In the end, the Delgados did move. They weren't forced back to Mexico City; they moved on purpose to the far-flung Los Angeles suburbs, Covina to be exact, where there were big lawns, wide streets, and kids playing in the streets from the afternoon to the purple-tinged smoggy evenings. There was a junior high with football and basketball teams and back-to-school nights, Friday night dances, and science fairs. It wasn't until later, when Jess had almost graduated from high school and was headed to Berkeley, California for college that he noticed the few Mexican and black families in town lived on his street or on two nearby cul-de-sacs. He'd been so happy to live there, he hadn't noticed they'd all been red-lined, pushed to the outer rim of the town, hidden away.

It took his leaving L.A. for him to notice that he'd never really been there at all.

Chapter Thirteen

Kellogg City, Nevada
May 2012

As Tanya took notes, Peach Tanver sat in her gown. The plasticky fabric crackled as the girl struggled to find a comfortable position on the hard examination table at the tribal clinic. She and Tanya both waited for Doctor Desmond to return to complete the physical exam, Tanya recording Peach's small weight loss progress. She smiled at the girl, noting her fluorescent pink toenail polish, and tried not to wonder how Peach was able to reach all the way to her toes. It was a hard reach, Peach a mound of round. Her arms and legs dangled with flesh. Even her feet were fat. Since she was fourteen, Peach had been a patient of the clinic—almost two years now—the Kellogg City High School nurse recommending Tanya's health and exercise programs. "She's a smart girl," May Stove had said. "If you can find her in there."

Peach had made it to her appointments at the clinic, but she'd been skipping out on the exercise part at the Kellogg City rez gym.

"I swear I stopped drinking all the soda," Peach said. "I'm drinking orange juice instead. It's healthy, right? Fruits and vegetables are on that food pyramid the doctor made me memorize."

Tanya raised her eyebrows as she read through the doctor's notations.

Weight: 268 lbs.
Height: five foot one.
Blood pressure: 145/120.
Blood sugar level: 192 mg.

Peach lived on the Kellogg City rez with her mother and two brothers, and she loved to read. She hoped to be a writer after college, and her favorite books were *Wuthering Heights* and *Middlesex,* a title that surprised Tanya, assuming that Peach had said *Middlemarch*. But no, the story of the in-between girl/boy and her family was the story Peach had read five times. Tanya asked Peach about *Wuthering Heights*, too, but the girl hadn't wanted to talk about it, blushed and blurting out, "He's so angry. I want to fix him."

Tanya put down her pen and looked up at Peach, a pretty girl with a clear, smooth complexion and brown eyes flecked with amber. Her smooth, shiny hair was long and dark and pulled back in a loose ponytail rope. With the gown spread out over and around her, it was harder to see Peach's girth. So here, right now, she was just a beautiful teenaged girl.

Outside the closed door, a nurse laughed and then walked by, the soles of her sensible shoes squish squishing as she walked. Then there was the clattering sound of wheels rolling over the hard floor, a machine being pushed to another exam room. Peach looked toward the door and then smoothed the gown over her thighs.

Since being enrolled in the tribal diabetes prevention program and despite weekly clinic appointments and nutrition classes as well as monthly home visits, Peach had lost and regained the same twenty pounds four times. Her blood sugar levels had steadily risen past normal and into the danger zone. One more month or maybe even a week like this, Peach would be on medication, maybe oral meds. Maybe even insulin. Insulin therapy, as the doctors called it.

"Peach," Tanya said, picking up the pen and tapping it on the folder. "Orange juice has as much sugar as soda."

"No way. It's like fruit."

"Yes, way," Tanya said. "And it's not fruit anymore. Besides, the only good things about an orange are the vitamin C and the pulp."

"My mom doesn't buy the pulpy kind. That's nasty shit," she said. "Sorry."

Tanya waved a hand. "Then all that's left is the sugar. How much of it are you drinking?"

Peach shrugged, looked over at the poster of the female reproductive system. "I don't know."

"So maybe you should have a half cup a day. Maybe. Total."

Peach studied the salmon-colored vagina and uterus, while Tanya sat back in her chair. Probably Peach's mother bought a couple of gallon juice jugs at Walmart and left them in the fridge, the kids drinking it like water.

Peach's mother worked in an insurance office in Kellogg City and with the three kids and work and life in general, she didn't have time to monitor Peach's food much less her juice consumption. But someone had to just say the things that were true or else the worst happened. Actually, the worst always happened but sometimes with warning, the worst could be made softer or take longer or not hurt quite so much. There was no way Tanya could change this girl's life totally, but she might be able to alter it, move the worst to the side for a bit, let Peach get out of high school and maybe enrolled in a college somewhere.

This was what Tanya would have hoped for in Peach's shoes, though of course she'd never undo Dwayne. Birdie tried to fix things, but long after Paul Tall Weather headed back to San Francisco without knowing about the pregnancy, much less Dwayne's birth. And none of his Nevada family could have told him, so hermetically sealed was the scandal, Birdie shushing it all up so well that no one ever asked Tanya much less Birdie or Auntie Wanda where the baby's father was.

No one, that was, until Dwayne.

Tanya stared at Peach, followed the plump line of her cheek. "Remember what you said to me about Heathcliff?"

The girl turned back to her, her eyes wide, a blush crawling up her cheeks. "Um."

"The part about wanting to fix him?"

Peach waited, eyes unblinking.

"That's how I feel about you."

Peach stopped smiling, her face shifting to upset. "I don't need no—"

"Yes, you do, Peach. You do."

The girl clenched her hands, her hair hanging in front of her face.

"Do you know what diabetes looks like?" Tanya asked.

Peach looked up, Tanya noting the girl's heartbeat in her carotid, a quick one, two.

"Nothing. It doesn't look like nothing," Peach said finally. "It's inside. It's all internal and shit."

"Really?"

"Yeah," Peach said, not apologizing for her swear word this time. "Everyone knows that."

Tanya's heart pounded, the way it did before she did something wrong; the way it used to when she was little and thought her mother was about to give her that famous, open stare. But Tanya ignored the warning, swiveling in her chair, and yanked a binder from her bag. She'd never used this last-ditch effort before, though she'd always intended to, working on it at night at home, the TV or music on in the background. She'd been collecting images, photos and diagrams online, and then printing them out at the clinic and organizing them into an escalating portrait of diabetes doom, often staying up late enough so that Dwayne got a look at her work when he came home.

"Jesus, Mom," he'd said, backing away from the table as he caught sight of an ulcerous foot, blackish rot digging down all the way to shiny white metatarsal. There were more of these. One, two, three feet bitten and chewed by the disease, red, purple, black, any color but skin. Lord knows what Dwayne would do if he saw the hearts or the kidneys. "What the hell is that? And why the hell do you have it?"

Tanya had it so she could show it to Peach, someone she wanted to fix. Her Heathcliff for today. She opened the binder right next to the sweating girl, slapping open the pages.

"So you're right. Diabetes is inside. Your heart and veins? One treatment we have is insulin. But over time, it's poison. You can stroke out. Your kidneys suffer. Some people end up on dialysis. And sure, you can hide some of this. No one will know unless you drop dead in class."

"I'm not going to die! I'm sixteen." Peach's words came out in soft grunts. "You're just saying all this to make me stop eating."

Tanya swallowed hard and flipped through the plastic covered pages. "But there are things you can't hide. See this eye? All fuzzy like an old dog's?"

Peach puffed out a surprised "Oh."

"That's glaucoma. You can get cataracts, too. So much that you are almost blind."

Tanya looked up at Peach who blinked, as if checking to tell if she could still see.

"And then the teeth. No matter how much brushing you do, your teeth start falling out. You could be wearing dentures by age forty."

"I go to the dentist," Peach said. "He hasn't said anything—"

"What about amputations? See this foot? That hole right there under her big toe? See that sort of glistening white spot? That's her bone."

Now Peach stared straight at the page, her mouth open slightly. "That's bone? What happened to make it like that?"

"Insulin's not great on the system. People stop feeling their limbs. Sometimes, you hurt yourself or step on a pin or cut your toenail wrong, and it gets infected. But you don't feel it because you don't feel anything. And then one day, your foot has this kind of sore. It's rotting, and there's nothing to do but cut it off."

Peach twitched her fluorescent toes. "There's nothing they can do?"

"Not by this point. How can they fix that?" Tanya pointed to a foot, black, swollen, oozing from a huge sore. "Hard to wear a sandal for sure."

"That's just . . ." Peach began. "That's not going to happen to me!"

"Honey, you just want to believe that everything is going to be all right. You want to be young and eat and drink and do what you want, but really, trust me. There are consequences that last forever."

"There are consequences to your action," they'd told Tanya in a terrible chorus, the four white women leaning over her. "You don't want that baby, dear. But you're lucky. You have options that we didn't. You can at least give it up for adoption to people who could really take care of it."

Tanya had stared at them the way Peach stared now, wanting—like Peach—to tell them—her—to fuck the hell off. She'd hated them all. What arrogance! People who could really take care of *it*, as if her baby were an it, an object, a thing. Right then, Tanya knew she could take care of it, him, her. Would. Could. She'd been helping Auntie Wanda with the ranch animals since before she could remember. Besides, she wasn't alone. There was her auntie. Uncle Stanley. And when her mom was home, Birdie, too. They were people who could really take care of things.

But here was Peach, no one really taking care of her. And she'd gotten the message somewhere that she should be healthy, beautiful, and trim. Where was the support for that? The money? No, she'd been left on the side of the American road with no other instructions than a bottle of Coke, a bag of Chips Ahoy, and a greasy paper bag of McDonald's French fries. Somebody had to tell Peach the bad way this story could end.

"Look, Peach. I'm not trying to be mean even if I am trying to scare you. It is really scary. No lie."

Peach's eyes fixed on Tanya's.

"I want you to remember someone told you the truth. I want you to remember these photos. Because I am telling you what's for sure and real. You are about eight blood sugar numbers away from needing a drug that will wreck your insides. It might keep you alive, but in the long run, it might not."

Peach was looking at the last photo, the close up of rotted away, black foot, and crying. "I hate being like this. Hate it!"

"Sick?"

"Fat," Peach cried out, as if the last two years of clinic visits finally made sense. "Gigantic! I have to wear my grandmother's pants! But I can't stop. I don't know how to, even though I know I should."

Tanya put her hand on the girl's shoulder, felt her desperate sobs, her yearning, and remembered her own. "You can't stop eating, Peach. But you can slow it down and eat better. Make little changes every day."

Peach sniffed and whisked tissues from the box Tanya held out.

"I'll be here," Tanya said. "I'll help you."

And again, like that, Tanya was back on the porch of the ranch house clutching a wad of wet, torn tissues and filled with a load of self-pity. Auntie Wanda sat next to her, not saying the words Tanya had just told Peach but feeling them. Her aunt's hand on her knee was dry and warm and steady, just as it still was. The Ruby back then leaned her old smelly dog body against Tanya's back, and as the sun set, the ranch turned from yellow white to pumpkin orange to a shimmering purple. The sky rose black and speckled with a million stars, and Aunt Wanda had sighed and said, "We can find a crib at that Goodwill in Kellogg City. There isn't anything they don't have."

Weeks later, as Birdie had paced the kitchen floor, going on about abortion clinics in California, Wanda put together the crib.

"Too late." Wanda pulled up the guard rail and stared at the tiny mattress. Tanya ran her hand on its small rectangle softness.

"This is Tanya's time! This is her young womanhood. She doesn't have to be strapped with a child." Birdie sat down at the table, opening the phone book for a number she'd never find.

Her aunt moved close to Tanya as they touched the crib's wooden railings, Tanya's stomach pressed up against the slats.

Now Tanya grabbed Peach's fat brown foot and squeezed; the girl startled from her tears and looked up.

"It'll be okay." Tanya wanted to make it true. For Peach. For Dwayne. For the Mapp Ranch. For Aunt Wanda, who needed to live in that one-room house on those 800 acres until she died. For Nevada and the tribe and everything and everyone. For her mother whose yearning and desire and drive came from some place deep and buried and mysterious. But Tanya wasn't Birdie. Not even close. Tanya didn't believe in total, entire, 100 percent change. She believed in small possible moments. Good weather. No fires. Healthy animals. Her son home before midnight, sober, unharmed, smiling. Her aunt standing on the front porch. And maybe, someday, a nice guy sitting across from her at a restaurant table, ordering them each a glass of wine. A celebration of something.

So Tanya was pinning her hopes on this fat girl in a small room who wanted to lose half herself and stay alive to go on a date and wear her own pants.

Chapter Fourteen

Kellogg City, Nevada
May 2012

KelloggCityFreePress.Com—The Daily Donnelly
Kindness by Em Donnelly

Kindness is like a freak summer rainstorm or a folded ten-dollar bill on the sidewalk or an email from an old friend: unexpected, surprising, a jolt of adrenaline. Back East in the commute and crowds, I wore of suit of emotional armor just to get to work. So I wasn't looking for kindness in Kellogg City. When I first moved here, I saw all the big trucks with tires that look four sizes too big, I heard all the head-banging music pouring out of The Silver Club on Second Street; I stared into the faces of people who've been working hard all day, and I thought, not here. No, my Bostonian self didn't imagine this was a place of kindness. But something simple tipped me off about Nevadans.

Drivers stop for pedestrians. No big deal, you say? Well, let me tell you that in Boston, driving across a crosswalk packed with school children isn't a random occurrence. The name of the game is: Can I Make It? No driver really wants to hit anyone, but hey? If there's a chance I can get across without having to stop, I'll give it a go and peel off.

In Kellogg City? My first week in town, I'd stand on the curb anxiously looking back and forth without realizing that traffic in both directions had come to a grinding halt. For me! Even if I hadn't wanted to cross the street, I would have, so grateful was I that anyone was paying attention. These drivers weren't even mothers in cars with kids. No, these were miners with their red flags waving, their trucks covered in dirt and dust. Motorcyclists. Semis. Wow. Even a year later, I still wave to those who stop, thankful and almost embarrassed I'm going to the other side of the road.

More personally, just last week, I ran over a four-inch pointed bolt (I don't want to know what it is for, but I hope it's just part of the new construction going on west of town instead of used for some gruesome weaponry). I zipped into D and D Tires on Utah Street, and in about twenty minutes, Michael (the manager-owner) had jacked up my beat-up Jetta, taken off the tire, and patched it.

"No charge," said he, brushing his hand along his spikey punk hairdo.

Then he sent me on my way.

As a struggling journalist without a lot of spare change, this kindness was more than an adrenaline jolt but brought overwhelming feelings of gratitude. How kind. How thoughtful. How truly unexpected. But how can this kindness play out in the bigger struggles our communities face? The new mine? The effects of cattle and chemicals on the land and water table? How can kindness help solve the housing crisis? If the kindness is there on the street and in the pedestrian crosswalk, it's there everywhere. So all you new arrivals in town wanting to cross the road? Just wait. Someone's ready to stop so you can get to the other side.

Chapter Fifteen

Devlin, Nevada
May 2012

The fire station days stretched out hot and beige. Even the stolen internet connection went wonky, Nick only able to contact Megan or his mother from his phone on the days the engine crews drove to Kellogg City. Sometimes, he had a fantasy that Megan would pull into the station yard in a rental car, hot and exhausted but actually here.

There she'd be, just as she had been freshman year, back when she still loved him. God. How happy he was to see her after class. She'd laugh and pull him to the large wide lawn by the library. They'd share a cup of tea, as she read aloud something funny. How they loved to be together. All the time. And now when he pictured her walking toward him at the fire station, she was that beautiful brown-haired girl, that happy Megan. Seeing just him. Not caring about the guys all around. She'd kiss him first, hold him and not pull away. Finally, he'd look at her face, not finding one second of reproach or blame. Finally, she'd accept his choice.

Sometimes, Nick even caught himself waiting for the sound of tires on gravel, but when it came, it was never Megan. Just Thompson's girlfriend driving in from Las Vegas, Hamm's brother from Tahoe, Wick's high school friend who lived in a double-wide in Wells.

Finally one afternoon as they were finishing up lunch and Schraeder's engine had just returned from the Ely station, Nick heard the tone— the three odd wobbly pulses that sounded like a badly played and partially broken Casio keyboard—coming from the loud speaker. Over the radio, dispatch said, "First two Federal engines out of Devlin. Water tender 21. Please respond to possible wildfire. Mile marker 244."

Nick stilled. The dispatcher repeated the instructions.

Jarchow got on the phone for more details, and Nick turned to Hamm, blood skittering in his body like ants.

"That's us, right?"

"Damn straight." Hamm jogged toward the garage even as he answered. The other firefighters in the room pounded down the hall.

"God damn," Mac said. "Fucking finally!"

Nick stilled, his whole body hearing Jarchow say, "Two engines."

Schraeder's crew was just back from the run and not prepped. So it was Wicks and Thompson.

As Hamm started the big engine, Nick buckled in, fingers shaking. He had the things he needed. In his lap, his helmet was full of his wadded up Nomex and his safety glasses. His newly organized pack was in the back of the engine, along with tools he'd personally cleaned and sharpened. Hose packs. Water. But everything in his mind was from a book or lecture or practice, the most of the firsts in his life had been: riding a bike, taking the first terrified freestyle strokes during swim class, going to school, driving a car.

He'd survived all of those.

According to the reports, the fire was just off of I-80 near Battle Mountain. As they rumbled up Immigrant Pass, Nick saw the rising smoke, a thick white thermal column that had begun to fan out and fill the sky. Then he smelled the tang and burn.

"Grass," Hamm said.

"Really cooking," Thompson said.

"God!" Nick said, leaning forward and looking through the windshield. Just as they dropped into the valley, he saw that up ahead, all four lanes of the highway were closed, the westbound two lines of red taillights. Smoke hugged the highway like fog.

"Go around them," Nick said. "Drive down the right side."

"Shut up, asshole," Hamm said. "I'm driving here."

"At least turn on the lights," Nick said, his voice catching in his throat. Hamm shrugged and flicked them on, the whirling red light from the top of the engine bouncing back off the smoke.

"Do what the newbie said and go down the side," Thompson said. "You know it's the only way we'll get there."

Hamm pulled off the highway onto the shoulder, the engine barreling past two Nevada Highway Patrol cars. For a second, Nick felt a ridiculous but true thrill at being able to rush past them. They were here on official business, on the same team as the NHP and paramedics. Official.

Past the stopped traffic, Hamm pulled the engine back onto the highway, and they raced on toward the fire. Then slowing, they pulled alongside the other Devlin engine as well as a volunteer water tender, a truck with the sole purpose of carrying water.

Calm and sure, Thompson turned back to look at Nick. "We're going to pinch it off. You and Mac are on one hose. Wicks and I'll man the other. Evergreen, you're behind Mac. Swap out when needed."

Nick jumped out of the engine and nodded at Mac, who was listening to Wicks probably telling him the same thing. As Nick put on his pack, Hamm prepared the pump. The wind pushed hard, the flames spreading alongside the highway. Nick tried to pay attention to everything Thompson and Wicks were telling them as he and Mac grabbed the hose, ready to pull it from the reel. But he couldn't keep his eyes off the fire burning only yards away. It had crossed the entire highway and was now in the flats, popping in the grass. Trouble was, if the wind picked up, the fire could just take off and go.

"Get your heads out of your asses," Thompson yelled sharply. "Get going."

With Hamm and Lehman driving the engines along the perimeter of the fire, Nick held the hose behind Mac as they walked the fireline, staying in the black as they doused the flames. As he stepped on the burnt blackened ground, Nick could feel the heat under his boots. He gripped the hose tight, his eyes smarting from the smoke, but soon he got used to the rhythm of engine, water, hose, and movement. They were taking the fire down, yard by yard. After only a shaky moment, Mac directed the water totally textbook: bottom up, the fire flaming out, sizzling, flickering, steaming. They were going to knock it out, keep it from moving up the hill. Traffic would reopen and people would be able to go on with the rest of their lives, saving the business millions it cost to stop the massive I-80 corridor for even an hour.

And then, like that, the wind died, the flames flickered into nothing, the ground smoking and then smoldering before they even got there. Mac and Nick swapped positions, Nick taking the heavy hose onto his shoulder, working the metal nozzle, Mac behind. Under his hands, the force of the water. He gripped hard, straining as he held the nozzle above him, directing it toward burned sagebrush, whirling the water in slight circular motions, changing the spray pattern from narrow to wide as needed. Flecks of water and ash peppered his face. His lungs pulled in the wet heated air.

"Keep at the perimeter," Thompson shouted.

They did, enough so that they had to refill both engines from the water tender. Then they put down the hoses and started in with the tools. The fire was inactive now. Nick stood at the fireline and took off one glove, the cool air on his skin a relief. He pressed his palm against the black earth and then the burnt remains of a sagebrush, feeling for heat. The branches were twisted and black, and at first touch, he felt the residual heat, as if fire hid in the core of what it had mostly killed, a whisk of smoke coming from the singed roots.

Nick put his glove back on and looked over at Mac who was testing the earth the same way. Behind them, Thompson and Wicks held the hoses, valves shut, ready to direct a wide spray.

But first, Nick dug around the sage with his combi, splitting the stump, knocking out any flicker of heat that lurked there waiting for a chance to burst forth. He could see and feel fire. He could tell with his own hand if there was any life left or not. He could beat and dig and spray it dead. Nick could dig the fire's roots all the way down. He wanted to reach to the very bottom, get it done. Leave nothing behind.

"Evergreen!" Thompson called from the engine. "Any day now."

"Done," Nick called, backing away, heading to another smoking sage. Thompson flipped the lever and directed a wide, soaking spray. Then Wicks was spraying, too. Testing, splitting, digging, and spraying, the four of them patrolled the perimeter of the fire, working their way into the black.

They'd been at it for about an hour when Wicks started yelling, motioning for the rest of them to come back toward the engines.

"The SEAT's coming. Time for the air show."

"Awesome!" Mac said.

"Why do we need a plane?" Nick yelled back. "This fire's over."

"Jarchow ordered it when the fire was still active," Wicks shouted as he jumped out of the engine cab with his radio and some orange flagging. "Anyway, too late to call it off. Loaded up and ready to drop. Won't hurt, that's for sure."

The radio pressed to his ear, Wicks walked out to the fireline with Thompson next to him, both looking up. As they gazed skyward, Wicks rolled up his sleeves, a sure sign that the fire was over. But Nick followed their gaze, spotting the SEAT, the slow noisy plane flying like a fat bumble bee through the smoky sky. Lifting the flagging to indicate wind direction, Wicks directed the SEAT in by radio.

The plane came toward them for a dry run, Wicks yelling into the radio, waving directions. The plane blared over them and then banked right and headed back.

"Pull out," Thompson shouted at them all as the noise receded. "Real stuff now."

Nick and Mac grabbed their tools and shot behind an engine.

"I've got to take a picture for my girlfriend," Mac said. "This is amazing."

"What's amazing is that you have a girlfriend," Nick said. Mac shrugged and slowly raised his middle finger. Nick laughed, shook his head, and looked out toward the horizon.

The plane wobbled back toward them, low and slow, and then slid by in a noisy whir as it headed to the fireline. Then a trail of red, slurry fire retardant spilled forth, a sudden soup storm splatting the ground, the smell chemical and sour. Nick and Mac watched as the plane then lifted up almost impossibly, banking right again, its roar diminishing, finally disappearing. Then there was nothing but wet, soggy Nevada earth and a dozen miles of cars waiting to get back to the business of driving across the middle of nowhere.

As soon as the plane was only a dot in the sky, Thompson walked over, tucking his radio in his pocket, a relaxed smile on his face. "Okay, this is basically over. Time to grid. Just like you were doing. Work ten feet in. Make sure it's cool. The edge is the most important."

The two engine crews spent the next couple of hours gridding the line. The work was sweaty and long, and they were working too far away from each other to talk. Nick became the pound of his combi on the sodden soil, the sound splitting roots, the swoosh of water.

"Now you know the secret," Hamm said during a water break.

"What secret?" Nick asked.

"The truth about firefighting," Hamm said, wiping his mouth and throwing his water bottle toward the engine. "Ten percent excitement. Ninety percent pain-in-the-ass. They don't hip you to that on the district website, do they?"

Hamm laughed and picked up the hose. Nick shook his head and walked back into the black, chopping away at a steaming stump. No, that secret wasn't listed on the job description, but wasn't everything 10 percent excitement, 90 percent work? No secret at all. But the heat? He looked up at the sky, light now, free of smoke, bright and clear. Only a wet dank smell remained. How hot it was under all this clothing was a secret, also left out of any job description.

Finally, after the ground was still, dead, black, and cool, Thompson and Wicks talked with Jarchow and then the NHP officers, and within minutes, cars were whooshing by as if there had never been a fire at all.

"Sorry about that girlfriend crack," Nick said later as he and Mac washed the engines. Ever since he'd said the thing about Mac's girlfriend, he'd felt bad, but the apology stayed inside until now, when he and Mac were alone.

They'd soaped and rinsed engine 1344, and now they cloth dried the driver's side, Mac following behind Nick in a swirl of rags.
Mac seemed ready to flip him the bird again. But then he shrugged. "Actually, you're right. It is amazing Sarah hangs out with me. She's great. Organized. Focused. Totally hot, too. She's studying nursing at Nevada State College."

"She must be smart," Nick said. Megan had taught a freshman comp class to nursing students at Mills. They'd beaten out a lot of people to get accepted into that program.

"That's the thing. I couldn't even get admitted for fall semester. So I applied for this job. Took the two-week training. Here I am making cash. Sarah wanted to kill me. Said, 'I go to school to learn how to save people, and you're going to end up being the person I help in the hospital?'"

"So why did you do it?" Nick swiped the large green door, moved around to the front left fender.

"My dad was a firefighter. Started when he was twenty-one. Retired last year. He and my mom moved to Boca. He fishes. Golfs. But he always told me firefighting was it. Thing is, not wildland. He's structural. But he keeps sending me advice."

"What would he have said about today?" Nick wiped the front bumper, his back throbbing.

"Who knows? He says, 'Get out of the grass.' He says, 'That's where the danger is.'"

"What about the forest?" Nick stood, stretched, and threw his wet towel in the bucket. "Isn't the canopy worse?"

Mac wiped on. "Not according to Mac Senior. From the comfort of his fishing boat, my dad says we're all a box of fireplace matches. Reassuring, huh?"

Mac looked out around the station and then went back to work. Nick turned to face all grass around the station and then beyond, the hills to the north brown all the way till they met the tan edge of the evening sky. Not even the irrigated patch in front of the station was green anymore.

That night in his bed, Nevada a silent flatness all around the station and Devlin, Nick stared up at the ceiling instead of at the flaring fan of the Milky Way outside his window, visible this moonless night. He didn't need more stimulation. His whole body was jumping with nerves, sharp hot pins and needles. His feet and hands twitched every so often, feeling boot and tool, reliving heat and wind and dust. He blinked, trying to keep his eyes open because when he shut them for even a second, he could still see the flames, smell the smoke, hear the whoosh and crackle of the fire.

He wasn't sure why he was so hyped up. The fire wasn't what he'd imagined while reading and studying in the weeks before he headed to Nevada. In fact, it had been a little disappointing the way it had just died, pulling up short before it might take off. Of course, wanting fire to burn on and on was ironic and probably immoral. What did it say about him? Wanting the trouble he was supposed to stop? But it had felt good to finally get out and have something to do. Working next to Mac had been exhilarating. In a sense, they'd all been united, as if at war. They'd been fighting an enemy that could kill but had no brain, only wild energy.

When he'd been mopping up, digging for hot spots, Nick hadn't thought any of this, nothing intruding on the work at hand. He'd been following or leading Mac, listening to orders from Thompson and Wicks, blinking through smoke, his nose and mouth burning. But no one had been in any obvious danger. There were escape routes and safety zones. Both engine crews had followed the Ten and Eighteen. Hell, they'd been right by the interstate. If there'd been a blowup, all they would have had to do was run to the pavement and hunker down, no shelter deployment necessary. Worst case, they get in the engines and drive away.

Nick got it now. Fire might not have a brain, but it moved like a living thing, a creature wild and untamed and full of nothing but need. Arcing, undulating, hissing, crackling. It was waiting.

Chapter Sixteen

Northern Nevada
Mapp Ranch
June 2012

Wanda headed down Dempsey Mapp Road in the truck, her eyes flicking now and again to the hills surrounding the Crescent Valley. Here it was only June, and everything was parched, crisp, gone to seed and an early death. The sagebrush was a dirty, dusky olive green, one second away from brown. Even the wild roses that grew by the house had flared to withered sticks and blood-red rose hips overnight. Wanda had lived a lifetime of summers on this ranch, and she'd never seen so much blond in a season that often held onto green until July, at least in the gulches and gullies. Some wet, cold years, the mountain ridges carried snow on their humps until mid-summer, wildflowers blooming in August like late Easter egg surprises.

Since the council meeting, Wanda had been thinking. Not her usual job. But Birdie had called from DC the night before, saying things were going slow. Meaning, Wanda knew, the ruling about treaty rights had been delayed.

"Back soon," Birdie promised. "In no time." Behind Birdie, in the background, Wanda heard the murmur of important conversations.

"Um hum," Wanda had answered, knowing Birdie's "soons" and "no times" often took days and weeks and sometimes years, both statements other ways to say, "Whenever I can."

Wanda couldn't wait. Dwayne was like the summer fire that hadn't come yet. For sure, Wanda had to get to him before the match did.

Wanda decided to talk to Len Dunning herself, when Dwayne was out with the herd, Tanya at work, Stanley on the couch with his movies and an open bag of tortilla chips. As Wanda had clomped down the porch, Ruby had whined to come along, and now she sat on the passenger seat, her graying snout pointed out the window, her tail wagging a slow, contented side to side on the cracked leather seat.

Wanda gripped the wheel, nervous about the moment she'd leave Dempsey Mapp Road and turn right on Highway 306. She drove around the ranch just fine on the ATV and in the truck, but the highway? No sir. And now she was paying the price, what with the sweat sliding down her sides, under her knees, and across her forehead. Why had she given up on highway driving, something she still needed? She wasn't dead yet, and she could ride a horse the same fine way she did when she was twelve, drive an ATV, and take command of a truck when she needed to. She was alive. Mostly.

As she pulled slowly onto the highway, a little brown turd of a car honked at her with its baby flute horn, but Wanda kept steady, using the gas, pressing onward. The drive to Kellogg City was imprinted on her, even with the highway improvements and sign changes and whatnot. She knew the curves of the road, the landscape alongside the asphalt, the houses, buildings, the slant of the sun at all hours of the day. She knew the surprise cool of the Devlin tunnels and the pop of sunlight at the end, the curve at the Hunter exit, and then finally the exit for Kellogg City's business loop. No big darn deal.

After only a few minutes of road behind her, a semi blared—a clarion of heat and anger—and Wanda's heart thudded against her ribs. She gripped the wheel hard and glanced at her speedometer. Forty miles an hour. She pressed down on the accelerator, glad she was able to get Stanley to help her with her boots today. She waited, watching the speedometer hit higher speeds—forty-five, fifty—and then she was almost flying at sixty. Fast enough to keep the truck-devils off her tail, she thought, laughing a little, almost enjoying the feel of the road.

As she approached the city, she exhaled and took the Kellogg City East exit, driving slowly onto Utah Street, through the intersections and turns, staying safe until she was on Ruby View Drive and for sure headed toward the reservation and the store. In the midday glare, Kellogg City seemed uglier than usual, like a city that'd had way too much to drink the night before. All these new buildings were rectangles of concrete and glass, with giant signs that promised coffee, gas, grease, or a grand dining experience, though nothing behind the shiny doors was more than slop on a white plate. What had happened to the buildings that had housed The Wagonwheel Motel and the Three Jugs Tavern and the Brewer's Saddle Shop? What about The Stumble Inn?

She put her hand into the paper bag next to her and pulled out half a peanut butter sandwich, tearing off a little for Ruby and eating the rest as she went through traffic lights that mercifully allowed her to go under the speed limit. No one honked at her the rest of the way, and soon enough she made it to the reservation. She waved at Warren Piffero who stood in front of the Sinclair gas station talking with Susana Leto, who was all angry arms and arched eyebrows.

"Something in her craw again," Wanda told Ruby. "Let's move on by."

A few more minutes, and Wanda pulled up in front of the convenience store, Barn Owl Foods and Smoke Shop. The big joke about the convenience store on the Indian reservation was that no "real" Indians ran it, the kind from Calcutta or some such place. Just the American kind.

Wanda pushed open the creaking truck door and slowly slid out, the pavement radiating heat. Ruby galumphed past her, shaking herself free of that ridiculous drive and wagging her tail next to the store's double door. Inside, Wanda could see Len behind the counter, leaning on his elbows, reading a car magazine and flip, flip, flipping the pages.

She stared at him in profile, a tall, strong young man, tall like her father had been, tall like Dwayne. But Len was tightly muscled as well, big in the way young men could be, all that young animal flesh tight and firm on long bones, the skin plump with health. One day, he might run to fat—shoulder and chest muscles dumping down into big beer belly—but maybe not. If Len could do something with himself and get out of the store and off the rez and out of Kellogg City, he might not end up being some kind of statistic in one of Tanya's studies. If Len and Dwayne could turn their anger toward ranch work or college or plain old life in another state for a spell, something good was bound to happen. Harder to make something good happen here. Look at the work Tanya did at the clinic. But she had to learn the world's ways to come back and fight them here on the rez. She had to turn around and come back.

"Hi there, Wanda," Merce Muckleshoot said as he came out of the store clutching a box of Marlboros and a loaf of white bread like bad twins. "How's the family?"

"Good, Merce," Wanda said. "Yours?"

He nodded. "Whatcha doing all the way up here?"

"Never too early for a Coke," she said, and Merce cracked a small tight smile and then walked past.

Wanda took in a breath and pushed through the door, Ruby scooting in ahead of her. The automatic ding-dong of greeting echoed in the store as the door closed behind her. Len looked up. For a second, she could a see a twist of feeling on his lips. And then just like that, his face shifted back into boredom, a lethargy young people thought was "cool." Dwayne had worn that same look for all of high school, so much so that Wanda had all but forgotten his smile.

"Hey, Ms. Mapp," Len said.

"Len," Wanda said, moving closer. "How're you?"

"Been better, been worse." He flicked a page. "Not so great since the meeting. I'm about to get run off the rez by Darlene Hightower and her buddies. People ready to buy me a car just to get me outta town."

Wanda moved closer to the Hostess rack. A couple years back, Tanya had rallied to get all the sweet foods banned from the store, and that particular tribal meeting had almost been as bad as the last one. What a fuss! Mines or Twinkies. Which was worse?

"So you're not up here to buy fruit pies, I'd guess." Len closed the magazine and stood up straight.

"Good guess," Wanda said, watching Ruby sniff the store's perimeter, her tail going a mile a minute.

Len crossed his arms in front of him, looking at her.

"What's your angle?" Wanda asked.

Len shrugged a little.

"There's one," Wanda said. "Always is."

"You can't be okay with all this," he said. "The corruption."

"I've never been okay with any of it." Wanda put her hand out to the counter, holding on for a little support, her knees feeling wobbly.

Len noticed, his eyes widening, and waited. Then he said, "You can fight back."

Wanda shook her head, feeling how fight had left her, and so long ago, it might not have ever been there. She couldn't remember what it felt like. How did it still flow through Birdie's veins, almost eighty years of it inside her? Fight wasn't what Wanda wanted except maybe against weeds in the garden patch. She sighed. "Nope, Len. I don't have any more. But I'm worried about Dwayne. He needs to move forward."

"Forward can be through." His expression advertised what flowed through him. Resolve. Indignation. Hatred. Fear. She'd seen that look too often on Birdie.

"Forward can also take a left and never come back," Wanda said, thinking about Birdie in DC. She swallowed, glanced back at Ruby, and gripped the counter. Her left arm was all a tingle.

"Are you okay?" Len asked.

Wanda nodded, but she really did need something to drink, Tanya's study be damned. "I could sure do with a Coke," she said.

Len rounded the counter and headed for the refrigerators. Wanda heard him talking to Ruby and then the clink of cans pushing forward in their little cold chutes. He cracked one, and she heard the tumble of the ice dispenser, and then he was back, holding the cup out to her. She took it and drank a few big sips, closing her eyes, letting the pop-y bubbles settle on her tongue and then slide down her throat, soothing her with sugar and carbonation. Little white blots of light scuttled in front of her eyes like see-through crabs, but as she waited, watching, they began to disperse, disappear, and she breathed in a few times. She took another sip and then another, and she felt almost back to normal.

After a moment, she put the cup down and nodded her thanks to Len. "All I can say is just don't let anything happen. His momma has been through a world of story with that boy."

"He's no boy."

"Maybe not," Wanda said. "But—"

"His decisions are his decisions," Len said, behind the counter again, flipping open the magazine, the pages slick and shiny with gleaming cars. He was back to his old self, wishing her away from the store and his life.

"Someone can put choices in front of him. Good ones. Bad ones, too."

Len shrugged. "Like I said, he's no boy."

Wanda wanted to say that everyone younger than she was seemed like a child. She was as old as the Cortez Mountains, old as the gold veins running through every ridge, old as the sunrise that kept coming day after day. Len looked like a newborn. Fresh and brown and long and lean. One day out of diapers. One second away from his mother's breast. How could anyone as young as Len and Dwayne make decisions that made sense?

But then Ruby was winding around her legs, sniffing, looking up as if to say, "Let's blow this pop stand! Let's go chase cows!"

Wanda leaned over and scratched Ruby behind one soft ear. This old girl was likely her last Ruby. For a second, her throat constricted by the sadness of a world where there were no Rubys to find and drive with.

"So?" Len stared at her, waiting for something. Probably, she was waiting, too, yet she had no idea for what.

"Thanks for the Coke," she said, fumbling in her pockets for a bill or two, but Len shook his head and held up a hand. "Thanks for remembering what I said."

Len met her gaze true. As she drove away from the shop, Ruby's nose out the window, her eyes slit closed, Wanda hoped what she saw in Len's eyes was real, a portent of a better future.

Once she pulled onto Dempsey Mapp Road, bumping back home to Stanley, the afternoon sun now cutting like razorblades on the grass, Wanda knew her hope when she left the store was probably just relief from having made the drive successfully, finding Len, and hearing what she needed to. But when she walked into the house, it was clear she'd been fooling herself. The first sign was that the television wasn't on. The second was that Stanley was gone from the couch, not watching Marissa or who-the-heck-else performing daily histrionics. Wanda put the keys down on the table and looked around for other clues, but all she found was an empty package of Marlboros, Dwayne's brand, nothing more. She walked over to the couch, imagining she'd find a note, though it had been years since Stanley had put anything to paper. Dwayne hadn't written a Took Uncle Stan to Kellogg City or a Going to a meeting or a Heading to the feed store.

Nothing. And the small house had never felt so big. For the first time in as long as she could remember, she was the only one at home. She sat on the couch and looked at the dead eye of the TV, wondering what old Marissa was up to today, probably just her usual slinky gyrations. But with Stanley out and about, she might go to the barn and work with the animals, maybe even ride Six later before the sun started to set.

Wanda put her hand on the sofa, angling to get herself back up to vertical, when she noticed the lighter, a slim flick of plastic, bright red, on its side on the coffee table. Dwayne likely left it here, forgetting for about three seconds that he needed it to smoke another Marlboro. But then she saw the lighter had a logo. *Barn Owl Foods*. She picked it up, shook it a bit to see it was full. Brand spanking new, picked up this morning while talking to Len about something he shouldn't. Plans, protests, civil disobedience. Worse. Arrests. Murder sometimes, too.

Len looked her in the eye and let her believe that Dwayne was okay.

Birdie, Wanda thought. Come home.

Chapter Seventeen

On the Road
South Dakota/Wyoming
Late Winter, 1973

Birdie didn't have one thought, not from Wounded Knee, South Dakota till about Casper, Wyoming, when finally, she couldn't bat away the flickering images: Gunfire. A flash of a bullet wound, half a head blasted, gone. She grasped her throat, squeezed her eyes tight. Arms flying wide open, a gaping hole in a strong back. Birdie came undone, wailing. She shuddered her car into the shoulder, lurching to a stop.

What wrested free was something she'd never heard from herself, a guttural snarl of grief and terror, the howling a sound and then a feeling and then an ache and then all of that over and over again, the air in the truck cab hot and stifling. The past three months came crashing out of her with huffs and moans, and she fought off the visions of the two dead men, Buddy Lamont and Frank Clearwater, both shot dead by federal marshals. Buddy by a sniper when he was on his way to the sweat lodge. Shot down like he was a Nazi or a Viet Cong or a terrorist. Frank when he was sleeping next to his wife.

But no. She couldn't think of them, but then she did, and that made her scream even more.

Buddy had flown at that first shot, the bullet pulling him right off his feet and throwing him back.

Frank's wife polka-dotted with blood.

After about fifteen minutes, she leaned over the wheel and just plain sobbed until her teeth chattered and her lungs felt raw and drained, her body empty and stretched like a knot yanked flat and useless. She sat up and leaned against the seat, looking out at the long vastness of American nothing in front of her, road and air and rushing cars. Birdie put her hands on her thighs, certain she wasn't really there and that her palms would touch beaten up upholstery and cracked leather instead of body. But she was still there, alive, all of her intact, skin, muscles, nerves, bones, blood.

She didn't deserve it. If anyone, she deserved to be dead because she'd believed too hard, too much, told everyone that the Indians were right and just. Despite all her belief, Frank Clearwater was shot in the head, his pregnant wife curled in a C next to him. Despite Birdie's avowals of conquering and change, of bringing back the native way of life, Buddy Lamont was hunted down like a quail.

Why hadn't she stayed in Nevada with Wanda and Stan to fight over grazing rights and broken treaties? Her family needed her. But no. All of Nevada wasn't enough, so she'd left for other Indian disasters. She'd joined the Oglala and the American Indian Movement activists and sat superior in the town of Wounded Knee, certain that now, finally, it would happen. On the land her mother came from, the AIM would reclaim the very spot where 300 Indian men, women, and children were butchered in the last massacre of the Indian Wars. Here she believed there would be rebirth with dignity. Here the home of Red Cloud and Sitting Bull and Crazy Horse would be reborn as the place of Russell Means and Dennis Banks, the AIM leaders. Here the US government would be forced to take notice and repair what they'd been breaking since the first white settlers arrived. It was the 70s, for god's sake. Everyone knew that Vietnam was wrong, America finally protesting the killing of Asian people half a world away. Nobody was being held back. Women. Blacks. It was the Indians' turn now, and Birdie wanted to be there when it all cracked open, everyone free at last.

Birdie took in a few long breaths, swallowing down her remaining tears and wiping her face with her palms. Outside, the sky was wide and blue, nature going on with her regular business. Just like the people passing Birdie in their cars, headed to work and school and wherever. She smoothed her hair, pulling at a lock at her temple, the strands coarse under her fingers. She relaxed against the seat. How had it ended this way? She'd believed in this cause more than anything she had in her life, leaving the ranch and spending most of the last year protesting the "Trail of Broken Treaties," a car caravan across parts of the country, a motorcade tour of spots where the US government had broken one treaty after the other. She'd been with AIM when they busted into the Bureau of Indian Affairs office in DC and held it hostage. And there she'd been with the two hundred Indians who'd caravanned into the hallowed town of Wounded Knee, taking over on a full-mooned night and blocking the roads with cars, men and women leaning over hoods with shotguns and rifles. They'd stripped bare the trading post, taken over the church; they'd fired at and then argued with the FBI, making their demands. They'd battled against tribal chairman Dick Wilson and his goons. The AIM was going to wrench back control from the corrupt Indians and the white politicians. Wounded Knee would be their badge, flag, symbol of strength and resiliency and courage. They'd get back their lives, land, and languages.

During the day, men with feathers in their brims walked the line behind the barricade, rifles cocked, talking to the media. Birdie worked inside with others behind boarded-up windows planning their next moves. During the night, they sat, eagle-eyed, waiting for an ambush.

It was a war zone. Cop cars and tanks. Choppers flew the skies like ravens.

Birdie wiped her eyes on her sweater and then gulped water from a canteen she'd brought from home, an old tin thing her father had kept around in the barn. In her flurry of escape, she'd managed to grab a couple of wool blankets and her duffel bag. She tossed everything into the cab at three in the morning, coasting down a slight hill before bumping into gear. Then she lurched around the burned-out car hulls blocking the roads, sped past federal and county vehicles, and made it out before the marshals sealed off the town.

Maybe Birdie had believed in the movement, but she'd deserted it, too, running away fast without telling anyone, not even stopping in Pine Ridge to tell her Aunt Edie or any of her mother's family.

Birdie took another sip of water. There was nothing else to do but go home. She'd failed in South Dakota, but maybe at home she could fix things. Wanda needed her. Dempsey Mapp had died when she was in DC, but Birdie hadn't even gone home for the funeral. What she was doing was that important. She didn't have time to help her sister run the ranch, not even when Wanda wrote that the BLM was breathing down her neck about the herd or that Stanley was acting odd, as if he were deaf, and the clinic doctor was recommending tests.

So Birdie was missing Stanley's world turning dim. She'd missed calves and foals turning to yearlings, and then all of that happening over again. The old Ruby died, another now in her place. Snows fell, spring came, the grass dried out. Everything spun on without her. Her father used to say, "Let's have our berries on our earth. Let the water run. Let the grass grow again." Back on Mapp Ranch, the earth had burst forth and died and done it again and again. And Birdie had been too busy to pay attention.

"If we can change things at the capitol," she'd told Wanda from the telephone in the AIM headquarters, the call expensive, long-distance. "Things will change on the ranch. You'll see."

"Barn needs repair," Wanda said.

"We'll finally have a say in this country," Birdie said.

"BLM's trying to count the herd. This and that about grazing rights. Now Dad's gone, I'm running out of excuses to keep them off the land."

"When we get done, there'll be no more talk about grazing rights," Birdie said.

"Stanley's going to Reno for tests," Wanda said. "Halona Walker's going to take him."

"Everyone will be able to see when this is over, Wanda. I promise. Gotta go."

Birdie went. And she'd been wrong. People were dead. The movement was dead. All that was left to her was a home she didn't deserve. But there was nothing else to believe in now but her sister and brother and the small house Birdie had lived in almost all her life.

Something rapped sharp on the window. Birdie jumped, hand to her throat. She turned to see a highway patrolman, his hat off, his eyes behind dark sunglasses. She rolled down the window and tried not to spit. He was one of them. The men that kill.

"Everything all right, ma'am?" He lifted his glasses to look at her. In his gaze, she could see he didn't recognize her as Indian but as a woman, a pretty woman. He tried to keep his smile north of sleazy, but he couldn't help himself.

How can you? she wanted to scream, but if she did, he might ask her more questions, put two and two together in that pea-sized brain of his and ask her where she was coming from.

Birdie blinked, swallowed, batted away images of Buddy and Frank. Again, she wanted to scream, but then she thought of Wanda and Stanley at home in the ranch house, sitting around the table, eating their soup. Stanley telling a joke. Wanda raising her eyebrows. Ruby on the porch wagging a stumpy tail. The Cortez Mountains frosted with snow, the sky the color of gunmetal, the bristlecone pines hoary with ice.

"Yes," she said, biting her cheek. "Fine, thanks. I'm going home."

Chapter Eighteen

Devlin, Nevada
June 2012

"Evergreen," Jarchow called out into the yard where Nick and Mac were polishing the chrome on Engine Two.

"Now you're in for it," Mac whispered. "He wants you to clean the toilets."

"Or your skinny ass," Nick said. "I'm going to use Drano and a Brillo pad."

Mac laughed a little, rubbing the chrome to a sure shine. Nick put down his rag.

"Yes, sir." Nick stood up straight and blinked against the slash of morning sun sliding across the land to the west. The day was going to be bright but moderate—the temp somewhere in the mid-eighties, the relative humidity high. Earlier in the day, the sky swirled with plates of lenticular clouds, but they'd disappeared behind the mountains, taking their storms with them. A light breeze whisked across Nick's forehead, and he wondered if there ever was going to be a big fire. After the Cross Creek fire on I-80, all they'd done was follow behind a Type II handcrew, mopping up used-to-be fire, scratching the barely warm earth with tools, sweating nonstop over the shorn black earth. Sure, a week ago, they'd put out a cigarette fire on I-80 down near Deeth, a quarter acre grass fire that burned up from the shoulder fast. But the NHP hadn't even closed the road. The rest? Mop up. Nick had spent the hours bent over like an old man, digging at soil with the combi at all but non-existent hotspots.

"Put on your district shirt. Tuck it in. We're going to pay some calls on ranchers. Time to do some prevention."

"Prevention?"

"PR work on fire preparedness. Got the order from District."

"But—" Nick began, trying to figure out how to get out of forced confinement with Jarchow. What the hell would they talk about? Besides, if he stayed at the station, he might get toned out to a fire. But Mac whispered up from the large front rim. "Thompson's going to make us clean the entire station. If I were you, I'd go."

"Yes, sir." Nick headed toward the station house, trying to find a manly, polite, firm smile that read, "Awesome!"

But Jarchow turned back before he could give it a go, and Nick felt his shoulders slump, the hope that today might be the day they'd fight a real fire evaporating like the morning dew that almost never happened anyway.

"Problem is this," Jarchow was saying as Nick finished his text to Megan:

On a ridiculous drive. don't worry today.

Nick didn't know why he bothered with the daily updates. Due to the spotty cell coverage and worse Wi-Fi, their conversations had been terse, tense. Nick kept his sentences short, knowing that at any moment, they could be disconnected. They talked about known things: Seattle, college friends, their parents. Of their separate realities: the new apartment, the station. The weather: rain, dry. Then a silence full of questions. Then nothing but air and buzz as their conversation broke apart.

"We've had three years of drought," Jarchow said as if beginning a lecture. "This year's snowfall melted by the beginning of March. Rivers and creeks started running dry in May. Fuel is high, and there's a pine blight in the mountains. The forest floors are covered in dead needles. Not to mention the dead trees. So bottom line, we can't allow ranchers and farmers to do any controlled burns. No brush piles. Tree limbs. Whatever. There are some ranchers in the Crescent Valley we need to enlighten, and most of them don't want to talk to us."

Nick turned to face his supervisor. "They hate the Federal Government? Or the BLM?"

"Both." Jarchow flicked on his turn signal and got into the slow lane. An ancient Volkswagen Bug gave them a "Fuck you" *honk honk*.

"Because?"

Jarchow shook his head. "Long list. Mostly it's about property. Lots of people are working land that doesn't officially belong to them. So we're the assholes who get to do the dirty work when the DOE." He glanced over at Nick. "The Department of Energy. Or even the Bureau of Indian Affairs sometimes needs people 'relocated,' to use their word. Folks aren't angry at fire per se. But we all wear the BLM label. Anyway, first we're going to Mapp Ranch. And I've been told to treat them with kid gloves. That's why you're here, college educated and all. Supposedly well-spoken. Because one time, Stanley Mapp tried to light himself on fire just to get us the hell off his land."

"Did it work?"

"No," Jarchow said. "We took him and some horses. But apparently the BLM guy in charge almost shit his pants afterward. "

Nick nodded, though he knew little about land grants and the reservations, especially in Nevada. The only difference he could see was that in most states, the Indians or Native Americans or indigenous had gotten the shit land, the crap leftovers. But in Nevada, the entire state seemed like crap leftovers, except maybe parts of the Sierra Nevada.

He'd had first choice servings his whole life, due only to his parents' hard work. But he was only two generations away from a third-grade education and a life in Mexico. At least on one side.

"You're not expecting any human torch today, are you?" Nick shivered a little despite himself, the thought of fire touching bare skin something he tried daily to ignore.

"Not really. The guy's old and pretty much deaf and blind now. But you never know," Jarchow said. "At least we're in an engine. Plenty of water to put out a nutbar."

Nick laughed, and Jarchow glanced at him, his quick gaze level, and then he asked, "So, where you from?"

"Um, you know. Oakland, mostly."

"Got that. I mean *from* from."

Here we go, Nick thought. He looked out at the landscape of nothing dotted only with oases of gas stations and Burger Kings.

"You mean, what am I?" Nick asked.

"Yeah, okay. To be blunt," Jarchow said.

"My dad's Mexican. My mom's family were boat people."

"Huh?" Jarchow looked over at him with rare emotional expression, eyebrows arched, eyes wide, as if he expected Nick to suddenly appear Vietnamese or Cuban.

"You know. Big old boats. Mayflower on one side. Steamers from Poland that landed at Ellis Island on the other. Settlers. If I were a woman, I could be a member of the DAR."

"What?"

"Daughters of the American Revolution."

Jarchow smirked.

"Seriously. Call me Betsy Ross, and I'll sew you a flag."

Jarchow shot him a glance. "I would have said Italian, but Delgado's Spanish, right?"

Nick wasn't brown-skinned and black-haired, like many of the Mexicans that worked in the cavernous kitchens in Las Vegas casino hotels or in Kellogg City, Sparks, or Reno. Nick was a foot taller and five shades lighter than the men and women who came from the small villages in Oaxaca or Chiapas. His own grandfather Victor was dark and short but strong as Popeye with arms that seemed capable of lifting whole engines from the guts of cars. At home, Grandpa Victor spoke only Spanish, unless confronted with someone like Nick's mom.

Jarchow couldn't know that Nick's father never spoke with an accent. Nick could never admit how he didn't know or had forgotten how to connect with his father's side, the part of him that wasn't white, the part that could never be truly Mexican. And it would be humiliating for so many reasons to admit he'd flunked Spanish twice in high school.

When his parents moved back to his mom's hometown on the other side of the Berkeley Hills, he'd been glad he looked . . . what? Greek, Jewish, Italian? Vaguely ethnic? No one really had asked, and he'd admitted nothing, ashamed to admit, embarrassed by his shame.

And so the years in white world went on. He'd listened to the other kids talk about Mexicans, as in, "That guy looks like a Mexican waiter" when talking about a guy in a small suit jacket. Or "Come on. Let's bail. It just belongs to a bunch of Mexicans," when Nick's friend Tyler hit a truck filled with gardening tools and then drove off, laughing. Mexican this, Mexican that.

The only person Nick had ever clocked was Tyler. A week later. Over a missing textbook.

"Fuck, dude," Tyler had said holding his cheek. "What the hell was that?"

Clipped, trimmed, and controlled, Jarchow wouldn't have a clue about any of this.

"That's right," Nick said. "Name's from Spain, but not my people. Mexico City, actually. What about you?"

Jarchow shrugged a little, and Nick could tell that for some reason, this wasn't a question he liked either.

"German. My dad's family came over in the 1800s. Moved to Minnesota. Farmed a lot. Turned into Americans."

"What about your Mom?" Nick asked.

"Venezuelan," Jarchow said, and Nick suddenly saw it, the darker skin, the shorter stature, the brown hair that was harder to notice when buzz cut. Jachow's ethnicity was masked, transformed by muscles, tattoos, ironed uniform pants.
Vaguely ethnic, just like Nick.

"*Hola!*" Nick said, panicked as he did that Jarchow would come back at him with a stream of Spanish, the way his father's family would sometimes, forgetting he knew nothing. But Jarchow only nodded. Maybe, Nick thought, they'd have more to talk about next time.

As they headed down I-80, neither of them spoke, the free day taking hold of Nick as the engine pushed through the fine, clear air. Even if he was in the middle of Nevada, it was nice to be out and about, not cleaning the engine or running in the hills or listening to Hamm and Lehman argue. Living with so many people was a shock; it had been years since the Evergreen dorms and all the shared noise and mess. Jarchow was isolated, solitary, liked silence. Turned out, a good person to drive with.

Past Kellogg City, they turned off on Highway 306 and traveled southwest, passing Beowawe, a mostly ghost town with a functioning library (open Thursdays from 10-2.30 according to the painted sign) and then the town of Crescent Valley. Finally, they turned east on Dempsey Mapp Road and headed toward the mountains. Nick looked around, forced to admit that despite the tractors left to rot into rusty artwork, the land was beautiful. Definitely not crap leftovers. The sky was an ocean blue that went on forever and was streaked with startlingly brilliant clouds. The flat land slapped right into hills and then mountains that rolled with dry grass and shrubs with golden flowers. Yucca or some kind of palm-like plants grew on the sides of the road. He half expected to see cowboys and burros, and then he did see burros, two skittering down a path, disappearing into a gully.

To the left, a herd of cows, and as they drew closer, Nick spotted the cowboys, both on horses that they reined up when the engine passed by.

"Good thing we aren't in a patrol unit," Jarchow said as he waved at the men, one tall in his saddle and with an intense dark glare Nick could see from the passenger's side. He turned back to get another glimpse, but dust filled the road behind them. "We'd be lassoed and dragged all the way back to the station just for getting off the highway."

"Maybe we should start a fire just to put it out and look like heroes." He wished back the words the minute they were out of his mouth. He was an idiot to joke about fire, especially to Jarchow, whose face had darkened. Nick swallowed hard and clenched his jaw.

"I didn't mean—"

"A fucking dumb ass thing to say." Jarchow said. "Look at this place. Dry as dirt. A valley boxed in by hills and mountains. Not a lot of fuel, but that fuel is three years dry. Kellogg City wants to put patrols on the ranch, and even if the Mapps let us, the damn patrol cars could set off a fire. This whole area is waiting for just one spark."

The air actually smelled like spark, almost like flame. For the Mapps' sake, Nick hoped that lightning didn't strike even once.

"Sorry," Nick said.

Jarchow cut him a hard glance. No hola there now. "Got a call yesterday from George Anderson, District's fire investigator. Turns out that the Cross Creek Fire was probably arson. They sent the incendiary device to forensics—"

"Device?"

"Yeah, so to speak. Wooden matchsticks wrapped around a cigarette."

"Shit." Nick thought about that first fire. If what he'd read about arsonists was true, whoever lit that terrible bundle had probably been watching. Maybe back in the line of waiting cars on I-80. "That's insane."

Jarchow nodded. "Damn right it is. We've got a high risk season and a psychopath all at the same time. Nothing funny about that."

After a few more minutes bumping down the two-track dirt road, Jarchow pulled up in front of the smallest house Nick had seen, a cube with a roof and a slanting porch covered by a tin awning. They stepped out of the engine, Nick re-tucking his shirt into his pants. He wasn't nervous, but he felt as though he were trespassing, which, he supposed he was or would be, once the Mapps told them to get the hell out.

"Hey there," Jarchow said as an old woman pushed open a screen door and stepped onto the porch. She was followed by a scruffy dog who wagged its tail and trotted down to Nick.

"Hey there," Nick said, imitating Jarchow, but the dog seemed happier to see them than the woman did. Nick knelt down and gave the dog a quick scratch behind the ears. Gray-snouted, bright-eyed and happy for the attention, the dog licked his hand, and then Nick stood and walked over to Jarchow.

"Ms. Mapp?" Jarchow began.

The woman stared, her face not like normal faces, with expressions and everything. Her eyes were steady, her mouth stern, her hands at her sides. She seemed ready to not believe anything either of them said for the rest of her life, which, Nick realized might not be that long. She was small and round, her hair short, too, a gray bowl on her head.

"We're from the Ruby District Office. BLM Fire. We hope you'll let us talk to you about the fire danger this year."

The woman stepped off the porch, one, two, three careful steps, and whistled. The dog rushed back toward her and leaned against one leg. The woman was really old, maybe one of the oldest people Nick had ever met, older than even the folks he used to drive around for the convalescent home back in Oakland.

"We know all about it," she said.

"Ms. Wanda Mapp?" Jarchow asked, unfazed by her preemptive strike. He stuck out a hand, his arm and bicep seemed almost bigger than the woman's head. She didn't extend her hand in return.

Instead, the woman—Wanda— nodded.

"Ma'am, Andrew Jarchow. Fire Operation Supervisor. Devlin Station," he said and then nodded over to Nick. "Nick Delgado."

"Nice to meet you." Nick watched her unreadable but clearly unfriendly expression.

The woman gave him an odd stare and then nodded again, and the dog jangled back to Nick and sat on his foot, wagging its tail in the dust.

"Who's this?" He leaned down again to scratch the dog, who panted, pink tongue hanging out.

"Ruby," Wanda said. "Ruby Treaty."

"Sounds like an important name," he said.

"Not so much to anyone anymore, at least outside of this speck of Nevada." She spoke slowly, almost musically, something in her cadence reminding Nick of his Grandma Rosa's accented English, the rhythm of another language—maybe another meaning—underneath the words.

Jarchow's fingers twitched as if he really were in a western film, ready to pull the trigger. "We've had some extremely dry weather. The county is calling for locals to take extra precautions. Could we come in and go over a few things with you? Your ranch hands?"

"Ranch hands?" Wanda said. "What do we look like? A big operation?"

Jarchow shrugged. "We have a list of recommendations we'd like to talk about."

He glanced over at Nick, and Nick stood, put his hands in his pockets, the dog's soft weight still against his shin. "Dangerous conditions," Nick offered.

"You said it," Wanda said, her quick look skirting over him. "Come in."

Jarchow raised his eyebrows at the moment of victory. Nick patted Ruby once more and then started toward the house. Nick was unsure, suddenly, whose side he was on. He wanted to turn Jarchow around and get him off this ranch. They had no business telling the Mapps what to do and how to live. As if anything in their glossy BLM pamphlet was news.

Keep woodpiles away from buildings.

Insulting for someone who has lived out here as long as Wanda Mapp.

As they headed to the porch, the screen door opened and this time, a young woman stepped out, her hand over her eyes to block the glare. Nick stopped walking and took in breath. She glittered, her skin, hair and eyes the finest shades of pale. As if determined to make up for a lack of color, she was dressed in a sleeveless black dress and sandals, a thin purple scarf hanging around her slim neck like a necklace. He glanced from Wanda to the woman and then at Jarchow, who was staring at the women the same way Nick was.

No way there were two more different people in the same place at the same time anywhere on the entire planet.

"Hey," the young woman said.

"Hey," Nick said.

Jarchow nodded in his cool, simple way.

Wanda stumped up the stairs. "Em Donnelly. Meet the BLM."

"Oh, the bad guys." She smiled, clearly not thinking anything about Jarchow was bad.

"Big Bad Wolf." Jarchow smiled, flashing bright teeth Nick had barely seen before.

"You're lucky the other Mapp siblings aren't here," Em said, her smile as white as Jarchow's. "Then you'd really have some explaining to do."

Inside, the house was surprisingly cool. Nick wasn't sure what to say, but he sat with the others at the small round table in the kitchen area, polite enough to take a glass of iced tea and a small round powdery cookie, smart enough not to stare into the smallness of the house that generations of this family had lived in. His face felt hot, his stomach jittery, more so than when he'd been on the fire and for no apparent reason whatsoever.

Nick licked his lips. Sweet. The cookie reminded him of something his Grandma Flo used to bake at Christmas. He took another bite just as Em glanced at him. He gave her a powdery nod and wiped his hands on the paper towel napkin.

Em made small talk in a big voice, enough so that Nick sat back to listen, almost surprised. Megan was a small woman with a quiet personality. Em was small, too, but with special effects, wide-open eyes, laughing mouth, hands punctuating words. A chop at the end of a sentence. A wave during a story about a road after a rain. Thumbs up about a tow-truck driver.

Niceties over, Jarchow started his spiel about the dry weather, Nick took furtive glances at the neat, buttoned-down room. All these years, this one family had lived on this ranch, their pots and pans and plates and bowls in order, the floors swept, the windows clean, the large glass squares allowing light to shine on the old furniture, the hutch, the table he sat at, the couch as broken down as an old swaybacked horse.

Nick sipped his tea, eyes on Wanda Mapp, noting her small hands, both curled into knotted Cs. Dark sun spots dappled each, but she was strong, calluses on her index fingers. She used tools, her body marked by strenuous repetitive movement. She wasn't sitting around knitting socks. No, she could grab things in those hands. Maybe even a fire hose.

"Delgado," Jarchow said, sharp as a slap.

Nick sat forward, put down his glass, and pulled out the BLM pamphlet from his front pocket and laid it on the table. He looked up to see Em watching him with those pale eyes, Wanda's expression something between a frown and a laugh but not exactly what he'd call happy.

"The big worry is the wildland urban interface," Nick said, his voice tight. He coughed and then picked up his glass and gulped, trying not to notice Em's gaze, her head cocked. "Basically too many cities are close to open space. The District has come up with these recommendations for this fire season. If everyone followed them, we'd reduce fire risk, wildland and otherwise. The homeowner is the most important person in preventing a house from being destroyed by wildfire. And around here, it's dry. The Cortez are a tinderbox, and the Hand-Me-Down and McDuff creeks have already run dry."

Wanda stared at him, unblinking. Em was clicking away on her tablet.

"What are you writing?" Nick asked finally when he realized that her jabbing at the screen mirrored the pace of his words.

"She's a blogger," Wanda said. "A journalist."

Jarchow stiffened, sat up straight. "Blogger for what?"

"Local news. Kellogg City mostly. Battle Mountain. Ely. The reservations," Em said. "Let new folks in town know what's going on."

"No, I mean, what's the blog name?"

"KelloggCityFreePress dot com," Em said, setting her tablet on the table.

"Free?" Nick asked. "No one pays?"

"Does anyone in Nevada ever pay for anything? State's ripe for the picking," Em said, her blue eyes now the color of a morning moon. "Anyway, the blog's part of the *Kellogg City Free Press*. Pretty much everything's going digital."

"The mines," Wanda said.

"Come again?" Jarchow said.

"I've been wanting to interview Wanda's sister Birdie about the mines," Em said.

"Birdie's flown the coop," Wanda said, this finally with a smile in her eyes.

"You seem to be my real story," Em said to Wanda.

Nick wanted to inquire after Wanda's brother, the one who almost set himself on fire. Maybe he'd flown the coop as well. To Nick, how Stanley Mapp failed to catch fire sounded like the real story.

"I want to know how the locals feel about the new lease," Em explained. "There's going to be another gold mine in the mountains."

Jarchow sat back, shaking his head, his booted foot tapping hard under the table. "Need that like a hole in the head."

"I'm interested in this dangerous fire season, too," Em said. "I heard about it at the tribal meeting."

Jarchow turned to Wanda. "Okay. So at least you know I'm not fooling you."

"No, sir," Wanda said, spreading her hands flat on the table. It's not a BLM plot. And we've stopped burning scrub. Got rid of the woodpiles. Cleared the brush. Keeping an eye on gas cans and such. We've been through this a few dozen times before."

She reached out and took the pamphlet. "But I'll keep it in mind."

"What's your biggest concern?" Em asked Jarchow.

"Lightning," Jarchow said. "And people driving off road. Sparks. Cigarettes. Because of all the work at the mines, there's no affordable housing left in Kellogg City. Too many workers. Greedy landlords. So people are camping illegally in the Cortez. Threat of campfires going wild."

"Sounds like you're worried about everything." Em tapped away.

"Pretty much," Jarchow said, and he smiled at Em again. Nick saw her glance at Jarchow's tattoo, her eyes following the lines of flame.

"And when lightning strikes." Em winked.

"Can't stop it."

Nick suddenly hated Jarchow's teeth and smile and perfectly tanned skin. He breathed in, wanting to be back outside petting the dog, Ruby Treaty.

"So why aren't you out patrolling now?" Wanda said. "I've got 800 acres ready to burn."

Good point, Nick thought. Here we sit. Your tax dollars at work.

"We have low temp and high humidity today. No storms, so no

lightning. District thought we could do some good by meeting with folks. Headed over to the Samuels' place next, spreading the good word."

"Consider it spread," Wanda said, and in that, Nick heard the message to stand up. So he did, Jarchow and Em following suit. Wanda took the glasses to the very low kitchen counter, just perfect for her. As she rinsed the glasses, Nick noticed her clear movements, the surety of her, something he'd never noticed in the older folks he'd driven to Trader Joe's and Heather Farms Park. They'd wobbled and dithered and sometimes fallen.

Em turned to Jarchow. "Can I come and interview you about the fire danger? I'd like to know more about it. Like what the district does to prevent the fires. Maybe come along on some of your calls?" Nick was not imagining her Jarchow-inspired gaze and smile. "Or even just come to the station? Work up some firefighting stories?"

"We're pretty busy," Nick blurted, feeling his face flush, so he silently sucked in a huge breath and prayed she wouldn't notice. Thank god, both she and Jarchow were already walking toward the screen door and then pushing out into the heat and light.

He watched her, hands moving, eyes focused. She crackled with interest about everything. Weather, Wanda, fire, horses, Nevada in general. Nothing seemed hidden. Nothing mysterious and full of subtext. Nothing unsaid.

"Hard to miss what's going on here," Wanda said. "She's a nice girl, sure enough. Though I can tell you, I missed my chance. I just turned away from the barn door and never answered Jake's question."

Nick hadn't seen Wanda sidle up to him and stand below his shoulder. "Who?" he said.

"A mistake."

"I'm sorry. I don't—"

"I could have said 'Yes.' But I never learned how. At least not to Jake Tenday."

Nick felt as though he missed a rung in a thirty-foot ladder and was now dangling by one hand.

Wanda gave him a little smile and said, "Let's go."

Nick shook his head and followed Wanda outside to the porch where Em and Jarchow stood making plans. Sunlight glowed off Em's hair, and she turned to ask Wanda about past summer fires. Nick looked away and whistled at Ruby who trotted over, tail wagging. *What kind of crazy was he? It was the mile-high altitude. This goddamn, no-good thin air.* He couldn't think straight sometimes.

In his pocket, his phone buzzed. Probably Megan. Or his mother, though she was likely not worried today, having already checked out the temperatures and the Ruby District dispatch website for fire alerts. His mother knew more about the district's fires than he did, texting him acreage info she pulled off the website. She was still obsessing about fire shelters.

"I know they don't always work, but you have one?" she'd asked during their last call. "In your pack, right?"

Nick could only imagine the next calamity his mother would uncover. Firestorm. Blow-up. She'd never believe he was on a rickety porch watching his FOS flirt with a reporter. He kicked at a rock, scattering it with a few others down the path. They needed to leave. And Wanda? How could she tell he'd been looking at Em? And what the hell was she talking about? Barn door? Jake Who-the-hell? Nick wanted to get back into the engine and get to the Samuels' ranch, then back to the station. He needed a fire or a call to Megan. Megan with her steady gaze. Megan who always knew what they both should do and when.

"Oakland," Megan had said at the end of their junior year at Evergreen. "I'll apply to Mills College. You'll be closer to your parents. You can figure out your next step there. Cal has a great history department."

And in due course, she was accepted, and after graduation, they moved into the Lakeshore apartment. The only thing was it took two years for him to figure out that next step part. Megan never understood why Berkeley or any history department was never an option.

"Sometimes you need to stay at the barn door," Wanda said, shaking him out of his thoughts. "Maybe engage in some chat."

Was she speaking in metaphor? What could she mean? Megan was the English major. He couldn't speak this language, if it was anything other than an old woman's nonsense. But she was nice and kind, so he turned to her and went with it. "Sometimes you just need to go home."

"Like I said, I'm good at that."

Nick nodded, and they both watched Jarchow and Em finish their conversation. The sun beat Nevada hot. A hawk screamed overhead. He could feel his breath and even Wanda's as they stood, blinking back the dust.

Chapter Nineteen

Kellogg City, Nevada
June 2012

Kellogg City Free Press—The Daily Donnelly
by Em Donnelly

So who among you—locals, even—have gone to a tribal meeting? I just did, and I'll admit it: I thought it would be more, well, tribal. Probably I can blame National Geographic videos in grammar school or old textbooks in social studies (god forbid, I should blame my own ignorance). But before I moved to Kellogg City, I had the wrong idea about both what a tribe and a tribal meeting were. Here's my idiotic former notion: folks sitting around in a circle. Maybe not smoking peace pipes and wearing feathered headdresses, but to be honest? In my imagination? To be real? To acknowledge Hollywood? I've either got some kind of shaking, wild feather-clothed whirling ceremony from Papua New Guinea or Dances with Wolves in my mind. Call me caught in stereotype, but I never thought a Native American tribal meeting would invoke Roberts Rules of Order, a gavel, and creaky folding chairs.

So knock those assumptions off the list, but this meeting was anything but orderly once the mining situation came up. Mining is a touchy subject around here because it's part and parcel of Nevada's history. But for the folks living on the Kellogg City reservation, mining has become way too personal. Thing is, without the entire reservation community knowing what was in the offing, the tribal council granted a fifty-year lease of part of Mount Aurora to the Northern Nevada Mining Company. Worse—and objectionable for many reservation and tribal members—is that Mount Aurora is a sacred ceremonial spot.

When contacted by this reporter, Council president Darlene High tower had no comment (basically, she didn't return my calls or emails). But local resident and former reservation resident Len Dunning had a few things to say. Now twenty-one, Mr. Dunning grew up on the Yomba and Kellogg City reservations and knows about reservation life as well as the government's way of dealing with the people who live on them. He lives with his girlfriend Eva, and sources tell me that they are expecting a baby. Mention of this is the only smile I got out of Mr. Dunning. But to Mr. Dunning, a lot of miners, and just as many ecologists and tribal members, starting a mine isn't anything to smile about.

Mr. Dunning has been a vocal protestor of mining interest in the Ruby and Cortez mountain ranges, arrested twice for "failure to disperse" and trespassing. My same sources tell me he's heading up a local group to challenge the mining company. But Dunning skirted around this issue, focusing on alleged financial improprieties.

"They don't bother telling with us. They do whatever the hell they want, and we scramble around figuring it out," Mr. Dunning said. "Some tribal members know how to work the system, too, you know? They don't tell us anything either. So there's money going into some pockets and money not going to the reservation schools or clinic, you know?"

But fighting a mine in Nevada is like fighting the casinos. Both bring gold. And jobs. And local spending. These are all things most Nevadans will tell you are good for the state. Gold production isn't about to stop, either. In fact, almost eight percent of all the gold in the United States is mined in Nevada. For the year 2009, that was 5,640,000 troy ounces (12 troy ounces equals a pound. Don't ask me). I'm scared to do the math, but I believe that's 470,500 pounds of literal solid gold.

And most Nevadans will also ignore the environmental and human costs to mining because we are in bad times. A job puts food on the kitchen table. When you're hungry, who cares about the water table?

So if no one wants to talk about it and if your own tribal council won't tell you how the deal went down or when the mine will open, what do you do?

"You go over their heads," Mr. Dunning said. "Or you work around them. You go to the source. You don't stop until you have answers or until you stop them dead in their tracks."

Calls to the Northern Nevada Mining Company have likewise been ignored, but I'm not finished with this story. Stay tuned for more answers and likely, more questions.

Chapter Twenty

Northern Nevada
Mapp Ranch
Summer 2012

After her every-morning call with Birdie, Wanda hung up and stomped over to Stanley to wake him up, her neck roped tight. She was tired of Birdie's "need to know" policy of communication.

"What do you know about the new mine?" Wanda had asked her.

"All this here will be over soon, sister," Birdie had said. "Then I'll be home."

"But what about the soon that's now?" Wanda asked.

Birdie paused. "I'll call Tanya. Have her come over."

All this waiting for some answers. Years and lives of it, and there seemed to be even more waiting now that there was less time to do it in. And here was her brother, seventy-four and sleeping in a nest of ancient quilts, his breath one part Coke, three parts whiskey.

"Brother." Wanda sat down on the couch, her right thigh over his feet.

"Ataa," he mumbled, trying to turn and wrest the blanket over his skinny shoulder.

"Birdie called," she said. "She didn't say anything about the new mine."

Stanley closed his eyes tight.

"The ruling hasn't come down," Wanda said. "She's still in DC. Not coming home for awhile."

"Hmmm," Stanley exhaled. "I'm tired."

"Yeah, all that late night business with Dwayne."

"Hmmm," Stanley mumbled as he fell back into instant sleep, his dream almost visible.

"And what business was it?" Wanda asked loudly. "Getting home at two. It's a whole 'nother day by then, brother."

Stanley opened his eyes and blinked. "Go away. I'm tired . . . ." His voice trailed off in a grumbling murmur.

Who wasn't? Wanda thought. Right now, Wanda could sleep for a hundred years, die, and then sleep for a hundred more. And after all that rest, she'd still wake up as stiff as a floorboard. But she couldn't rest today. She'd been out in the barn by five-thirty and then worked barbed wire down by Copper Creek. Dwayne hadn't even gone home, sacking out on the cot by the stalls, but he was now out with the herd. A world had already happened, even though it was only eight a.m.

"Get up," she said, grabbing his shin. "I want to take a drive."

"Oh, take it yourself," he said. "Jeez, Wanda."

"You'll go driving with Dwayne, yeah? Not me?"

"Why right now?"

Wanda rubbed Stanley's warm blanket between her fingers. Why now. Maybe it was Em's map, all that mountain spread out to see on the wooden table.

"Morning," Wanda said. "Time to do something."

"You'll kill us out there for sure," Stanley said. "You drive like a pirate."

Wanda laughed, squeezing Stanley's leg. "At least a pirate has one good eye. Come on. I want to go see this mine. That blogger girl pointed out the spot on the map.

She felt Stanley go still, his mind at attention, his dream floating away.

"We can look for fire danger, too. I've been reading that BLM baloney," she said, though it wasn't baloney at all. It was true, every single warning. Mapp Ranch was full of danger.

Stanley moaned but then sat up, rubbing his eyes.

"Coffee," he said.

Though three doctors had tested him and found nothing—not even ear wax—Stanley had stopped hearing things years before, a sporadic, undefined deafness that came on during family dinners and tribal meetings and moments of terrible pain. A few years back, he stopped reading the morning paper and missed the top porch step six days in a row. The Reno doctor hadn't been able to find anything definitive, but finally Tanya took him to the eye doctor at the clinic and then to a specialist in Las Vegas. But the clinic doctor had been right. Stanley had macular degeneration, his vision disappearing from the center, a circle of black no matter which way he looked. And neither doctor had a cure, though for a few months, Tanya had Stanley slurping that fish oil, smelly yellow liquid morning and night. Then she went on a salad kick, bringing over armfuls of greens that Wanda had never seen before and Stanley wouldn't eat, no matter what health promises Tanya made about them.

So Stanley usually stayed put. In the darkened house, shades drawn, the television on, he said the dark circle in the middle of everything felt less apparent, the world sort of dusky. But outside, Wanda knew it was hard for him to not see what used to be right in front of him.

"Grandpa Mapp probably had it, too," Tanya had said when she and Stanley returned from the specialist. "Mom used to tell me how in his last years he stopped doing a lot of things he loved."

"She wasn't here for his last years," Wanda had said, slamming her lips shut after saying that, wishing she hadn't.

Tanya stilled and stiffened, and then her shoulders relaxed. "Don't I know it?"

She dropped her bag and Stanley's new prescriptions on the table and turned to fill the kettle with water, her back to Wanda. But Wanda knew, saw her breathing quicken, her hand wiping away the old tears, the old story. All Birdie's missing years. Tanya's childhood and Dempsey's death. Things Birdie couldn't make a speech about.

Toward the end of his life, Dempsey had bumbled around in a peculiar way Wanda now understood because of Stanley. Pretending he wasn't literally in the dark, Dempsey had held onto counters and truck doors and bed posts and fences when all he'd ever needed before was his two feet to get anywhere. Who knew how long he'd been having trouble seeing? It might have been years. When Wanda finally brought it up, he'd waved his hand and told her, "I see what I need to."

Dempsey didn't notice the government was circling the ranch, his younger daughter had run away to become an activist, and the independence he and Margaret had fought for was dying. Dempsey died before his way of life did, so it all worked out for him. All he could see was his ranch and family and a Ruby by his side, leaving the rest for his children to deal with. Never once in the years of encroaching blindness and arterial sclerosis did he worry about the future. No, he was in the past, back in the time when he and his wife worked their own land. Back in the time when he kept his children out of Catholic schools and kept the tribal ways alive through stories, song, and ceremonies. Through powwows and dances and handgame. Through living on this patch of land treatied to them. Hunting pheasant. Tending horses and herds. He lived in a time that had disappeared for everyone but himself.

Stanley dressed, mostly awake, and sitting next to her, Wanda put the truck in reverse, the balding tires spinning for a moment and then finding traction. She gripped the wheel and accelerated, the truck popping and chugging as they headed down the driveway toward Dempsey Mapp Road. Ruby sat on Stanley's lap, panting from a last minute jackrabbit chase, which she lost. Stanley stared straight ahead, his arm around the dog, his fingers absently scratching under Ruby's collar. If he could see everything, what would Stanley look at? Or, she wondered, what didn't he want to see? Maybe he imagined that if he looked straight ahead at things, whatever was caught in his circle of blindness would literally disappear, poof! Magic.

As they headed up the road toward Mount Aurora, Wanda rolled down the window, catching the last of the morning air. The past few days, the weather had been cooler than normal, and some neighboring ranchers scoffed at the BLM's warnings. But Wanda had been around longer than most and knew this trick of Nevada summers, hiding in late June and sometimes parts of July before running out screaming with its hot sword in August, September, and sometimes October.

"Doesn't seem like fire now," she said. "September maybe."

She felt, more than saw, Stanley's shrug.

"But you know that thin air. Heat."

His head bobbed in her periphery.

"You remember when we were little, right? The fires in the hills?"

She didn't even have to turn to know he was nodding again.

"When lightning struck, Daddy let the fires burn, long as they were on Mapp Ranch land. He said fire was here before people. He waited for nature to do what it had to. Remember?"

Stanley cleared his throat. "It needs to burn out. Nothing grows unless it's burned to the ground."

Wanda felt a rush of heat as her brother spoke, this man she'd known for seventy-four long years. All those decades of conversation, only to have him clamp down unless it was about soap operas.

"The wildflowers! Remember that, Stanley?"

He turned toward the window, breeze tousling his wispy hair. Wanda pulled onto Mill Canyon Road and gripped the steering wheel hard as the road bumped into rough dirt tracks. They drove in silence for a while, Wanda feeling each rock lurch and stutter under the tires. Then Stanley grabbed her arm.

"That way," Stanley said.

Wanda jabbed the brake to the floor, looking in her rearview mirror, thankful that there wasn't a tractor or truck following behind.

"How do you know where we are?" He couldn't see and he'd never come out to the mine site. And then, of course, she knew he had.

"Who took you?"

"It's not a mine yet."

"Was it Dwayne?"

Stanley hugged Ruby, kept looking forward.

"Or Len?"

Stanley blinked again.

"Both?"

"Hmmm," Stanley mumbled.

"What were you doing up here?"

"*Ataa!* What are we doing up here?" Stanley said, turning to her. "No one, not even you, wants this mine, yeah? For sure you're wanting to cause some kind of something."

He leaned toward her over Ruby. "Or sister, is this your way of seeing what you already know is true? Maybe you've been pretending to be as blind as me."

"I just want to see what's going on," Wanda said.

Wanda swallowed and tightened her grip on the steering wheel, ground pounding to hip and thigh and spine. She looked over at her brother and then back at the road. He was right about one thing. She might not have any bad ideas now, but when Em had shown her the mine location, she noted it was upstream from the ranch. When Wanda stared at the point below Em's slim finger, her blood beat like a ceremony drum.

"This is the area leased out by the tribe," Em had said, tracing the map grid. "Len Dunning was right. Looks like it's going to happen, though if some folks challenge the agreement, it might get delayed. Gold's the thing."

"Used to be silver," Wanda had said.

"The Silver State, right? Well, it's changed color."

"Price, too."

"Gold mines," Em said, "don't have to pay rights on Federal lands."

"That's right," Wanda said. "Guess they ran out of free land and had to come to the tribe. At least these days, they pay us. Or some of us. A hundred years ago, they'd have redrawn the reservation."

Then as she and Em were leaning over the map in silence, the BLM firefighters had driven up in their green engine. The taller one with the big brown eyes had been familiar. She'd met him before or maybe he just reminded her of everything that was wrong with being young: blind hope, utter confusion, too much strength but no way to know how to use it. If she could, she'd jump into his all-long-bones-and-muscle body and go riding for hours up in the Cortez. She'd work a hard day with Dwayne and his buddies with the herd. She'd go to that damn beach with Birdie, fly on the plane and put her feet right there in the water. She'd do all the things she used to do and the things she never did.

Even if she had her youth back, Wanda knew she couldn't knock sense into anyone. And here it was. All these years after the treaty, a Mapp was sitting at a table, listening to the government tell them what to do. Sure, they were nice young men with their good manners and short hair. But as she sat with them, Wanda hadn't been sure how to hold in her frustration and anger. The government would let business destroy the land with giant pits and cyanide but didn't want it to burn from lightning strikes even though fire enriched and fertilized the soil. Mining with its leaching and poison and traffic would harm the water table, erode the top soil, kill off plants, much worse than a few extra head of cattle or a few hundred wild horses or a quick day of wildfire. No matter what the BLM said.

But locals wanted mines because mines hired people—Indian people who always were first in line for dangerous jobs. Half the tribe was employed at the Devlin mine. After a long day at work, they'd come home to drink tainted tap water. Then they'd fry up the steak and drink the beer they bought on payday. Sure, gold mining wasn't as bad as uranium; Birdie had met folks in Utah and Colorado who'd died from mining that radioactive rock. Mining gold was pure poison, but it took longer to kill, Wanda guessed. Time for more steaks and six-packs.

"There it is," Stanley said, pointing ahead, right through the black hole of his vision.

Wanda pulled over to the side of the road, put the truck in park, and turned off the engine. As the dust settled, she looked at the mine location, nothing but a gate and fence to mark the spot. For now, it was hill, grass, sagebrush, twirled and rusted wire, and lizards. For now, it was the place that still held all their songs. But before work could start, they'd have to pave the road, construct buildings, and bring in all the machinery. This rounded, smooth brown hill would be nothing but a hole, a pit. A weeping wound.

Stanley opened his door and got out, Wanda hurrying to do the same, tsking Ruby to stay where she was. She met Stanley on his side of the truck. Both of them stepped carefully toward the gate, Stanley holding tight onto Wanda's arm.

"Remember we used to come with Daddy for the Sunrise Ceremony?" Stanley asked.

"Oh, my," she said. "How do you even remember that?"

"Because people were fighting about it. White people wanted to stop it. Said it was illegal. Hah! We did it anyway."

How wonderful it had felt to sneak out in the pre-dawn morning, right here on the mountain, surrounded by people mostly long gone. Oh, she'd been to many other Sunrise Ceremonies in other locations, some before, most after of course. But here, their ceremony had meant something. Maybe knowing that the white folks in Kellogg City thought it was wrong made it more important. Her daddy seemed to think so, wresting them out of bed and into the cold truck cab, even though they moaned and complained and argued, Birdie pinching Stanley to get him to stop crying.

Once they'd arrived, the tribal elders lit the fire in the stone circle before first light. The flames leapt and crackled, warming Wanda's thin legs. She held onto Birdie and Stanley, Stanley's little hand in her left, Birdie's in her right. In the bushes and shrubs, the birds began to wake up, trills and cries out into the chilly air. Dempsey sat next to Chief Dean Roundhorse, who beat out a thin rhythm on a flat skin drum as he sang his welcome to the sunrise, to the year, to the hopes that most were afraid to have. Then other men joined in, chanting along with him, even Dempsey, a man who rarely sang. He never even hummed when he worked in the barn. But here, on the mountain, he had hope and words for it.

Our morning star coming up
Clear sun rays streaming out
Star sitting lightly

"We should do it again," Wanda said. "Soon."

"More like time for Sun Dance."

"Sun always comes up."

"People forgot what to welcome," Stanley said, moving forward again. "They say hello to the wrong things."

"Sun always comes up," Wanda repeated.

"One day, might not," Stanley said.

"People want money," Wanda said. "Times are hard."

"Times were hard before the mines. And they'll be hard after. Those who come to fight for the jobs will leave with the money. Nevada's that way, for sure."

Stanley shook his head, pulled on Wanda's arm, urging them closer to the gate.

"What's it say?" Stanley was pointing to a posted sign.

"A bunch of legal gobbledlygook," Wanda said, but Stanley stared straight ahead, waiting.

"Okay, just a second," she said, leaning in close, her reading glasses back at the house. "*This mine site is designated off-limits by the Mine Safety and Health Administration. For safety and health reasons and to prevent hazardous and unhealthy conditions, MSHA's regulations prohibit entry except to authorized personnel.*" She took in breath, gazed out at the slow slope of rounded mountain, rock and grass and then cloud. "Some smaller print. Legal stuff. An ordinance. Phone number."

"So it's a done deal," Stanley said.

"Looks like," she agreed. What would it all look like in a year, two?

"Hell pit," Stanley said. "Right here on the rez."

Her brother breathed in hard, the air ragged and noisy in his throat. Wanda glanced around and heard the ceremony song from all those years ago on the wind and in the grasses and scraggly trees. Her father's voice here, along with her own. Her voice had been filled with mother-loss, but by then, her father had stopped drinking. Wanda was on her way to being okay. And maybe she never had a life anyone else wanted, but she liked it well enough. She'd had her family. She'd lost Jake Tenday there at the barn door, but she'd held baby Tanya. Wanda had felt all those warm animal bodies in her hands. And these mountains were part of that all goodness.

"Done deal," Stanley repeated, his arm clenched with anger. Wanda caught a flicker of that younger Stanley, the one on the truck bed, yelling, "Mother Earth is not for sale!"

She'd thought that gas-slicked man had disappeared. But maybe he'd just been hiding.

Glancing back down at the mining sign with its warnings and regulations, Wanda knew that yes, like everything else—even souls and hearts and minds—Mother Earth was on the market, sold over and over again to the highest bidders for whatever treasure lay inside her.

Wanda looked out at the site and the mountains beyond, all the way to the horizon dusky with smoke from some far off fire. She breathed in heat, felt the touch of sun on her face. How to pull this tiny section of the whole world off the market for good?

On the way home, Stanley was silent as usual, but then he said, "Remember that story 'bout Wolverine? That one from the Crow Fair powwow?"

"Didn't go, brother. You went with William Beechey, years back."

Saying the name of Birdie's long-ago husband was like remembering an ancient language. Wanda could still say his name, but she'd almost forgotten what he'd meant to the Mapps. He'd barely been there, unable to hold onto Birdie, jealous of her sense of freedom, just like everyone else.

"That Wolverine," Stanley started. "He wanted fire."

"That so?" Wanda said.

"Wolverine and Wolf, they're out hunting one day. Wolf is the smart one, Wolverine tagging along like a little brother. But together, they make magic for sure. They pile up some dry wood and jump over it a few times, and it explodes into fire. Wolverine can't get over that kind of power. So he asks Wolf if he can make the magic on his own.

Wolf says, 'For sure, brother. I'll give you some.'

So all by himself, Wolverine tries it, jumping over the wood, but there's no explosion. No fire at all.

Then he tries it again, and he finally makes fire.

Wolf says, 'You have the power now. Just don't play with it.'

Wolverine says, 'I promise. I'll only start a fire when I need to. Emergencies.'

Course, Wolverine is lying. He can't help himself. Every time he sees dry wood, he has the desire. The need. He has to make fire. He pretends he's cold, throws a few sticks on the ground, jumps over them, and they explode. He does it over and over again, laughing each time. Finally one day, Wolf sees all the burned up piles and gets mad.

'For sure my little brother is making fun of me. I've got to stop him. No more fires for him.'

So the next time he jumps, Wolverine can't make fire. He tries again. No luck.

One morning, he goes up the hill and sees a lot of fires. All kinds of animals are making different fires all by themselves. There's different smoke, different flame.

And him? Nothing. And for sure, this time he's cold. He finally really needs the fire!

He's so mad and jealous, he hollers out, 'Brothers! Sisters! I don't have the power to make fire. But one day, there'll be people here. They'll be wanting your fire for themselves. And you know what? They'll start hunting us when they see what we can do with fire. They'll clean us out!'

The animals listen and agree. 'That's true. If there's going to be people, they'll hunt us dead.'

So they holler back to Wolverine. 'Okay, brother. No more fires.'

That's why there's no fire for the animals. Otherwise, they'd be hunted out."

Stanley nodded as he finished the story, mumbled something under his breath, and then turned to look out the car window. Ruby leaned against him and closed her eyes, her pink tongue hanging out in pant.

All that potential for fire gone to waste. Wanda was pretty sure the storyteller wasn't on Wolverine's side. But was it fire gone to waste? Or was something dangerous tucked away for safekeeping? Or for safety?

"What's it mean?" Wanda asked.

Stanley shrugged, his gaze unfocused on the dryness all around them. Ruby curled into the U of his armpit and closed her eyes.

Wanda turned back to the road, watching it roll right on under the truck. Wolverine might have wanted all the other animals to hide their fire because he didn't have any of his own. He was jealous and too stupid to control himself. Or maybe he was right, his thinking true. Something that important needed to be guarded close. The animals hid what was best, tucking it away out of fear. That's how things were for real.

Chapter Twenty-One

Northern Nevada
Mapp Ranch
1973

After her long drive from South Dakota, Birdie wanted home to feel like home, but it felt like more waiting. Those first seconds back, she pulled the truck in front of the house and almost tumbled out of the cab into her sister's strong arms.

Thank God, she thought she said, but later, Wanda told her she didn't say a word. Instead she followed Wanda into the house and fell onto the bed, waking a day later, hoping Wounded Knee was all a dream or someone else's story.

At least I'm in this old house, she thought, the place that was supposed to surround and protect her, muffling the sounds of gunshots and screams that still rang in her head. Home was supposed to make her forget. But home had changed. Her father wasn't here anymore, his boots no longer scuffing the floor as he banged out at five a.m. to get to work. The only whiff of him was his tobacco on the mantle, the dirt and sweat on his coat dangling limp on the coat rack, the hay and spilled coffee in his truck cab. The months Birdie had been gone, Wanda and Stanley had filled up the house with themselves. Wanda had taken over the top dresser drawer, part of Birdie's side of the closet, and the middle medicine cabinet shelf. Stanley's new television blared its terrible eye, packing the entire living area with blue light and loud sound.

"We're kind of modern type now," Stanley said with satisfaction. "Got a remote!"

But what did Birdie expect they would do while she was gone? Life always fills in the empty spaces.

"Come to town," Wanda said after a week or so. "People want to see you. When they come to visit, I say you're sick."

"Can't," Birdie said, unable to tell Wanda that *can't* meant everything: getting out of bed, taking a shower, washing her hair, eating more than crackers and toast. Wanda wasn't lying to anyone. Birdie was sick in the heart, what piece of it was left.

Wanda stared at her for a couple more days, and then one morning, Birdie felt Wanda and Stanley lift her out of bed and take her to the small bathroom, leaning her against the pink and white Formica shower stall.

"She's scrawny as Cock Crow," Stanley said, referring to the rooster they'd had as children, red, stringy, fast as a roadrunner, mean as an attack dog.

"Get her some clean clothes," Wanda said, and he left the two women alone in the bathroom, Wanda pulling off Birdie's nightgown.

"It's time to get up," Wanda said.

Wanda had it backward. It was time to let go, give up, fall down, let life have it all back. She was done fighting things, even her own body. She wanted to melt into the puddle of herself and let this mess go on without her. Her hair, skin, blood, bones, guts could funnel down the drain into the septic tank and then the earth and dark nothingness.

When the cold slash of water hit her, she sputtered, trying to breathe, unable to fight her own need for air.

"You need to wake up." Wanda lathered Birdie's head with shampoo, her body with soap. Later, she slicked oil on Birdie's tired feet, lotion on her arms and legs and face. As she had when Birdie was little, Wanda combed out Birdie's long dark hair. Then she yanked and tugged it into one thick braid. Birdie felt the stretch at her eyes and temples, the air on her neck.

"Good thing you got up now," Wanda said. "You're going gray. If I left you in bed any longer, you'd turn into Grandma Spider."

Wanda dressed her in clothes Stanley found in Birdie's duffel bag, and then she was at the table eating hominy with whole milk poured from a glass bottle and brown sugar scooped from the cracked crock, the porridge one of Birdie's only memories of her mother. Later, after Wanda and Stanley finished with the animals in the barn, Wanda made dinner. Afterward they all sat out on the porch watching the sun pull itself away from the sky, leaving the moon to do her work alone.

It was the moon that did it. Round, white, and watching her. Birdie breathed in, her eyes taking in the ranch around her. The bowl of the dark sky. Her body beating into itself. Hands, feet, belly, full and not from Wanda's beet root hash.

"Back, huh?" Wanda asked, after Stanley went in to get another soda, the screen door closing behind him.

Back? Birdie didn't know how to answer. A part of her had never left Mapp Ranch. And never would. A part of her was always going to be a motherless little girl chasing after a Ruby. This earth and air and the seasons of grasses and trees and flowers were in her as much as she was in them.

Part of her, though, had flown away. Like a hawk, knowing the exact location of her prey. But this hawk had swooped down and pulled up nothing but grass and twigs, the rabbit scampering down the hole.

"We need you," Wanda said, lifting one tan hand, age spots dark constellations running up her forearm. "This land is too big for just Stanley and me."

There should be children, Birdie thought. Lots of children. A whole tribe could live on this ranch.

Birdie hadn't really been here, not for years. Their land—what she was fighting for—was underneath them right now. Here it spread out, grasses flickering silver. The hills humped smooth and sleeping. The herd. The horses. Raccoon growl and chatter. Coyotes slinking just past the porch light. Flap of bats skittering between barn and house. But to keep any of it, she'd had to leave. Over and over again. Maybe now it was time to live in the fight in the truest sense by staying put in the center of the center.

"Yes." Birdie stared out at the cloud-stippled sky. "I'm back."

But it wasn't that easy, the map back to herself a labyrinth, a maze, a slow winding trail. On her good days, Birdie woke up before six am, showered, helped Wanda and Stanley with chores. She saddled up, road the ranch, tended the herd. But she kept to herself, avoiding the neighborly calls from the various female Dailys, Circles, Greasewoods, and Tendays, all carrying bad casseroles, their sharp eyes scanning for gossip.

In the afternoons, Birdie walked the land just outside the house, bending down to study new blooms, listlessly picking sage buttercup, desert parsley, biscuit root. Without her noticing and despite her sadness, spring had cracked open. As she walked, Birdie felt like a dark reed, weaving above the mallow and lupine, dipping and swaying, the breeze catching her thoughts and taking them away before she saw Buddy Lamont's body again. The image of his wound would fill her mind, but then the push of wind would hold her and she'd stare at the flowers in her hand. She'd bring the blooms to her nose and breathe in their delicate perfume, the scent on her fingers, dark green, resinous, medicinal.

Some nights under that bright moon and in the dark still air tipped with winter snow chill, Birdie couldn't forget. She'd wail, mourning the dead, all those killed and silenced. And she sang for her parents and their parents and their parents, all the ancestors back to the time when there weren't any ancestors to weep over.

But after three months of sticking close to home, Birdie felt an inkling, an itch that started in her shoulders and moved into her stomach and traveled down the currents in her body to her feet. Her body suddenly too big for the small house. She wished she were like Wanda, content with this known air, the past lined up in the house like old books. Birdie wished she could eat her hominy and live each day like the next, safe and tucked in this valley. If only she could be content with the daily inside and out of ranch house and barn. But when she was out with Wanda and Stanley, rattling around in the truck, she began to look up from the ranch soil toward the horizon. For the first time in months, she could imagine the feel of the steering wheel under her palms and her feet on the accelerator, pushing down.

Chapter Twenty-Two

Cortez Mountains
July 2012

Nick was pissed, even though there wasn't anyone to be pissed off at but himself. He was the idiot who'd agreed to take the broke-ass chase rig down the fire road and into the Cortez, past the new mine site, and toward Highway 306. Somewhere to the east was Mapp Ranch, but no light beckoned, no road familiar. He drove on, his mission to deliver sandwiches and supplies to Wicks' engine on patrol status. All he needed to do was hand over the coolers filled with ham and turkey sandwiches, thermoses of coffee, bags of chips, and cookies. Though the early morning was still and calm, there'd been a wild wind the night before, the fire only seconds away from total conflagration. And the hills were parched. Each booted step reminded Nick of Rice Krispies, everything underfoot a snap, crackle, and pop. Even plants that were heat and fire adapted looked brown, the juniper and sagebrush dry and brittle, papery skeletons.

When they'd put out the camp fire gone haywire, two crews mopping up the last of the three acres, nothing else to do but sit and watch, Thompson said, "I need you for something."

Nick had looked up, his headlamp shining on Thompson's face. As always, eyes fierce and serious, even now when the fire was all over but the shouting.

"Patrol crew needs food."

Nick wanted to do what needed to be done, and food was necessary. The chase rig, though, had been in its last year for at least six years now, all of it held together with hope, twine, and the promise of a new federal budget.

For a second, Nick had thought Thompson might ask him to look for hotspots. For a second, he'd had hope. But instead, there Nick had been, sitting behind the wheel of the junker, rattling around in the middle of nowhere, the yellowy-green tang of mustard and pickles filling the cab. The patrol crew was nowhere to be found.

When he'd called back to Thompson, the damn radio had gone out. His cell phone spiked out somewhere on the Cortez, and then as he turned the truck around, the engine churned, rumbled, and stopped dead.

"Fuck," Nick mumbled now as he walked toward the crew's last known location. If they'd already left, he'd have to make his way to the 306. He'd thought to go to the Mapp Ranch somewhere down the road, but a surprise early BLM visit might make them edgy.

Nick walked on in a sea of nothing. For a moment, he imagined he heard the rumble of an engine. A car. A flicker of lights, maybe headlights. He paused, waited, but then nothing. He started walking again. No, there wasn't anything but dead grass, cattle, and coyotes for miles and miles and miles, the world at high noon nothing but a disk of burning sunlight and heat waves that barely parted for oncoming traffic. Right now, bothering the Mapps sounded a lot better than a walk out to the highway. By the time Nick got to the asphalt, it would probably be almost 90 degrees on its way to over one hundred. But some rancher would stop. At least in his work pants and covered in soot and smelling like fire, passersby wouldn't think Nick was a rapist murderer. Actually, they'd probably think he was a hero and buy him a meal before talking him back to the station in Devlin. Patting him on the back and telling him they'd write in to the local paper, his photo on the front page of Em Donnelly's blog, Nick shaking hands with Kellogg City bigwigs and Ruby District brass.

Meanwhile, the engine crew would be hungry for the sandwiches that would curdle in poison mayo in the blazing hot truck cab.

Nick had left his helmet and jacket in the truck, though he'd slipped the radio into his pocket, taking it out now and again to talk into its utter deadness. Periodically, he clicked on his cell phone, holding it over his head, trying to catch a signal, but no luck. No one could hear him now. When Nick got back to the station, Hamm would never let him forget his nighttime wandering. "Poor little Delgado. No radio. No rig. All by his lonesome."

And this wasn't the kind of story he wanted to tell Megan. This wasn't the story he needed to show her their separation was worthwhile.

Nick kept walking, his boots scuffing lumps of dusty dirt. The hum of night was slowly replaced by the sounds of the waking world, a dove cooing close by and a rooster cock-a-doodling from a ranch house he couldn't see, possible objects and out buildings all mysterious gray lumps and bulges on the landscape.

But then he turned, seeing a flash. Lightning? Fire? What use would he be now? The sandwich-filled truck was almost a mile back, useless, another gray lump. He stopped, held his breath, waited. The light shone again, disappeared, and then again, brighter now. A noise, motor, engine. Nick stumbled back, off the road, running a little.

An ATV chugged toward him. The driver yanked the handles, swerving a little, skidding to a stop. The engine gurgled and then lugged, one, two, until the driver slowly let the engine settle before turning it off. The air filled with the smell of gas.

"Holy moly," the driver said. "What are you doing out here so early?"

"Ms. Mapp?"

Nick walked toward the bubble of light around the ATV. As he stepped closer, he couldn't see her features clearly, but it was Wanda Mapp, with her telltale gray bowl hair. Behind her, Ruby sat up in a cardboard box and stared at him with her black eyes. Nick thought he could hear her wagging tale whapping the box.

"Didn't mean to scare you," he said.

"Where's your engine?" she asked, her voice clipped and sing-songy all at once.

"There's a fire." He wasn't making sense, but that's how he and Wanda seemed to communicate. He hoped she wouldn't bring up the barn door or Em this time.

"Oh, yeah?" Of course she knew about the fire, the smoke blowing through the entire valley.

He cleared his throat. "My truck broke down about a mile back. I'm headed for an engine on patrol status." He paused, unable to admit his food delivery mission. "But I got turned around. I thought I'd walk out to the highway for help."

"You have a radio, don't you?"

He reached a hand into his pocket and pulled out the useless thing, shaking it a little as if it had a loose screw, a broken top. "Stopped working. No cell phone coverage out here."

"Don't I know it," she said, laughing a little "Heh" sound. "I've got some work to do, but I could take you back to your truck. Check it out and see what I can do. If that don't work, I'll take you up to the highway."

"Oh," Nick said, wondering how he could get out of the "her looking at the truck" part.

"I know my way around a truck," she said. "Don't look so surprised."

"You probably know more than I do," Nick said.

"Sure as heck better." Wanda got off the ATV, helping Ruby out of the box, and then taking the box and putting it on the side of the road. Then she got back on the ATV, Ruby nestled in her lap.

"Get on now," she said. "I got to get stuff done before the rest of the ranch wakes up. Birdie's still not back. Lots to do."

He wasn't sure what to say about that, having a hard time imagining a ranch run by two ancient women, one of whom drove around before sunrise and fixed trucks, the other not even at home.

Nick always found it weird to be on a vehicle where you have to hold onto someone else in order to stay on. Here he was, sweaty, smelly, smoky, holding onto Wanda who was surprisingly sturdy, hardy—her sides like iron—who smelled more like the outside than this outside. Green and moist and maybe even flowery.

The sky lightening, Nick saw how far he'd walked—much farther than a mile—the dirt road opening up with the sunlight.

"Holy moly," Wanda said as they rounded a bend and found the truck. "Bad parking job."

And she was right. The truck was canted to the left, one wheel on a slight berm. "Yeah," Nick said. "It was dark. Wasn't sure where I was."

"No fooling," Wanda said, as she slowed and stopped.

Ruby jumped down and went sniffing and wagging to the truck's giant back tires. All around them, the sky seemed to tease, the hills around them starting to light up gold, yellow, the sun peeking over the mountain range.

"Open it," she said as Nick got off the ATV. "Let's see whatcha got."

Nick walked over to the truck, first opening the cab, and then unlocking the hood that burst open with a deep metal pop. He came around front, seeing that Wanda barely came up to the top of the hood. She'd produced a couple of tools, and she held them in her small brown hands.

He stared at her, confused.

"Just get me up there. I've seen the top of a truck or two," she said, laughing, that little "Heh" again at the end of her sentence.

Nick kneeled down and made a foot step with his palms, Wanda placing her slippered foot in his hands. With a muttered "One, two," he had her up on the truck. She flicked on a flashlight and peered into its wrecked guts.

"Jeez," she said, her voice hard. "Thought the BLM had more money than this. Government takes everything but doesn't seem to spend it."

There was actually no money for anything, but Nick didn't want to say it. No one at the station but Jarchow had health insurance. All of them lived at the station. Housing was the big perk, unless you counted the hazard pay and overtime, which he was getting right now.

But what was Wanda's issue with him? Why the sarcasm? He hadn't asked her for help. Nick tried to hold his breath, pressing a large hand on his stomach as if he could keep in his words, but he couldn't.

"What do you want from us?" he blurted.

For a moment, Wanda didn't move or speak, everything stilling, just as things do in books and movies before bad things happen. In the silence, Nick didn't even feel or hear her breath. He looked away, noticing that in the short time since they'd gotten back to the truck, the entire sky had filled with golden light, everything visible, the ranch, Nevada, the entire country opening up all around him. For a second, he could almost imagine this is what the first people would have seen, nothing and everything spread around them like a grassy blanket.

Nick knew he shouldn't have said anything. Of course he knew what the Mapps and the tribe wanted: what was theirs. He should have just shut the hell up. But he was punchy from lack of sleep and days of fighting fire. He'd been demoted to sandwich bringer and now he was waiting for riddle-talking, irritable Wanda Mapp to fix his truck. His fingers tingled, the back of his neck pricked like it did when he was nervous or angry, but he was surprisingly neither. He felt strangely content, as if in this perfect, unbroken morning light, something ridiculous and new was possible.

Wanda worked this big favor, bending into the engine, her hands full of tools that clicked and dinged in the early morning silence. As he waited for her to answer him, the space between them stilled. If he lit a match, whatever it was might explode, roar into blowup, burn bright, high, hot and wide, needing smoke jumpers, helicopters, and dozens of engines to put it out.

He stepped back, swallowed, wished for the first time since he arrived to be in Seattle where it was wet and damp, where he could be surrounded by Megan and books, safe in a small house doing not so much, certainly not this.

Wanda suddenly jerked up, turning to look at him, her facial features blurred in the dull light, only her eyes clear, focused, staring at him. She waited, looked some more, and then said, "What I want is breakfast."

Nick sighed, and the tense moment cracked and fell to the earth like confetti. "How about a ham sandwich?"

Wanda nodded, as if expecting him to say just that. "That'll do."

Nick leaned into the cab, opened the cooler, and grabbed a sandwich labeled H. He brought it to Wanda just as she slid down off the hood, landing with surprising grace next to the right front tire. Ruby came and sat, leaning against her leg, wagging her tail in the dust. He handed Wanda the sandwich, and she opened the wrapper and took a bite and then gave some to Ruby.

"There's some cookies, too," he said. "Oatmeal. And chips."

"You save them for your ride home," she said, chewing.

"You fixed it?" he asked.

"Maybe not," Wanda said. "But give it a try."

Nick jumped into the cab, sat down in the seat, and after waiting for Wanda to move to the side, started the truck. At first, he thought it wouldn't catch, the same not-catching stutter as earlier that morning. But then, with a deep diesel rumble, the motor turned over, roaring throaty and alive.

Nick found himself smiling from the inside out, relief releasing the tension he'd been carrying in his shoulders and face since the truck broke down. Now he could get to Wicks' engine without anyone giving him too much shit. The golden sunrise hadn't been just advertising. Today wasn't going to completely suck.

By the time he got out of the cab, Wanda and Ruby had finished the sandwich. He handed Wanda a bottle of water, and she put it in her deep pants pocket. He bent down and gave Ruby a good scratch under her chin, her eyes closing in pleased slits. Then he patted her head and stood straight, stretching a little.

"Thanks, Wanda," he said. "I didn't mean to be rude. I'm just—well, I shouldn't be out here with no radio or a broken down truck. Managed both in one day."

She watched him, and then he thought maybe she was going to tell him something else confusing, metaphorical, and symbolic. But she just gave him a slight nod.

"Okay, then," she said. "Come on, Ruby."

Nick knew he should get back in the truck and get his ass and the vehicle in gear, but he stood by the truck, watching Wanda, who suddenly seemed like an old woman again. She was so tiny, her strides short and slightly stiff, as if she had pains. But then she got on her ATV as if she were a 12-year-old boy, her dog in her lap.

"I expect to see you later, Nick Delgado," Wanda said. Then she started the ATV, moving the vehicle in a small circle in front of him, almost tenderly driving away into the morning, Ruby looking back at Nick as they moved down the road. He watched them until they rounded the bend and all he could see was spun-up dust.

She'd said, "I expect to see you later," as if Nick were going to show up at the ranch house for a beer in the afternoon. As if he were going to show up to play cards and eat fry bread on the porch. There was something hopeful in her words, as if there was more to expect from everything, as if things that were good would be that way again, later, more.

Nick breathed in sharp and hard and tried to focus as he headed toward the crew digging in the burnt dirt for that last ember. The sun up, they'd be worrying about wind, the day's heat, relative humidity. Mostly, though, they'd turn when they finally heard the truck, their stomachs empty, growling. For about five seconds, Nick would be today's firefighting hero.

Chapter Twenty-Three

Northern Nevada
Mapp Ranch
1973

"Don't mind if I do," Birdie said when William Beechey offered to buy her another bourbon, neat. They sat at the long wooden counter of Three Jugs Tavern, Birdie in a simple blue dress, her hair brushed out smooth and dark over her shoulders and down her back. She'd lost some weight since she'd come home—her stomach hard and flat—and she felt sexy in an alien way, like women in glossy magazines, their legs slim, long, and lean. Her breasts pressed against the front of her blouse, unbuttoned at the neck.

"One more," William said to the barkeep. "And one for me."

"You like bourbon?" she asked.

"I like you." His smile was so wide and bright she could almost hear it. Birdie had grown up with William's older brother Percy, but before high school, the family moved to Las Vegas and she'd never met William, the younger brother by seven years. No one had ever talked much about this Beechey boy, no long savored, juicy gossip about him at tribal meetings. Percy had been ordinarily useless and mostly boring, now working at the gold mine. But here was young William, strong, thirty-three, and all smiles, announcing himself when he sat, his eyes the color of caramel, his skin perfect and unlined.

At forty, Birdie knew she looked a decade younger, no one ever guessing her age. White women told her how lucky she was to have "Such good genes!" At fundraising parties, women in DC and Manhattan admired the very things they probably didn't want themselves: permanently dark skin, dark hair, boyish body, small breasts and slim hips. They told her she looked like a model, should be an actress, had a glamorous career in front of her. After confiding they were so sorry about what their people did to her people, they brightened, saying, "Did you ever consider going to Hollywood?"

"You're so lucky," they'd said. "I wish I looked like you."

"You could play all those mysterious roles," they said.

"Westerns," they said. "Maybe even foreign films."

She became their pet, their go-to liberal symbol. A couple of women insisted on taking her shopping and to beauty parlors and health spas. Once in a waiting room filled with canned music and decorative ponds dotted with cucumber slices, a woman asked, "Isn't a sauna just like a sweat lodge?"

Birdie wondered if it were possible to nod and howl at the same time.

Dark, different, and odd at rallies and informational meetings, Birdie had felt an outsider at worst, exotic at best, a caged animal put on display, like the Indians brought to cities in the 1800s for research and show. But for the sake of the movement, she shook hands, made nice, took their donations.

But here in downtown Kellogg City, sitting next to young, strong, handsome William Beechey, she felt like a true, real woman. He wasn't a tall man, but he was put together nice and neat: muscled and wiry and strong, his pretty skin stretched just right over his bones, his hair long but tied right in a ponytail, his shirt tight but not too. Here he was, exactly what she needed. Birdie leaned in, closed her eyes, and breathed: sun, sex, sweat, and something else. She knew it wasn't just the bourbon heating up her insides. He had been waiting at the end of the journey. He was the prize at the end of the struggle. Maybe all that out there was meant to lead her to this dark bar and William.

"We can always drink Picons," William said, referring to the notorious Basque cocktail made of grenadine, herb and orange peel liqueur, and soda water.

"The first two are terrible," Birdie said. "But that third one's delicious."

They sipped their bourbon and laughed.

"Don't know what you're going to do," Wanda said months later, as Birdie was draped rag doll over the toilet, her morning sickness taking over everything. Nothing was left inside but burn and sick and the tiny growing creature at the center.

"Me, either," Birdie whispered, letting Wanda pat her face with a cool, wet towel.

From behind the closed door, Stanley said, "I'm going to kill him."

"Don't know what you're going to do," Wanda repeated, and Birdie pushed away her sister's hand, needing air and space. She knew what Wanda was really asking. Everyone could get an abortion now, the Supreme Court ruling on Roe versus Wade earlier that year. But even as Birdie struggled to stand and then held onto the sink to rinse out her mouth, she knew that this child was hers and William's, made out of sadness, bourbon, and lust. Whoever this was inside her was Indian. There's been enough killing of Indians for now.

"I'm going to kill him!" Stanley cried from behind the door, banging on the wood with a fist. "Somebody has to!"

Birdie brushed her teeth, washed her face, and decided that day to drive to Carson City.

"Let's get married," William had said the night before, his mouth at her ear, a hand on her belly. "Make it real."

If it was going to be real, Birdie needed Wanda tucked into the backseat of the truck to serve as witness.

Birdie had never been fooled by honeymoons, watching her friends drive off after wedding ceremonies, tricked into believing in that magic. A honeymoon is a period of time, not really an adventure or even a place. It's when a married couple holds back all that is true from each other, letting joy, sex, and maybe love and probably hope take over. If the married couple is lucky, Birdie knew, the honeymoon is a promise. If the couple were her and William Beechey, it was three nights in Reno.

Months before the baby was born, Birdie realized she didn't love William. He was beautiful but weak; fierce but misdirected. He made friends easily and lost them just as fast. His smile was the only truly nice thing about him. Despite her husband's flaws and her lack of love for him, Birdie had another idea: the successful Indian family was part of the revolution. Russell Means had a philosophy about intermarriage and how it diluted Indian ways.

She'd heard him say it weakened the respect people had for themselves and their traditions and undermined spiritual clarity. This clarity was now her mission. She was going to bring up her child steeped in Indian ways, culture, and lore. She was going to study Lakota, her mother's language, and teach it to her baby. William had his father's language, and she was going to make sure the baby learned that, too. She wanted her baby to be familiar with tribal meetings, ceremonies, powwows as well as horse-riding, cattle-herding, and hard, outdoor work.

The Beechey family was going to do it all.

"What?" she said to Wanda. "You're looking at me like a tree full of owls."

"It's just." Wanda put down her fork. They were sitting at the small dining room table at Birdie's apartment in Kellogg City eating the coffee cake Birdie had made from the recipe on the back of the Bisquick box.

"Just what?"

"Just that," Wanda said, sitting back, her eyes clear and sharp, even as she was trying to be careful and kind. "This seems too small."

A fist lodged in Birdie's throat, just below the tender swallowing place. She wanted to tell her sister that she couldn't possibly know how it felt to be carrying a child, a girl she hoped, who would be the one to take up Birdie's work. A baby was as close to the truth as Birdie had ever gotten, never feeling like this even in the midst of her tribe and clan members, when all of them fought together for freedom.

"It's the biggest thing in the world, Wanda," she said, and even as she did, she wished she could swallow the words to the bottom of her stomach.

"Okay." Wanda looked down at the sad brown cake.

Baby Tanya never slept. Eight weeks old and plump as an early fall berry, she screamed every two hours for milk or a change or for Birdie. Anything other than the small bassinet Wanda had bought them. The first time it happened, Birdie was a one, two, three too slow to get out of bed. William's fist came at her like a projectile, a surprise attack, Birdie sprawled out on the cold wooden floor.

The wind knocked out of her, Birdie struggled to breathe even as Tanya screamed on, louder now. Moaning, her breasts leaking, Birdie pushed herself up to all fours, taking in a deep breath once her lungs forgave her. Stars flickered and popped behind her eyelids.

William helped her to her feet. "Lord, I didn't mean to. I must have been dreaming."

Birdie leaned into him as he walked with her to Tanya's bassinet. He sat her down and brought her an ice pack, pressed it against her cheek as Tanya nursed.

The three of them together on the couch, William stroked the baby's soft black hair and cooed. He kissed Birdie's cheek, apologized, got up for more ice. She felt his absence at her side. Tanya opened her eyes but then sucked on. Birdie lifted her hand to her ice-cool cheek. It must have been a dream. All the crying. He was so tired, working so hard. Like he said, he didn't mean it.

Before going into town for groceries the next morning, Birdie concealed the purple welt on her cheek with makeup. She turned this way and then that in front of the small bathroom mirror. Nothing could really cover it up. At best, she looked like she hadn't slept for eight weeks, rocking the baby from dusk to dawn. But Birdie forgave William, let him kiss her goodbye on his way to the mine, promised to make him fried chicken and potatoes for dinner.

Then it happened again. And again. And not at night out of a dead sleep. No way to blame dreams anymore. It happened enough that Birdie found herself hiding out in her apartment, the same way she'd hidden at the ranch after Wounded Knee. She avoided visitors and neighbors, even Wanda. Especially Wanda.

When William's sister Micah came to visit from San Diego, Birdie learned the history that no one had bothered to tell her during the parade of after-wedding family visits. The Las Vegas Beechey years had been filled with bailing Willie out of juvy, putting Willie in outpatient treatment for alcohol abuse, dealing with Willie's girlfriends, some pregnant, some not, other children questionable or unknown, at least for now. Until he'd landed back in Kellogg City, Willie's prior life had been a dot-to-dot of disobedience, defiance, and, of course, his dick. Birdie stared into Micah's round, untroubled face. The William who held Tanya in his arms and sang to her before laying her softly to sleep was the same William who slapped her for burning the grilled cheese sandwiches the day before. He'd held Birdie in his arms and rocked her, too, but then pushed her against the wall, his eyes slits as he yelled about the baby toys on the floor, the water bill, the stink of Birdie's milky blouse.

"Francine? Oh, yeah. She used to throw baseballs at our windows," Micah said, oblivious, eating handfuls of popcorn and drinking beer from a bottle. "She told him she was pregnant, but then there wasn't no baby. Anyway, she was just one of them. Dee Dee came crying that he'd hit her, but she was always a liar. I never saw no broken arms or busted eyes."

"He hits me," Birdie said. "He's busted my eyes."

Micah's expression didn't change. She grabbed another handful of popcorn. "Ah, he don't mean nothing by it."

Birdie had fallen for William's smile and eyes and body just like the rest of his conquests, but she wasn't a liar. He hit her, and she told Micah about it. But he did so for the last time on a Friday night just before Tanya was eight months old. He'd come home late from the mine and tripped on a baby blanket, drunk from his after-payday six-pack.

"Goddammit," William started, his eyes wild. He let the beer drop, wrested off his jacket, his eyes on Birdie.

But he didn't see Stanley at the table. Her brother jumped up and knocked William to the ground, flatly saying, "This time, I am going to kill you."

Stanley could have, too. He still had his vision and was strong from working the horses, but Birdie just shook her head.

"Am I going to call the sheriff?" Stanley asked, his arm tight around William's neck.

William looked at Birdie, and in his drunken, angry, sad glare, she saw another failed cause, her Indian family just another broken treaty.

"No," she said.

"I'm going to lock him in the damn trunk until you're ready to go. Don't matter what you say."

Stanley yanked William to standing and lugged him out of the apartment, William's shoes banging on each step. Birdie waited and listened for the creak and then slam of William's Buick Regal trunk before she packed up all of Tanya's and her own things, stuffing everything into grocery sacks and pillow cases. She opened up the kitchen cupboards to stare at their few wedding presents, mostly Kmart plates and cheap, brittle juice glasses.

Probably the ranch house could use all the new things, especially the set of Revereware pots Mary Tenday had given them. But Birdie closed the doors and went to pick up her sleeping baby, the only part of this marriage she needed.

A month later, Birdie heard that William Beechey had clattered out of town with the wedding presents in the backseat of the Buick and headed down Highway 278 to San Diego and Micah, who probably added the Birdie story to the litany of Willie's wild adventures.

Tanya would grow up without a father, but Birdie was grateful he'd left without an angry drunken visit. No threats. No demands. Her relief at his departure started to feel like hope.

Stanley set up Tanya's crib by the woodstove and the playpen by the front window where she could see everyone in the house as she banged her toys around. Wanda stood at the periphery at first. But slowly, Birdie watched her sister move forward and in, pick up the round, happy baby girl and plop her on her knee, make the sounds that belonged to most women around babies. As Wanda moved in, surrounding Tanya with coos and love and smiles, Birdie felt herself detach, like a dirigible slowly unmooring from the docking station. Oh, not all at once, but one loosened line at a time, and as the months passed and her divorce was finalized, she started going to tribal meetings again. Pretty soon, she was camped out at the BLM offices waiting to argue mining leases and grazing rights. And it didn't take long for the AIM to contact her, her friends and allies wanting and needing her back in the fold.

One night, Birdie sat in the glow of the woodstove and watched Tanya sleep, perfect and whole and content. At Birdie's touch, Tanya sighed, reached out a tiny hand, even in sleep yearning for touch.

Her hand on her baby, the night quiet around them, Birdie understood that Wanda had been right about her all along. She was broken for the normal things. Birdie wasn't the type for this quiet family revolution. Despite the safety of the known Mapp Ranch routine, at night, Birdie ground her teeth. Each day as she watched Tanya smash noodles and squash into her mouth, an urge built inside her, something strong that felt like it was almost in her throat, ready for words. Birdie was not a quiet small person. She had big ideas and big hopes, but maybe that made her empty in some way. Just like William Beechey, she was flawed. But unlike him, she was strong and good in the ways that she could be good, which she knew were many. She could fight for her family, tribe, people. Yes, good Indian men had died at Wounded Knee, but now the world was watching. This wasn't the time to hide. It was the time to push forward. And because of her fight, her daughter would grow up a whole woman, unafraid of the government—unafraid of men. Her daughter would never be abused by a single man or a whole set of unfair laws. Her daughter would never, never put up with it.

So Birdie spread her arms again, but this time, she didn't fall down flat. She grabbed for more. Wanda, on the other hand, picked up Tanya. Wanda made her squash soup and broke tiny bits of soda crackers on top of the orange surface. She put the girl on her knee and spoke to her in the little bit of their mother's language she had left, lulling the toddler. While Birdie was on the phone or in DC or picketing some office somewhere, Wanda sat with Tanya on the porch, a Ruby by their sides, both of them looking out at the ranch land in front of them. When Birdie sat with tribal members in Kellogg City, Wanda and Tanya went out into the waist-high fields, looking for flowers. During July and August, they searched for mullein, the leaves and flowers used for a tea drunk with milk and honey, good for a winter's cough. As Birdie plotted inside, outside meadowlarks flung past, gold on the wing. The cottonwoods lost their leaves. The snow fell on the mountain tops and then it melted, filling Ruby Lake to bursting blue. Then fields flashed green and crackled into almost white. Tanya held up her arms to be picked up, and Wanda lifted her high, swinging her around and around, both of them whooping, Birdie watching from inside the house.

As Tanya slept in her crib next to the bed, Birdie began to miss her child. She began to leave her even as they both slept. Her nighttime heart beat to the pain she knew she was creating for them both. That little girl baby body against her shoulder would be the memory she'd have to carry with her into places Tanya couldn't go. Not now. And maybe not ever. Her throat ached at the thought of all those days and months and maybe years she'd spend without her child. She clamped her eyes shut at the idea that her absence was what Tanya would grow to expect. And want, too.

Tanya grew big and tall and beautiful, while Birdie went out and away, getting in her truck and barreling up Dempsey Mapp Road, a plume of dust behind her.

Chapter Twenty-Four

Seattle, Washington
June 2012

Nick texted Megan in the early afternoon: Got one. Love to you both.

One meant a fire.
Both meant her and his mom Sue.

Just this single message. Then nothing. She sat in the living room of her—in a few months their—newly rented apartment on 17th Avenue, only a block away from campus. Her laptop was on the coffee table, open to one of the web sites Nick had told her about. If she knew the name of the fire, she could search for it. But he hadn't texted her that info, so she couldn't pick from the current list of Black Mountain, Trinity, Green Range, Casen's Ridge, Meadow Fire, or Pinetop. Who knew? The fires were named after ridges, ranges, towns, gullies she'd never seen. She barely understood Nevada, a strangely upside down triangular state she'd avoided her whole life, shoving it into categories like prostitution, rednecks, and gambling. Maybe showgirls, Cirque du Soleil, and Celine Dion, too. Everything wrong in the universe was located in Nevada. It was over-kill and over-statement, filled with bad environmental policies, poverty, and empty tract houses. Also, it burned every summer like a stupid teenager at the beach, darkly crisp, brittle, and dangerous.

It was early June in Seattle, so of course it was overcast, the air thick with almost rain. The grey sky hung low and close to the ground like a needy friend. She was that needy friend, feeling alone, which she really was, so at least she wasn't making up that part. She wanted to whine or maybe even cry on someone's shoulder, moping and sniffling that her boyfriend had finally found the job he'd always wanted, that she was waiting to start grad school and sitting alone in her apartment.

Wah, wah, wah.

The good news for her high school and Evergreen friends was that they had come home and left again, traveling to internships in Chicago, Manhattan, and Raleigh. Closer to home, some had jobs in Seattle or Tacoma or Portland, which, of course, they were at right now, plopped down into the action of the world. Her parents were at work, and all she had was pre-grad school reading and a lot of time and the space that Nick once filled.

"Why don't you get a car and go and see him," her best friend Holly (safely located in Amherst, far away from Megan's angst) had said on the phone the day before. "Just ask your parents if you could borrow their Honda, for god's sake. It's like, what? Ten hours? Eleven? Not a totally big deal."

"That's a long drive, and—"

"So fly into what? Salt Lake? Or Reno. There's got to be a good hotel there." Holly laughed. "I'd rather stay at the station though. All those bearded guys in ass-kicking boots."

"I can't stay at the station." Megan heard her own whining, but she couldn't stop herself, her words elongating with all her selfishness: *sta-tion.* "I mean, there's nowhere for me to sleep. Legally."

"So camp out at the nearest Motel Six and wait for the fires to be put out."

"Like some kind of Army whore."

"Exactly," Holly said. "He's your boyfriend. You go to Nevada for him."

"I want him to come home."

"Nick's got a life, too," Holly said.

"Finally." Megan bit back the word, but it was too late. Not that she'd been very supportive as he searched. After all, how many times could she ask, "Graduate school?" without him getting angry? Maybe, she had thought, some office job would tide him over, lure him in. For a while. Long enough for him to forget the job he didn't even know he wanted. But some web search led him to fire fighting. That was that.

"So, yeah. It took him awhile. But there he finally is. And what is he supposed to do? Watch you write papers? Like forever"

"No. No. Of course not," Megan said, shame thick at the back of her throat. "He's got his own life."

"So go."

Megan found herself telling Holly she'd talk to her parents about the car thing, but when she hung up, she knew she wasn't going to drive east, over mountain ranges, down into Oregon and then Idaho and then the hot flat palm of an ugly state she'd never been to before. And then what? Would she really stay at some crappy motel in Kellogg City, while Nick was up at the station? And even if he had a few days off, it would be her luck that a huge fire would burn down the world and call him away. All she'd be able to do is get back in her borrowed, rented, stolen car and drive home.

So instead, Megan rented an apartment and arranged for their furniture to be packed and shipped from Oakland. Everything now put in its proper place, she hoped Nick would like her choices, couch here, table there, photos on the wall. All there was left to do was wait, just as she'd waited for him all of freshman year when he tried to get away from that Claire. Now here she was, waiting again. She wasn't reading or studying but Googling Devlin's weather and seeing enough to scare her: high temperatures, low relative humidity, and threatened lightning strikes, the very things fires love best.

Her phone vibrated again, and she grabbed it, blood pounding in her ears, her throat, staring at the screen, hoping to see:

False alarm. Going back to the station.

But it was only her mother, checking in with a cheery: Hope you're having a great day in your new home!

Megan tossed her phone on the couch and looked around. Home wasn't where she was right now. Home used to be with her parents. But for the past five years, home was with Nick, and he was gone. So she was homeless. Megan wasn't feeling sorry for herself but being honest and true. She didn't know how she could find her home with him working so far away for so long without her, five, six months away each and every year until he got tired of the life or decided what was more important to him.

She stood up and walked to the window, watching the cars drive by on the street below her. When Nick got the firefighting job, Megan had thought she was worried about him because she loved him so much, as she had since the second he'd popped up on the Evergreen Facebook group, all blinding white smile, dark eyes, curly hair. And those status updates? This one about the hipster panhandler:

This one about the hipster panhandler:
If you're going to panhandle on the side of the road with
a sign that reads "broke" don't do it wearing your very
clean loafers, skinny jeans, and v-neck shirt while standing
in front of your brand new bike.

Or this:

Watching a laser disc copy of the bmx bandits in a derelict
asbestos plant, drinking Olde English out of a sippy cup,
wearing man capris with a Christmas sweater and yacht
shoes, all while my new unicorn tattoo heals.
I love my new life.

Or the picture of the rabbit wearing the glasses and holding a ray gun.

Cracked her up. Besides, she loved rabbits. So she had no choice but to friend him. And then just like that, they were just together all the time, friends despite his girlfriend back home. At the dorm, in the cafeteria, on the lawn in front of the library. In his dorm room watching YouTube; in hers reading. At the Reef, sitting in the ripped up, lumpy booths, drinking bad coffee and eating worse pancakes, and talking for hours about anything.

That whole long year while she waited for him to decide to break up with Claire, break up with Claire, and get over his break up with Claire, she knew that she might never meet someone as kind and honest and funny as Nick Delgado. If she hadn't waited, she would have lost him.

And then, she had him, finally, that first night in her dorm room. Both of them in her bed, naked, finally, touching, his body just as she'd imagined, all heat and strength and kindness. His hands firm, his back strong. Lips and fingers and warmth.

So when Megan read what happens to flesh in fire, she'd been horrified into silence, at least for a while. One book described what it was like to burn from the inside out, fire so hot it sucked the air and water and life out of people before it burned them to charcoal bits. Their lungs were crisped like burnt paper. In every chapter, one firefighter after the other ran up hills as the power of flame chased after and caught them all. Thankfully, the books didn't show photos of the dead people, but they presented the perfectly blackened, bloated, intact bodies of deer and squirrels and birds, all of them like stiff coal statues, something out of Greek myth. The sad photos had been like an accident on the freeway. She hadn't been able to stop looking.

But now, Megan knew what her upset back in Oakland had been about, all the worrying and crying, the sleepless nights, the clinging to Nick in the middle of the night as he slept, listening to the steady one two of his heart. She'd not just been trying to save Nick from heat and fire and hot, ugly death. But herself from being alone, without him.

Chapter Twenty-Five

Devlin, Nevada
July 2012

Nick learned not to be fooled by a fire at dawn, temperature and humidity low, winds calm, crews fresh. Even when the fire was small, the flames scattered and sparse, Nick could see the sharp yellow edges, swords masked as paring knives. One wind shift, one subtle degree drop in humidity, knives sprang up as swords clattering forward in a sharp, flickering army.

He'd heard stories of firefighters taking naps next to a fireline and then wham! a roar like a freight engine, the thunder of a stampede. A blow-up. The world on fire. Or a wind shift might push the fire into a patch of light fuels, and then firefighters were running uphill, looking for an escape route and safety zone, the big black that didn't exist. They'd deploy their shelters and not live to tell about the small fire that suddenly, without warning, blew up.

Yet Nick knew that there was always warning, and he didn't want to sleep through it. He watched every fireline as if it were spreading up a steep slope, wind shoving it along. A week ago, two Devlin engines had been sent to a big fire in Idaho, and even though they were just griding line, Nick had seen the flames, felt the wind, watched as people laughed and joked around when only yards away, the fire burned through grass and shrub.

"It's not a textbook, Evergreen," Mac had teased as they dug hard into the still hot and smoking soil, using the stupid nickname everyone else was. "You can't know about it from reading anything."

"Fuck off." Nick didn't want to get into it with Mac. Not that the guy even knew what he was talking about. Thing was, fighting fire was like reading a book with the same beginning and end, every single time. It was the unpredictable middle he worried about, the middle that made people write up rules that most firefighters broke in the literal heat of battle. Nick didn't blame them for that because the rules didn't always make sense. Not with something so violent and volatile and manipulative, not with something that could hide its power, smoldering and simmering until it wasn't.

One warm July day near the end of an impromptu kickball game, Jarchow walked out onto the porch to watch, his hands on his hips.

Nick tried not to notice because he was irritable and didn't want to feel self-conscious, too. Schraeder was whining like a princess and mincing around, mocking Nick's last kick, a weak strike to right-field that almost veered out-of-bounds but not quite.

"It's just a kickball game," Nick said to Hamm, as they stood at first base. "Like we're a bunch of kids."

"It's PT," said Hamm, not meeting Nick's gaze.

"Yeah, fine," Nick said. "But not the World Series."

"Take it seriously," Hamm said. "You could've made it to second."

"Maybe." Nick shrugged. "But really? Kickball?"

"Yeah," Hamm said. "Fucking kickball."

Thompson was up, and Nick leaned over, hands on his kneecaps, ready to take the game seriously. Jesus. He could play, but he'd always disliked team sports. The egos. The politics. The waiting. His own growing, gangly body. But he'd put up with softball, volleyball, flag football, basketball. He swam. He ran track one year. On the weekends, he and his father would hike, Nick's body making sense during the climbs, no odd, random ball coming his way, no hand-eye coordination to consider, just one foot in front of the other.

This kickball game was a surprise, a game he'd hoped he'd seen the last of back in what? Sixth-grade?

Clearly serious, a grim-faced Thompson took Wicks' fast, rolling pitch and kicked the ball past Cowley in left field. Nick ran the bases hard, hitting home, and jogging to the bench, barely out of breath.

"Delgado," Jarchow called out from the porch.

"He really hated that run," Mac said, his voice low. "You'll have to wash the engines as punishment. Spit shine."

"Wait till he sees yours," Nick said, punching Mac in the shoulder. "You'll be scrubbing the toilets for weeks."

Nick headed over to Jarchow, who gazed out at the game.

"I hate kickball," Jarchow said. "I'd rather play dodge ball with a rock."

"Ouch," said Nick. "What's up?"

"Remember that journalist we met at Mapp Ranch?"

Blush flamed from Nick's jaw to his cheek. He brought a hand to his face, trying to look thoughtful and maybe interested, hoping to cover his embarrassment. Since that day on the ranch, he'd tried not to think about Em Donnelly. But there she was behind his eyelids before sleep, her image keeping him awake. Nick kept seeing her looking right at him, interested in what he was saying, asking him questions. Then he'd think about her hair, the way she tucked it behind her ears. Her dress, the way it fell down body. Her slim, strong body, which he could see more clearly than Megan's at this point.

A few dozen rounds of this, and he'd toss off the blankets, feeling hot and guilty, sweat trickling down his temples even with the AC on. He'd turn on his computer hoping he could catch a wave of Wi-Fi. But no Wi-Fi. So no Megan. Only the heat in his body, Em's face in his mind.

"Yeah."

Jarchow nodded. "She's coming to the station today for that interview."

"Okay," Nick said, turning back to the game in time to see Schraeder zip past first and head toward second amid whoops from the bench.

"I want you to give her the tour. Tell her more about the BLM outreach. All the ranches we visited. You know. The BS smorgasbord of BLM concern."

"Why me?" Nick remembered the way Em and Jarchow sparked, their repartee, the smiles, all while Nick watched them and listened to Wanda Mapp's cryptic comments about Jake at the barn door.

"I don't have time for it," Jarchow said. "But having the community on our side is important. Turns out her blog gets read. District gave the go-ahead. Anyway, I'm calling you in. My reinforcement. Take care of her."

Nick took in a quick breath and laughed a little, nodding as Jarchow prepped him on what to say. But his mind was a fire whirl. Em next to him as they walked around the station. Em asking him a lot of questions. He making her laugh. Maybe a follow-up to this interview. In town. Even as he listened to Jarchow, he was unable to keep Em off his mind because she'd be real. Also real was the fight he and Megan had the night before on Skype.

He'd wangled a sudden, fairly strong Wi-Fi connection in the left-hand corner of his room, and they started off having a great conversation. He hadn't seen her face in weeks, and finally, there she was, a small smile on her lips. It didn't matter that there was a lag in the visual, her movements behind her voice, her face pixilating, breaking up entirely, and then coming back together.

"You'll like it here. Not as hot as the Oakland apartment. And a parking space."

"No more parking a mile away on a Friday night."

"And the laundry's close."

But when he asked her when she was going to visit, it wasn't pixilation that changed her expression.

"You wouldn't have any time to go anywhere," she had said. "Not that there's anything to do."

"I've typically got Monday and Tuesday off," Nick said, stung. To him, her visit wasn't about seeing anything but her, and her seeing him. Who cared about landmarks and tourist traps after such a long separation? "I can stay with you in—"

"Kellogg City?" Megan asked. "I did a Google search, and it doesn't look promising hotel-wise. There's one actually called the Thunderbird Motel. Really. It's insulting to the tribe."

"Which tribe?" Nick asked.

"Every tribe." Her voice was flat and negative, filled with no.

"So you don't want to come."

"I can't," Megan said. "For one thing, I've got to get ready for school. I've got a ton of reading."

"You could bring your books with you, you know. Strange like that, books."

"Just stop it, okay?"

Nick had stared at her impassive face, hoping that the dull flatness in her expression was the fault of the computer screen. He was used to her big smiles or her blazing glares, but not this passive mask. The Skype seconds went by, and he waited for the Megan he'd known for years to push aside this imposter and say the right things: *I can't wait to see you. I'll be there this weekend, and we can hole up in the room and eat take out in bed. Then later, I want to see your station and meet all the firefighters. I want to hear about the fires.*

"I've gone over this," she said. "I can't drive that far by myself."

"You could fly. I'd drive to meet you halfway."

"I don't want to fly," Megan said.

"You mean you don't want to fly to see me." He shook his head. "If it were you out here, I'd—"

"I'd never leave you for six months."

"That's the way this work is," Nick said for what felt like the millionth time. "I'm not making it up. It's not like it's my choice."

"You're the one who picked it."

Nick felt the urge to click off the computer and go into his room and stare at the ceiling. Here they went again. "What else was I going to do? I don't want to go back to school. I love history, but I don't want to teach it. I don't want to work in an office. Okay?"

"Firefighting is the only thing in the world you want to do."

"But in Nevada?" Megan asked, her voice a whir of pained upspeak.

"It's where the work is. If you were the one working far away, I'd come every weekend and—"

"You're a better person," she said. "That's already been established."

"No it hasn't," Nick said. "I never said that."

Megan sighed. "Remember, I'm the one here waiting for you. I've always waited for you."

"I'll be there."

"Eventually. But don't forget you're the one who decided to go out to the pit of the United States and work for five months. Not me. I'm following the old plan. I found the apartment, hooked up all the utilities, and moved us in, okay? So this isn't about me being the bad guy."

"It's not about being bad." He wanted to say, *It's about you not loving me enough.*

But he didn't need to hear that, not even from his own mouth. When he was finally able to click off from their conversation, he was left with her face, scrunched up in what he could only call distaste.

Now as he listened to Jarchow talk about the interview with Em, Nick felt relieved. Here was something he could excel at, adept with facts and figures and information, history major—*Evergreen*—that he was.

"Just don't fuck it up," Jarchow said. "The last thing we need is the

Kellogg City Free Whatever reporting that the BLM is whacked out and harassing the locals."

"No problem." Nick pulled his sticky wet t-shirt away from his chest. He needed to take a shower and change clothes. Even though the game had been ridiculous, he was drenched and probably smelled bad.

"And Delgado," Jarchow said. "The game means something. Schraeder can be a shitbird, but it's more than grammar school stupidity. It's a metaphor. How you'd be out on a fire. It's not about kickball."

Nick looked out at the field. Bugs and dust floated above the dried sod. The heat of the day stuck on his neck like glue.

"You don't want to be the one out there searching for the ball alone, right?"

Jarchow crossed his arms, his flame tat gleaming vermillion in the morning sun. Then he shrugged and walked back into the stationhouse. Nick turned back to the game. Mac was on the sidelines yelling at Lehman, who was running around the bases, arms pumping, dust flying. His strong right-field kick was somewhere out in the scrub, Johnson booting angrily at sage and grass. Hamm cupped his hands around his mouth and yelled at Lehman, who flipped him off, and the rest of them either jeered or rooted him on. It was just a game. All of them wanted a home run, a smooth sail around the bases. Lots of cheering. A total win.

Nick showed Em the inside of the station (she'd been interested in the radio and the large relief map of Kellogg City and environs) and now they were in the garage, looking at the gleaming engines, all three spit-shined after they'd come back from Idaho. She looked out of place in the cement and steel, dressed in black shorts and top. She wore black sandals, flats decorated with little gem stones. But she was all business, asking about the equipment. He'd given her the low-down about the models and water capacity—everything he learned in Kellogg City at the beginning of the season—and she was now examining the tools on the shelves. Nearby, he could hear Hamm snickering as he sharpened a Pulaski, but Nick forced himself to answer Em's questions, covering mostly what he and Jarchow had already told her and Wanda Mapp during the visit at the ranch.

"Seems like wildfires are getting bigger and bigger." She turned away from the rows of tools, her wide white-blue eyes staring at him. "Every summer, the stories are worse."

"You're right." Nick glared at Mac—who gave him an excited little girl wave—and then led Em out into the shade of the garage overhang. A light sheen of sweat lit her face, her light skin reddened. He noticed a mole above her left eyebrow, perfectly round.

"Why?" she asked. "It's not like anything's changed."

"Yeah, it has," he said as they sat down at the picnic table. "Twentieth-century fire suppression theory and then practice made forests more combustible. Before, fires burned wild until they burned out. There was no one here to notice. But after a few killer fires, instead of letting things burn, the Forest Service reacted. Remember those Smokey Bear ads? Yeah, well, they worked. Forests grew heavy with fuel. Seasons and seasons of growing branches and leaves and small trees and bushes. So when there were fires as there naturally would be, they burned like crazy."

"The policy prevented fires but made the fires that did start worse?" Em clicked away on her phone.

Nick shrugged. What he knew came from Jarchow and all the books and websites he read while studying before and after firecamp. "Probably. But also there's this wildland/urban interface issue. People built where they shouldn't have. And they keep building all the way into the wilderness. It's not just in the US, either. South of France. Australia. LA's the worst, though. Think about Malibu."

"I don't know how to think about Malibu," Em said. "I'm from Boston. As the old timers would say around here, 'California can go have that.'"

"Come on! Didn't you ever see *Baywatch* reruns?"

"I was too busy for TV, reading the classics and writing long sad stories about girls in psychic pain." Em winked at him. "But anyway, tell me about Malibu."

Nick paused at the idea of Em as an English major. His mom, Megan, Em. He couldn't escape them. Something Freudian, he imagined, though his mother wasn't dark and subterranean like Megan or as inquisitive like Em.

Maybe he just needed people to read with.

"Malibu?" she asked.

"Oh, so it's a lush place. Lots of biomass." She cocked her head, her fingers still on her phone. "Fuel. The climate's great, but there's the Santa Ana winds down south. They're amazing, powerful, relentless. So you have a fuel-filled ecology, low humidity, high temperatures, and constant winds. And then, fire. Before people settled there, the fires burned. Some of the plants in the environment are fire-adapted, needing that fire every so often to re-seed. All that was fine for millennia, but then we showed up."

"*Baywatch,*" Em said.

"Exactly. Everyone starts running around in their red string bikinis and scary Speedos and building houses. The place turns into an enclave for the rich and famous, and surprise! They don't want their big beautiful houses to burn down and manage to convince federal and city agencies to protect them at all costs. The wild was just fine till it turned urban."

"In Nevada, there was all that suburban sprawl in the nineties."

"Right. And it wasn't just Nevada. All the west. There are houses that have no reason in hell to be where they are, other than the view. They're built on fire-adapted terrain. People are always so surprised when things burn. I've seen pictures of forest fires stopped right at someone's back door, and to save that house cost what? A couple hundred thousand? More than the damn house."

Em nodded, taking notes. Her fingers tapped, her brilliant hair lit and dangling in front of her face. She had some light color on her eyelids, a flick of mascara, and blue toenails. Nick found himself staring at them. Megan never painted her nails—fingers or toes—and it was rare that she wore makeup, usually just for English Department parties or Christmas dinner celebrations with her persnickety Washington relatives or Nick's family.

It all seemed natural on Em, even the black clothes in Nevada during the summertime.

She sighed, looked up at him, and then glanced over at the station house, probably hoping Jarchow would come out so she could go over and talk with him. She shrugged. "Nevada's a mess. I've been looking into that whole mining situation. Done some sleuthing."

"What did you find?"

"Not as much as I need to. I'm waiting for Birdie Mapp to come home for her thoughts. But she's in DC trying to keep her lands from being confiscated."

"How can they take Mapp Ranch?"

Em gave him a glance. "*We* take."

"Okay, right. *We*. But how?"

"The government claims they paid the tribe for the lands and that the Indians living there should pay grazing rights," Em said. "The Mapps and others have refused, saying they didn't take the money the government offered. So the government said that if they don't pay the grazing rights, off they go. Back to the reservation or wherever. The whole mess has been in court for years, and now, finally, it's at the Supreme Court."

"From the way she acted, I would've never known the ranch was on the line." Nick didn't mention Wanda's cryptic advice about Em or her amazing truck fixing skills. There was something Wanda wanted, though. Both times he'd been with her, she tried to tell him something he wasn't quick enough to grasp. But confusing as she was and despite not knowing her well, Nick found it hard to imagine the ranch without her.

Em shrugged. "Me, either. But I'm not sure you'd see it. She seems pretty, well, Zen, if that makes any sense. We'd actually been talking about the mines. They're terrible for the earth. The water table. Everything. You know there's one right here in Devlin."

Nick nodded, shifted a bit on the bench. "Never been."

"Not a pretty sight. Or site for that matter. Open-pit mining. It's more confusing than Malibu."

Nick smiled, though it really wasn't funny. It was easier to think about horrible environmental practices when he was far away in California. He'd been raised in the land of the politically liberal and correct, and in Nevada, nothing was correct, as far as he'd seen in a few short weeks.

"Do you want to see the mine?"

"You can get us up there?"

Em smiled, her teeth straight and perfect. A perfect match for Jarchow. She was about to say something else, when the tone rang in the station house, the sound echoing outside.

"What's that?" she asked, her eyebrows pale arcs over her wide eyes.

"Fire. Somewhere. Hold on." He listened, and there were the three tones for Devlin.

"That's us," Nick said, and they both stood up. "Getting toned to a fire. Better go."

"I kept wondering when that was going to happen. It was making me nervous." She laughed and slipped her phone into her bag. "So I'll text you about that mine visit, okay?"

Just then, Mac jogged by, excited, smiling. "Dude, let's go. Get your bucket. Fire in the Crescent Valley. Looks like we might be sleeping on this one. H-pay for the whole weekend!"

Nick nodded at him, and then turned back to Em, catching his breath. But how not to? The afternoon sun held her backlit, her hair, skin and eyes, even the tiny fake jewels on her sandals, glowing.

"Bucket?" she asked, cocking her head. "I know you don't put out fires with buckets."

"Hard hat."

"H-pay?"

"Hazard pay."

"Oh," she said. "Okay. Well, let me know when you want to go to the mine."

"I will," he said. He would have said more, but the sounds of the firefighters, the lugging roar of the engines, turned back toward the station, fire taking over everything.

Chapter Twenty-Six

Kellogg City, Nevada
July 2012

Kellogg City Free Press—The Daily Donnelly
by Em Donnelly

Three weeks ago, I wrote about the tribal meeting where, among other things, I learned about the fire danger this summer. There have been three years of drought, a beetle infestation, and some low humidity to blame. Maybe even global warming. I'm not a big weather watcher, but from that meeting onward, I started scanning the local forecasts. No surprises: dry with chances of thunderstorms. For those of you new to the Kellogg City area—miners and mine executives and administration as well as their families—or those just not used to Nevada weather, these summer thunderstorms don't produce much moisture but do create lightning. And lots of it. In fact, on my way home from the meeting, the sky was a zing of spider web lightning strikes, each promising the chance of fire. The good news was that nothing caught. At least, not that night. But in the days since that meeting, ten incidents have been called into Ruby District dispatch. Since the current fire season started in mid-May, over 78,000 Nevada acres have burned on public, private, Forest Service, and BIA Tribal Trust lands. The district anticipates the 2012 fire season will run all the way through October and maybe November if this current weather pattern persists.

So folks, if I'm doing some averaging and math correctly, we have another 78,000 acres left to burn, more if something catches and can't be caught. Some of the rules I learned while a member of Girl Scout troop 415 seem to apply here. Here's one: Let's keep those campfires in check, people.

But what, really, do I know about wildfire? Born and raised on the

East Coast in totally urban areas, my only bonding with fire came from the aforementioned troop and our camping trips to Bumpkin Island and Myles Standish State Forest. There I sat with my marshmallow and stick, attempting to keep the flames from burning the best part of a s'more. Fire was the enemy in this case. But I was really more concerned about mosquitoes and spiders. Not to mention sneaky Missy O'Leary, who would, in fact, pour water in my shoes. So in order to learn more, I arranged an interview at the Devlin Station, and yesterday, I sat talking with firefighter Nick Delgado, a first-year firefighter from Oakland, California, a city that knows a bit about fire. Remember that devastation in 1991?

Nick might be new to firefighting as a profession, but he's read the history of how we've fought fire in the United States. Actually, fighting fire didn't become militaristic and regimented in the West until the beginning of the 20th century after The Great Fire 1910 in Washington State. Of course, this attempt at suppressing fire comes with the expansion of Western cities and towns. Houses are built up to prime burning areas. As Nick says, "There are houses that have no reason in hell to be where they are, other than the view."

He calls this backdoor/forest fire meeting the wildland/urban interface (which sounds a bit too technological for me). But the scoop here is true: we are building too close to lands that will and should burn.

I checked out some books and blogs, and what Nick says is now pretty much common knowledge, though practice has not accommodated this new fire prevention theory. More and more, we should let fires burn. Many local ecologies thrive (and did long before we were here) with burns every so often, ranging from every year to once every twenty. But also, we need to be real. We all do live here and would like to keep doing so (but please, God! make the AC work all the time). We don't want our houses to burn down, but if we can keep fires from raging out of control, we have to accept some burning. This newer firefighting practice allows for such where there is little to no threat to homes and businesses, humans, cattle, or protected wildlife.

Makes sense to me. No more fighting the fires in the middle of nowhere where no one lives and no one cares. And where actually, the land might thrive with a good meltdown.

We made it through the 4th of July without a wildland weenie roast. Every fire has been contained with minimal structural loss and no loss of life or limb. Let's try to keep it that way. So people, watch those campfires.

As Smokey Bear said, "Only you can prevent forest fires."

He might have also said, "Some fires need to burn. Just be safe.

Chapter Twenty-Seven

Northern Nevada
Mapp Ranch
Summer 1938

On hot summer ranch nights when it was too miserable to sleep—when even the porch bench was uncomfortable, and all Wanda, Stanley, and Birdie could do was sit on the stoop and drink ice water or lemonade in tall plastic glasses and suck the ice—their father told stories. Wanda's favorite was about Cottontail, the rabbit who wanted to kill the sun. Under the moonlight, Wanda understood that desire. She was prickly and irritable and so desperate for coolness that as her father wove his stories, she imagined the fields were water, waves of it, the tide constant and lulling.

Dempsey was hot, too hot to smoke his pipe, and he sat on the porch bench behind them, wearing his t-shirt and pajama bottoms.

"You know," he said. "The sky here. It used to be really low. The sun hung too close to the ground and burned everything. And just like tonight, people back then said, '*Ataa!* It's too damn hot.'"

Stanley gaped, but Wanda and Birdie were old enough to know it was just a story.

"So," Dempsey said. "Cottontail decided to kill that sun. He was going to be a hero, for sure. He and his friend Sand Rabbit got up one morning and walked toward the east. They went over the Rockies and the Appalachians, though no one called them those names back then. This was before there were names for a lot of things, you know? No matter what mountains they went over, Sun always came up the next one to the east. Finally, Cottontail and Sand Rabbit came to the ocean and stopped."

"Why?" Stanley always asked.

"Because you can't walk on water," Birdie said.

"Oh," said Stanley, nodding.

Because of the woman who taught religion at school, Wanda knew

Jesus walked on water. Why couldn't Cottontail, she wanted to ask but didn't. Her father had fought against them going to "that goddamn Catholic school," so he probably didn't want to know how the church lady came on Wednesday afternoons to the reservation school.

Dempsey sipped his water. The porch creaked under his chair. Out in the field, Wanda heard animals pushing through the grass, rustling through the sagebrush like Cottontail and Sand Rabbit.

"So Cottontail had an idea. He said, 'Dig a tunnel.' And they both buried themselves, right there, in their tunnels. But here's the thing. Cottontail made a twisty, turvy tunnel. Sand Rabbit was tired and lazy and made a straight tunnel. But they scooted in and stayed in their tunnels. Sun came up, but they didn't, hiding like prairie dogs. They stayed down deep for nine days."

"How did they breathe?" Stanley asked. Wanda thought of the silver miners, who went down into the ground.

"Air goes down, too," Birdie said.

"Oh," Stanley said.

Dempsey cleared his throat. "Finally, at the end of the ninth day, Cottontail got all his arrows ready. When Sun came over, he shot at him and then jumped back into his tunnel. But all the arrows burned right up. Not one hit Sun, you know? So Cottontail did some big thinking. He took a long roll of sage bark and shot it at Sun. And what do you know—"

"Sun died!" Stanley yelled.

"That's right. Sun died, but it's hard to put out even a dead sun, you know? When Sun fell to the land, there was a huge explosion for sure. Everything caught fire. Water boiled all over the earth. Cottontail saw what was happening and jumped back into his tunnel and kicked dirt behind him to keep out the fire, except some fire got to him and burned his neck, wrists, and ankles."

"That's why Cottontail has black ears!" Stanley shouted.

"Is not," Birdie whispered.

"That's right," said Dempsey, cutting a glance at Birdie. "But you know, here's the thing. Poor Sand Rabbit only dug down about six inches in his straight hole. He was roasted to death."

Wanda looked down on the ground, wondering how deep she'd have to dig to save herself from Sun's death.

"So his friend was dead, and it was dark everywhere," Dempsey went on. "Cottontail knew he had to do something. He decided to make another sun. First he cut out Sun's gallbladder, but it had some green spots on it, so he made the moon out of it instead. Then he took Sun's bladder. It had been all beat up during the fight, but Cottontail patched it and made a brand new Sun. But here's the thing. The sky was still too low. So Cottontail stood up on his hind legs and pushed the sky up with his head. Then he did an amazing thing. He threw the new Sun up into the sky. And you know what?"

"The sun wasn't hot anymore!" Stanley shouted.

"It's still hot," Birdie said. "It was one hundred and eight degrees today."

"Smarty pants," Wanda whispered.

"Imagine what it was like when the sky was too low," Dempsey said, he and Birdie arguing as they always did about how things were or were not, about how something was right or something was wrong.

Back and forth, Dempsey and Birdie, Birdie and Dempsey. Didn't matter what they thought about the sun. High or low. Blazing hot or just hot enough. It just was. People just had to deal with it.

Wanda drifted away from her father's story, her mind taking her back to the waves of the grassy ocean, the moon a silver light on imaginary waters. Blowing off the mountain and across the valley, she caught the notes of the song *Eagle's Wing is Skying*. Her old grandmother singing grass *upon waves, grass upon waves.* But then the water calmed, stilled, the moon whole and white. This image was what finally cooled Wanda down, let her stand up and walk away from her family, and go inside and to bed, the ebb and tide of their voices lulling her to sleep.

Chapter Twenty-Eight

Northern Nevada
Mapp Ranch
July 2012

"I talked to Dwayne," Tanya said as she and Wanda swept hay from the truck bed. Dwayne and his friend James had just left, heading back to the herd and the cowboys they'd hired to help out for a bit. It was late afternoon, the sun arcing down the sky but still bright yellow, heat wafting in wiggles in the distance.

Wanda stopped and slowly stood straight, leaning on her broom. "What did he say?"

Tanya pushed a lock behind her ear, her hair long and shiny black as a young girl's.

"He and Stanley have just been checking out the mine site. Len Dunning is just an old friend." Tanya wiped her temple with a swipe of her forearm. "According to him, I have nothing to worry about."

"Believe it?" Wanda asked, the hope in her heart wanting to sit down and stay awhile.

Tanya sighed. "When Dwayne was in high school, I used to ask 'How're your grades doing?' Dwayne would look at me and say, 'Nothing to worry about.' I'd ask him, 'Are you and your friends getting into any trouble?' and he'd say, 'Nothing to worry about.'"

Tanya stabbed at the truck bed with her broom, her strong brown arms golden in the light. It was so long ago that Tanya came home from the hospital with Dwayne, holding him like a grown up woman, not a girl of almost sixteen. Confident and sure, even though her whole life had changed. There she was breastfeeding and changing diapers and waking up at night to walk Dwayne on her shoulder. But she'd been so young, a mother still needing to be mothered. She hadn't learned all she needed to teach her own child. Now, Wanda knew that Tanya felt Dwayne's failures were hers personally.

Tanya shook her head and looked at Wanda, half her mouth smiling. "You know how well high school and Dwayne got along. You know what he and his friends did all those years. If Len Dunning is a friend, then there is something to worry about."

Wanda stabbed the broom against the truck bed. "So what should we do?"

"I have half a mind to have a party." Tanya pushed the last of the hay off the tailgate and lightly tossed the broom to the ground. Then, after she jumped out herself, she held up her hands to Wanda who had no shame accepting the help.

Safely on the ground, they leaned against the truck, looking into the open barn door. Wanda heard the horses snorting and stomping, Six letting out a high fine whinny.

"A party?"

"A potluck," Tanya said. "Neighbors. People from the clinic."

"What for? How will that help?" They hadn't had a party at the ranch house since Birdie turned seventy. What a hoo-ha that had been. Stanley went missing during the night but later crawled out from under the porch where he'd slept off whatever he'd been drinking.

"Shake things up in the right way," Tanya said. "Get Len relaxed and make him tell us his plans. Maybe get me relaxed, too. My antennae are up 24/7. But Dwayne's deep undercover."

"So we invite some of the tribal council? Things might get explosive."

"Can't not have Ruth Eagle."

Wanda snickered, remembering the way Ruth had stormed out of the meeting two months ago, her husband following behind her like a failed parade.

"Dave, for sure."

Tanya smiled.

"Who else?" Wanda asked.

"What about that journalist we met? The one who wrote about you? She might ignite a spark or two."

Wanda nodded. Tanya had printed out the nice article Em had written. Over the years, lots of people had written about the Mapps, some not so nice, especially about Birdie. *Indian Activist Causes Trouble for Locals.* That kind of thing. As if being here forever wasn't damn local.

But Em's piece seemed personal. Interested in what was true. When Wanda read it, she looked up, half expecting Em to be sitting right there, round the kitchen table bright and sparkly. All those articles before, most about Birdie and all her good works and far-flung travels. But this story? It gave Wanda a warm little butternut of a feeling because it was about her. There was even a photo of Ruby, dog-happy and alert-eared.

It would be nice to see the girl again. Wanda thought they wouldn't meet up until Birdie came home from DC with all her political this and that, Wanda of little informational use.

"What do we tell them all it's for?"

"I've thought of that. It's the time of year for a Sunrise Ceremony," Tanya said. "Start off with it. Then come down to the house for a picnic. Let the party go all day. Tug-of-war. Handgame. Need to set up a tent for that."

"Could we get two teams together?" Wanda asked. "Darlene Hightower will smack her gavel and call for bingo instead."

Tanya went on arranging, but Wanda had floated into the game tent with her family and friends, sitting across from the other team, who tried to hide the bones in their hands, under scarves. How long had it been since she'd played, listening to the tap of the sticks on the chairs, heard the call of the music: *ye ye ye wi ye o e.*

Birdie always guessed right, knew who clutched the bone. Oh, how she sang out, her voice like moving water. Birdie was good enough to sing anywhere. She could have danced, too, tall and thin and graceful. But Birdie didn't want to dance. She wanted to learn the horses. Then she wanted to "Learn us some new traditions. The kind where no one takes advantage of us anymore. Where we're not some kind of show people pay five dollars to see. That's something we should practice."

She'd practiced those new traditions her whole life. And when the rez school wanted to enroll Tanya in shawl dance lessons, Birdie refused, giving her a new saddle instead.

"Birdie's not here," Wanda said, letting go the sound of the music she had almost forgotten. "She does most of the party arranging. Bakes all the berry pies." Birdie was a pie whiz, her motto very clear. "Butter, flour, fruit, and sugar. Buy good ingredients and stay out of their way."

Tanya turned back to face the barn, her lips pinched. "If we'd waited for Mom to come home, we'd never have done anything. I can bake pies just fine."

"She does loads," Wanda said, pushing away from the truck. "Without your mom, the courts would have our land by now. We'd be on the rez or living in an apartment in Kellogg City. And besides, Birdie being gone so long probably means things are changing. The decision might go our way."

Tanya shot her a quick glance. "You know about the ruling?"

Wanda snorted. "Have to be worse off than Stanley not to know Birdie's business. All she does is talk on the phone when she's here. Not so careful with her secrets."

"At least some of them."

"Don't be mad at her, girl. She's doing her best for sure."

"I know," Tanya said. "And really, she didn't want to keep you in the dark. She just didn't want you to be upset."

Birdie was still protecting her, but she alone couldn't hold back the US government. If they wanted Mapp Ranch, they would have it, one way or the other.

Tanya flicked her ponytail behind her shoulders and sighed. "I'm sorry, Auntie. I just wish she'd been here more."

Wanda brushed hay off her sleeves with her old leather gloves, nodding. "Never was in her, save for those few months that brought you to us. Home's deep inside your mother, but being at home isn't."

Tanya looked like she had more to say. A lot pent up, being Birdie's daughter. A lot of lonely time, weeks and months without her own momma. Birdie not there for school girl fights or crushes. Dances or powwows. Every day times around the table talking about this and that, the herd, Dwayne, college. Tanya deserved to talk for two weeks straight about this injustice. But instead, she took Wanda's arm, and they headed up to the house, Ruby standing up from her tiny shade spot next to the barn, stretching, and following them, tail wagging.

"When do you want the ceremony?" Wanda asked.

"First Saturday in August?"

Wanda looked up into the distance at Mount Aurora, the view murky through the particulate matter that hung in the sky like someone's dirty laundry. It was dry as burnt toast and only July. It would be pretty dangerous to light a fire in August, and even though she disliked the BLM, she could still hear that young firefighter's warnings, the way he looked at her with his serious smart eyes. Sad, too. But he'd known what he'd been talking about. Anyway, it might be too late to welcome the summer as the land had already moved into crackle.

"The wildflowers are already spent. Stalks like old bones," she said.

"So invite that fireman."

"What's he going to do? Bring his own engine? What I seen, BLM can't spare one."

"No, but he'll keep an eye on the fire without us even having to ask. It's in his nature, I suppose," Tanya said.

If he can get his truck to run, Wanda mused, smiling a bit. That ham sandwich sure had been good. Nice surprise in the early morning.

"A party then," Wanda said.

"A party. We'll do some sleuthing. But we'll have something to look forward to. Set us back to normal."

"Like taking off dirty socks and putting on clean ones."

Tanya laughed, a sound so loud and full of joy, Wanda knew if she had it in her, she'd say any funny thing to keep the sound coming.

As they walked up the steps toward the porch, one of Stanley's television shows blared out the front door and into the air around them. Just like always. Maybe nothing was going on, Wanda thought. Maybe all this worry about Dwayne and Birdie and Tanya and the ranch was just her imagination. All there was to do was plan a party, invite the guests, and buy some good ingredients and stay out of their way, just like Birdie always said.

Chapter Twenty-Nine

Kellogg City, Nevada
July 2012

Kellogg City Free Press—The Daily Donnelly
by Em Donnelly

In a room full of yelling, upset people, don't get upset. Instead, look for the one calm person. That's how I met Wanda Mapp, long-time Crescent Valley resident and local treasure. There she was in the midst of a volatile tribal meeting, listening intently to all the disagreement. I couldn't stop watching her and sort of invited myself to Mapp Ranch for a talk.

Every day, 84-year-old Wanda gets up, makes breakfast for her brother Stanley, 74, and her sister Birdie, 78, and then heads out to work on the Mapp Ranch, 800 acres of Northern Nevada land. Located in the middle of the valley, the ranch bangs up against the Cortez Mountain range and has been home to the Mapp family since 1878 and the signing of the Ruby Valley Treaty. Her father Dempsey and his father Dempsey before him raised cattle and horses, and Wanda and her siblings do the same.

"When we old ones go, we'll be passing on the ranch to my niece and her son," she told me as we walked to the corral. Wanda wanted to introduce me to her horse Six. "And hopefully, my great-nephew will get some kids soon, and the Mapp family can hold onto this ranch till there aren't any more of us."

Wanda may be 84, but she moves around her ranch comfortably, the animals, the buildings, the land itself known and familiar. She is solid and strong and open. Like no other person I've met, she seems to be paying attention, her gaze steady and sure. Even my mom (yes, I know you're reading) doesn't seem to wait as patiently for what I'm saying (and really, can I blame her?). And while Wanda must have the aches and pains that come from living as long as she has, she's confident as she marches from ranch house to barn to ATV—which, mind you, she drives herself, her dog Ruby in a box strapped to the back. Out on the ranch, she tackles projects herself. Let me tell you this: I've never even touched barbed wire. I'm scared of the very idea of it. But Wanda? She twists it in her gloved hands as if it were a balloon animal.

Her days are long. In the morning, she's out helping her great-nephew Dwayne with the horses or she's repairing fences. Seriously. I watched her chug around on her ATV from broken spot to spot. When I imagine myself at 84, I'm usually in a cozy chair, reading a book. I'm not doing much of anything and people have to help me do the very basics. Actually, to be truthful, I can't quite picture myself much past fifty, but when looking at Wanda, I see a way of living that long that is really living.

When she introduced me to Six, it was clear that she and the horse are deeply connected, Six whickering and expecting a handful of oats, butting Wanda gently with her soft nose.

"She gets bored," Wanda told me. "Needs a good ride out in the open."

And I think Wanda was really talking about herself. The Mapp Ranch is huge, wide open, and pretty damn hot. But that didn't stop Wanda taking me on a long truck ride around the property.

"Government claims they paid us for this land already," Wanda said. "We're expected to pay them a grazing fee for letting our herds on our own property. My sister has fought this all the way to Supreme Court. We'll see what those old buzzards say when it's over."

It wouldn't be hard to look around, shrug, and wonder why this hot, dry, arid land was worth all the decades of struggle. But as I watched Wanda's competent hands on the wheel, saw her steady smile as we passed a renegade pair of burros, listened to her point out landmarks of her past, I felt her need to stay exactly here. The Mapps deserve to pass this land on to the next generation. Granting people the rights to what is already theirs isn't too much to ask for.

"Look there," Wanda pointed as we finally headed back to the ranch house, my palms still gritty from feeding all the horses.

I looked up and saw a flock of swifts whirl in the sky, first a ribbon, then a straight line, a soap bubble, and then a W, as if sending a message just for Wanda.

Chapter Thirty

Devlin, Nevada
July 2012

"A miner can earn one-seventy a year," Em said, her small hands tight on the wheel of her Jetta, an older model she probably got as a going-off-to-college gift, now a faded black. The engine emitted periodic, strange noises that she steadfastly ignored. She'd picked Nick up at the station, and now they were bumping along on an unmarked dirt road, heading up into the hills above Devlin, each rut bouncing them in their seats. In her red leggings and black cotton dress, she looked unsuited for mine spying, but Nick couldn't help but notice her lean legs under the fabric, the thigh muscles flexing as she shifted gears.

He watched her thighs flex for one second more and then turned away.

"For that pay, no wonder they're willing to camp out in parking lots and in the hills," Nick said as he looked out the window. "Can't blame them."

"So weird to be doing so well and not have a home. I guess I'm lucky I found a roommate."

"The miners make for a good story." Nick took in a quick breath and turned back to her. "My father always tells the hard-scrabble stories of our family. His, really."

"What do your parents do?" Em asked, and Nick told her about Jess' life in pharmaceutical sales and about his mother teaching in the local high school.

"Your mom's an English teacher?"

"Yeah, and Megan. My girlfriend. She wants to be one, too. Well, a professor." Nick felt the words *my* and *girlfriend* stick in his mouth.

Em glanced at him, her short hair pushed up off her forehead, sweat glistening on her hairline. "I was going to do that. Actually, I was in grad school for one semester. University of Virginia. I finished my first and only fall semester finals and never went back."

"Why?" he asked.

"It didn't feel, well, enough. Probably, it just wasn't what I wanted to do. Just something I slid into. You know. English major track. If I want, I can finish later. But I wasn't ready, so I looked on Craig's List and found this job. The newspaper had just started their digital edition. Wanted an outreach column for new arrivals. All those miners and their families. Kellogg City seemed like the place to start fresh."

"You'd probably make more at the mine," Nick said. "Me, too. For damn sure."

She laughed, and Nick tried to remember this was just a drive to the mine, not much different than the interview at the station. He'd told her things about fighting fire, and now she was showing him what he didn't know about mines. As she drove, Em detailed the history of mining in Nevada (silver and gold, silver and gold, just like a childhood song he couldn't put his finger on). Above ground, there was no evidence of anything priceless, nothing around but fence posts and barbed wire and mangy scrub, the land denuded, bare and stripped of trees, the bones of the land articulated and visible under relentless, uphill waves of undulant brittle grass. He couldn't even imagine it with trees, this ugly dead look somehow natural.

After a few miles, he noticed deep tire grooves in the road and fluorescent yellow signs for the truckers, arrows and warnings and admonitions: *ahead, stop, yield*. Nick was surprised that anyone could drive on the roads leading up to the mine. He remembered the gravel pit in Oakland, that rusty, triangle-shaped slash above the intersection of Highways 13 and 580. Once he and his father had stopped to check it out, but the road was barricaded with a twelve-foot, barbed-wire-topped chain-link fence strewn with red warning signs and guarded by a man in a shack who wore a gun on his holster.

The guard nodded at Jess and Nick, but then he said, "Turn around."

Jess had looked at Nick, a flicker of protest in his dark eyes, but then he shrugged and did as he was ordered.

Em's contact told her to drive up to a pull-out after the third yield sign, and then hike up and slightly east to reach the lip of the mine. As long as they didn't go all the way up to the front gate, they could see all there was to see. But if they wanted a guided tour from the stiffs in the shirtsleeves and hardhats, well, there were applications and permits and such. But according to her contact, the general workforce turned a blind eye to the lookie-loos.

"One," Em said, pointing to the yield sign.

"Two," Nick said as they passed the next. "Three."

Em swung the Jetta into the pull out, and then looked at Nick. "Do you have your phone?"

Nick patted his jeans pocket. It had been awhile since he'd been out in the day in his regular clothes, most of his time off conscripted to overtime. Not that he complained about that. For the past three weeks, he'd spent his free Tuesdays digging line and mopping up fires. Wicks' and then Schraeder's engines took turns at a fire in Colorado Springs that seemed to have no end. The Tuesdays Nick did actually have to himself, he was either driving to Kellogg City for supplies at Raley's or Walmart or hanging around the station doing the usual. The biggest thrills of late had been furious ping pong battles with Lehman and Tomb Raider death matches with Deb. Back home with Megan, most days were days off. After a run or a hike, there he'd sit in that stuffy living room, reading as Megan labored over her studies. He'd think of things for them to do—a movie, the farmer's market on Grand, a walk through Lakeview cemetery, his parents' house for ribs and beer—but there was a 95 percent chance she'd say no.

But now, here, he felt like himself, a normal person who would go out for the day. But, of course, it wasn't normal for him to go to a gold mine.

"Ready."

Em tucked her purse under her seat, and they both got out of the car. Em locked it with a high-pitched beep that was suddenly drowned out by a truck's huge rumble. They backed up to avoid the dust and diesel fumes, the trucker giving them a stalwart wave as he croaked by.

"Jesus," Nick said. "That's more exhaust than a fire engine."

"Work horse." Em tugged on his arm and turned him toward the summit. "They're up and down this hill 24 hours a day."

"No neighbors around here to complain," Nick said as they started walking up the hill. He noticed she matched his strides, breathing hard but not too much.

"You work out?" he asked.

"Yoga," she said.

"Yoga? That's not aerobic, is it?"

"The way I practice it, it is," she said, smiling. "Downward dog is the least of it."

"Downward dog?"

"Don't make me show you now," she said, laughing. "You know. Hands on the mat, butt up, legs straight. You've seen it."

He had, he knew, on television or online somewhere. He'd never done yoga (if *done* was the right verb), and Megan didn't exercise at all, unless he counted the Lake Merritt walks he'd cajoled her on. Megan was thin but soft, her skin and muscles pliant. Looking at Em, he could see that she might have soft places somewhere, but most of her was hard and tight.

Blood knocked around in his temples and heart, and he focused on the gravel under his boots.

"You have to be in shape to do what you do," she said. "And if your supervisor is any indication of the workouts he puts you through, my condolences."

Nick shrugged. Jarchow again.

"What's his story?" she asked.

Nick held back a sigh. "I'm not really sure. He's half Venezuelan. Actually, he's not what I'd call forthcoming about personal shit."

"Does he have a partner?"

It was just as well, Nick thought. He told her no, Jarchow was totally single. *Go for it. He's all yours*, he thought. *The coast is clear.* Even if Megan wouldn't come and visit him, Nick knew she loved him. Or said she did. No one on the planet—not even his mother—knew him as well as Megan did. And right now, she was waiting for him in their brand new apartment in Seattle. Sure, they were fighting. Yes, they'd grown apart. But he had no business being interested in Em Donnelly. In fact, he shouldn't even be here with her, climbing this Nevada moonscape in order to spy on a poisonous gold mine. But he was. Unafraid of breaking rules or heat or big, smelly trucks, Em had pulled him right up here, both of them now trudging up the mountain.

"I mean, it must be difficult for him in your profession."

Nick glanced at her, saw a bead of sweat form and then trickle down her cheek. "What could be difficult? Look at the guy!"

"Firefighting in general. It's pretty macho, you know? And if he's

Latino, well, that's even harder."

Nick blinked and thought back to his odd conversation with Wanda. He seemed to be periodically floating into pockets of Nevada confusion. "I have no idea what you're talking about."

Em stopped, put a hand on Nick's shoulder. Dust spun around them. He turned, saw her bright face, her wide blue eyes.

"What?" he asked.

"He's gay, right?"

"No." Nick stared at her.

"Are you sure?"

"No," he said, shaking his head, and then he felt a lightness, as if given permission to breathe. Jarchow was gay.

"How—did he say something to you?"

Em laughed. "Hardly. But there's something. Maybe it's his hair."

"He doesn't have much hair," he said.

"Exactly."

Nick thought back to Thompson's redlined statement. Wow. Everyone tidily packaged in one station house, minorities of every stripe.

But Jarchow? Gay? So, maybe. Okay. Nick must have known subconsciously. But how? The absence of a girlfriend? That was weak evidence. For all anyone at the station knew, Megan could be a figment of Nick's imagination.

"I'm—I don't know," he said. "My policy is to wait to be told before assuming."

Em laughed, and they started walking again. "That's a good policy. But my gaydar—" She looked at him. "Not me, but I have a sixth sense about these things. Can't really explain it. Journalist thing maybe. But there was a curious lack of heat when we were talking."

"Used to heat, huh?" He tapped her with an elbow.

"More heat than no heat," she said. "But there were other clues."

"Maybe it was his 18-inch biceps that tipped you off," Nick asked, knowing that not much about his supervisor screamed anything but ex-Marine or cage fighter.

"Maybe both."

"Might explain his lack of girlfriends. He's still a fucking hardass. He's a good FOS."

"Better be. He's leading you into fire. He has to know what he's do-ing, right?"

"I hope," Nick agreed, pausing. "I thought you had a thing for him."

Em laughed. "Really? Why?"

Nick shrugged. "You were nice to him."

"I'm nice to everyone," she said. "But I don't like everyone I'm nice to."

Nick wanted to ask her all sorts of questions. He wanted to say something smart but, instead, remained silent and tried to ignore the ex-ultant ting in his heart, a recurring *She doesn't want him.* He felt buoyant, but then, each booted foot landed on the solid, gold-veined earth. He was as unavailable as Jarchow. And besides, he had no idea about Em's love life. And he wasn't going to ask.

For a few minutes, they were silent. They struggled on the loose, rocky soil as the incline increased, Em slipping a bit with each step. Nick took hold of her upper arm, gently, for support, and they both pushed on. Just before the ridgeline, they heard the noise, the relentless sound of en-gines, trucks and other machinery. The air was filled with a smell he couldn't identify, tangy, metal, harsh.

"I suppose we should have brought gas masks or something. Don't you have those at the station?"

"We could've worn full regalia," Nick said. "Or space suits."

They held onto rocks and short, scraggly shrubs. Though she wore shoes with some traction, Nick let go of her arm and held out his hand, and Em took it, letting him steady and pull her as they worked their way up. Then, breathing hard, they were at the top, looking down onto the entire mining operation, caught in a vortex of roar.

Em pulled her hand away. Nick tried not to notice the loss of her smooth heat, focusing instead on what was in front of him.

An inverted pyramid, the pit was at least a half mile wide, slightly elliptical and stepped, the tiers leading downward toward a spiraling center. Empty trucks headed down on the right side of a winding road, and com-pletely filled trucks—heavy with soils—churned up the left side, snorting out exhaust. From where they stood, Nick couldn't see the eye of the pit, but he knew that was where the gold was, the road leading to the money.

"It's so ugly," Em said, her hand in front of her mouth to ward off the dust or odors or horror. Or all three.

Nick agreed, but in a way, the mine reminded him of a Mexican ruin, maybe Chicen Itza or maybe even Teotihuacan, the City of the Gods and the site of the Pyramids of Sun and Moon. He wasn't sure how this comparison could be true, a god-awful mine and archaeological treasures. But when did something go from being a blight and an evil eyesore to being an archaeological Mecca? Both of the enormous Sun and Moon pyramids rose out of the Basin of Mexico, thirty miles northeast of Mexico City. He'd gone there with his parents and his father's uncle Chato during eighth-grade spring break. Chato picked them up from the downtown Four Seasons Hotel in his clankety Granada, and at one point, the highway interchanges were so confusing, Chato ended up driving on the wrong side of the road. Jess finally leaned over and wrested the wheel, yanking them to safety. On the way back, Jess had driven, Chato silent and sullen in the back seat with Nick. Years later, Nick would realize that his great uncle had smelled of Coke, brandy, and lime, the ingredients of Chato's favorite cocktail, a *Cuba Libre*.

But after the ride of terror to Teotihuacan, and with Chato resting on an ancient bench in the shade, Nick and his parents climbed to the top of both pyramids, holding onto the ropes and pulling themselves up and up, until they could look around and see that these structures were rising out of nothing, a flat, dry landscape of scrub and cactus. Probably the people enslaved to construct the buildings and the long straight Street of the Dead didn't think it was a marvel to exclaim about. Life in that hot flat place had been heavy and hard and oppressive. And what about the ritual human sacrifice when the buildings were dedicated to the gods?

What to think about this mine, though? Nick glanced at Em, who had taken out her phone and was capturing the noise and dismal vista.

"I can't use this on my blog, but I can post it on YouTube," she said. "People will want to see how ugly it all is."

"It is ugly," Nick agreed. "But architected. Thought out."

Em reared back a little at that and then looked out at the mine. He watched her take it in, her gaze sharp and smart. Her shoulders relaxed.

"I guess you're right. Sort of, well, like an upside down pyramid."

"That's what I was thinking."

"But with poison in the middle. Pyramids don't have that surprise."

"True," Nick said. "And I've never really gotten it, anyway."

"What?"

"Gold. You know. It's a mineral. Pretty and shiny. And it rules the world."

Em looked away from the mine and straight at him, nodding. "People believe printed paper is worth something, too. We're all a bunch of idiots," Em said, slipping her phone into her dress pocket. "We believe in things that in another light are just a bunch of rocks or wads of paper. Anyway, come on. Let's walk the rim."

Nick reached out to help her up onto the lip. This time, he let go first. If she slipped, he could grab her. Or her him. As they made their way, he waited for someone to yell at them to get the hell out, but no one bothered to look up.

So much of life, he thought as he followed behind Em, was about things that weren't even real. What they worried about might only be a dream. Money, gold, heaven and hell, success, failure. That's why Nick had always loved the work of the body, something he could feel. That's why he loved to fight fire, too. Fire was real and fierce, even when it just crawled around, a spider web of heat. It could be defeated and destroyed, the result obvious and clear. Fire left a mark, something people could go back and look at later and know it had been there. Fire was permanent. Eternal. Sure, it was put out. But it always came back, again and always.

As they walked along, Em stopped to take a few photos. Nick took a couple of shots as well, thinking he might send them to his dad.

"What are you going to do about this?" he asked Em. "And, I guess why are you doing it?"

"I'm going to write about it," she said. "Protest the new one they're planning on Mount Aurora."

"Are the locals protesting?"

"There's a movement afoot," she said. "I just don't know what the plan is. But, hey." Em actually struck her forehead with the soft pad of her palm, a cartoon-like gesture, but endearing. "I almost forgot. The Mapps are having a Sunrise Ceremony on Mount Aurora next week. They invited me to come. Said I could bring a guest."

"What's a Sunrise Ceremony?" Nick asked.

"Wikipedia says it's a fire lit before first light. And everyone sings and chants and prays to heal the land."

"From what?"

"From us. Humans."

Nick laughed.

"What?" Em said. "Don't tell me you don't use Wikipedia. That and Google constitute my brain mass."

"One day, let me tell you about Slippery Sam Randall?"

"Who?"

"Never mind," Nick said, savoring the idea of later telling her how he and his college dorm-mate, Mitch, made up a historical soldier named "Slippery Sam" Randall, who supposedly fought in the Indian Wars. Six years and counting, no one had deleted Sam. In fact, when he Google searched Sam, he discovered that some researcher had used the Indian Wars section pretty much unedited.

"Anyway, it's a greeting to the day. Done in summer to celebrate the season," Em said. "Starts before dawn, and afterward, the Mapps are having a party. There's going to be a handgame."

"A ball game? Softball?"

"No, it's sort of like a song slash hiding a bone slash guessing game."

Nick waited for Em to explain. But for once, Em didn't have all the facts.

"Hide the bone," she said.

"Excuse me, Ma'am?" Nick asked, feeling the smile pull his face even as he tried not to because Em was blushing. Flaming really, a bright red from chin up.

"Okay, that sounded bad."

"Not so much," he said, his tease light as air.

Em took in a breath. "I don't really know. We'll find out. But guess what Wanda

told me is on the menu?"

Nick tried to conjure forth Native American food. Nothing in his mind but corn, dried buffalo meat, and acorn patties. What was Native American food, exactly? What were those three sisters? Beans? Pumpkin? Corn? But that was back East. What did they have here in Northern Nevada? Pine nuts? Sage leaves? Sumac? Or was that from Mexico?

"I have no damn idea," he said.

"Prairie dog."

"Seriously?"

Em smiled, shook her head. "No lie."

"Is that even legal?"

She made a face as if tasting the little animal. "I really hope not. They're so cute."

"I bet this shindig isn't happening on a Tuesday," Nick said.

"Saturday," she said.

Saturday was Hamm's day off. It would be almost impossible to cut a Saturday-for-Tuesday deal, even though Hamm was easy-going.

"I'd have to work some magic to get the day off," he said. "And if there's a fire, it won't matter what day it is. But I can try."

"Good," Em said, scanning the mine once more. "Well, I guess that's all there is to see here for now."

She smiled again, even in the face of ecological disaster. She had no idea, not a clue, and he could never tell her the sappy and ridiculous truth that when she was around, there would always be more to see.

He couldn't stop watching.

Chapter Thirty-One

Northern Nevada
Mapp Ranch
August 2012

On the Wednesday afternoon before the party, Wanda sat at the kitchen table with Tanya, going over the shopping list and adding last-minute items. After dropping his mother off at the house, Dwayne had taken Stanley out, "For a drive."

Drive? Some drive. Stanley didn't push out of the house quick like that for a drive or anything, really. More like big talk with a whiskey chaser. Though Wanda worried about what the two of them were doing out in the world of trouble, it was a blessed relief to have the television off, the house calm, just her and Tanya doing the ordinary work of planning a party.

"Plastic cups?" Wanda asked.

"Haven't you seen that movie about red plastic cups?" Tanya asked. "They waste more energy to make than anything!"

"Don't tear, though," Wanda said. "Can reuse them."

Tanya shook her head, her pencil tip on the word plastic, and then the phone rang.

"Got to take this." She scooched her chair back and walked out onto the porch, the long cord trailing behind her. From the tense way Tanya held herself, it was likely Birdie on the other end.

Tanya put a hand on her hip. Her voice got louder and then even a little louder still, Wanda making out, "You know what's going on around here! And now Dwayne's into something." Then there was a long pause as Birdie seemed to fill her daughter's ears with the right words, Tanya scrunched up again—free arm wrapped around her chest—listening, head cocked. That's how that relationship was. Anger, acceptance, lull. Then it started all over again.

Wanda pulled Tanya's list close and read her niece's clear script. Mostly, they needed plates and forks and their own baked offerings for the table. They had the napkins and the red-checked tablecloths. There would not be a shortage of food, folks driving up to unload truck beds and trunks. For instance, at every potlatch, party, and powwow, Violet Tenday made rock chuck, gutting a half-dozen pesky prairie dogs, wrapping them in foil, and putting them in an oven for a few hours. The end product was greasy and smelly (and in no way on Tanya's approved clinic diet), but Wanda had to admit, soft and tasty. But the process was unbearable. Violet would come with her bag of carcasses and take over the kitchen, disgusting Wanda with the smell of singed fur and the stink of the cooking meat.

"Good lord!" Birdie would say every time, if Birdie were there. "We don't have to eat those poor creatures anymore! Hasn't Vio heard of buying three pounds of hamburger?"

"It's cultural," Wanda would say with a straight face. "Our traditional meat."

"But the smell. It's a charnel house in here. Can't she cook it outside?"

"At least we're not hunting walrus."

"*Ataa*," Birdie would mumble, shaking her head. "Some traditions can take a backseat. Most everyone I know would rather eat chicken." She'd cast a stern eye at Wanda. "And don't you tell me prairie dog tastes like chicken. In this case, the old saying is wrong!"

But like Birdie, Wanda preferred other traditional dishes: barbecued venison or buffalo, corn balls, fry bread, smoked-bucket chicken, sweet potato bread, and chokecherry pudding. For the party that she and Tanya were planning, Wanda was in charge of the fry bread dough, made the way her mother used to, one of Margaret's recipes that truly lived on, all the way to Wanda's hands.

Wanda glanced out toward the porch, but Tanya had walked to the far edge. Craning her neck a little, Wanda saw her niece pacing back and forth, Ruby following behind her wagging her tail and sniffing the boards, as if Tanya's footprints were clues. Probably, they were. Probably, Birdie was giving Tanya the real news, the true update on the legal battle. Wanda pushed herself up from the table and walked over to the cupboards. She opened the one containing all the baking goods and peered in. After Birdie left, Tanya had stocked them up, the shelves full of flour, salt, walnuts, corn meal, bran. Bran? Wanda shook her head and pushed aside the bag that would likely be found unopened after all the Mapps had died. Her hand circled around the red can of baking powder. Not the brand with the Indian on it, but the other that sported a tiny US flag on the side. Wanda pulled out the can, her shoulder creaking as she did. She shook it a bit, but nothing moved inside. Full.

Strange that baking powder could be so political.

"Stanley Kubrick knew it was offensive," Birdie told her a few years back as Wanda measured out flour, baking powder, and salt for pancake batter.

"Who? And what?"

"The movie director. He put Calumet baking powder cans in his movie The Shining. He was sending a message."

"To who?" Wanda stirred her batter.

"Us. The indigenous. And the world."

"Why that movie? The one with the ghosts and the strange little boy?" Wanda asked. She and Stanley had watched it on television. It was so scary, Wanda had held up a pillow to block the TV screen and then gone to bed early. With that film, Stanley was lucky he couldn't see much.

"Using his art to let us know his politics."

"Big message on a little can?"

"I won't buy it," Birdie said.

"This is trouble then for our breakfast. One brand comes in a white can," Wanda said. "You know what that means."

Birdie shook her head.

"Supremacists," Wanda said. "And that other red can?"

"What?"

"For sure it's communist."

"Oh, hush yourself," Birdie had said. "Just make the pancakes, okay?"

Seemed as though Tanya had settled on the inoffensive red can brand, too, and it was a good thing. Wanda could make thirty batches of fry-bread or more with this jumbo-sized one, and they had more than enough all-purpose flour and salt. She just needed to write vegetable oil on the list—probably a gallon or maybe two. Thank goodness fry bread was traditional or Tanya would for sure put it on her forbidden list.

Wanda walked back to the table and wrote down oil on the list. Outside, she heard the roar of Dwayne's truck rumbling over the dirt and gravel. Wanda looked up from her list and out the window. There they were, the two of them, sitting in the cab, Dwayne and Stanley talking quietly.

Tanya walked over, the phone at her ear, but then she must have hung up because she was all hands and voice as she talked to Dwayne through the open window. Dwayne argued back, and Stanley opened his door, one leg and then two swinging out of the truck.

Wanda went back to her list. Tallow. She wanted tallow, using it the way her mother had, frying the bread in the fat rendered from their own butchered beef. There was nothing like that crisp, delicate golden brown. Wanda closed her eyes, and saw her mother right in front of her, her apron tied in a bow over her blue flowered dress, her arms moving as she rolled out the round of dough and then put them in a cast iron skillet. So many years later, Wanda could still smell the crackling softness of the bread, still see her mother turn from the stove and bring her the first piece out of the pan, the bread hot and puffy and rich. Birdie was next, but Stanley was too small to eat one by himself. He banged his cup against the table and hollered, so while her mother worked, Wanda would scoot over and feed him bits, Stanley taking in the bread like a baby bird would take in seed.

Wanda sighed and studied the list. Oil and flour and red plastic cups, those evil stars of their own horror movie. Some folks wouldn't be here, those who accompanied Birdie to DC. But Wanda could count on the rest to bring everything else. Wanda laughed a little, surprised at the tingle of excitement about the get-together. And just like that, she thought of Jake Tenday by the barn door. If only life could be in the time before the wrong thing happened, in the spot before everything went one way for good and forever.

Jake had moved off reservation when he was eighteen. Wanda heard tell about him, first in Reno and then in Las Vegas, both places better to leave than to visit. But then he made his way to the left edge of the continent. Before he enlisted in the army, he'd been living somewhere in Washington State. What would he be doing if she'd said the right thing all those years ago? Would he be out at the truck, arguing with Dwayne about who should be finishing up the repairs on the barn or working on those fence posts? Would he grumble as he walked back in, saying, "Kids these days."

Or maybe sitting out on the porch just watching Tanya work her magic, Dwayne shaking his head but heading to the barn.

Tanya came back in the house with Stanley, who avoided Wanda and stomped to the bathroom.

"What were they up to?"

"Not enough of what needs doing," Tanya said. Wanda watched her trying to rearrange her face back to party planning mode but it wasn't working.

"What's wrong?" Wanda asked. "Not Dwayne?"

Tanya sat down, and Wanda reached out to touch her niece's hand.

"Oh, Auntie," she said, the word throwing Wanda back to the days she carried Tanya in the crook of one arm as she walked through the barn introducing the toddler to the horses.

With those words, the entire ranch disappeared, pulled out from under Wanda's feet like a huge rug.

"We lost?"

Tanya shook her head. "Oh, no. Not yet. At least, it's just that Birdie and her group withdrew our claims for individual occupancy rights."

As Wanda considered the phrase and then the words separately, she saw the ancient ones running on land that wasn't theirs but all of theirs, tribal, communal, shared. So Birdie and her group said no, this ranch wasn't Mapp Ranch per se but Tribal lands.

With that move, the government would believe Birdie had given up. Abdicated. The black crow judges would think she was signing away the land. Those Supreme Court Justices would think Birdie was saying, "None of it belongs to us individually. So how can we fight for what's not ours at all?"

But there were layers of ownership, an order, even when something couldn't really be owned. Like with Tanya, for instance. She was first Birdie's and then Wanda's and then probably Stanley's, too, especially the Stanley of thirty years ago, the one who taught Tanya to ride a horse and drive a truck. Maybe Dwayne thought he was first in the Tanya-ownership line, but he wasn't. To be fair, she was also William Beechey's, though he'd done nothing to stake a claim in her heart. Truth was, Tanya was foremost her own self, owned by no one. Just like this ranch, this whole state. The land might not be Mapp or tribal, but it was more theirs than the government's.

"She says claiming we own this land makes us just as bad as the government."

Exactly, Wanda thought. *Yes.*

But Tanya didn't understand, all her emotions playing out on her face—irritation, anger, frustration, sadness.

"So far, though," Tanya said. "Birdie says no one on the other side has proposed an honest solution."

Mom, Wanda thought. Say Mom.

"Your mom's not coming home soon," Wanda said, using the word herself.

Tanya shrugged and then said, "No."

"I guess she'll miss Vio's rock chuck." Wanda laughed. "I'll save some for her in the fridge. Smell good and strong when she gets home."

Tanya looked up, started to laugh, but then she stilled, her eyes welling, and she started to cry, putting her forehead down on the table.

"Oh, baby," Wanda said, moving her chair closer and rubbing Tanya's back. Wanda wanted the ranch to always be Mapp Ranch. Communal and theirs. Tribal but Mapp through and through. But more than anything, she wanted Tanya to be happy. To not give up when there still was a chance that Birdie would find a way. Wanda was almost 85 years old, and she was still here, wasn't she? "It's all going to work out. Or it's not. But one thing's for sure, worrying won't change a thing. So have your cry, but then let's make a party here, okay? Let's buy us some red cups."

Chapter Thirty-Two

Northern Nevada
Palisades
July 2012

"Goddamn moon," Nick yelled from his sleeping bag. "Turn the fucking thing off."

"Jesus, Evergreen." Mac was wrapped tight in his own bag next to Nick. "No one swears at the fucking moon."

"The moon is our friend," Lehman said in a mock teacher voice. "Didn't your parents read you that book?"

"Read if it's so fucking bright. Just shut it."

"Goodnight, Evergreen. Goodnight, Mac," Wicks minced, clearly juiced on some stashed flask of Jack. "Goodnight asswipes."

"'Your mother was a hamster and your father smelled of elderberries,'" Lehman began, trying to encourage someone to join him in Monty Python quotes. Last summer, Nick learned, the crew had almost made it through the entire Holy Grail movie script during a single fire.

"Everyone shut the hell up," Hamm said.

"'I fart in your general direction,'" Lehman continued.

They lay on cold dry ground, the scorched earth just yards away, burnt, wetted, doused with retardant, and then beaten to death with Pulaskis and combis until nothing was burning. A bug couldn't have survived this fire. The hill was silent and totally dead. But here they were, on patrol, lest some tiny spark burn the last sagebrush. From Nick's sleeping bag view, the ground looked eerie, grey, and flat. But underneath him, Nick imagined he could feel the drumbeat of fire, a pulse of heat just under the surface.

The Devlin crews had been at the Palisades Fire for two days, the section of the fire they'd been on contained. Here on the burned earth, cell phones spiked out, Nick was pretty sure he would miss the Mapps' party. Mister Fabulous Moon wasn't going to let him forget that. But he wanted to see what this Sunrise Ceremony was all about. And Wanda Mapp was trying to tell him something. Not that he would ever figure out what she meant. Mostly, though, it was about Em. Since the moment she dropped him off at the station after their mine visit, she was constantly in his thoughts, behind his eyelids, on either side of him, whispering something funny into his ears. He thought about her hair, her fingers, her laugh, her lips.

The more he thought about Em, the more he thought about not thinking about Megan. Then he'd think about her anyway, the things he'd been trying to avoid, the big one the fact that she wouldn't meet him—literally—half way. By the time he got back, they wouldn't have seen each other for five months. Maybe more.

And instead of imagining a happy Megan running into his arms when he opened the Seattle apartment door, he thought of her hunched over her studies, work he didn't understand and would never be invited into.

The fire, at least, had kept him from thinking much about either of them. The day before the fire, there'd been lightning strikes near Palisades, a ghost town about twenty miles southwest of Devlin, and a couple caught. When the call came, they'd driven two engines out to the staging area. Thompson went to confer with the incident commander, but even Nick could tell there was no way they could get two engines up through the hills, the terrain unpaved, rough, uneven. But a large ranch with several structures was threatened, and from the way Thompson stood as he listened to the IC, arms crossed, face impassive except for quick, curt nods, Nick knew they weren't going to get kicked loose.

But instead of driving into the fire, they waited around for hours. Finally, something. A helitack crew's saw broke, and they needed able bodies to do what the blade could not. The Devlin crew gave their flight weights to the pilots—body and packs—and they were briefed, loaded up, and flown into the hills.

Dropped off at the helispot near the fireline, they put on their packs and hiked up and worked hot spots on the back side of the fire, cutting brush. The choppers dropped water, and the crew cut line, working until their shirts were soggy. They ate M.R.E.s for lunch on the ridge, and then patrolled the line until dark. The moon hadn't risen yet, so they had hiked back toward the drop spot with their headlamps lit.

It was a long walk. Nick chanced to turn back as they headed down from the ridge. Far off on the horizon, the still burning section of the fire was a beacon, the flames reflecting off the remaining storm clouds, the sky glowing orange, gold, crimson, the world lit up like a hellish miracle or the most beautiful sunrise ever.

"It's sorta beautiful," Mac had said.

"It's fucking fire," Hamm said. "Come on. The GPS says this way."

"The damn thing's broken." Wicks preferred maps, and he unfolded his, his headlight shining on it, one big hand holding the paper flat.

In the lamp light and from the corner of his eye, Nick saw a slippery flick and twitch. "Rattler."

Thompson must have seen the S of the serpent tail, too, and in a second, in a flash of Thompson's shovel, the snake was headless.

"Jesus," Mac said. "Good peripheral vision."

Nick thought of his father and all their hikes in the hills, the way Jess had shown him to watch and listen as they moved through the grass, a snake always possible.

"This way," Hamm said. Wicks shrugged and folded up his map.

So now at the drop spot, they huddled like sad caterpillars and waited for morning and their ride back to the staging area. Their part in the Palisades Fire was all over except for the damn shouting, which is what Wicks was doing now. Or it was more like yodeling out into the great expanse of the night sky, the moon shining at them with its wide, ugly eye. Nick tried to get comfortable in his bag.

"Do you think we'll get out of here tomorrow?" Mac asked.

"I goddamn hope so," Nick said. Hamm had even agreed to the frowned-upon day-off swap, actually wanting a Tuesday off in order to run "important" errands in Kellogg City (Nick read errands as "Gloria's Dancing and Diddling" and/or "Downtown Casino"), willing to argue with Jarchow if they were caught. "Seems like it's almost controlled."

"I thought this was gonna be a big one." Mac sounded forlorn. "Five-day show. Days, maybe. Weeks."

"Dude," Nick said. "Think about the experience. You got to work with a helitack crew. We wouldn't have even been asked if a saw hadn't broken."

"Yeah, I guess," Mac said. "It was cool."

Nick wanted to tell Mac to stop wishing for something bigger, more intense. But Nick had wishes, too. Here he was on a mountain, wishing for someone he didn't have. Em was like this moon above them, looking at him full on, never turning away. She wanted more of everything around her, asking one question after another. Of course, that was her job, but Nick was pretty sure that not all journalists roamed the planet asking, *Why? What? Who? How?* Em's eyes wide and focused, interested, completely opposite from Megan, the dark side, the one turned away, hiding herself, unseen, unseeable.

Just like Mac, Nick wanted more, and the thing they both wanted was fire, literal or otherwise.

"Go to sleep," Nick said.

"I'm not dead . . . I'm getting better . . . I feel fine. . . I feel happy,'" Lehamn called out.

"Good night, Moon," Wicks trilled in his fabulous falsetto.

"'Bring me a shrubbery!'" Lehman sang.

Camelot, Nick thought, staring into the moon's bright eye. *'Tis a silly place.*

"Good night!"

This time, Nick picked up Em, driving into Kellogg City at five am, running lightly up her Willow Street apartment stairs. The world was morning silent, neighbors' apartments dark. His breath was a small white flume as he huffed up onto the landing. At his quick rap, Em opened her door. He blinked into the hallway light blazing behind her.

"Thought you might oversleep," she said.

The possibility of sleeping into next week had crossed Nick's mind. They'd made it home late the night before, all of them dirty and exhausted. His sooty, smoky clothing strewn on the carpet around him, he'd texted Megan, starting and then erasing it three times, the lie and the autocorrect making even one sentence impossible. Finally he came up with:

Going to Kellogg City tomorrow

A half-truth, incomplete. A lie.

She wrote back:

Are you going to The Shoe ☺

Ha ha! he typed.

But Megan would understand his going to The Horseshoe Club to watch strippers more than she would his hanging out with Em.

After their texting was over, Nick had taken an industrial-strength shower and then set his phone, clock, and computer alarms, all of which bounced him out of bed at four-fifteen. He didn't mention that he probably really woke up about a mile into his drive here.

"Good news for me you didn't sleep in!" Em handed him a couple of laden bags and locked the door behind her.

"You're pretty awake for this hour."

"I love the morning," Em said as they started down the stairs. "Everything good is still possible."

They loaded the car with her things and then headed down toward Highway 306 to the Crescent Valley to meet up at the Mapp Ranch, a big group headed to Mount Aurora for a six am Sunrise Ceremony. He was jittery, either from lack of sleep or Em's proximity, his hands tight on the wheel, his face frozen in a smile he felt all the way in his toes.

Em, however, seemed completely herself—at least as far as Nick could tell from having been with her all of four times. She smelled sweet and sugary and warm like one of Nick's Grandma Flo's sugar cookies. She was dressed in black layers she would likely later peel—leggings, a tunic, a sweater, a coat—as well as sturdy black boots and wool hat, but her neck was wrapped in a brilliant magenta scarf.

"How can you be wearing only a t-shirt?" she asked, as if reading his mind about her attire. "Aren't you freezing?"

"We're in Nevada?" Nick's neck prickled with a wash of gooseflesh. "It's summer?"

"Not until eight am. Until then, it's snow season. But fear not. I have something perfect for you. Might not quite fit," she said, holding up a yellow sweater with stitched rosebuds at the collar.

"Cute little number. But I'm good." Nick knew if he were cold for about fifteen minutes in the Nevada summer morning that would be the extent of it.

"Don't you like it?"

"Very fetching," he said, feeling Em's swift glance.

"Fetching," she said. "That might be my favorite word of all time."

She put away the sweater and began to tell him about the Sunrise Ceremony, but he was caught up in the glow in his chest: her favorite word of all time! Nick knew it was stupid, but he felt beyond pleased.

". . . And then the sun comes up, and it's over," she was saying. "Then we all head back to the Mapps' place for the party."

Nick nodded, gripped the wheel that didn't need more gripping. Suddenly, he was pushed back to high school, just before he'd hooked up with Claire, feeling anxious, unsure. Often he sat in math or English and wished he could transport himself back home to the family room couch, the television on The History Channel, his mother talking in the background as she made a meal, one of his favorites, maybe spaghetti and meatballs. Then senior year, finally with Claire, he'd been a part of a couple, someone, somebody, known. Of course there was the bobble of trying to break up with Claire over and over again his entire college freshman year, but then there was Megan.

"Have you ever been to a Sunrise Ceremony?"

"Ha," Em laughed, punching him lightly on his shoulder. "Me? Boston to the core? More like I've been to a tea party. So this is totally going on the blog."

Nick nodded, turned onto the freeway onramp, the gear in the back clinking and jingling. Em looked back at the pile stashed behind them.

"What is making that noise?"

"What?" Nick wished he'd wrapped a blanket around it.

"This," she said, leaning even further into the back seat. "A small submarine? An incendiary device?"

"The opposite," he said. "A portable pump. Basically, a fire extinguisher."

Em snorted. "Really?"

"Well, yes."

"Hardly a traditional item."

"This isn't exactly a traditional outing." Nick prickled with embarrassment. When Jarchow questioned where Nick was going, he pitched his type of fit—raised eyebrows and wide eyes, wider stance—and said the only way he wouldn't follow him to the mountain in an engine was if Nick brought along the pump. Nick knew he'd feel like an asshole carrying it up a hill—the damn thing clanking as he lugged it—but at least the celebrants wouldn't have the BLM swarming all over the mountain. "Lighting an ill-advised fire on the top of a dry hill may be traditional but maybe not-so-smart in these conditions."

"It's tribal land," Em said. "Totally legal."

"Thought I'd be prepared."

"Were you a Boy Scout?"

"For one year. Cub Scouts. The little car my father and I made for the Pinewood Derby lost, and I quit."

"Fit of pique."

"More like fit of pine," he said.

"Ha!" Em smiled and righted herself in her seat. "It makes sense. You invite a firefighter to a fire. What else would he bring? Not a potato salad."

"I hate potato salad," he said.

"It's the mayo, isn't it? Me, too. Disgusting stuff. Sort of obscene, don't you think? White and blobby and full of fat."

Nick laughed, but he felt something else inside him, and it wasn't the thrum of nerves Em brought out in him. As they drove deep into the dark morning—talking and laughing, he tried to figure it out. What else was in the back seat with the green salad and the pump? Was it this thing between him and Em? Or the fact of his guilt from lying to Megan about where he was going and with whom? Something else? The oddness of the unfamiliar ceremony on the dark mountain? The threat of being other, different? Growing up, he'd fended off the Mexican cuts and slices from his friends. But in the Crescent Valley, he was the power, the oppressor. The BLM and "white," at least as far as the celebrants would be concerned.

As they headed up into the mountains, he felt the same way he had at fire-camp. His body tingled as Chris lit the flame, his breath fast and tight as the fire broke loose and free.

So dangerous.

So exciting.

"Are you ready?" a beautiful woman asked Em as they walked toward the Mapps' ranch house. She stood on the steps under a porch light, dressed in jeans and thick fleece layers, a blanket thrown over her shoulders, scruffy old Ruby nearby wagging her tail. The woman reminded Nick of his father's family, specifically the clutch of glimmering Mexico City cousins—eight sisters with shiny red fingernails and waxed upper lips.

"I have no idea," Em said. "But we come bearing supplies and food. Tanya, this is Nick Delgado. Nick, Tanya is Wanda's niece."

Even in the weak yellow light, Tanya's black hair and eyes shone. When she smiled at Em, Nick saw her resemblance to Wanda. It was more than her nose and lips and cheekbones but also Wanda's flicker of a laugh floating across her face.

Tanya asked. "You're the firefighter?"

Nick nodded, shaking Tanya's hand, which was strong and hard. He was fumbling for words when Em said, "And he has the fire extinguisher to prove it."

"Really?" Tanya's eyes lit up. "No kidding?"

"Better safe than sorry," Nick said. "Just be thankful I didn't bring the engine."

"Or his bucket!" Em said. "That means helmet, by the way. I'm becoming fluent."

"Don't make me go back for both," Nick said, pointing back toward Devlin's direction.

Both the women laughed, and Nick felt himself relax.

"Smart move, really," Tanya said. "We're lighting up a big fire. Anyway, my aunt will be happy to see you. She wanted you to come. Imagine that. A tiny soft spot for the BLM. Who knew?"

They turned when the screen door banged closed, and there was Wanda and a slightly bent-over old man holding onto her arm. His gaze was focused on the porch as they creaked across the porch, his balding head pale with sprouts of hair. He was only a bit taller than Wanda, but seemed shrunken, as if from inside, something strong pulling what was left of him back inside. The famous Stanley Mapp.

Wanda walked out slowly onto the porch and looked at the crowd. Stanley wasn't smiling much, and if Nick hadn't known he was blind, he'd probably think the old guy was ignoring everyone.

Even with his hard gaze, it was impossible to imagine this was the man who doused himself with gasoline and threatened to light himself into a human torch. This guy was the rebellious activist? But then what was an aging activist supposed to look like? Maybe just like an aging rock star. Both, if they were lucky, managed to get old.

Wanda smiled that smile Nick remembered from the morning she'd fixed his truck, the one that indicated she knew the world was pretty damn ridiculous, but she wanted to see what would happen anyway.

"Mr. Firefighter." She let go of her brother and moved toward him. "You're here to welcome the sun? Or maybe something else?"

"I always welcome it." Nick ignored her last question, hoping she'd steer away from barn door discussions for now. "Except when it's 110 degrees with no relative humidity."

Again, the women laughed, and he felt himself relax even more.

"For sure," Wanda said, turning slightly to look at the old man. "This is my brother Stanley."

Stanley nodded, shrugged, and started to blink.

"Hi." Em stepped closer. "I've heard so much about you, Mr. Mapp. I sure would love to interview you sometime."

Stanley could clearly still smell even if he couldn't hear or see. In the bubble of Em's attention, he started to smile open-mouthed, as if breathing in her sugar sweetness. Nick couldn't blame him.

"Wanda read me your article," Stanley said. "For sure, I know a story or two about the old days."

Nick heard the steps before he saw the person, but then out of the gloam came a tall lanky dude, his long braid thumping against his back with each strong stride. Nick stilled, remembering him, the guy from the protest at District, the one with the treaty sign. The same guy who was on the horse the day he and Jarchow came to talk to Wanda. He was lightly built but looked strong, as if he threw bales around and built barns daily. The kind of guy Nick would prefer not to meet in a downtown Kellogg City alley after an argument and a drink or two. Even now, Nick noticed the guy's clenched fists.

They stared at each other for a beat, but then the guy turned toward Tanya. "Let's go." He gave Em a quick and slightly aggressive once over, his eyes heated, dismissive, interested. "I've got the truck running."

"This is my son Dwayne—" Tanya began, but then Dwayne turned and headed back toward the cars. "He's our ride. We'll see you up on Mount Aurora. Follow us."

Tanya called out to the rest of the assembled group, all of whom started to drift back to their vehicles. Wanda said, "Brother?" and then she, Stanley, and Ruby followed Tanya, walking carefully to a rattletrap truck, the dude with the braid now behind the wheel glaring at Em.

But Em didn't seem to notice. Or maybe she didn't care. Maybe after her year in Kellogg City, she was getting used to such looks. Instead, she took Nick's arm, squeezing it. "You okay?"

Nick rubbed his face. Despite his shower, he still felt the fire on his skin. Soot and oil and wind. "I have no idea."

Nick nodded as he opened his car door for her. It was an experience to be out in the middle of the dry, dusty Nevada nowhere with people he didn't know, off to possibly burn down the world as the sun crept up the sky. He had no idea what was going to happen next. But as he got in the car, turned it on and blasted the heater, he hoped it was nothing bad.

Chapter Thirty-Three

Northern Nevada
Mount Aurora
August 2012

Dwayne wanted to kick someone's ass. He wasn't sure whose, but probably it was the BLM dude's, the one Dwayne had stared down the day of the protest. Guy had been all crouched up in his fire truck, hiding. Guy had been lucky Len had told them hands off. No broken windshields. No fighting. But why had Aunt Wanda asked him to the ceremony? When Dwayne saw him, he could feel his fist against the guy's face, imagining he was some kind of Indian wannabe. Problem was, he actually looked fucking Indian or something. Mexican maybe. Or at least part. But he brought Miss Starlight Wonder, the white-as-hell reporter Dwayne had seen at the council meeting. She was so pale, just looking at her reminded him of milk or cheese, things heavy and awful in the mouth. Government cheese, the kind his mother used to bring home when he was a kid. Heavy, like a brick. And he'd eaten it until his mother decided Indians were lactose intolerant.

But still. The girl. Big white cheese. He wanted to get close enough to scare her, stare his dark anger into her pale eyes. But getting close was dangerous. She was so shiny. So glittery, even in the dark. He might want to reach out and touch.

Fucking white people. First they tried to stop Indian ceremonies. Then they wanted to join in. The only damn time they told the truth or made sense was when they kept their mouths shut.

"*Ataa*," his Aunt Wanda said. "Slow down for sure. There's cows out here."

Dwayne nodded, listened to his mother, aunt and uncle talk about the ceremony and the party, all of it for nothing. No one could stop the mine now.

His mother pointed at the humps of landscape outside the window, gray, unclear mounds of earth and buildings. In his rearview mirror, Dwayne searched out Len's car in the darkness. He wished his friend was with him now, able to hear his family's hope even when there wasn't any. His mother was one hundred percent all the time certain education and a good diet would fix everything. Aunt Wanda thought that hard work was the answer. That or a good ride on a fine horse. Uncle Stanley? He was deep, hidden behind TV shows and blindness. But Dwayne knew what Stanley thought. Only Stanley agreed with him and Len.

"*Ataa*, Dwayne," Wanda said from the back seat. "There's old people behind you in worse cars than this."

Dwayne sighed, lifted his foot a bit off the accelerator and sat back against his seat. Right now, he needed more than Ruby leaning next to him, panting in his ear and smelling of dirt and dog chow. He needed courage. This ceremony had no use, not in the world Dwayne lived in. That's what Len said. It was time for action. Time to get people to stop and pay attention. Only his grandmother would really understand. She totally got it, but she wasn't here. Dwayne was the only one with any sense.

He glanced back again for Len, but all he could see was a line of headlights following behind the truck, a bright dot-to-dot of friends, neighbors, tribal members, even that fat girl his mother went on and on about. "She's lost twenty pounds! She's working out at the gym!" But it didn't matter who they were. They were all fucked.

"Crank the heat," his mother said, but she didn't wait for him to do it himself. She reached over all irritated and fiddled with the controls. A waft of hot stale doggy air filled the truck cabin.

Dwayne shook his head and kept driving. Len had got him into Russell Means, a righteous Indian that Grandma Birdie actually knew from the 70s from all sorts of protests, the incident at Wounded Knee for one. Means was one badass motherfucker. Means saw right through this land ownership bullshit and said it right: *If all human beings were taken away, life on earth would flourish.*

People were like rats, eating everything, over-breeding, and shitting on the entire planet. But which rats should go?

His grandmother wasn't around to give him her good advice. Dwayne wasn't even sure he'd have known how to ask. Since he was a kid, Birdie had scared the shit out of him, always talking at him, telling him what to do. But now he needed her to lay something on him. She was like an oracle, a chief, a warrior, but somehow protected, isolated, alone. When he was little, Dwayne learned to walk as silent as mice, not wanting to stir her to a lecture about tribal land trusts or broken treaties. He was screwed if she started in on The Trail of Tears. He wished he'd paid attention. Now something had to be done. Russell Means knew that. Len knew that. Stanley used to know it as well, ready to give up his whole body for Mother Earth.

"What's got into you," his mother complained. "You're not late for anything. Give the road a rest."

Again, Dwayne lifted his foot off the accelerator, glancing at the speedometer. He'd been going almost fifty on a two-track dirt road. He sighed and looked in his rearview mirror one more time. Instead of seeing Len barreling behind him in his Ford truck, he caught Stanley's blind gaze. Stanley knew Dwayne was watching him, and he watched back. His uncle raised his chin, sat up straight, gave a slight nod.

His mother was wrong, though. They were probably too late to do anything to fix their lives. But they wouldn't go down without making a mess. People would remember that.

Chapter Thirty-Four

Northern Nevada
Mount Aurora
August 2012

If he stopped listening, Nick could imagine he was camping with his father in the Sierra foothills or on Mount Diablo, a fire in a rock ring wicking up into a dark sky, crickets and deer in the trees behind them, the earth cool under his feet. But there were no camping chairs, hot chocolate, or burned hot dogs on a stick. No tents or what Nick would call regular campers around him. And he couldn't imagine away the rhythmic beat of the drums and the chanting, a truly tribal sound, a one-two beat of stick banging on stretched leather. How he knew anything was tribal, he wasn't sure, but nothing in his life had sounded as indigenous as the ongoing chant filling the morning sky.

Nick couldn't make out a word. The shaman or medicine man or chief or whatever sang a continuous song, his voice alternating between deep and throaty and then wavery and high. He was a small man, bent over his song, his face glowing in the firelight. At certain points, he'd cry out and hold up his hands, sort of like a priest. All his childhood, Nick had been forced into attending epic Catholic masses with his father's family, mostly his grandparents. But not one had gone on this long.

On the way up the mountain, Em had told him that before 1978 and the American Indian Religious Freedom Act, it was illegal for American Indians to practice their religions. But how could this ceremony be illegal? All they were doing was standing in a huge circle around a big fire holding hands. On one side, he was pretty much in heaven, Em's small hand in his. He pressed his palm against hers, memorizing the feel and heat of her skin, as if her hand were the key to the rest of her. Then the thought of the rest made him take in breath.

But his other hand kept him from going too far away from the ceremony. On his left side, he was a kind of purgatory, his hand deep in the sandpaper mitt of a wizened woman. She'd smiled at Nick at the start of the ceremony, pushed her way close, and latched on. Now, she grabbed hard on his fingers, chanted, and pulled Nick forward and backward as she swung her arms. Nick held on tight to the woman, too, wanting to be a part of the ceremony, even if he didn't really understand what was going on.

Actually, since the ceremony started, he'd gone with it all, ignoring the glares from Tanya's son Dwayne and his tall friend. Dwayne stood straight, almost rigid, his mouth firm, his hands clasped with others, but his arms not swinging much. Every so often, he cut Nick glances so sharp they hurt even in the dusky light. Nick wanted to break the ring and walk over, and say, "Listen, I'm Mexican," or, "You're not the only oppressed one around here," or "Lighten up, dude." But to present as Mexican would leave Em all white and out in the cold by herself. And truthfully, how Mexican was he anyway?

Now as the celebrants moved up and back, swinging their arms, Dwayne and his friend were in his view and then not, in his view and then not. As the sun pushed against the edge of the horizon, the ceremony seemed to be intensifying, the old man keening, the people moving closer to the fire, some of them shouting out a word or two. And the fire kicked up flames two feet tall, sparks flickering like fireflies, the wood roared and hissed as it surrendered to the flame. The air warmed, the heat of the day revving up, and Nick was glad he was only wearing a t-shirt. It was going to be a scorcher, dry, no dew on the ground.

"It's coming!" Em said. "Look, Nick!"

As he turned to glance east, from the corner of his eye he saw something else, not the sun, but something bright hurl toward the fire—or maybe it flew out of the stone ring toward the circle of celebrants. But that was impossible; no one was scattering to get away from it. Someone must have thrown something into the ring. A flash of arm and object. An arc glimmering and then gone. The group swung closer to the ring, the chanting louder, the flashing, bright thing consumed in the fire. The sun burst orange-yellow all around them, fully welcomed. Now they moved back out into the wider circle, and there were another sounds, murmurs, yells, a break in the chanting.

"*Ataa!*" someone called out.

"Oh, shit," someone else yelled.

"What's happening?" Em asked.

Nick knew in his legs and arms before he knew in his brain. He knew in his heart before even his eyes saw the glow that didn't come from the sun bursting over the horizon. This was the glow from Idaho and I-80 and Palisades. Fire.

He dropped the hands that held him and ran to the spot he'd stowed the pump after the humiliation of dragging it half a mile uphill. The crowd shouted, but he focused on the heft of the machine as he yanked it toward the fire, which was spreading fast and wide around the ring. Already, it cupped a small orange palm over the hill, heat licking his face.

He glanced at his hands. No gloves. No Nomex. No goggles. No boots. And already, the fire was roaring, the sound he'd first heard at firecamp, the animal in the center awake and ferocious.

At the edge, in the black, Nick turned on the pump, his fingers sure on the machine. He had to stop this now. How had it grown so large already? It didn't make sense this early in the morning. But it was fire, and his hand was on the nozzle, aiming low, spraying, just as he'd been taught. Bottom up, dousing the fire at its roots, killing it before it had a chance to grow into more. Twisting up and through the brush, it was a snake uncoiling, so Nick worked the line, its shape, and then it was daylight, the sun wide open, and the fire was nothing but smoke. He emptied the pump, making sure to fully cover the former hotspot.

"Water." Nick glanced up. "We need to get some water here. Dump it where it's smoking."

Most of the group seemed frozen in surprise or fear, except for a heavy girl who pushed forward with a bottle of drinking water.

"Like here?" she asked.

Nick pointed, and she poured. Tanya followed behind her with another, and she poured, but it wasn't enough.

"Does anyone have a shovel? A rake? Or stick?"

"I brought this to stir the fire," said an old guy, holding out a small rake.

Nick nodded, took the tool, and began to pound out the line of fire. He turned the earth, blonde crisp weeds, black scorched brush. Another man came with a bottle of water, dousing the ground, and Nick kept at it, sweat on his neck, forehead. Two guys joined in next to him, digging with sticks. Four others walked the fire's perimeter, stomping on smoldering clods. After a bit, Tanya, a bit winded, handed Nick a shovel.

"Found it in the truck." She traded him for the rake, and together, they worked the soil, flipping the clods, breaking up any place where the fire could hide. Together, the rest of the group quiet on the edges of the burn, their movements became the ritual, the ceremony, the process, everyone surrounding them instead of the fire ring.

Eventually, Nick stopped digging and surveyed the burn site.

"Looks good," he said to Tanya.

She wiped her forehead with a forearm. "Think so?"

"But I've got to watch it," Nick told. He stood up straight, stretched his back, and wiped his face with the bottom of his t-shirt. "For a while at least. It could ember. Or else I need to call it in."

"God, no." Tanya waved her hands. "That's the last thing we need publicity-wise."

"Okay, but someone needs to bring me some more water. I want to saturate everything."

"I'll send Dwayne and his friends back up with a couple of barrels," she said, turning behind her, looking for Dwayne, who must have walked back to his truck without his family. "Maybe some beer, too."

"A lot, okay? Of the water, I mean. If this went up? It'd be bad. See how the wind might push it?"

He pointed to where the fire could spread, heading over and down the hills, right into the Crescent Valley and Mapp Ranch.

"That was smart," Wanda said. "You're a real firefighter, for sure."

"Thank goodness you were here," Tanya said, turning to look around. "We would have had to turn the party into an evacuation zone."

The celebrants-turned-firefighters talked at the edge of the burn, pointing to the fire ring. One made an arc with her hand, the jump that Nick had seen the fire make as well. One older man put a tremulous hand on Nick's arm and nodded as he shuffled by. The rest put down their sticks and walked away, looking back and waving. Nick almost called to them to watch for sparks when they started their cars. He raised his hand, saluting them and the fact that the hill wasn't crispy fried.

"Hard to top this," Em said to Tanya. "I'm surprised you don't want to go home and take a nap."

"About that party. Could you take Em back with you?" Nick asked. "She shouldn't miss it."

"Hello! Excuse me? I'm not going without you." Em shrugged off her sweater and unwound her scarf. "This is a story!"

"Yeah," Nick said, looking around the now hot bare hill, nothing left of the ceremony but a fire ring and a black flag of burn. "Title the story 'Hot and Dead on The Mountain.'"

Em shook her head. "No. That's not the story I was thinking about at all.'"

Wanda nodded, winking at Nick. "Come on, Ruby."

"See you later," Tanya said. "Make sure it's out, but then come on down. You don't want to miss the rock chuck."

At Nick's grimace, Tanya laughed. "So the prairie dog's out of the bag, huh? Thought we'd be able to pull one over on you."

"Remember, I'm hanging out with a journalist," Nick said. "She knows everything. Tells all."

"She tells all in the right way," Tanya said. "She's okay, that one."

She took Wanda by the arm, and the two of them and Ruby went down the hill toward the truck.

"So what can I do?" Em asked as she and surveyed the burn site. "It doesn't look bad. It's like what? A few yards wide?"

"Fire is sneaky. One minute everything's calm, then there's wind. Next thing you know, all of Oakland's on fire. Mount Aurora in this case."

He held out the rake, and she took it. "We need to turn over the soil. Break up anything burned. Clods. Clumps."

"Sounds like guys at my high school," Em said.

"Hit them hard, them. And when we get more water, we'll douse it again. Turn it over. I think it'll be fine."

"And then we can go eat rock chuck?"

"Damn straight."

They got to work, Em with the rake, Nick with a stick. The sun was hot, the ground warming, but it was still comfortable. He moved along the spot, the sound of their tools and small birds in his ears.

"So," he said finally. "High school wasn't your best time?"

Em laughed, but they both kept at their chore. "I was the journal-ism, English class, drama geek girl. Still am." She stopped and leaned on the rake. "But now I don't care if people tease me. Unless you start. I'm trapped out here."

"I'm not going to tease you," Nick said. "I would've been sitting next to you in the cafeteria. Along with the chess champ and computer nerd."

"What kind of nerd were you?" she asked.

"I was pretty much a generalist," he said. "An all-around, all-purpose nerd, with a focus on history. Actually, military history."

"I would've tapped you for a basketball player. A jock."

"Right." Nick hit at a clump of burned weeds.

"Tall, strong. Kind of good looking, too," Em said. He looked up, saw her smiling. "I would have pegged you as a cheerleader dater."

"My high school girlfriend wouldn't have even tried out."

"What about your current girlfriend?"

Nick beat at another clod, watched the dirt spatter. "Always the bookish type," he added.

They were silent for a bit, working, until Em stood up and wiped her forehead with her sleeve. "So how does it work?"

"What?"

"You and your girlfriend? Being apart. Being in really different occupations."

Nick shrugged, shook his head. "I'm not sure that it does, really. It's been confusing. Maybe I thought that by not doing anything about it, our relationship might fix itself magically."

Megan and Nick. Nick and Megan. Living together. Moving to the Bay Area together. Planning their lives together. Nick hadn't even questioned moving to Seattle until he'd landed in Devlin. Tunnel vision to the extreme. But as he slid down the tunnel toward the known future, what was he missing? Who?

What had Wanda said to him?

"I could have said 'Yes.' But I never learned how."

Had Wanda ever had the chance to meet up with that boy by the barn door, the one she was trying to tell him about?

Nick put down the stick on the burnt earth and looked at Em. Below them on the road that wound up the mountain, he could hear the hum of a truck, full of angry young men, probably, and barrels of water, hopefully. Under his and Em's feet, simmering heat, fire still possible.

He walked closer to Em, took her elbows, looking at her, into her blue eyes, seeing her *Yes*. He pulled her to him and kissed her.

Chapter Thirty-Five

Northern Nevada
Mapp Ranch
August 2012

As Wanda walked out of the ranch house door, she glanced back at the crowded kitchen. Tanya and Peach Tanver were frying up the flatbread dough Wanda had made earlier. Dozens of pieces lay hot and crispy on paper towels, the dense smell of slightly burned oil in the air. Kestrel Jackson and Ruth Eagle stood by the oven, pulling out pans of tomato-y meat sauce that folks would later ladle on the bread, making Indian tacos. On the kitchen table were tubs and tins and pans full of guests' contributions to the party fare—casseroles, beans, brownies, cookies, sliced watermelon, pasta, potato and Jell-O salads, and red-flecked bowls of sauces for the tacos and barbecued meats, the smells dense and deep and perky with vinegar.

"I'm going to check on the horses," Wanda called out. Tanya glanced up and nodded, but then went back to her task. Peach listened to Tanya's every word, standing at the ready with her tongs. The girl was short, wide, and round, her long hair cupping her body like a thick dark leaf. Peach didn't need one single bite of fry bread, Wanda thought, though she should at least know how to make it. And then, feeling uncharitable and mostly crotchety, Wanda revised, deciding everyone needed fry bread, at least once in a while.

Outside on the porch, Wanda gazed out to the assembled party-goers, folks arriving as she stood there, cars floating in on clouds of dust. People talked and laughed as they opened up and erected tents. They unfolded metal tables and covered them with red and white-checked paper tablecloths and set out huge coolers and filled them with ice. Kids started running around, looping around their families and then scattering down toward the barn and the creek, which was dry now but filled with shadows and possible treasures.

The sun skimmed the peaks, a blaze of sunflower light. All around her, the grass was a susurration of whispers, blowing in the windy whoosh of midday. Overhead, a late hawk cried; in the bitterbrush, bobcat, coyote, various vole.

Birdie need to be home for this. They would win or lose the case, but this? The happy clatter of kitchen sound behind her, Wanda gazed at the party goers. Birdie enjoyed all these people. Pulling them close, telling them what was what. But laughing and playing, too.

Something in the fields of tall dry grass beyond caught Wanda's eye, a rustling, a movement, like maybe a hunter stalking a rabbit. A dark head bobbed just under the grassline followed by three more. For a second, Wanda thought for sure it was kids, holding play spears, whooping into the wind, playing a game older than time. She thought to tell Tanya to keep the kids closer to the house. Who knew what dangers hid in the grass and under the sage? Coyote bones, rusty nails, rusted gas cans with jagged metal teeth.

But then she looked again and the would-be hunters were gone.

Wanda stared out at the ranch, feeling her arms tingle, an ache from jaw to index finger. Somebody was out there. But who?

The temperature was rising, and she wondered how Nick and Em were doing on the mountain. By now, Dwayne and his buddies should be on their way back, water delivered. The fire had only burned a couple square yards, so all the embers and such must be beaten into black dust. Nick and Em should be back soon, too. There was likely nothing close to burning on Mount Aurora but Em Donnelly's pale Irish skin.

Wanda didn't know how the fire started outside of the ring, and no one seemed to want to talk about it, much less solve that mystery. Was it just a prank gone wrong? Kestrel had brought all her grandkids. That oldest boy was trouble. Even now, he was on top of a bale of hay, teasing one of his little siblings. But a fire? No, all that one needed was a leather strop, the one her father used to mention whenever they were acting wild.

Wanda walked toward the stairs. One of Len's friends. Or Len? Though she'd tried to keep herself from watching him like a hawk, she'd not been able to keep her eyes off him. But all he'd done for the entire ceremony was stand in between Dwayne and Bebe Mudgett, chanting and looking mighty handsome and regally Indian, the portrait of a man who might actually be a good chief one day. When the flame burst wild, he'd looked as surprised as everyone else.

"Flew out of the ring" was all Tanya had to say about the fire as they drove back to the ranch.

Stanley had shrugged.

Dwayne said nothing.

By the time Wanda thought to examine Stanley for excessive blinking, he had turned toward the window.

"It flew," Peach Tanver had said, using her hand like a bird. "Or jumped."

But how? Fire wasn't lightning, though Wanda knew it could move. But there needed to be wind to give it lift, dry air to give it wings. That's not the way it was this morning, the air still and dark when the fire jumped all by itself like a fairytale frog or a myth from the old days. Fire frog wanting to burn down the mountain.

Under the porch swing, Ruby twisted on her back, legs up, snuffling in all the picnic smells, but when she saw Wanda, she grunted, righted herself, and trotted over. Wanda patted the dog's head and turned to look at Vio Tenday who Tanya had forced outside. Vio was cooking her rock chuck in a black metal barbeque her husband had driven over the night before.

"Won't taste the same at all," she'd said, and Wanda didn't have the heart to tell her that was a good thing.

But now, the waft of the dense, greasy meat slunk low and mean toward the house, as if desperate to work itself inside, no matter what.

"Come on, Ruby girl," Wanda said, taking the stairs carefully, waving to Darlene Hightower and saying hello to those she had to pass on her way to the barn. She made excuses as she walked along slowly, told everyone she'd be right back after she checked on a couple of things, directed people with blueberry pies and platters of roasted meats to the ranch house, and then stole inside the dark barn, the coolness a relief.

Six poked her head out right away, nickering Wanda over. After snorting and spraying hay with her head, Ruby turned three times and curled up in the pile. Wanda headed toward Six's stall and took out a carrot from her pocket.

"You knew this was coming, didn't you?" she asked as she snapped the carrot in two. "You heard me think the word."

Six nuzzled Wanda's palm, her nose warm and soft, her tongue and teeth taking the vegetable and crunching down, the sound of chewing awakening the other horses to their own carrot need. A goose waddled out the open door and commenced to honk at the new arrivals, more visitors slamming car doors, laughing, clanking furniture and beer bottles.

"What are we going to do?" Wanda whispered, Six nudging her for the rest of the carrot. "What's going to come of all this wrangling?"

Six didn't tell Wanda that Birdie's team would win the case or that the BLM would pack up their nosiness and leave their herds alone. Six's dark eyes didn't hold the answer to Tanya's and Dwayne's futures or let Wanda see all their happiness. Tanya finding someone to work alongside. Dwayne an education and a good woman. Both of them safe and whole for years to come. Six wasn't revealing any truths about the dry summer, how no spark would catch and hold and hurt the land.

"Come on, girl," Wanda whispered, but Six only pressed her nose closer.

She held out the carrot, and Six snuffled and chewed once again, her dark brown eyes on Wanda. How easy to fall into the easy rhythm of the horse's chews, this one, two, three four, back and forth of strong jaw. All known and expected and so much easier than anything people ever did. The other animals stomped and stirred. Bats swung in the rafters, pigeons cooed, the spiders spun their big webs. Wanda leaned against the stall, her hand on Six's short, bristly coat, feeling the big beat of the animal's heart under her palm, the pound of the muscle matching the pounding in her head.

There was some fandango by the barn door, Ruby up to something with her scratchy claws. Wanda pushed herself straight and headed toward the door. It wasn't Ruby, though, but a man pushing wide the barn door, or a shadow of a man, his body backlit, his wisps of hair lit up like sunrise.

"Wanda girl?" he asked, moving forward, his boots pushing hay.

Wanda put on her very slight but true party smile, ready to direct this person back to the house, but then something caught her. It was the smell of wood and sage and maybe a spritz of whiskey, tangy and dark like cologne. It was his voice—now going round and round in her head—deep and with the lilt of their people. Now as he came more fully into focus, she could hear the music from that night so long ago, remember the way he came to her then, right here in the very same spot.

"Jake?"

"Wanda." He walked forward, his hands in his pockets, just like the way he used to. To school, toward her. Jake.

He certainly wasn't the Jake of her childhood, dreams, or memories, the Jake she turned over in her mind like a stone in a polishing drum. He was an old man, just as she was an old woman, both of them shrunken, gray, and stooped. But in her most secret, deep insides, Wanda felt the way she had seventy years ago: expectant, hopeful, happy.

"How could you be here? I thought—"she began. "The war. In Korea?"

"Don't believe what Vio tells you," he said. "Didn't I always say that?"

"The teacher's underwear?" Wanda asked, remembering how Vio swore their elementary school teacher Miss Trebuchet wore red pantaloons. Made sense that Vio was the woman still cooking up rock chuck and swearing it was the best dish ever.

"That and everything else. So you can believe it," Jake said, closer now, his face familiar through the wrinkles and time. "You can believe in me. For sure."

Wanda reached out her hand to touch his arm. Under his shirt, she felt warmth and bone. He was here, Jake Tenday in the flesh, after all these years.

"I don't know how to believe. And I for sure didn't know then," she said finally, looking up at him. His almost-blue eyes were watering, sad like, tired but full of relief. "I was scared."

"Me, too," he said. "Don't you know I could have tried harder? I could have said the other words, the ones that would've worked."

And for a moment, Wanda was the young, ordinary, not-even-plain girl standing by the barn door waiting for the boy she had a crush on hard to talk to her. All she'd wanted those afternoons on the way home was a wink and a smile. That night, at the dance, he'd come to her, just as he was here, right now.

What should she have said then? If she'd just but nodded, followed him to join the swirling dancers, this world right now wouldn't exist. A year or two later, she might have followed Jake to Washington State. Had her own kids to take care of. Back home, who would have taken care of Stanley and Dempsey? No matter what, Birdie would always have been Birdie. But if Wanda hadn't been here when Birdie rushed home from Wounded Knee, maybe there'd have been no Tanya. No Dwayne. So this barn, this land, this ranch, might all just be scrub pine, sagebrush, and cheatgrass.

She'd hadn't given up everything for nothing. But still. Here Jake was, all over again. Wanda hadn't known what to say then. What to say now?

"Would you like to come to the party with me?" he asked, moving even closer, near enough that she could see the still-gold flecks in his eyes. "You Mapps always throw a hell of a shindig."

Wanda felt a smile on her face she'd never worn, at least not for over seventy years. Her arm tingled. Her whole body tingled. "You might have to eat some of Vio's rock chuck."

Jake tipped his head back, laughed, squeezed her hand. "For you, Wanda Mapp, anything. For you, I say yes to that."

Yes, Wanda thought, as Jake pulled her into his arms, into the embrace she'd waited for. And it was as good as she imagined. There'd been good. Better than, even. Baby Tanya in her arms. Laughing with Birdie in the bed in the early morning hours. Scratching a joyous Ruby on a warm summer porch. Riding Six through the grass, the wind blowing her hair away from her face, the sun behind her, the shadows long. Her father's strong arms throwing her up and catching her, her laughter filling the small house. Those long ago images of her mother, a feeling that was more dream than memory.

But this? Nothing like it.

She lifted her own arms and held Jake in return, his still strong body under her hands. Wanda pressed her face against his chest, his shirt scratchy, but smelling of pine, wool, and a future she could almost imagine.

"Wanda, girl," he murmured, pausing and drifting away before moving closer, his voice loud, louder. "Wanda. Wanda. Wanda. Wanda."

"Ms. Mapp," the Kellogg City Hospital doctor said, turning from his computer to face Wanda as she lay on the emergency room bed. Tanya stood at her side, one calm hand on Wanda's shoulder. Wanda had already forgotten what this doctor's name was—she'd seen a couple already—and she couldn't read his itty-bitty name tag stitched over his breast pocket. For some reason, she couldn't really concentrate, and she bet it was all the damn clatter outside her curtained room, clangs and beeps and sounds of pain. The ER smelled like blood and alcohol. Not isopropyl but day-old whiskey wicking off thick skin, as if just behind the curtain were a raft of old-timers sleeping off life-long benders. Clorox and plastic. Wanda needed to get out of here. She was fine, though she felt exposed and awkward in the hospital gown, the neck tie scratchy and too tight, the sheet flimsy like old paper.

"What did you find?" Tanya asked.

The doctor looked at Tanya and then Wanda, and Wanda nodded, knowing that Tanya would make better use of any information than she would.

"The MRI and your neurological exam suggest you had a mini-stroke." He pointed to some fangled image on his computer, her brain a blobby jellyfish, his pen on a little white dot floating there like a wild fishy eye. "Here we can see there was a very small clot. Your niece was smart enough to give you aspirin right away. Your treatment at home and in the ambulance seems to have made all the difference. We're going to keep you here for observation—"

"I'm going home now," Wanda said.

"Ms. Mapp, a mini-stroke means you have an increased chance of another. It's highly likely this wasn't the first. We need to get you on an anticoagulant and see how you tolerate treatment."

Wanda looked up, not liking the sound of that co-ag word, something stuck and negative inside it.

The doctor added, "Keeps the blood from clotting. Coumadin is one drug we may try. Then we can provide suggestions for lifestyle changes."

Wanda stared at the doctor, his face calm and serious, though he was a little round under the chin and on the cheeks and looked tired and blotchy, as if he'd been in the hospital for days, eating vending machine food and drinking coffee the color of ginger ale. He needed some lifestyle changes himself.

"I'm eighty-four," Wanda said. "Almost eighty-five. Something's got to get me."

"But it doesn't have to get you yet," the doctor said. "Your other stats are excellent for a woman your age."

"She's in great health usually," Tanya said. "I couldn't believe it when they found her. She hadn't complained about anything. No headaches. No double vision. Nothing."

"Are you in a health profession?" the doctor asked, finally smiling a little and managing to be almost good-looking.

"I work at the reservation clinic," Tanya said. "With those at risk. That's why I knew what was going on."

"Great catch. But I do need Wanda—Wanda, I do need you to relax and stay with us a couple of days. Just to be sure."

"Auntie," Tanya said. "I'll be here with you the whole time. But you have to stay."

As the doctor and Tanya talked, Wanda breathed in the barn, felt Jake's arms around her. A sorrow keened through all her bones, and she swallowed back the sound, lest Tanya worry. But he'd been there, real and true, as solid as Six or Tanya or anyone. She could still smell him, feel his shirt, hear his voice. How could he have been part of a sickness? No way she'd had a stroke and fallen down against the stall door, Dave Eagle finding her when he went out to show his grandkids the horses. Maybe she'd had a bit of a headache and perhaps her arm had been tingling, but she was fine, no matter what direction this computerized brain map pointed to. She wanted to go home and sleep in her own bed.

"... will need to keep up her activity level but avoid strenuous work. Driving. Riding horses. Those changes and the meds will probably be enough. And we will keep close tabs on her."

Tanya nodded, shook the doctor's hand, and then walked out to the hall to confer with the nurses, that gaggle going on and on about whatnot. Wanda turned to face the curtain, behind which another poor person was being kept against his will.

How could Jake have been just a teeny weeny blood clot? It was impossible. He'd been in the barn—and really, even if he hadn't, he'd been with her. Her yes to him was in her. She'd finally said yes, the answer she'd been trying to give him her whole life. Now that she was old and clotting up and forced to stay in the hospital, she could say yes.

"Heh," she sighed, feeling a little laugh in her at the stupid joke.

But Jake hadn't been a joke. Not before when he was real, and not now, when he was a ghost resurrected from the battleground in Korea. Vio hadn't been making that part up. Not back then when she'd driven to the ranch to tell the Mapps the terrible news. Jake Tenday has been dead for almost sixty years. He was part of her now and then and until some lurch in her body took her down for good.

"Sister," Birdie said on the other end of the line. "I'm coming home."

The phone had awakened Wanda, and for a few floaty moments, she struggled to remember where she was, the hospital world coming back to her slowly despite the bustling noise. She looked around for Tanya, but remembered her niece had gone down to the cafeteria.

"Don't come to the hospital," Wanda said finally, pressing the phone tight against her ear. But she wished hard that Birdie could just move through the wires and pop up in the hospital room. Birdie would be a sight better than the old girl next to her, her and her snoring and noisy relatives. But Birdie had her important business that didn't seem to be done yet. "I'm going back to the ranch."

"You aren't done with tests, are you?"

"Not if the doctor can help it," Wanda started, trying to find a joke but landing on nothing. The phone air was filled everything Birdie wasn't telling Wanda, but from the shape of the silence, Wanda knew the news was bad.

"*Ataa*, Birdie—" Wanda said.

"Listen, I'll see you at the hospital and at home." In fact, Birdie's voice was different somehow, a nervousness that gave Wanda pause. Maybe Wanda was about to die, so it was time to rush back before it was too late. But Wanda wasn't ready to die. Like the doctor said, death didn't have to grab hold of her yet. "Anyway, I've already made my plane reservations. I'll be home in two days."

"I'll try to hang on," Wanda said.

"Hush," Birdie said. "You don't hang on, and you'll have hell to pay."

They both laughed a little but not as much as usual, not like they did in the middle of the night, both of them chuckling as they stared up at the cracked ceiling. "Come get me out of here," Wanda said. "The air smells like a dirty sponge."

"All hospitals smell bad," Birdie said, and in the criticism, Wanda heard Birdie's regret at missing important hospital visits, mostly those to

Dempsey during his last weeks. How hard it had been to see their father shrivel up into himself and die in a bed just like this. How hard not to have Birdie at her side.

"I miss the animals," Wanda said, feeling the empty spaces at either side of her that Ruby and Six usually filled.

"Don't worry. Dwayne's taking care of everything."

What everything, Wanda wondered. Dwayne had been such a fighter lately, angry, itchy, ready to pull the gun he didn't even carry.

"Ruby's probably sniffing him up for treats as we speak," Birdie said. In the background, Wanda heard the noise of an office or courtroom hall or meeting room, loud, arguing people, the sound of business far away.

"Sister," Wanda said. "I'll be alive when you get here, but I'm not promising I'll be at the hospital. I've already planned my escape."

"Old biddy in a gown on Highway 80 will be quite the sight."

"My wrinkled behind gets me rides. Just you wait and see."

There was another pause, and Wanda could hear her sister's grief. But this time, Wanda felt selfish. She wanted Birdie back, the need fierce in her heart, that old, worn girl of a muscle.

"Okay, Sister," Wanda said. "I expect to see you later."

"I expect you will."

Wanda hung up the phone and sank back against the stiff mattress and the sad little square pillow. Out in the hall, she heard Tanya asking the nurses questions, organizing everything just as Birdie always did. Things would go on, with or without Wanda, with or without Birdie. Tanya, Dwayne, Em, Nick, all the young ones, even poor fat Peach Tanver would take over the roles she, Birdie, and Stanley would leave behind, just the way they'd filled up their mother's and father's. On and on it would go, all of them cycling through the land, which would be there, no matter who claimed it as their own. Snow would fall. The grass would grow. The fires would start and burn and be put out. Over and over again.

"Auntie," Tanya came in, holding a tray, whatever was on it wiggling. "A big treat. You have to promise me you won't tell Uncle Stan. Gross green Jell-O! The kind with walnuts and cottage cheese. Your favorite."

Wanda let Tanya adjust her pillow and then took the little plastic cup and the spoon her niece handed her, nodding like a child, biding her time.

Chapter Thirty-Six

Kellogg City, Nevada
August 2012

Kellogg City Free Press—The Daily Donnelly
A Real Firefighter Fights Any Fire by Em Donnelly

A wise woman recently related her now-deceased father's aphorism for our silver state: Nevada: No One's Watching. After a day filled with emergencies of various kinds, I'm here to tell you that though the wise woman's father's saying is pretty darn true, it's not entirely correct. Yesterday, a Devlin firefighter was watching and watching hard and fast and because of his quick thinking and the help of a few locals, disaster was averted.

At a get-together in the Crescent Valley, a fire started but was put out within minutes. You, careful readers, will remember my blog that related our dry woes that continue at this writing (temperatures up, humidity down). Yet at the get-together, neither of these conditions was in place.

Fire is scary when let out of its cage. I hadn't realized that before yesterday. In my past, fire was always held tight in candles, barbeques, fireplaces, and the rare campfire. Wax, rocks, bricks, rings, boxes—all good things for containing fire. So I was in awe of how this off-duty firefighter responded. A portable pump (yes, he carries one with him if necessary) and a strong fast attack on the flames. Then nothing but smoke. Locals helped with the fight and the mop-up (I know the lingo now), and then even after more than an hour of beating down the charred fire site with tools, this firefighter didn't feel safe leaving the site and called his fire operation supervisor, who radioed it in and then drove down from the station personally to assess.

"Good work" was all this supervisor said as he looked around. Truly a man of few—but good—words.

Whew.

The fact that he drove down to look at the scene shows a lot about his commitment and the need for vigilance. According to the supervisor and on the record here, this area is one good lightning strike or barbeque gone wrong away from a nasty fire. Scary how just starting a car on a grassy lot can get things going, too. And how many of you travel with a firefighter and a portable pump when you go to a Saturday picnic or get-together that necessitates a flame out in the open? How many of you bring a trusted fireman to weenie roasts and fires by Ruby Lake on summer evenings? How many of you have any idea of how to actually put out a fire other than throw water on it?

Yeah. Just what I thought.

So once again with the public service announcement: It's dry out there, folks. Really dry. Watch the matches and cigarettes. With this fire, no one really even knows how it started, so I guess watch out for everything. So far this summer, forty-two percent of the Ruby District fires have been human-caused. We can do better than that.

Chapter Thirty-Seven

Devlin, Nevada
August 2012

The internet signal was wonky, so only the voice portion of Skype worked, the screen black, Megan's voice sounding far away, adrift on a raft in the middle of the Pacific.

Nick was in the common room, his chair in the special Wi-Fi corner turned to the wall, his head phones on. Thompson was the only other crew around, reading a book at the dining room table. Everyone else was on the patio watching the ping pong showdown between Hamm and Wicks.

"When do you come home?" Megan asked. "It's almost the end of August."

"We have another month," Nick said.

"Can't you leave early?"

"I don't want to leave early, Megan," he said, his voice riding a surprising edge. He'd almost said, "I don't want to come home," and he was glad he hadn't said those words, unsure if they were really true. What he knew was that he'd lose respect for himself and from his crew if he bagged the end of the summer. Besides, the station needed him. There had been no relief in the dry, hot conditions, and thunderstorms were forecast for later in the week.

Also, how could he face her after kissing Em even if that had been all that happened? Minutes later, Dwayne literally barreled up, Nick's breath quick and not from fighting fire.

"I feel like I'm on my own," she said. "Like I'm single."

Nick almost blurted, "I've felt like that for two years," but he didn't.

"I want you here," she said.

"For what? Really? To watch you write papers?"

"To be my partner? To be my boyfriend? You know, the things you're supposed to be?"

"The things we haven't been for months, Megan."

"Well, so why can't you say it?" Megan asked.

He couldn't say anything yet.

Nick half-hoped Megan would read his mind, the way she could sometimes, seeing the truth. The kiss and Nick's confusion. Fear, too.

"What?" He heard what he could say: *I want to break up. I'm falling for someone else. You don't love me anymore, anyway.*

Megan sniffed, paused, fiddled with her keyboard. "That you like it there. You like Nevada."

Nick rubbed his face, wishing he could whisk away his fatigue. "So what? What's wrong about liking Nevada?"

"Really, Nick. It's not like you could live there permanently."

"How do you know that?"

Megan was silent, a world of staticky weirdness coming from his computer. "You need things. Bodies of water. A view. And bookstores."

"There're bookstores here."

"Right. Really. Come on. Your job is seasonal. Temporary. Part-time. Replaceable. What's really keeping you there?"

Here they were again, back at the core, the crux: You left me for that. No, you left me for that. Every fight landed here on schedule.

After a silence, Nick turned the conversation, asking about Megan's parents. But he was thinking about another conversation, this one between his mom, her cousin Kim, and Grandma Flo just before Nick left for his first fire camp. His mom and Kim were about the same age, but unlike ordinary school teacher Sue, Kim had gone straight through Cal and then UCSF dental school, setting up her own dental practice in Lodi, California, marrying a local man, and having three children even as she built up her clientele. But her perfect life hadn't gone as planned. Kim's husband lost his job and turned house husband during the children's school years, and now they were relocating to San Francisco, where Kim was setting up a new cosmetic dental practice. Over lunch as they all caught up, Sue explained how Megan would graduate from Mills and then attend the University of Washington, and Nick would go to whatever fire district would hire him.

"A PhD in English?" Kim said.

"She's a smart one," Grandma Flo said.

"But how will that work?" Kim asked. "Really?"

"What do you mean?" Sue asked.

Kim took a sip of her champagne cocktail. "Will she be okay taking a fireman to literary banquets and university parties?"

"How do you feel taking your unemployed husband to dental soirees?" Grandma Flo had asked without a beat. Kim had flushed and backpedaled. Later, Nick's mom gave Grandma Flo a big high-five as they drove home.

"What a snob!" Sue said when telling Nick the story. "She's always been such a bitch!"

But maybe dear snobby cousin Kim was right. Sure, Nick was a reader and did, in fact, need a local bookstore, but what would he be able to say to all of Megan's new UDub people? Even at Mills, he'd felt off, other, even more than at Evergreen. Since they'd been apart, Megan wasn't doing anything they could share, her books and her studies hers alone. And everything Nick had been doing, she didn't want to hear about, all of it too dangerous, including the Em part.

"I don't want to talk about my parents," Megan said suddenly. "I want to know what you're going to do."

"Do when?"

"Do, Nick. With your life. With us. Are you going to come back and just sit here?"

"What are you doing?"

He stared at his blank Skype screen and listened to Megan's breathing. "I'm waiting."

Waiting. For him. For her semester to start. For the rest of whatever was going to happen.

"Me, too," Nick said, and he knew then he was only waiting for himself to decide.

They were long past their early days, unsure, naïve freshman, when sitting together and studying was enough. When holding hands in the quad and at The Reef over bad flat pancakes was enough. When watching French movies on long relentless wet winter days was okay. Even in later years when being together was better than being alone.

"You're going to wait so long you're not going to come home."

Nick opened his mouth, paused a beat, his breath stuck.

"I've got to go," Megan said quickly. "We'll talk later."

"Don't hang up. Wait. Megan!"

But she'd clicked off and then the whole internet connection was lost, floating away back toward the volunteer fire station where it belonged.

Nick closed his laptop and pulled off his earphones. She'd always rushed him. Be my boyfriend. Move back to Oakland. Come with me to Seattle. Decide, decide, decide. Again, her need for him to figure it out seemed rash. As though she were waiting for him to make her decisions for her. Behind him, Thompson closed his book, and Nick swiveled around to face him.

"Man." Thompson stood up from the table. "And I only heard half of that conversation."

"Yeah," Nick said.

"It's hard being away," Thompson said, shrugging. "Girlfriends and wives feel like war widows or camp followers, depending."

Nick nodded.

"What's interesting is if you find out that being separated for five months is better than not." Thompson picked up his book. "That's when shit gets weird.

Nick breathed in. All these weeks and months he'd been wanting to see Megan, and yet that longing was only in his head. The big heart and meat and bone part of him was fine with her in Seattle. And all of him—head and body—was happiest when he was with Em, even if it was for only an hour or two.

And for the first time since he'd met her, Nick couldn't share his happiness with Megan.

"Well, goodnight," Thompson said.

"'Night."

Nick watched Thompson walk down the hall to his bedroom. He heard the bedroom door close and music flare, and Nick swiveled back to face the wall, slumping in the chair, feeling like the internet connection that was neither here nor there, not one place or another. His stomach ached, the way it always felt when he was caught in the middle, unsure, certain only of disaster.

Chapter Thirty-Eight

Northern Nevada
Cortez Mountains
August 2012

Stanley held onto the door handle as Dwayne blasted up the dry hills, driving off-road, the truck tires grabbing earth and spitting it back. Stanley couldn't see where they were going, but he could almost smell the new mine site, a space no longer sacred.

His nephew took him up to the mine site often, where both of them sometimes sat in front of the main sign, thinking hard about ways to stop it.

This time, he and Dwayne had taken a detour on the way home from visiting Wanda in the hospital. The whole visit, Stanley could only see his sister from the edge of his vision, her small body in that big white bed, like a little doll, her skin so fragile and thin under his hand, her bones like a starling's.

"Take me home," she'd whispered in his ear, her hand cupped, her breath close, warm, secret. She grabbed his forearm hard. "Get me out of here. I won't tell anybody."

"Okay," Stanley had agreed, wanting his sister out of this terrible place of death that smelled like melted plastic and vomit. But Dwayne had nixed that, saying the doctors and his mom would have his hide.

"We'll come back tomorrow, Aunt Wanda," Dwayne said. "I bet by then you can come home for sure."

"Nephew." Stanley reached over to the bed, feeling for Wanda's arm.

"No, seriously, Uncle. Mom'll have my ass."

Stanley shook his head, waiting for the lump in his throat to pass. He swallowed. "Don't stay here too long. I'll expect to see you later."

He moved his hand along his sister's sheeted arm, resting on her tiny wrist and squeezing a little.

"I expect you will," Wanda said. "Can't wait to see what that

Marissa's up to on your show."

He'd tried to laugh, but he couldn't find the sound inside himself, nothing funny about anything.

Stanley hadn't spoken to Dwayne the whole way back but finally did agree when Dwayne wanted to go up the hill to check out the new mine site, as if they hadn't been checking it out for months.

"The thing that would fucking help is a casino," Dwayne ranted, continuing his litany of what was wrong. "But goddamn, wouldn't you know, we live in fucking Nevada where it's already legal for whites. How are we supposed to compete with the Bellagio and that whole Las Vegas scene? Kellogg City can't even do a real casino. Len says Russell Means says we should try to overturn legal gambling in Nevada. Len says ...."

Len says, Stanley thought. Len says what other Indians have said for years. It was true now and true then. And look at what's changed? Nothing. The tribe's still fighting for land.

"Grandma Birdie's coming home, and she can get going on this. Once she wins that ruling in DC ..." And Dwayne was off again on how things were going to get better fast, better forever.

Len says, Birdie says. Russell Means says.

Birdie was one thing, Len another, but Means was a long-time carnival freak show performer, a cat with 15 lives, popping up when there was a nearby circus.

Outside, the air smelled sharp and hard, ready to crack wide into something else, something that hurt. The air was like Stanley's heart, full of a rage he'd felt for so long, he couldn't remember when he'd felt normal. The only thing that took his mind off anything was TV, but lately, he couldn't take any more of the damn shows either. The court case. The last horse round up. The mine. His sisters—Birdie's graying hair, Wanda in the hospital bed—still having to fight. Dwayne growing to manhood in a world that hadn't changed. It burned inside him. His legs itched, his arms tingled. All parts of him were ready to burst. Maybe he was going to have a stroke, too, just like Wanda.

"We can get some kind of injunction, or whatever," Dwayne was saying, as he slowed down and stopped, the engine idling. "The law might actually be on our side."

"Your grandparents weren't even US citizens when they were born."

The truck slowed a little. Stanley heard the slide of Dwayne's hands on the wheel. "What do you mean?"

"No Indian was a citizen until 1924. How long had Indians been living on this continent?" Stanley asked. "Since before the white people got here and made it a country none of us had heard of. The 1600s. So it took three hundred years for them to give us a piece of their pie. I'm not looking for an injunction in my lifetime."

"It's not the old days, Uncle."

"What's the difference?" Stanley said. "We protest, and Indians are still ripped off. Still dying. Talk to your momma about that. And look at you!"

"What about me?" It wasn't Dwayne's fault. He was just caught up in it all like the rest of them. Stanley wanted to scream his old scream. Indians died in mines; they died by alcohol and sugar. They died poor in unheated HUD houses. No one paid attention, ever, and now it was probably too late to fix what was broken. Look at Dwayne. He was half in and half out of his own culture. Wasn't succeeding inside or out of the tribe. No schooling in either world had stuck, bad English, no Indian, not even the small bit of Lakota Stanley had.

Who was this boy Dwayne, anyway? How could he be Indian when everything that made him Indian was being taken away?

Even their Sunrise Ceremony had been invaded by the BLM, that firefighter and his girlfriend standing down there at the bottom of the circle trying to fit in. Why did Wanda invite them? That's why Stanley had done what he had. He'd been forced to stop it. No sunrise should be welcomed by the BLM. This time, Stanley had gotten hold of a lighter he could flick into action.

For a second that day, the fire sprang from the wadded up rag. Len may say a lot, but he let Stanley let go of his hand without a word. Stanley lit the rag and threw it out of the circle. As it caught and burned, Stanley had seen how fire might have changed everything.

"Pretty soon, all this earth will be dug down and out," Dwayne said, striking the steering wheel with his right palm, a thump, thump, thump in the cab.

Like they're digging out our hearts, Stanley thought but didn't say.

"Len—"

"Len," Stanley said. "Len can't do a damn thing."

Dwayne began to reply, but then he slumped a little. "Oh, Uncle."

Stanley nodded, and Dwayne put the truck in gear and accelerated, the tires spinning, one caught in a hole or ditch or some such, dust and grass bits flying. Dwayne accelerated some more, the engine roaring and banging.

"Shit," Dwayne said suddenly, and Stanley knew it wasn't about the tire. "Christ!"

"What is it?" Stanley asked, searching out the corners of his eyesight, unable to see around the black orb in his view, the world a flicker of ground and some slight blue sky. Dwayne was all a helter of twisting and turning to see behind him.

"I—" Dwayne started, but instead of finishing, he accelerated one more time, and the truck lurched and rumbled away from the mine site.

"It's—Shit!" Dwayne said, pulling the truck up aways and then creaked open the door, leaning out. "Fucking fire!"

Stanley turned around, casting about in his vision to see it. He swung his head until there, yes, back a bit, a wisp of smoke, a lick of fire. He could smell it now, too, a new fire burning hot and clean.

"I got to put it out." Dwayne jumped out and ran around to the back of the truck, tossing things about looking for what? A pump like that BLM kid had? A blanket?

Slowly, Stanley opened his door and got out of the truck.

"No," he said. "Stop."

Dwayne ignored him, cans and tools crashing around as he searched for the thing he wouldn't ever find.

"Don't," Stanley said loudly now. "Let it burn."

"Are you crazy, Uncle?"

"Yes," Stanley said. "For sure, I am."

"We can't let it burn," Dwayne said. "People'll get hurt."

"No wind today. Air like gauze." Stanley remembered that long-ago lighter in his hand, the way his thumb rolled smooth across the striker. Even that hadn't lit anything. "It'll go slow. It'll burn up this site and that mining trailer. It'll send a message. Let it burn, Dwayne. Let it burn."

"But—"

"We'll wait. We'll drive back Kellogg City and call it in." Stanley held up a hand. Nothing but still, hot air. "The fire will say what it needs to say."

A fierce course of hate and rage buzzed through his body. For a second, he wanted it all to burn. The mountain, the mines, the ranches, the towns. The casinos and brothels and motels on the interstate. The reservation and its sad convenience store. Even his father's house. Burn down this house! he wanted to scream, the house not just the sad one-room shack he'd lived in his whole lifetime, but the house of the world built wrong from the start with its bad foundation and crooked, rotten walls.

"Don't worry, nephew. The BLM'll get to it."

Bit by bit, Dwayne stilled the noises from the truck bed, a mere rummage and then nothing. Stanley closed his eyes against his shattered vision. And in a minute, even he could hear the crackle of flame as it burned away from them, see the message that the fire would send.

Chapter Thirty-Nine

Devlin, Nevada
August 2012

Before anyone else in the station was up, Nick headed to the engine and pulled his pack out of the back, sitting on a bench so he could reorganize it. They were going to take off at six for a three-mile run with packs, humping over the hills before the sun broke hot and wide. First thing, he took his fire shelter out of its bag to look at it in its clear packaging. He made sure it hadn't been damaged, which could happen because he usually clipped it to the bottom of his pack. But it looked okay, intact, no holes; not worn or dusty or full of pinpricks where fire could slash in as it roared over. Nick put it back in its bag and clipped it back to the pack and then carefully put everything else back in: two M.R.E.s (chili and barbeque pork), six quarts of water, first-aid kit, spare gloves, eight fusee flares, bandana, headlamp, rain poncho, and an extra long-sleeved shirt. He'd used the extra shirt the night they'd slept out under the terrible moon, the temperature falling to under thirty degrees that night.

His pack organized, Nick had sat down on his bed and stared at the mound of it, this bag that could make all the difference.

"Rumor is you tried to burn down Mount Aurora all by your lonesome." Hamm punched Nick in the right shoulder, hard but not as hard as he could have, Hamm with his truly huge ham fists. "I'm so glad we traded days off."

"That's me," Nick said, avoiding Hamm's gaze. "A righteous fire-starter."

After their run, Nick, Hamm, Mac, and Thompson had headed to the small weight room next to the garage. Nick spotting, Mac struggled to bench press 135 pounds. Even though they were inside and protected from the sun's razor glare, the spotty air conditioning could barely keep out the pulsing heat, the day dry and still at nine am, the air sharp and brittle. Mac was red, sweaty, and grunting.

"Twisted firestarter, more like." Hamm slammed down the 65 pound dumbbells in the rack and wiped his face with a sorry looking towel. His biceps were pumped, veins popping.

"You heard we have an arsonist?"

"For real?"

"Same device at Cross Creek and Deeth Fires," Hamm said. "Plus a sighting of the arsonist on Highway 306."

"No shit?" Nick said.

"Exactly, Sherlock," Hamm said. "So what were you doing up on Aurora, anyway?"

Mac racked the bar and exhaled, his chest heaving, his eyes slightly bugged out.

"A ... woman," Mac said. "Kinda hot."

"What other reason would there be to cause mayhem?" Thompson added. "Poor Nick here just needed a little attention."

"What about a brothel? A lot easier than burning down a mountain. Faster, too," Hamm said.

"I've heard that about you, Hamm." Thompson turned and winked at Nick and Mac. "He's a bit fast, our guy here. Quick Draw McGraw."

Nick saw Hamm cobble a comeback but then keep it to himself. Thompson was his engine captain, after all. So instead, Hamm turned back to Nick.

"If I'm fast, Nick's got to be a jackrabbit."

Nick waited a beat and then another. "Oh, wait. I get it. You're just a time-released smart ass."

"Nick's no rabbit. A turtle," Mac said, his breath slowing a bit. "He's had two dates with her and nothing!"

"Evergreen's waiting for her to propose," Thompson said.

"He wants a ring," Mac said.

"Maybe I should let this drop." Nick jiggled the bar over Mac's chest.

"What will he do next?" Thompson twirled the jump rope with one fast hand, slapping it rhythmically on the concrete floor. "First a fire and then what? Blow up the mine?"

"Yeah, yeah, yeah," Nick said, shaking his head. "Bingo. You all got me. Now shut the hell up."

The guys laughed and went back to their workouts. Nick focused on Mac's next set, noting the dude's shake and wobble, the bar jerking back and forth as he strained to extend his arms. The two iron plates at either end of the bar clanked as he struggled. No matter how hard Mac tried, he couldn't seem to bulk up or gain strength. Just yesterday, he barely managed to do seven pull-ups during morning PT (and Jarchow was counting), even though they'd all been working out every day since the fire season started. Mac would never qualify for anything other than engine work, not that Nick could really imagine him on a hotshot, hand, or helitack crew. The tension and fear and waiting for fire had gotten to him. Sometimes he thought Mac might not be asked back for next season. Sometimes, Nick knew he was just as scared as Mac.

"Steady," Nick said, his fingers just under the metal, ready for Mac to drop the bar rather than push it all the way up. "Breathe. Steady. Okay, you got it."

Mac racked the bar and sat up wearily. "I can't do anymore."

"Dude," Nick said, but Mac was walking away, his shoulders slumped, and then he was out the door.

"Jesus," Thompson said in between jumps. "He's phoning it in."

Nick shrugged and walked over to the leg press. When Nick arrived in Devlin, Mac had been so gung ho hyper, but lately, he was on autopilot, as if wanting to coast the last six weeks of the season. He'd stopped hoping and dreaming for the fire of all fires and didn't volunteer for overtime assignments. Last night, he'd been on the phone with his nursing student girlfriend back home in Henderson for hours, and the writing was on the station house door that he would ask to go home early, the first day temps and humidity shifted into fall patterns. The way things were going, Jarchow would hold the door for him. But Mac might be the lucky one, not waiting for every tone, eager to get out there and beat back the flames. Despite his father urging him on from the Florida sidelines, Mac hadn't been seduced by fire.

Closing his eyes, Nick pressed the weight, the stress in his quads, his back, his stomach. He'd never seen the apartment Megan had rented, he'd left Oakland behind—twice now—and Devlin was a temporary fire season stop. Even if he came back next year, the station would never be where his heart was. How could it be? How could Devlin be the home for anyone?

But, of course, someone must love it. Or it wouldn't be here.

"Hurry it up," Hamm said, flicking his towel at Nick. "Or let me work in."

"Fine."

Nick released the plate with a clang and stood up. He watched as Hamm added more weights to each side and sat down, knees up, quads pumped.

Wiping his face with his towel, Nick glanced out the small weight room window. No, Devlin wasn't home. But Megan was right. There was something here in northern Nevada. Something calling to him other than fire, and it wasn't just Em Donnelly, though she seemed to be attached to Nevada, too. All her reporting and blogging showed her interest in these people, this place. She might be over-eager for some stories—some conversations feeling like interviews—but she wasn't self-serving, out to make a buck or a name for herself in the blogosphere. She wouldn't be living in Kellogg City if she were, living in her over-priced shoebox-sized apartment. Somehow, she was happy working almost for free and driving around in the heat.

Takes all kinds, as Grandma Flo would say.

"What the hell you smiling about?" Hamm said, the weights smacking together with his last rep. "Not that woman again?"

"Oh, just mulling over how I'll take your job next year. I've got engine operator written all over me. In fact, I've had some t-shirts made up."

Hamm snorted and stood up. "Lemme take off the extra weight for you, sweetie."

Nick rolled his eyes and sat down, trying not to hear the word: Sweetie. Megan called him that. Sweetie, sweet, sweets.

Em called him Nick. Nick with a K.

He pushed against the weight, hoping the memories of Em would move away like the huge metal plate, but there was no stopping them. Em on the mountain, looking up at him. Em's warm mouth and bright eyes; her small hands on his waist as they kissed. Em smelling like flowers and feeling entirely different from Megan.

It had been months since he'd kissed Megan, felt her against him.

She'd been too sad, too upset, too worried to have sex the night before he drove to Devlin, holding him but keeping him away, too, her hands on his chest like a barrier. How easy it would be for him to just float away from Megan and land next to Em. Assuming that's what Em wanted. He wouldn't go to Seattle. He'd find a job in Kellogg City between the fire seasons. He'd let life tell him what he was supposed to be doing.

"Jesus, Evergreen. Are you lifting weights or jerking off?"

Nick looked up at Hamm, who stood akimbo next to him, impatient and irritated. As Nick tried to find words, the tone out blared. The men stilled, and then came the crackle of the radio. Dispatch: "Wildland fire. First two federal engines out of Devlin. Reported wildland fire. Mapp Ranch."

Nick's heart thumped as dispatch repeated the call.

Mapp Ranch.

"Who's on it?" Hamm asked.

"Schraeder's crew went to town looking for a pump valve. So it's us and Wicks. Come on," Thompson said.

"Game on," Nick said.

"Damn straight," Hamm said as they ran into the station house for their gear. "Gonna make poor little Mac's day."

The fire had started in the Cortez Mountains above Mapp Ranch, the two engines forced to drive up in the hills off Cottonwood Canyon Road, which was more dirt than road. Their rig was behind Wicks', and they were eating dust, Hamm forced to close the windows even though they were sweltering in their gear. Thompson was on radio with dispatch, swearing at the static. Nick joggled and bounced in his seat, holding onto his helmet as Hamm negotiated the giant holes.

"There." Thompson pointed to the obvious smoke about a mile away. "Volunteer engines at the base. The ridge road is a good place to fight it. But there's no wind. Minimal fuel. Could be worse."

Thompson conferred by radio with Wicks. Nick wiped his forehead with a shirt sleeve and stared out the window. It could be worse. But everything about a fire could change so fast, Nick needed his whole brain every single second. And now, he was anxious, jittery, unsure as he'd been on day one. Probably the fight with Megan. The kiss with Em. Maybe the long days of nothing but heat. Whatever it was, he'd found himself worrying his sleeves, rolling them down and buttoning them as they headed out. Even now, he had his gloves and helmet on, as if he expected there'd be no time to put them on when he jumped out of the engine. Maybe the fire at the Sunrise Ceremony had made him jumpy. Even though he'd been able to put it out pretty fast, he'd gasped as the fire tried to slip out of his hands like an angry cat.

The road rocked them, various metal objects clanging in the cab. He was thrown against the door, his phone pressing against his thigh. Shit, he'd forgotten to text Megan and his mother as he usually did when he was called out, so now as Thompson and Wicks decided where to park the engines and while he could catch the last wave of cell coverage, he pulled out his phone and scrolled through the texts. Em's number and words were at the top of the list:

So much fun at the Mapps. Amazing party!

And his:

Not as amazing as you.

He shook his head and smiled at their conversation, tapping in a new message, his anticipation of the fire smoldering as he did.

At fire above Mapp Ranch.
No worries for the Mapps but close by.

He watched the screen and then there she was:

Shit! Is it bad?

My engine captain says it could be worse.

Good! I'll call Tanya

Prbly knows. But not bad idea. Got to go

Be safe, Em texted. I need you to take me to that brothel, remember? The Shoe!

Always angling for the story

You betcha ☺

Got to go

Text me when it's over. Be safe.

K

He was about to shoot a text to Megan, but then Hamm pulled up next to the other engine, Lehman behind the wheel, both big motors blowing dust and heat. Behind them, a tender pulled up with extra water. The road had led them up the hill to the ridge line, the fire coming toward them. It had started at the bottom of the hill, and the plan was for the volunteers to stage at the heel of the fire and mop up what had already burned. The Devlin Station engines would start a mobile attack, using the road to hold the fire at the ridge line, working the edges as the volunteers pushed up.

"Over in a few hours," Thompson said.

Nick watched the fire, breathed it in even through the closed windows, thinking of the 18 watch-out situations he'd studied about in fire camp. This strategy was clearly breaking number ten: Attempting frontal assault on fire. Not smart to stand in front of open flames. A flare of nerves shot through him all the way to his gloved fingers. But like Thompson said, the weather conditions were stable, winds calm, humidity low but not crazy low, and they had an escape route just behind them. Besides, the fire was just stumping around, making slow, no-big-deal pushes up the hill headed northeast. Even if it began to burn northwest, there was nothing around for miles and miles, the ranches, Mapp Ranch for one, in the entirely other direction.

Hamm jumped out of the driver's seat, and Nick followed, closing the door behind him. The sun glared through a hazy yellow filter, the air full of the tang of smoke and particulate matter. Mac and Lehman stood by the other engine, while Wicks and Thompson both talked on their radios. Nick heard Wicks asking for reinforcements. "We need a hand crew. Engine 1346 clear at eleven hundred hours."

There wasn't going to be an air show today, not with this no-big-deal fire and no planes to spare anyway.

Thompson was talking to Jarchow, who was down at the base with the volunteers.

"1344. Affirmative," Thompson said before pulling the radio away from his ear and looking over at Nick and Hamm. "Evergreen, get your pack and the hose."

Nick went to the left-hand side of the truck where Hamm was working the control panel, priming the water pump.

"Ready to go," he said, after a few seconds, nodding at Nick.

Nick picked up the heavy nozzle, hoisting the hose onto his shoulder, and waited for Thompson to give his orders. But instead, Thompson got behind him and hoisted the back of the hose.

"Fire's not burning evenly, so our engine's going first, skipping the smaller spots. Wicks' engine will follow behind, getting what we missed." Nick faced the fireline, walked forward as the hose filled, a giant quivering snake on his shoulder. They were breaking another rule, number eleven: Don't keep unburned fuel between you and the fire. A fire could rear and gallop forward; a fire could jump from one source of fuel to another. There was no telling what might happen. Thompson knew this, and yet, here they were surrounded by tall dead grass, brittle trees, dusty sagebrush.

But as they walked along the road, first he and Thompson with one hose and Mac and Wicks with the second, Nick saw that they could put this fire out quick. The flames were low, scattered, sparse. As soon as he shot water on the clumpy bases of burning shrubs, the flames died, no wind to carry a surviving spark. The air sizzled with steam, swirled with smoke, black flakes hit his face. He heard Thompson's boots clomping on the sodden earth, and behind Thompson, he knew Mac and Wicks were working the fire the same way. Hamm and Lehman in the engines had their backs, water for it all. Six firefighters, a volunteer tender, and two engines. Soon this would all be over, and he'd be headed home.

But where was home? Wherever Megan was used to feel like home: the dorms, their rental houses, the Oakland apartment on Lake Merritt.

He would sigh with relief as he walked through any door she was behind. But the thought of driving to Seattle at the end of September and opening that new apartment door almost hurt, the taste of no no no in his mouth and throat. They'd barely communicated since she hung up during their last Skype session three days ago, and Nick couldn't even blame the lack of internet connection for their silence.

But he couldn't keep depending on another person to make a home for him. Home had to be a place made out of land and sky and work, too.

They worked this way for a while, the fire going nowhere except out. The sun beat down as heat from the fire pulsed all around them. Nick was drenched with sweat, his shoulders ached, his eyes streamed, but he focused on the fire. Unlike on Mount Aurora, he had the right tools and fellow firefighters. Also, if things went wrong, Hamm wouldn't be able to give him shit about this one. No way was Nick burning down this mountain range by himself.

When he and Thompson swapped out hose positions, Nick thought he felt a breeze, a finger of air slipping across his slick neck. Where they were standing, the smoke had almost disappeared, even though the fire was smoldering. But Thompson didn't seem to notice anything, nor did Wicks, and they all went back at it.

Thompson's radio crackled, and someone was on the other end speaking fast and loud. Thompson turned to look down the hill. Nick followed his gaze and that's when he felt the wind on his neck, saw the clear sky above him.

"Fucking wind," Thompson yelled. "Goddamn it."

Nick kept the hose on the fire but saw how it gained body as the wind paused, and then it straightened and leaned the other way, growing and heating up, taking off down the unburned right side of the hill, away from the ridgeline and past the black. Even if he started running, Nick couldn't have caught up with it.

"How?" he started to ask, but then sudden heavy gusts buffeted him, the kind of wind only suited for flying kites or hang gliding.

"Keep moving. Keep spraying," Thompson said, but Nick could see that they wouldn't be effective, not by chasing a fire that was screaming back down toward the base of the hill, racing southwest. Toward the flats. Toward Mapp Ranch.

"Jarchow? The other volunteers?" Nick yelled.

"They've moved position," Thompson yelled back. The noise of the flame was loud, wild, crackling as it burned through sage and shrub and small pine trees.

Nick sprayed as Thompson radioed Jarchow again. Mac and Wicks came up next to him, Mac repeating, "What the fuck? What the fuck?"

Thompson tapped Nick on the shoulder, and then Nick felt the entire weight of the hose, but in a minute, both hoses were turned off. The silence was huge and wide, the ground smelled of wind and water and burn. They all stared at each other, waiting, breathing hard. The volunteers who drove up in the tender truck walked over, eyes wide.

Thompson, Hamm, and Lehman jogged back from the engines. Thompson was business-like but clearly angry, Hamm and Lehman both red-faced and sweaty.

"We're going down to the flats," Thompson said. "It's spreading like crazy. Reports say it might be two fires. Jarchow called in again for more reinforcements, but we're only getting an engine from Battle Mountain and maybe one from Wells."

"Two fires?" Mac said. "How's it two fires?"

Thompson shrugged. "Spotters got it wrong. Someone called in another one. I don't fucking know."

"What about Schraeder's engine?" Lehman asked.

"Don't want to strip the station." Thompson cut Lehman a glance. "Not yet."

"They're not going to tone-out the whole district?" Hamm asked.

"Not yet," Thompson repeated as he studied his GPS.

"Can't we call in to another district? Or call the NDF and get a couple of inmate crews?" Nick asked. "If it's that big?"

"Middle Stack fire's taking up all the resources. Anyway, we'll make do until the other engines show up."

"What about a SEAT?" Nick asked. "A couple good runs would slow it down. Then we could go out and mop up."

"Jesus, Evergreen, Jarchow's got it under control, okay?"

Nick stepped back, took off his helmet, amazed at the sudden lightness, as if the worry weighed as much as the plastic.

Okay, he thought. All right.

"Come on. We need to get down to the fire." Thompson strode off toward the engine.

"How big is it now?" Mac asked, his voice louder than necessary, as if the fire were still burning all around them.

"No idea about acreage," Hamm said. "Rapid growth potential, though. I'd say it's about twenty acres. Who knows about this other fire? Could go all the way to two thousand if we don't get our shit together."

"The ranches?" Nick thought of Wanda and Ruby not far behind her, snout to the ground. And Tanya, working hard next to him on Mount Aurora as they mopped up the fire. "They've been evacuated?"

Hamm nodded. "Come on. Let's go."

Nick started to follow, but Mac grabbed his arm hard. Nick turned around to face him. The guy looked freaked, as if he might run all the way back to Devlin. Nick breathed, realized what he saw in Mac's face was living inside him, too, just waiting.

"Mac," Nick said. "Jim. Look, it's going to be okay. Come on. Chill out."

As Nick stared at him, he saw how Mac's emotions could go one way or the other, calm or flat-out hysterical. Nick took Mac's forearm, squeezed, waited, and released. Mac didn't look him in the eye for one breath, two, but then he did. And just like that, he was back, calm, ready.

"Okay," he said, nodding as if trying to believe himself. "Okay."

Chapter Forty

Kellogg City, Nevada
August 2012

During her "rest" after Stanley and Dwayne left (damn Coumadin made her tired and cold), Wanda had kept her ears and eyes open a tiny crack, which was smart considering Tanya was holding down a big secret.

One minute Tanya was sitting in the blue vinyl chair across from Wanda, reading a tattered People, and the next she was in the hall punching a number into her phone and talking in a whisper so low it was completely audible. People never remembered that about whispers, Wanda thought. They're louder than yelling.

"They've what?" Tanya hissed. "It's where? What about the animals?"

There was a pause filled by nurse and patient noises, muffled moans, and the clatter of IV stands scuttling across the waxed floor. Then Tanya muffled a surprised "Oh, no," and then rattled off names of other ranchers close by: McDuff, Peterson, Samuels. More whispers followed, phone numbers, a strategy for keeping Wanda in the dark, as usual.

All smiles, Tanya walked back in the room, tucking her phone in her purse.

"What?" she asked Wanda.

"I didn't say anything," Wanda said.

"Oh, right." Tanya sat down and took her phone back out of her purse, texted something or another. She bent over her phone as if praying, her long, beautiful hair falling into her lap. How many times had Wanda combed that head of hair, braided the long thick ropes, pulled it back in one ponytail, smooth and sleek? She'd known every inch of that baby girl, and even now that Tanya was full grown and heading toward the curve of middle age, Wanda saw her as she always had.

Had Wanda told Tanya enough times the things in her heart? Had she said the word love as many times as she'd thought it? Had she smiled and nodded at the times she should have? Did Tanya know how much she'd given Wanda by just being born? Had she told her how proud she was of Tanya's studies and work at the clinic? All those long hours. All that care. All while raising up Dwayne.

Wanda wanted to reach out and touch her niece's hair and say the words that needed saying, but then Tanya's phone rang again. Without looking up, she skirted out of the room, but this time she went further down the hall, away from Wanda's open eyes and ears. But it was too late. Wanda already knew.

Fire.

There was fire near the ranch, and all the way in Kellogg City, Wanda could hear Six in her stall, feel Ruby's warm dog body on the porch. She could even smell the fire, dark and hot. Underneath her blankets, Wanda tested out her legs, flexing her thighs and calves and feet. Maybe a little creaky and groany, but she could roll out of this bed contraption. She found the control and slowly lifted herself to sitting upright and took in breath. She was still alive. A very good sign.

Tanya rushed in, her face set in a pleasant lie. "Auntie, I need to go to the cafeteria for a bit. I've told the nurses where I'll be."

"Okay," Wanda said.

"They'll watch out for you," she said, finally looking at Wanda, her eyes black and huge and brilliant, a whole world of stories in them.

"I know." While she still had time, Wanda reached out and took Tanya's wrist, feeling the strong bones and smooth skin under her rough old bear of a palm. "Thank you, niece."

Tanya swallowed, leaned down, kissed Wanda on the forehead. Wanda closed her eyes and breathed in a combination of butterscotch and yellow flowers and warm earth. The one thing in this life she would never understand was how Birdie could have left so many times, over and over, giving up being near Tanya when every second was like daily sun.

Truth was, Wanda owned all the words now and could ask anyone anything. For instance right now, she could say she knew about the fire—the same way she knew that Birdie and all the legal Indians had lost the case. The answer had been in the tone of Birdie's voice, the forced high notes, the quick, sure way the conversation ended.

But Tanya's greatest gift was to protect, and Wanda wanted her niece to have that, even if it wasn't possible to keep fire or the US government from burning down everything.

"Get some rest, Auntie. All right?"

"For sure," Wanda said, attempting a small scoot down in her now upright position.

"I'll be back soon."

"I expect so," Wanda said.

Tanya kissed Wanda again and then left the room. Wanda's nurse peeked in and gave a little nod and a thumbs up and then left.

Now was the time.

Flexing her legs and feet again under the blankets and taking in deep breaths to fill her lungs and test her head, Wanda slowly shifted, letting one and then two chicken legs dangle over the hospital bed, swinging them back and forth, blood flowing, skin tingling. Then she slowly stood, the floor cold through her little hospital socks, the kind with the nubby rubber roads on the bottoms. One step, two step, three, Wanda made it to Tanya's chair and then the closet where she found her clothes neatly hung.

Once she was dressed and finished in the bathroom with a little spruce of water, soap, and a nurdle of pasty toothpaste, Wanda walked out of the hospital room. Her real clothes must have been a good disguise because none of the nurses noticed her, much less gave her a single concerned glance. One even held a door.

But just to be safe, Wanda tried to pick up some speed and headed down the hallway that led not to the bank of elevators that Tanya always took to go to the cafeteria but toward signs that said *Exit* and *Parking Structure*. On that elevator, she kept her eyes ahead, not staring at the man in the wheelchair or the two nurses in their rosy-colored scrubs. She gripped the rail, the air in her head full of pinpricks and sparks, and then they were in the lobby, and she flowed with a crowd out into the hot afternoon.

Now what are you going to do, Miss Know-It-All, she thought, looking around. She could probably steal Tanya's car—door always unlocked, keys tucked in the visor—but she'd already done enough harm by leaving. So what else? There wasn't a horse in sight, but to the left in a waiting row were a few parked taxi cabs. She put her hand in her pocket, feeling the money she'd slipped out of Tanya's purse the night before. She knew they were cabs because they were yellow and had "Taxi" written on them, but they were nothing like the last cab she took in Rapid City, sixty some years ago, from her Aunt Edie's house to the train station. What model had that car been? A Studebaker? A Ford? A Chrysler? This little bitty thing here was some import, a yellow bumble bee in a summer sky.

"You need a cab ma'am?" The man behind the wheel bent over, looked through the passenger's window. He had on shades, his red hair peeking out from under a dirty baseball cap.

"It's a long ride." Wanda looked over her shoulder, half expecting to see Tanya barreling toward her. Or a nurse or orderly. But the hospital doors opened and closed, spitting out and swallowing up the usual suspects.

"My favorite kind," he said, smiling. He got out and came around to let her in the car. "Where ya headed?"

"Crescent Valley. Mapp Ranch."

"Oh, my! You'll put my kids through college."

Wanda humphed and sat down on the hard back seat, breathing in the smells of cigarettes and body odor. Outside, people squinted against the light as they headed toward their cars. The cab driver got back in the car, pulled on his seat belt, and fiddled with the meter, the red digital numbers starting at 3.

"Costs just to get in," he joked.

"Everything comes with a price," Wanda said.

"Don't I know it," he said. He put the car in gear, and they pulled out of the traffic circle and onto the street, headed toward the highway.

Wanda sat back against the stiff seat. Tanya would be worried, and Wanda wished she didn't have to pain her niece, much less steal from her. But no one—not Tanya, Birdie, Stanley, or Dwayne, not to mention the doctors—would just let her go home, and she needed to be there more than any place else. Later, she would apologize, but for now she needed to get to the ranch. If there was time, she'd hitch up the trailer and load up the horses she could. Open the barn doors for the rest. Get Ruby and a goose or two in the cab and drive out of harm's way.

The cab driver pulled onto the highway in a lurch of 4-cylinders, and soon they were headed down to the ranch. Wanda stared out the window watching Nevada go by. The land outside was white blond, full of heat and what looked like violent wind, the grass bent over, tree limbs waving as if in warning. In the far off distance, a cone of dark smoke rising.

"Quite a day," the cab driver said.

She didn't answer. Somebody was still out there. Or something. She'd swear it. She blinked and looked hard because every so often, she thought she saw them, those little people from before the before, their dark heads bobbing through the tall grass. Sometimes in between the blasting radio and the whirl of air conditioning, she heard them whoop.

Wanda wanted to run with them all the way to Mapp Ranch, feet on the ground, summer air in her lungs.

Chapter Forty-One

Kellogg City, Nevada
August 2012

"Where's Dwayne?" Tanya asked Len, the phone pressed hard against her face. She sat hunched at a corner cafeteria table, a pulse in her stomach. All around her, people went on with normal hospital life, which seemed improbable on the best of days. Upstairs on every floor, people were sick and dying or even dead. And now there was a fire bearing down on Mapp Ranch. Ever since the McDuffs called to make sure Tanya knew about the evacuation notice, the hot knot of worry inside her went from simmer to burn. Even though she'd called his cell phone twenty times, Dwayne hadn't called back. No one picked up at the ranch, and when James McDuff drove by to offer Stanley a lift out of the evacuation zone, no one was home. James had driven off to other neighboring ranches to try to find him. But so far, no sightings of either her son or uncle.

Which was a good thing in terms of the fire, but where were they? Where was Uncle Stanley, mostly blind and deaf and maybe alone?

"Dunno," Len said. "Not on the rez."

Tanya rubbed her forehead. How could Wanda and she have thought this kid was behind anything? He couldn't even answer her question. She wanted to shake him silly. "No bullshit, Len."

"No bullshit," Len said, the sound of Barn Owl Foods behind him, the ding of the store's front doorbell, the clang of the cash register. "Why you asking?"

"Did you see what happened at the ceremony?"

Len paused, mumbled something to someone, and then said, "Saw the fire."

"Did you see how it spread?"

"Dwayne didn't do it," Len said.

"So you saw who did?"

Len paused again and then repeated, "Dwayne didn't do it."

"Did you do it?"

"Not me," Len said.

Not Dwayne or Len. So who? Fires don't jump. Only with wind or in myths. So who else?

"Stanley?" she exclaimed.

"Indian's a fighter," Len said. "Always has been. A real hero, man."

"How is a fire heroic?" Tanya shook her head.

"It's the way things are," Len said. "That whole talking, legal stuff doesn't work."

Tanya wanted to argue. After all, if what Len said was true, her whole childhood was a casualty of a faulty process, her mother all about the talking, legal way of dealing with the government. But then she remembered something her uncle said once, at another party, back when he could still see and hear and fight.

"Treaty is for entreaty, you know? We're always begging."

Yes, he'd been a fighter, but that was so long ago. How could Uncle Stanley have thought a fire at a Sunrise Ceremony could fix what was broken? And how had he done it? Tanya hadn't been looking at him. Then with Nick Delgado and his pump and everyone digging and later with Aunt Wanda's collapse, Tanya had almost forgotten about the flame. What a damn fabulous idea that party had been. And now all she could imagine was her uncle bumbling around the ranch alone, arms outstretched, calling out to Wanda and Birdie, the fire heading toward him and no one there to help. But if what Len was hinting at was right—Uncle Stanley a fighter, a hero—then maybe he'd started this one.

"There's a fire in the mountains," Tanya told Len. "I can't get a hold of Dwayne, and I'm worried about my uncle."

"The ranch okay?" Len asked.

"I don't know! That's why I'm calling to find Dwayne, Len." Tanya was almost yelling and felt the people around her flinch. "Look, I'm worried, okay. So if you hear from Dwayne, have him call, please."

"Sorry," Len said. "Really, I don't know anything. We're planning some protests about the mine. A blockade when it opens. You know, civil disobedience. Bodies in the way. Not burning down shit. But I'll keep my eye out for him. I'll call around."

"Thanks," Tanya said, clicking off her phone. She stared at the cold cup of coffee in front of her, the milk curdled, dark brown sugar dots on the Formica table, a splat of milk in the metal spoon. This was just the way it went. Her mother left for DC and everything at home fell apart. And before Birdie could even get back to visit Wanda, Stanley goes missing and the ranch burns down. All on Tanya's watch. Her mother would give her that terrible eye, purse her lips, look away. At least Wanda was getting better, asleep upstairs, safe and sound.

Tanya packed up her purse, pushed away from the table, and walked out of the cafeteria and down the hallway toward the elevators.

"Don't worry," Birdie had said last night on the phone. "We'll find a way. Like we always do. They don't have us yet."

But as always, the they seemed faraway. Unreal. Not like the fire surrounding their home right now. Anyway, Birdie couldn't cajole fire. She couldn't appeal to Mother Nature by cell phone or court case. The earth shook and burned and blew when she wanted. No amount of arguing could stop any of it.

Tanya knew what she had to do, even if it went against everything she'd ever believed in. In her mind, she could hear her mother speaking to her.

"Call those assholes," Birdie would say. "Use up those tax dollars and have them save the land they want to take from us, just in time for us to take it back."

She rode the elevator to her aunt's floor and stepped out, breathing in the air of sickness. Only a few more days in this stuffy place. Then she could take Wanda home where she belonged.

She nodded and smiled to the nurses, pulling her cell phone out of her purse as she turned the corner and headed toward Wanda's open door.

Even though her family hated the BLM, Tanya had to tell them about her missing uncle. They needed to know that a now-blind, mostly deaf former warrior might be wandering the ranch all alone, unaware that the world around him was burning to the ground. Tanya needed to call Sheriff Bryant and get his deputies out on the search.

Tanya put her hand on the door and pushed it wider, ready to tell Wanda she'd be back in a flash, right after she made a quick call. But Wanda wasn't there to hear anything, her bed rumpled, blankets pulled back, the bathroom door wide and empty. Clothes hangers stripped bare. Tanya threw down her purse. "Nurse!" she called. "My aunt!"

Tanya yanked at the blankets, searching for a clue. As if Wanda would leave one.

"What is it?" a nurse asked, breathless.

Tanya held up her arms, mouth open. But then she saw them. Her aunt's beaten-down, scuffed boots on the closet floor. The ones she wanted to wear every day, but sometimes couldn't get on by herself. That's when Tanya knew Wanda was really gone.

Chapter Forty-Two

Northern Nevada
Mapp Ranch
August 2012

Jarchow stood on the hill facing the fire, radio in one hand and binoculars in the other, surveying the terrain through the gauzy fog of smoke. Next to him, Thompson confirmed roads and landmarks with his GPS. Wet, tired, black with soot, Nick, the rest of the Devlin crew, and the five volunteer firefighters huddled in a half circle, waiting for directions. Nick's mouth was parched, and when he swallowed, grit dragged down his throat.

As Jarchow studied the horizon, Nick followed his gaze, his hands shielding his eyes, staring at the fire as it raced shimmering down the mountain like an ocean of rain. In less than an hour it had expanded rapidly—at first throwing spots and then merging into a river of red and yellow. All around, the wind pushed and yanked at the men, plucking at clothing, tossing hair, whipping exposed skin with flecks of grass, ash, and dirt. The two Devlin engines sat idling, and in the distance, another two engines headed their way, plumes of dust trailing behind them.

"The ranch is defendable." Jarchow pulled the binoculars away from his eyes. "Not a lot of fuel around the structures."

"How do we work it?" Nick heard his own anxiety.

"We're not getting any aircraft. Not for awhile, at least. Resources tapped out. We could do a burn and use the road that runs in front of the ranch as a fire break. The other fire is burning north, so we'll attack here. That'll check it. Two engines down at Mapp Ranch, and the other two at McDuff Ranch."

"We need a hotshot crew," Hamm said. "Better yet, a dozer. About ten."

"Not going to happen," Jarchow said.

"Jesus," Wicks said. "We used up most of our water on the ridgeline.

And there are some funky humidity readings. Mixed. The conditions are changing. RH is dropping."

Jarchow nodded, crossed his arms. "Structures are threatened. But there's a clear escape route. As for water, we've got the tender. I'll keep calling for reinforcements. But the burn out will do the trick."

Nick backed away and strode to the engine cab where he yanked out his pack. He pulled it open, his hands searching for known objects, touching and remembering the items he'd arranged so carefully. He forced himself to breathe in and out, trying to slow down time until his nerves could calm. Such a big fire. He closed his eyes, tracking the anxiety that whirled in his body, everywhere. Hands, arms, chest, thighs, feet, on fire, trembling, buzzing like flies. Another breath. Another. Everything was going to be fine. He had everything he needed. Jarchow was in command. Reinforcements were coming.

He breathed in, opened his eyes, and closed up his pack. He walked to the back of the rig, threw his pack in the back, and clambered into the engine. He sat jiggling one leg until Thompson and Hamm jumped in, doors banging shut. As Hamm accelerated, Nick tried not to imagine how Mac was feeling as he sat behind Wicks. If Nick felt queasy, almost light-headed, then Mac must be shitting himself. This fire was fast and hot and angry, flying with orange wings, spitting yellow flame as it sucked up everything in its path.

"Fucking A," Thompson said as Hamm sped down the hill, bumping and lurching over small gullies and dirt mounds and, once, a broken down fence, all the way to the two-track that encircled the Mapp ranch house. They pulled closer to the ranch house, and Nick glanced out the engine window as Hamm ground down on the brakes. The house, the barn, everything, seemed deserted, no one and not much in sight, not even Ruby. Behind the cottonwood grove at the back of the house, the sky was a swirl of smoke and fire, the mountains obscured, the sun, too, everything a pale gray. How lifeless and vulnerable without Wanda standing there on the porch.

"Get ready to burn off the road," Thompson said, putting on his helmet.

They leapt out of the engine, everyone slipping on their packs. Nick, Mac, Thompson, and Wicks grabbed drip torches, and Hamm and Lehman primed the water pumps and prepared to man the hoses if the burn went wrong, which it might. How many stories had Megan recounted for Nick where that exact thing had happened? Over-zealous firefighters screwing up tactically, the burnout fire going crazy and burning for days and even weeks?

"One hundred acres," she'd said as they read together in bed one night. "Turned into two thousand."

At firecamp, Chris made sure to point out that burnouts were dangerous but insisted they had to fight fire with fire.

"Water isn't always available. No fire-free option," Chris had said. "Take your pick. Controlled fire or uncontrolled wildfire."

Thompson walked them through the process, urged them to be "fucking quick about it," and they started lighting the fire that would be slowly drawn into the one headed toward them, consuming all the fuel and checking the main fire. The wind was pushing the fire fast, and the stubby burnout fire caught and held. Nick followed the road, using the drip torch to light small grasses and shrubs by the edge.

Move, Nick urged the fire. Go.

It was the burning hour, just after one o'clock, the air lighter, hotter, the time when fire could break free, nothing holding back the flames. Humidity was at zero, winds hard, brisk. The main fire roared forward, burned through the grasses. Crickets and butterflies flickered skyward as the heat and flame pressed close, meadowlarks streaming yellow and black out of the shrub. Probably under the grasses, snakes and rodents scrabbled for cool ground. Nick had never really thought about these creatures before. The bigger animals? Yeah, he'd even seen mule deer and elk bolt out of the path of flame. Coyotes, too. Squirrels, rabbits, and chipmunks zigging and zagging their way to safety. But there were so many live things under the grassline, all of them just wanting to stay alive like everything else.

He adjusted his glasses and put the torch to a clump of grass and watched it light, moving on as it took. Mac was ahead of him doing the same, Thompson and Wicks and the volunteer engines behind him. He saw both Devlin engines creeping alongside. They hadn't broken standard rule three: there was a safety zone and an escape route. Good news, too, that the wind and fire were behaving the way they should. If things kept going like this, the fire would miss the ranch and die out at the interstate, if not before. Jarchow had to have reinforcements coming by now. Nick forced himself to not look up for a SEAT and its load of retardant that could slow the advance enough for them or a hand crew to slow the fire. Or, if they were lucky, to stop it altogether.

So they lit and burned, the dead, dry grass going up in an instant, leaving nothing but black. They walked forward, focused, but then like a whisper, it happened again, just as it had up on the mountain. Nick felt the wind change, slightly, gently, the same slick finger of movement on his skin. He shivered, stood still, everything inside him falling into his stomach. But this time, he didn't wait. He turned back to Thompson and yelled, "Wind's changing!"

Thompson looked up and started, seeming to feel the air with his own skin, and then he hollered, "Stop."

Lehman jerked still and got on his radio, the channels overloaded with loud voices. Nick stopped to listen, hearing mostly "Transmission not clear" and "Please repeat." When Nick turned back toward the burn line, it was clear Mac hadn't heard Thompson and had moved far ahead, still holding the drip torch as he approached a large sagebrush. He hadn't noticed the way the fire was bending back toward the road.

"Mac!" Thompson called out as the wind now whirled hard. Just then the sagebrush burst into flame, the heat powerful enough that Nick felt it on his face, a pulsing gritty breath of burn. Sparks exploded into the air, landed and ignited the grass around the brush. Smoke swirled and obscured Nick's view, his eyes stinging, his lungs pulling in air hard. Mac appeared and then disappeared, there and then not, but another hot spot flared, shot forward leaning toward Mac with outstretched arms. It staggered as it lunged toward him. Nick stepped back once, twice, almost tripping.

"Mac!" he yelled again, finding his balance and moving forward. Mac dropped his torch and stumbled as he tried to rip his shelter out of its plastic.

"Don't deploy!" But now, Mac wouldn't hear him, not with all that fear in his head. Nick got that. The guy wasn't thinking. He was afraid for too long a second, and Nick had to stop him.

Mac juggled the shelter, but just when Nick thought he'd see a flash of silver, it fell to the ground. Then tripping and lurching, Mac ran backward and then turned and raced toward the road. Smoke filled in the space where he once was, Nick blinking against the sting to see him.

He was gone.

"What the fuck?" Nick said under his breath.

"Jesus Christ," Thompson yelled, running toward Nick. "Where did he go? I don't have time for this!"

"Did that shitbird deploy?" Wicks asked.

"No!" Nick said. "I swear. He didn't."

"What was he thinking?" Wicks wiped his face, soot swirling his cheeks. "Jesus."

He was scared, Nick wanted to say. *So was I.*

Thompson grabbed Nick and pulled him back from the fire line. Wicks ran to pick up Mac's still lit torch. The flames leapt around them all, smoke a whirl, but then just as it had started, the wind rearranged itself and shoved back at the burnout fire, pushing it forward again, the scary sagebrush still lit up but nothing to scream about.

"What a fucking moron," Wicks said.

"Should I go find him?" Nick asked.

"He's behind the fire break. We've got to keep at the burnout. The fire could jump the road," Wicks said.

"Once we get ahead of it, we'll get him. He's safe. He's probably in Kellogg City by now. Just finish the burn," Thompson said. "Jarchow radioed. Dozers are coming. If we're lucky, mop up might be in our future sometime this week."

Thompson could mean mop up Mac or the fire. Either way, it was going to be a hell of a mess.

Nick looked back one more time, hoping to find Mac loping back. At least he hadn't deployed his shelter. That would have meant a full report and maybe a district investigation. Already there were going to be questions about the wind and the two fires and the lack of equipment. But it was too late for Mac. Nick could already imagine how Hamm would sling insults at every possible opportunity. There would be nowhere for Mac to hide.

"Get going." Thompson put a hand on Nick's shoulder. "He'll be fine."

Nick turned and continued to burn along the road, lighting grass and brush, and started to loop around the ranch house. Behind him, the burnout fire had met the fire sweeping down the mountain. Both battled and then slowly tangled and diminished, though there was still a wall of flame to the north of the ranch. The engine pumps started, the two volunteers readying the hoses to start spraying.

As Thompson said, mop up might be in their future. Then they could all go home and deal with the Mac fallout.

Burnt grass crackled under his boots. The flames pushed northeast, but then, no. He almost moaned when he felt it again, that same subtle shift of air, the wind curling around him, the fire headed the wrong way again. As it had with Mac, a plume of sizzling heat pushed him back, a human-sized clump of sage bursting into flame.

Nick sucked in breath, backed up, turned to find Thompson. But in a flicker of peripheral vision something moved. As he spun around—thinking fire might be curving up toward them—he saw a small dark figure walking slowly but methodically from ranch house to barn.

Wanda Mapp, Ruby trotting behind her.

Nick hoped he was imagining things. Wanda couldn't really be here, could she? She'd had a stroke the day of the ceremony. By the time he and Em had made it down from Mount Aurora, the ambulance had come and gone, whisking Wanda to Kellogg City Hospital.

But the figure glanced over her shoulder at Nick and then started striding faster. No doubt, it was Wanda Mapp. He turned to alert Thompson, but the captain had run over to the Wells engine that had just pulled up, the crew jumping out and putting on packs and grabbing torches. Nick tried his radio, but the channel was still filled with chatter.

He spoke into it anyway, "Any confirmed civilians on Mapp Ranch?"

He looked up to see if anyone at the engines had heard his transmission, but they were taking direction from Thompson and Wicks, and moving toward the fireline.

"Caller on Red One. Please repeat," someone blared through the radio.

"Delgado. Engine 1344. Civilian on Mapp Ranch," Nick said.

"Jarchow here."

"Wanda Mapp is at the ranch," Nick said. "She's in the barn."

"Jesus." Static surrounded his words, and then other voices filled the airspace. Then Jarchow was back.

"Other civilians?"

"Thompson said the Mapps were accounted for. But who knows?"

"Is Wanda in danger?"

"Not now, but situation's changeable."

Jarchow asked more questions and then told Nick to stay on the line. Nick clutched the radio, blinking back the dank, swirling smoke, waiting. After a tense few seconds, Jarchow said something garbled and then there was nothing but static.

Nick kept an eye out for Wanda but went back to burning, checking over his shoulder now and again to watch the barn. There was no movement other than the wind and smoke, but then he saw one horse and then another gallop from the back door. Wanda was letting the animals free. Why hadn't anyone done that already? Shouldn't that have been part of the evacuation?

He pressed the radio button again. "1344 on Red One. Civilian and animals in Mapp Ranch barn."

Nick listened for Jarchow, but there was nothing but mess on the radio waves, rivers of static and occasional yells, something about the other fire? He flicked through the channels but heard nothing and got no answer. Nick glanced back at the engines. Thompson and the rest of the crew were still burning the line.

The smoke swirled, Nick's eyes burned, his nose itched and continued its permanent run. Ash caked his lips and teeth. He coughed and poured the hot oil over the grass, listened to the crackle and pop, his eyes watering under his glasses. His lungs ached and sweat slid down his neck and chest. He wished he could manage not to breathe, trying to take in small, shallow inhales as he walked. He finally took in a deep breath, the rasp of hot smoky air scratching his windpipe. He took in another and coughed. The radio scratched and blared in his ear. All Nick heard was, "Second fire," and then, "Wind."

And then someone shouting.

Nick spun around. Fire swirled down toward the ranch house, heaving up and throwing itself at the porch, a surge of heat, crack, and sizzle. Flames flew into the open door and windows, a palm of red and yellow grabbing the house, seeming to almost lift it off its foundation.

Dropping his torch and the radio, Nick raced toward Wanda and the barn over a hundred yards away, his arms and legs and body pulling him forward. Despite the weight of his pack and the fire at his back and to his side, Nick ran through the smoke.

Chapter Forty-Three

Northern Nevada
Mapp Ranch
August 2012

The barn was hot and smelled like burn, but it wasn't smoky inside, not like the house and the land around it. When she'd stood at the kitchen sink looking out the small, familiar window, Wanda waited as long as she'd dared, drinking one, two glasses of water as the sky darkened. She'd barely made it there in the first place, the cab driver reluctant to pull down Dempsey Mapp Road, what with the fire truck with lights whirling parked there, roadblock style. But as they drove closer, they watched an NHP cruiser pull up, but then it and the truck suddenly sped away, and Wanda convinced the driver to take her halfway down the road.

"Holy cow!" he'd said as they rounded a turn and saw the fire pouring down the mountain. "Damn, let's get out of here."

She handed him the money she'd stolen.

"I can't leave you here," he said, taking off his sunglasses and staring at her. "Your ranch. It's burning."

"Got to get to my animals," she said.

He shook his head. "Someone would have taken care of them, huh?"

"Drive faster," Wanda said. He did drive her a bit further but slowly, and then idled as they stared down at the ranch.

"You got to promise me you'll get out of here soon," he said.

"You've got to promise me not to tell anyone I'm here," she said, realizing her mistake once she said the words. Now he would tell, for sure. He might even chase down the fire truck. But he'd nodded, and she'd made it to the house. She coaxed Ruby out from under the porch and they went inside, Wanda struck dumb as the world outside crackled and flamed. Through the kitchen window, she'd seen the way the fire was headed, saw how it could turn, a carousel of heat and wind.

Now in the barn, her heart beat fast, her breathing a glug of in and out, air stuck under one rib or another. Her throat was parched from her trip from the house, and her eyes watered hard. Blinking away the smoke, Wanda strained to open the other door, letting in filtered dusky light that hung full of dust and ash. She leaned against one wall, and in dog sympathy, Ruby rubbed her side against Wanda's leg, just enough to show support.

"Thanks, girl," she said, taking in a deep breath. Her arm tingled and stars floated in her eyesight. Her bones ached from their hollow middles. For a second, she almost wished she were back in the stiff Kellogg City Hospital room, propped up in her bed like a scarecrow. But she had work to do. "Come on Ruby. Time's a wasting."

Six stamped and snorted in her stall, flaring the whites of her eyes. In her fear, Six didn't acknowledge Wanda, horse sense taking over. And all the other animals were ready, hooves and bodies thumping the wood trapping them. Wanda knew enough to stay out of the horses' way once she opened the stall doors.

She looked at Six one last time, right in the center of one brown eye. Her throat tight, Wanda resisted reaching out touch Six's coat.

"Run," she shouted. "Go!"

One after the other, she threw open the stalls, Six first, and then big warm flashes of black-and-white, brown and stippled spots that matched the stars floating all around her. None of them gave her a second glance, pounding out of the barn into the smoky afternoon until there was nothing left but their absence.

The sheep, the two billy goats, and the waddling geese followed after, Ruby chasing them with her rough snout. The mangy barn cat screamed out low and fast in a shot. And then there was only Wanda's daddy's barn. All those years ago, he'd built this himself. Dempsey Mapp and his friends, hammering nails and laughing, smoking their Marlboros and drinking Budweiser. But now there was fire coming down the mountain to take it back.

"Let's go, Ruby," Wanda said. But then a flash of color, a yellow burst flooded the barn. Jake was there, looking around wild-eyed. Wanda breathed in hard, a pain in her heart that radiated down her arm. Stabs of old but true love. He hadn't just been a stroke or a little eye of blood clot in her brain. He'd been real.

"We've got to get out of here," Jake said as he moved toward her, urgent, smelling of wind and water and burnt earth. His clothes were warm to the touch and smoking, a plume following him as he moved toward her. He asked no questions about why Wanda did this or that in the past. No questions about dancing. No thought about a kiss. As he strode toward her, there was a roar like the roundup she and Birdie had borne witness to in the spring, a thunder of stampeding hooves, but it wasn't coming from wild horses or the ones that had just flown out the barn door.

Jake grabbed her up the way her daddy used to and pulled her into his arms. "Ruby!" he called. Wanda thought to walk herself out of her daddy's barn, following the tracks that Six laid out for her. She put a hand on Jake's shoulder, and as she did, there was a crack inside her, a whip in her head. Wanda leaned against his chest and found herself light and letting go, relaxing as he stumbled and ran. To the beat and rhythm of his fast, jarring strides, she let go of the ranch and her worry about the animals. Her letting go had large, transparent wings that made her feel even lighter than a child. Wanda released her muscles and breath, her skin and her thoughts. She moved up and out of her body like she was a new thing, a creature made of light and air, flying above the ranch and the fire that was eating the side of the barn with big orange teeth.

And, oh! Here it all was. The answers had been right under her nose. For a second, she wanted to swim back down so she could tell Birdie. Because my goodness, what a sight it was. All the wrangling and nonsense; all the fighting and much worse. Wanda saw the needless blood spilling, the cracks of gunshot, the slash of knives. She watched the coming and goings and the thises and the thats. Just plain nothing for sure. How silly.

"Hold on, Wanda," Jake huffed as his body hurtled over the smoking earth. Wanda let her gaze drift, seeing a man next to Jake, a graying head. Her father. But no, someone older, not in age but time. And next to him, another person, a woman, both of them running with Jake. Her mouth opened as an old, unknown word floated past her teeth. Just as she understood what it meant, just as she knew the word she'd been meaning to say her entire life, something inside her yanked one final time. Instead of moaning or clutching Jake, she let go a little more. A final float, a wisp of whisper, nothing left, not even sound. Not even memory.

Chapter Forty-Four

Northern Nevada
Mapp Ranch
August 2012

Three fires. Two fires went nowhere; one was an accident he let turn into incident. One fire he'd let everyone know about. He'd wanted that fire to consume him. He'd threatened and done nothing but stand and scream. The last fire, he'd done everything and so had it, consuming his entire world.

Now the lights flashed. Now the ambulances screamed as they bumped down the road. Now the thing he'd wanted least was true.

Hands held him back, hands forgot, and Stanley wandered off, seeing only the edges of his former life. That's all he'd ever seen. Not like Wanda who had the middle and the edges covered for sure. But where was Wanda?

He followed the path from the barn to the house—a path he knew by heart—but it was a path to nowhere, the ground under his feet different and dead. Behind him, the authorities talked and talked, Sherriff Bryant's bucksome gums aflapping. Everything smelled like burned water, stank like a sweat lodge after a rain. The remains drenched with loss.

Stanley stumbled but kept walking. He could see it if he tried, the ranch of all his years. He closed his eyes, and there it was, his mother on the porch, an apron tied around her waist, her dress a flowered print, her shoes black and scuffed. She spoke in a way he could understand again, finally the words coming back.

"Son, come inside. Time to eat," she said in her language. Their language.

Stanley wanted to eat his mother's food. There'd be fry bread and maybe venison if his father had been lucky while hunting.

He shuffled forward, smelling the grease, tasting the bread, and there Wanda stood on the porch, holding a broom, her eyes on him. This was the place Wanda last drew breath, and somehow, maybe just like this, as a girl, she was still here. Maybe he was still here, too, in that other younger form, a boy without knowledge of how he'd have to fight and how often he would lose.

"Come on, Stanley," she said, her known small smile on her face.

He heard his own giggle, a sound from back then and only then. He was home. Ataa! He was home. For sure just around the corner, he'd find his father chopping wood, a cigarette in his mouth. Around the house and down in the creek he'd find Birdie and his cousins, all of them splashing in the last trickle of the summer.

"Come on, Uncle," Tanya said, her voice calm but harder than usual, blame in every syllable.

"I want to go home," Stanley said, a wail in his words, and he knew it was too late. It was done, all over. He would never sleep in this place again.

"I know," Tanya said. "But people want to talk to you, okay?"

One wrong thing had led to so many others, crimes stacked up in guilty piles. No wonder they wanted to talk.

Whatever they gave him, he deserved. Whatever happened, he would make sure he was the one punished. Not Dwayne. He, not his nephew, had made the decision to let it all burn.

Stanley nodded and let his niece turn him around, both of them walking back into the sound of his crime.

Chapter Forty-Five

Elko, Nevada
August 2012

Three days after the tone sounded at the Devlin station, Nick's finger pressed against the plastic doorbell. Right then, he realized he was shaking. And not just his hands. But he noticed it there first, feeling the tremor and rattle of his skin, muscles, bones and blood. Even his eyes felt jittery, though he didn't want to close them because every time he did, he saw fire. Blink again, he'd see Wanda.

"Nick!" Em gasped as she yanked open the door. She reached out both hands and drew him in, closing the door behind them and leading them to her living room.

"You're okay, right?"

He nodded.

"God. Wanda," she said. "I can't believe it."

He nodded again, unable to really believe it himself. How small and light Wanda had been. How she'd gasped. How she'd stopped, her face going slack, her mouth opening, one last word escaping before he could even begin to hear it.

Em turned to him and put her hands on his shoulders and then—with a move that made him inhale—on his face, her palms warm and smooth. He breathed in her sweetness. And then she looked at him, and the shake and jitter inside him turned to tears.

But he looked up and at her, holding her gaze. She kept her hands on him, her own eyes filling. "You risked everything," she said.

How could he tell her he didn't risk anything? It was his job. Of course, Nick knew what she meant, but running for the barn wasn't a risk. He'd been wanting to run since Mac had—or maybe even before. There was no other choice. How to say something like that and not sound like an idiot? And how to tell her that coming here to her apartment was more of a risk.

But maybe that wasn't even true. How could it be a risk if his relationship with Megan had already ended even though neither of them had said the words?

So Nick didn't say anything. He gave in. He took it all in and put his hands on hers and slowly lowered them, kissing her and letting this kiss last. She kissed him back. This time, neither of them was nervous about the newness between them or because angry men with barrels of water would show up any minute and interrupt them.

"Nick?" she said, pulling back for a second.

"Yes," he said, as his tears and trembles turned into something else, an excitement that deep and real and true. If anything, the fire had taught Nick living was for living. Being here with Em gave him the chance to live, and being alive made being with her necessary.

"Yes."

Chapter Forty-Six

Devlin, Nevada
Early September 2012

After dinner, he went out into the twilight and sat on the bench—a beacon of signal—and called Megan.

"You're breaking up with me by phone," Megan said after a punch of silence.

"I—"he began. "Look, I'm sorry. There's no other way. We're just not in the same place," Nick said.

"I'm not the one who left."

Nick pulled the phone away, knowing what it would feel like to hurl it into the dead grass to the side of the station. He looked up into the stars, bright tonight, smoke cleared from the sky.

"Can we not do this again?" he said when she was done with the song they'd both been singing since May. "We've had this conversation a hundred times. I left. You stayed. We haven't seen each other for months. Our lives have gone on."

She gasped, swallowed it down. "But I've been waiting."

"Probably not for me, Megan. Waiting isn't the same as wanting."

Again, she was silent. Out in the grasses, a nighthawk pee-yahed pee-yahed. The air turned down the temperature a notch, the sky darkening and opening up to stars and moon. Nick would feel amazing if it weren't for the fact he and Megan were going to end this call differently than when they started it. Nothing after this would be the same, even if the same had been pretty bad.

"I'm here with all your stuff," Megan said.

"Did you unpack everything?"

In her silence, he saw his whole life boxed up and tucked into a convenient corner. All around his books and clothes and music, she'd spread out and gone on.

"It'll be easy then," he said.

"And we can talk when I get there. I should be able to leave in a couple of weeks." Nick hoped he could hang up, end this for now. But Megan always knew what he was trying to do.

"Is there someone else?" she asked. "Is that what you really want to tell me?"

Nick stood, pacing the patio. What did he want to tell her? That he was so happy they'd had each other during college? That they'd grown up from teenagers to adults together? That she would always be with him, residing in memories deeper than thought? That there was no way he could really break them apart?

In a way, she was the exact person he'd want to talk to about Em. No one but Megan would get why he and Em fit the way they did. But there might never be the time or place for that conversation.

"There is," Nick said.

"That woman firefighter?" Megan asked, her voice tight. Nick could almost hear her fire station fantasy play out. Late night sneaking around from room to room.

"No. A journalist."

"How predictable. The fire. You as the great hero. Everyone in Nevada needs to know. Gotcha"

Her words hit him in his throat and stomach. He was no hero, he knew that. He hadn't been able to save Wanda. What was heroic about racing to safety with a dying woman as her whole ranch burned to the ground? He sat back down on the bench, elbows on his knees. Tears pricked his whole face, his whole body. A fire still roared around him, even though it had been out for weeks. But the truth was still the truth. Wanda Mapp was dead.

"I'm sorry, Nick." Megan's voice softened. "I didn't mean that. But aren't you going to tell me that it's nothing serious? Aren't you going to say that nothing's happened yet?"

Something, everything had happened, but what did Nick know? It felt serious, but everything did since Wanda died. Right now, he wasn't doing anything but being happy when he saw Em Donnelly.

"It's time," Nick said, sitting up straight. "It's well past time."

"I've—" Megan began suddenly, but then she stopped. Whatever she was going to say hung in the air, and somehow, they bumbled along through silences and flares of anger. Through the repeating of what both of them already knew, the repetition of the story they'd been telling themselves for years, the came up with the same answer. Up and down, over once more and then again. They talked till the night was a sheet of black against the sky, crickets filling the air with autumn.

Chapter Forty-Seven

Northern Nevada
Mapp Ranch
Late September 2012

"Some of you might think I'm the fighter for my family's land and for the tribe. But it was never really me," Birdie Mapp said. She stood on a platform in front of where the Mapps' house used to be, under a canopy made of fluttering red fabric decorated with strands of beads and feathers. Her long hair was pulled back, and it was still mostly black, two gray streaks on either side, both tucked behind an ear.

In front of the platform were rows and rows of folding chairs, all of them occupied, with a huge fantail of people standing and filling the rest of the space. Nick wasn't surprised to see the people he'd met at the ceremony plus dozens—maybe a hundred—more, but he was surprised to see the Kellogg City sheriff and deputies in dress uniform dotting the rows. To the sides and in the back as well as next to the platform, journalists stood or sat, video and digital cameras whirring and clicking, everyone wanting to capture the festive desolation. And on either side of the dirt road, three vans with satellite uplinks were parked next to the BLM and sheriff's vehicles, the talking heads with microphones keeping a respectful distance. Behind the mourners were folding tables and barbeques already smoking with beef and venison and chicken, the air filled with grease, smoke, and heat.

Nick sat in a row at the back, Em next to him. Today, her phone had mostly been in her bag, one of her hands on his, squeezing him a little as Birdie spoke, as if what Birdie was saying was upsetting him. But Nick was okay, even though Wanda had died in his arms. She'd been so light as he'd run out of the barn and away from the fire that spread north as fast as a train. At some point, Mac had turned around and come back toward the fire. Ruby at his side, Nick sprinted as fast as he ever had in his life, Mac behind him, both making it to the waiting engine. Jarchow jumped in the back seat with Wanda, helping an EMT from the Wells crew as they tried to save her. Nick threw himself in the captain's seat and grabbed the wheel, punching out up the road ahead of the fire toward a staging area where paramedics waited. But even as Nick roared the great engine over the grass and dirt and then asphalt, he knew it was too late. He'd felt Wanda leave while she was in his arms. He'd almost heard it, a sigh as she died. He might have seen it, too.

"My sister was the kind of person that comes around once in a lifetime," Birdie said. "If you find yourself lucky enough to be with someone like her, pay attention. Look her in the eye and listen to her few words. Each and every syllable could change your life. She changed all our lives. She was our rock. Our soul. She was the only one of us who knew that the true fight starts inside, at home."

There was a wave of approval, clapping, one whoop, two. Birdie put her hands on the podium and looked out at the audience, her face full of resolve and maybe anger, her features fighting her personal sadness and somehow winning.

"Because of budget cuts and bad government, because of poor land management and power struggles, because of racism and ecological rape, Nevada was ripe for burning. My sister was here alone, desperate to save what she could of our family home. And what did Nevada send her? A couple of crews? Some volunteers? One firefighter in particular, a good man, who happened to spot her, barely making it out alive himself."

Birdie held out her hands. "No planes. No heavy equipment, at least not in time. One man when all of Nevada is just one spark away from disaster? Where are you, Nevada? Why aren't you taking care of your own? The people who've been here long before the casinos and mines? Why do you care more for businesses than people? Why weren't you taking care of my sister? Nevada, I ask you. Why is no one watching?"

There were murmurs and assents from the crowd, a smattering of claps, one loud whoop. Nick looked down at his lap, swallowed down an irritation that wasn't his to feel. But he couldn't help but dislike what Birdie was doing. Suddenly, Wanda's memorial wasn't about Wanda but Birdie's agenda.

Em gripped Nick's hand tight as if she felt this, too, her body pressing close.

"My sister's struggle and her death have left me with further resolve to not give up, just as Wanda didn't give up. The Supreme Court may have ruled against our tribe, but I'm not done. I won't stop, just as Wanda didn't stop. We will not vanish. I will run into the barn of this country and free us from illegalities and broken treaties. I'll free us just as Wanda freed her favorite horse Six. Together with those like me who won't give up, I'll rebuild this ranch and our way of life. I'll do this for Wanda. For the Mapp Ranch. For all our people!"

After the service, Nick and Em mingled. Mostly, Nick walked beside Em as she talked with people she knew and some she didn't, asking about Wanda and the Supreme Court ruling. Nick was content to float and listen, but then he felt a hand on his arm, and he turned, almost starting. There in front of him was Wanda, but then not Wanda. Her same eyes, her small smile, but an energy that was strong and pulsing, just as her words had been earlier. But behind all that, sadness. The pricks of irritation he'd felt early slipped away.

"Thank you for helping my sister," Birdie said. "My daughter told me how you risked your own life."

He held out his hand to Birdie who took it. "Knowing your sister was my honor. I wish it had turned out differently."

Birdie nodded, watching him, her eyes dry. Meeting her closed the Mapp circle for Nick, but he saw she wasn't like Wanda or Tanya or Stanley. Dwayne maybe had some of her edge, but Birdie was unstoppable.

"What are you going to do?" Nick asked. They had turned to look behind them at the blackened ground, the cottonwoods dark skeletal fingers against the blue and white sky.

"Rebuild. Starting today. In front of the cameras." Birdie looked to the line of white vans. "We'll show the whole world that treaties can't be broken and we can't be stopped."

As she spoke, others turned to listen, Em close and now tapping away on her phone.

"Those of you who believe in our cause can stay to help," Birdie said.

She pointed to several big pickup trucks filled with plywood, sheetrock, two-by-fours, and bags of concrete just beyond the mourners and tents. The materials for a new house and barn had been here during the entire service.

"With Wanda in mind, we will rebuild the house my father built. This will always be Mapp Ranch."

People began to clap again, and Nick and Em were pushed out of the inner circle as neighbors and other reporters pressed closer to Birdie who continued rallying the group.

"Wanda may have been a rock, but Birdie's a force of nature," Em said, her mouth partially open in surprise or amazement. Or maybe something else. Nick wasn't sure what he felt now, but he could see that being a member of Birdie Mapp's family must be a challenge.

Nick and Em wandered the grounds, accepted full plates of fry bread mounded with a meaty sauce from a woman who stood behind one of the tables. They sat down under a tent on picnic table bench next to Stanley Mapp, who stared toward the Cortez Mountains.

Stanley and Dwayne had both been investigated about the fire. Turned out their truck had started the smaller fire. Dwayne admitted to it. An accident while driving up by the mine site. That fact had given Nick a few sleepless nights, thinking back to the Sunrise Ceremony and the fire that had flown from the ring onto the dry ground. Had that been Stanley? But the BLM investigation had covered a lot of things: the faulty evacuation plan, the bad intel on the second fire, the horrible radio communication. But no official asked any questions about that first little fire on Mount Aurora, and Stanley and Dwayne were found a little slow in their reporting of the fire they caused, but innocent of intent.

And it wasn't their truck spark that ended up burning down Mapp Ranch. It was the other fire, the one started by the arsonist. Fueled by the increasing winds, that fire was the one that roared up from the south and swallowed up the ranch.

Investigators found the same device—the bundled matches—up in the mountains that had ignited the highway fire. But they hadn't found the arsonist. Not yet. Nothing but a campsite. A fire pit. A chair. A dozen empty bottles. Evidence of a quick getaway.

Maybe, Nick thought, the arsonist was watching now, wanting to know all he could about what he'd done. He might be right here, standing on the burned earth, wandering through the crowd, listening to the conversation, eager to hear "That was some fire" or "What an inferno."

Nick scanned the crowd for a man no one would ever suspect, some one standing slightly at the edge of the crowd, eyes wide in anticipation of praise for his terrible work. But nobody looked out of place.

Em touched Stanley's arm. "Mr. Mapp? It's me. Em Donnelly."

Stanley nodded, absently petting Ruby. She had run faster than Nick and the fire, the old dog jumping into the engine with Wanda before being shooed out. Later, Mac cared for Ruby at the station until Tanya came to pick her up a week later. Somehow, his responsibility for Ruby had kept Hamm and Lehman off his case. But once Tanya drove down the driveway and back toward the Crescent Valley, the taunts started. Schraeder started calling Mac Dr. Doolittle. Nick tried to tamp down the teasing, but that train had left the station. It was a free-for-all until the day Mac drove off early before anyone else was awake. Later, Jarchow found his resignation letter on his desk.

Nick missed him. Would miss him next fire season. There was something about the guy's nervousness, stupidity, and honesty that was for real. His flat-out chicken shit response was a barometer of what was true. Without Mac, something authentic was gone. Something that was inside all of them when they were out on a fire. Next season, there would be a few new people at the station, the dynamic shifting but essentially the same, someone else being a Mac, but, he hoped, without running away from a fire.

Looking back at the crowd, Nick watched Dwayne, who now stood next to Tanya and the fat girl from the ceremony. He no longer seemed the angry man who'd dumped off a barrel of water on Mount Aurora all those weeks ago. Walking through the crowd, he stopped to talk and accept condolences, shook hands, and seemed to take on a family role. For a second, Dwayne glanced up, and Nick thought he saw him nod. But before Nick could nod back, the moment passed.

Nick took a bite of his taco, listening to the hum of voices, to Em and Stanley chatting. Jarchow, near Tanya and Dwayne, stood with his arms crossed, nodding as some old rancher in a beat-up cowboy hat talked. Undoubtedly, they were discussing the fire. Nick put down his plate and thought to join them when Stanley reached over and fumbled to grab both of Nick's wrists. The old man's hands were shaking, but he held tight, giving Nick a sort of double handshake. But it was more like Stanley was taking his pulse, pressing just under Nick's radial bones with his thumbs.

Nick almost jerked away, but he caught himself and relaxed, let the old man squeeze. Maybe Stanley was looking for traces of Wanda. It was possible he'd find her there. Wanda's neck had been on top of Nick's right wrist, the back of her legs under his left, almost exactly where Stanley held him.

"*Ataa,*" the old man mumbled, and Nick nodded.

What a responsibility to carry someone into death. The bearer of the most important thing, now gone. Nick's throat constricted, tears under his cheeks and in his eyes. For a second, he felt the events of the past month in his lungs like smoke. Gripping Wanda tightly as they ran out of the fire was one of the most intimate things he'd ever done with another person. In a weird way, like sex. Or maybe like being born—life and death so possible— but he didn't remember his own birth. All those stories were his mother's, and really, his birth mostly seemed to belong to her, she the one with the memory. Wanda was his to remember, and he would never forget her shifting from one state to another, no matter what.

Stanley held on. Nick glanced down at their four hands, and then looked into the man's eyes. Despite his blindness, Stanley seemed to see him, nodding.

"She went with the fire into the air," Stanley said. "But some of her, she's in you, for sure."

Nick paused, felt the warm air on his face. He got it now. That's what Grandma Rosa had meant all those years ago. "Every single thing you do, mi'jo, leaves a trace." Grandma hadn't been chastising him about being rude to his mother. She'd been reminding him that people left evidence, something people could touch, hold, see, taste. Affection, anger, grief—everything could be passed down and around.

Wanda's sacrifice and good natured bravery was on his skin, under Stanley's hands. Nick held on, felt the man's bones, thin but strong. Nick could feel Stanley's grief, a pulse as strong as his grip.

"Where do you go from here?" Stanley asked.

With everyone packed up and the station closing down tomorrow, Nick had thought about going to the Bay Area for a while. But the last thing Megan had said to him was, "Come get your stuff. I'm not taking care of it this time" before hanging up. So he'd go and get his stuff. What he'd do with it once he had was another story.

"I'm going to Seattle for a bit."

Stanley loosened his grip and finally let go of Nick's wrists. Nick glanced at Em and saw that she was watching them, her typing hands still.

"Bring Wanda back to us," Stanley said. The day pulsed hot and yellow, the air a surprise of laughter and hope. Nick turned away from Stanley's gaze and looked toward the road. For a blinking second, he saw himself racing up toward the engines, Wanda gathered in his arms, the fire roaring behind him.

Stanley leaned forward, his breath a waft of whiskey and spearmint. "Come back to Nevada. Come home."

⌘

Afterword

The world has always given me stories, and the universe gave me my sons. For this story, the world and the universe were in collusion. My firefighter son texted me one late spring day: Fire. Dann Ranch. Unable to contact him, I searched online for the Dann Ranch, and found parts of this story scattered around like gold. Without Julien Inclan's knowledge and guidance in every firefighting section (translation: I pestered him endlessly) I would have never imagined Wanda and Birdie Mapp, Nick Delgado, and the terrain of Northeastern Nevada.

Over the three plus years it took to write this novel, many people helped me in ways usually very large. For their comments and assistance in so many ways, I would like to thank Julien Inclan (again), Michael Rubin, Kris Whorton, Jesse Inclan, Warren Read, Julie Roemer, Judy Myers, Marcia Goodman, Keri Dulaney-Greger, Joan Kresich, Maureen O'Leary, Gail Offen-Brown, Carole Barksdale, Larry Smith, Stanley Rubin, Sarah Blaser Murray, Melinda Thomas, Linda Kerr MacKillop, Ned Hayes, Kevin Goodan, Suzanne Berne, John Holman, and David Cates. Most especially, Ann Pancake, Scott Nadelson, and Rick Barot.

This novel is fiction, and I've tried to create a small make-believe world populated with make-believe characters in the midst of the real Nevada. I read a lot of books, poured over maps, and had one computer screen constantly at the Google ready. My husband Michael and I spent a week in Elko and Carlin, Nevada, visiting Indian reservations, bars, casinos, fire stations, and driving in the hills and valleys of Northern Nevada, the land of gold mines and ranches. I have, I will tell you, sipped a Pincon, that dreaded Basque cocktail. Other than my son and his fellow firefighters, the second most important source for my imagination was two sisters—both Native American activists—living on their family's ranch in the Crescent Valley. While Birdie and Wanda Mapp are not these sisters in mostly every way, I studied the details of Mary and Carrie Dann's experiences as well as much of the information about the various legal battles the Western Shoshone have fought since signing The Treaty of Ruby Valley in 1863. But for the real story and more about the Danns and their struggles against the US Government, I suggest the documentary *American Outrage*.

Also Available from Urban Farmhouse Press

Ash (*Kilgore Trout Series*) by Kelly Dulaney, ISBN: 978-0-9937690-6-1

Booking Rooms in the Kuiper Belt (*Crossroads Poetry Series*) by Kenneth Pobo, ISBN: 978-0-993769-07-8

Curious Connections (*Cities of the Strait Chapbook*) by Karen Rockwell, ISBN: 978-1-988214-07-8

Endless Building (*Crossroads Poetry Series*) by Marvin Shackelford, ISBN: 978-0-993769-01-6

Home & Ghost (*Crossroads Poetry Series*) by Scott Weaver, ISBN: 978-1-988214-05-4

Jesus Works the Night Shift (*Cities of the Strait Chapbook*) by Caleb Tankersley, ISBN: 978-0-993769-02-3

Legacy (*Vintage Sci-Fi*) by Larry Schmitz, ISBN: 978-1-988214-03-0

Puppet Turners of Narrow Interior (*UFP Fiction*) by Stephanie Hammer Barbe, ISBN: 978-0-993769-03-0

Roundabout Directions to Lincoln Center (*Crossroads Poetry Series*) by Renee K. Nicholson, ISBN: 978-0-993769-01-6

Smack Middle in the Spotlit Obvious (*Cities of the Strait Chapbook*) by Laurie Smith, ISBN: 978-1-988214-06-1

CPSIA information can be obtained
at www.ICGtesting.com
Printed in the USA
BVHW081235300919
559784BV00001B/67/P

9 781988 214047